To the

Drown

for your

Sins

DIARMID MACARTHUR

Very best wishes

Contents

If we were absolutely certain of what lay ahead of us, what would we do? Would we stay at home, barricade the door and hide under the covers? But then, if we really did know, how could we possibly change it? Can we hope to change or to conquer fate...?

Prologue

Mystique

A perfect morning.

The conditions were at their very best; warm and windless, an azure sky streaked with wisps of feathery white clouds that reflected in the calm, still waters of Castle Semple loch. Already the morning sun was rising across the water, the long stretch of trees bordering the opposite bank catching its burgeoning rays in a verdant and bright late-summer display. As the day wore on, of course, the rising warm air would create a gentle breeze but, at the moment, the conditions couldn't have been better.

A perfect morning...

The two young women were already on the pontoon, their pride and joy, "Mystique", sitting calm in the water, blades securely fastened in the riggers. They climbed carefully into their sleek, graceful boat, pushed off and took a few gentle strokes; then they were out.

Annie White and Fiona Jackson were competent and experienced rowers. They were also great friends and had decided, towards the end of the previous year, to purchase their own boat, a top of the range Italian "Filippi". She had cost them a small fortune but, already, she was proving her worth.

Once they had rowed gently over to the buoy line, Annie, who was in stroke, turned her head slightly.

'Usual warm-up, Fee?'

'Yup, Annie, you call it.'

In no time they were past the one kilometre buoys, the calm water swishing under the boat as they glided across it, the pools of their blades evenly spaced and as gentle as if only a small stone had been dropped in the loch. Annie called out.

'Okay, build rate and pressure up to the end; three, two, one...'

Soon they were speeding past the little island on their right, the habitual cormorant perched atop the dead tree calmly observing their progress. Fiona steered confidently, varying her foot pressure to keep "Mystique" running straight, just a few feet from the line of buoys. She called out

'Watch out for the water lilies, Annie, you could almost walk across up here.'

'Okay Fee; twenty more. Final push. Go...'

They dug in for their final, gruelling drive. Five... ten... suddenly, there was a muffled thump and the boat lurched heavily, tipping hard to bow side. They tried their best to keep upright but to no avail. Over they went, sideways into the water. A quick pull on the cords securing their feet and they were free, emerging like two mermaids swimming amongst the water lilies. It wasn't the first time they had capsized, of course; they were experienced rowers, the water was warm and at no point was the loch deeper than about five feet (although the bottom was thick with slime). Annie grabbed the boat first, wiping her eyes and pulling strands of lily stalks out of her hair.

'What the hell was that? There shouldn't be any debris here, there's been no rain recently to wash anything down.'

Fiona grinned at her friend.

'Haven't a clue, Fee, but there was a definite bump as if we hit something. Don't see anything here. Listen, I'll go round the other side and have a look. We'll turn her over then get back in. It's warm, we'll soon dry out.' She started to pull herself round the stern of the upturned boat, checking for any damage as she went. Fiona called after her.

'Aye, you're right, the speed you had us going at we'll be bone dry by the time we're back at the pontoon! Must've had us up at about thirty-six strokes a...'

She was interrupted by a spine-chilling scream. She stopped mid-sentence, her mouth open, then shouted.

'Annie! Annie, are you okay?'

There was no reply; Fiona pulled herself round to the other side of the boat, where her friend was staring wide-eyed at the object that had caused their capsize.

'Oh my God!' Fiona screamed, before bringing up her breakfast.

Part One

I went again last night, just for a look, of course; I couldn't help myself. Well, if I'd really tried, I probably could have but, deep inside, I really wanted to, I really had to.

I sometimes think I'm obsessed. Actually, take away the "think". I am obsessed! There, I've finally confessed, I'm obsessed, I'm obsessed. Well, that was liberating— and poetic...

And who can blame me? After all that's happened, she's had a major impact on my life, in more ways than one! But it's odd; in a way I'd love to rid myself of her but I realise that, in some perverse, twisted way, I also need her; or want, maybe? God knows. That's what obsessions are all about, of course. It's a love-hate thing.

It was dark, but then it always is, because I go in the middle of the night. Couldn't risk being seen, after all, that would never do. I crouched in the shadows for a while, hidden behind some trees. No-one saw me. At least, if they did, I wasn't aware of it. Nothing. It was in darkness, no sound, no movement. I saw a fox, though. It seemed a lot braver than me!

I waited for an hour, watching, wondering. Wondering just why I was there in the first place, what I expected to see...I was tempted to pick up a pebble, throw it at a window, but that would have been really stupid!

I'll try not to go tonight; after all, I don't want to appear obsessed...

Maybe again at the weekend, though; just for a wee look...

O sleep again deceive me...

Chapter 1

The uniformed constable pulled a face as he waved the grime-crusted silver pick-up through the police cordon, then turned back to his post. As it trundled past him and into the car park, a deep voice boomed out.

'Constable, make sure those camper vans don't bugger off...'

The vehicle pulled in to a space and the imposing figure of DCI Grant McVicar got out, stretched and rubbed his hand over his shaved head as he stared out over the calm waters of Castle Semple loch; waters that today had been sullied...

He had wakened with a vague, undefined feeling of unease that he couldn't explain. No doubt it would come to him, but for now he turned his gaze along the car park, already a hive of activity; uniformed cops were taking statements from rather shocked-looking members of the public, SOCOs were busy on the three pontoons that stretched into the loch and there were a number of emergency vehicles parked indiscriminately, including an ambulance and a red van with an empty trailer attached. He presumed that the semi-rigid rescue boat was already out on the water. There were a few buildings situated at the far end of the car park, including Castle Semple Rowing club, outside which the activity seemed to be centred. He sighed heavily and set off towards the epicentre of the investigation; he would keep an open mind until he had spoken to his team, but already he had the feeling that it was going to be a murder investigation. Despite the implications, he felt the first frisson of excitement run up his spine...

As he approached, he could see the unmistakeable figure of Detective Sergeant Quinn issuing instructions to a couple of uniformed officers. He frowned. He still hadn't made his mind up about his new assistant...

*

DS Briony Quinn regarded the tall figure of her boss as he strode along the car park; she glanced surreptitiously at her watch; unfortunately, he noticed and rewarded her with a frown.

'Aye, I know, sorry...right, what have we got. Who all's here?'

"Mornin' Briony" might have been nice...

'Okay, Boss, two female rowers capsized at the far end of the loch after hittin' what turned out to be a body.'

'What time?'

'Just before eight, they reckon. Weren't wearin' watches, apparently.'

'Have you taken a statement?'

Of course I bloody have...

'Aye, but they're in shock. No wonder, mind you; the body was naked and they think that the hands and feet were tied.'

'Hm, definitely sounds like murder, then – how did they get back up here?'

'They managed to wade ashore – it's pretty shallow up there – then a local resident took them in and called us. There's a few bungalows up at the end...'

'Aye, I can see them from my house. Right, is anyone up there just now?

'Cliff took one of the rowing club's launches up, just to secure the locus. I've got uniforms along at the far end tapin' off the area, just in case. The place is a warren of paths, it's a bloody nightmare...'

'I know, I sometimes cycle down here...'

He suddenly realised that he hadn't. Not for months, not since...

No...

Their conversation was interrupted by the sound of a powerful Zephyr outboard – they turned and saw the Water Support Rescue Vehicle approach and draw in alongside the central pontoon, on which a number of figures had gathered. A black body-bag lay in the centre of the boat and Grant turned angrily to his sergeant.

'Who the hell authorised removal of the body. I always like to have a look...'

'Sorry, Boss, it was Doctor Napier. I said you'd probably want to see where it was found but she refused to wait any longer.'

His anger subsided slightly – even he wouldn't dare cross the formidable and experienced pathologist, Margo "Nippy" Napier. As he frowned in the direction of the pontoon, he saw her petite, wiry form step nimbly into the boat and unzip the body bag.

'Aye, fair enough...right, who else is here?'

'Well, as I said, Cliff's up at the end of the loch, Kiera is out co-ordinatin' the uniforms round the paths and Faz is on his way. Actually, I think that's him arrivin' now. Sam's in Dundee on leave, won't make it back until Monday.'

Clifford Ford, a young and enthusiastic DC, was a relatively new member of the team, still anxious to prove himself; DC Kiera Fox had been with him for a few years, her short red hair matching her short temper, especially where the criminal fraternity was concerned. They were capable officers who could be left to get on with the job in hand.

Grant looked back along the car park as DC Faz Bajwa jogged towards them. The black turban of the young Sikh officer contrasted with the white t-shirt and khaki cargo shorts that showed off his muscular physique and, as he approached, he flashed a wide grin through his dark beard.

'Morning Boss, morning Sarge. Sorry, was playing football; right, what can I do?'

'Get back along the car park and interview the occupants of those three camper vans. They've got German plates on them but they'll probably speak English and they might have witnessed something if they've been here overnight.'

Faz smiled again.

'Sure, Boss, Catch you in a bit.'

They watched as he jogged back along the car park.

'Bloody runs everywhere, that boy, eh.'

Grant gritted his teeth. For some reason, his sergeant's slightly uplifted east coast "eh" at the end of her sentence irritated him.

'Hm. Right, let's get down and see what Nippy has to say. Brace yourself...'

As they walked towards the pontoon, Briony turned towards him.

'What the hell's she wearing, Boss?'

Grant had wondered about the Doctor's outfit, a crisp white blouse and a grey pleated skirt – he had forgotten that she was a competitive bowler. Somehow he found it rather attractive, a feeling that immediately dissipated as the Doctor turned towards them with a scowl.

'Well, I could do without this – last damned match of the season and you manage to find me a swimmer.' Doctor Napier called any body found in the water "a swimmer".

'Sorry, Doctor...'

'Yes, well, let's get it over with...anyway, how are you Grant?'

He wasn't quite sure how to take the question. Face value seemed the best option.

'Aye, okay, just getting on... have you met Sergeant Quinn?'

The doctor regarded Briony.

'Not yet. I'll leave the formalities until I'm done here, if you don't mind. Right...'

Briony and Grant exchanged a look – Nippy was certainly living up to her reputation.

'Right, there's duct-tape over the mouth which I'm about to remove— bag, please... come on, I don't have all day...thanks.'

There was a rasp as the tape was taken off and Dr Napier placed it in the evidence bag.

'I doubt that it'll be of much use after the immersion...'

She continued her examination of the corpse for a few more minutes then stood up and stepped back out of the boat, pulling off her forensic gloves as she did so.

'Right, so far we have a male, probably mid-to-upper twenties, naked and with his hands and feet tied behind his back. Hog-tied, I believe it's called. Been in the water for possibly up to forty-eight hours but I'll get a more accurate idea after the post-mortem. There's extensive bruising on the torso, consistent with a beating, and the inside of the mouth is lacerated with a couple of loose teeth. I'd say he was fairly seriously assaulted before being placed in the water.'

Grant waited. There was usually an addendum.

'Oh, and although I can't confirm it yet, I'd say he was probably alive when he was placed in the water. The poor bugger drowned, I'm afraid.'

There was a slightly stunned silence, even the case-hardened rescue crew were shocked at the thought of the victim's last moments of life, assaulted, bound, gagged and left to drown. As always, however, the pathologist managed to remain detached. Grant wished he could do the same.

'Right, where in God's name can I get a cup of tea around here?'

Grant had been aware of Briony's phone ringing while the Doctor had been speaking. Nippy had favoured his sergeant with a stony glare at the intrusion. As she ended the call he turned back towards her, noticing the shocked expression on her face.

'What?'

'That was Cliff, Boss. he had a scout about up at the top of the loch, once the rescue team had left...'

Grant raised a dark eyebrow.

'...he's found another body...'

Fuck...

Chapter 2

It was another hour before the second body had been recovered and brought to the pontoon. Having completed the examination, Doctor Napier zipped up the body bag, stepped out of the boat and sighed.

'Well, as you can clearly see, pretty much the same modus, although there is more extensive bleeding inside this victim's mouth. Anyway, that's me done. I'll carry out the post-mortem examinations first thing on Monday morning and I'll be in touch...'

Following a further remonstration at having missed her bowling match, finally she had stormed off, her pleated skirt swinging angrily and leaving a waft of Chanel No.5 and the smell of cigarettes in her wake.

Grant looked at Briony. As far as he knew, this was her first murder enquiry and it was a particularly nasty one.

'You okay, Bri?'

The question took her by surprise.

'I suppose, Boss. Bloody brutal, mind you; I mean, what kind of sadistic bastard would do a thing like that?'

As they walked back up to the rowing club compound, he turned and looked at her.

'That's what we're here to find out...'

*

They had made some progress; Faz had interviewed the occupants of the three camper vans, all of whom spoke reasonable English. Two of the vans had only arrived the night before but the third had arrived on the Thursday and the husband had been aware of a vehicle passing when he had got up to use their cramped chemical toilet.

With characteristic German precision he had noted the time. Three-seventeen a.m.. *A snippet which may prove useful*, Grant thought. Other than that, despite the considerable police presence no further evidence had come to light.

The police diving team had arrived mid-afternoon but, other than a couple of ancient, waterlogged phones and assorted sunglasses, they had found nothing of note and they planned to return the following day to extend their search. Grant turned to his sergeant.

'Doubt they'll find much, to be honest. Right, I'll give the Mint a call, keep her in the loop...'

He stood for a few minutes talking to Superintendent Patricia Minto and bringing her up-to-date with the investigation so far. Briony could see the slightly pained expression on his face. His superior wasn't the easiest of woman to deal with. Finally he ended the call and put his phone back in his pocket. It immediately started to ring and he remembered that a call had come in when he was talking to the Superintendent. He pulled it back out and stared at the screen.

'You not goin' to answer that, Boss?' queried his sergeant.

He shook his head but remained silent, then looked back up, a distant expression on his face while he scanned the still-busy crime scene.

'Right, there's not much more we can do tonight. I'm calling it a day; I'll call in to Osprey House tomorrow, see what's what. Tell the troops to start rounding it up, make sure the uniforms keep the place secure...'

'I have managed a crime scene before Boss' she snapped back. 'I *do* know what I'm doin."

He sighed. She was right.

'Aye, I know, sorry, Briony, it's just... listen, I'll see you tomorrow. Cheers.'

As he walked away, his head down and his shoulders slumped, Detective Sergeant Briony Quinn wondered just what the hell was bothering the big man now. Maybe someday he'd tell her...

*

Grant was sitting in the lounge of his cottage, holding his phone in his hands. He shook his head despondently and looked again at his phone screen. The missed call had been from "Louise." His thumb hovered hesitantly over the call icon.

Louise Thackray.

Brian's widow.

Today would have been their wedding anniversary and he had

forgotten.

Fuck...

He pressed the button and the call was answered on the second ring.

'Grant?'

'Louise...'

Grant yawned, stretched and stood up before padding through to the kitchen and switching on the kettle. Saturday had been a gruelling day, both physically and emotionally, especially the phone call to Louise; he tried not to dwell on it, but as usual, failed miserably. After a quick coffee and a shower he headed in to Osprey House, the homogenous brick building just off Paisley's Inchinnan Road that served as headquarters for "K" division MITS – Major Investigation Teams. Cliff Ford and Faz Bajwa were already busy.

'Morning lads. Anything fresh?'

Faz looked up with his customary grin.

'Morning, Boss. No, 'fraid not. I've got everything uploaded on to Holmes but there's no mis-per reports, nothing, sorry.'

He checked his own computer and briefly shuffled through the pile of paperwork that lay on his desk; finally, deciding to take a trip back down to Castle Semple loch and see if Briony and Kiera had had any more luck.

They hadn't; despite walking the perimeter of the loch (as far as the path allowed) they hadn't found anything of relevance and, as expected, the police divers had recovered nothing more than another ancient phone and more sunglasses from the green-tinged waters of Castle Semple loch. He and Briony made a final, fruitless trip to the pontoons then headed back to his pick-up. He opened the door, sat down and lifted up one foot, glaring at his trainer.

'Bloody bird crap. Why do they shit all over the pontoons?'

'Don't know, Boss, but Kiera knelt in it yesterday. The stuff's stinking.'

He picked up a stick and scraped the offending excrement from the sole of his shoe.

'Right, I'll head back up to the office, see if there's any more news; mind you, there's probably not much going to happen until tomorrow, once Nippy gets the PMs done.'

He paused briefly.

'Thing is, if it *did* happen on Thursday, you'd think someone would have reported the victims missing by now.'

'Depends. Maybe they lived on their own, Boss. Or maybe they were a couple...?'

He hadn't thought of that.

'That's a point. Anyway, I'll see you in the morning. Cheers.'

A couple of hours later, he was home. He had planned to try and install the wood-burning stove that had arrived during the week but, instead, he flopped down on the leather couch, staring out at the spectacular view across the lush Renfrewshire hills and distant Ben Lomond towering majestically in the background. He barely noticed. Already there was something about this case that didn't feel right. Mulling over the facts, he put his hands behind his head and soon fell into a troubled, restless sleep.

Chapter 3

'Good morning, Domestic Services Agency. How may I help you today?'

Nothing.

'Hello, Domestic Services Agency, Delia speaking. How can I help?'

Still nothing...then a sharply-drawn breath...

'Hello, Delia here, what can I do for you?'

'Em...is that, em...the Domestic Services Agency?

Finally...

'Yes, it is. Is this the first time you've called the agency?'

'Em...yes, well, you see, what it is...a friend told me, and...Oh God...'

Delia smiled. She was used to this and knew exactly how to handle it!

'Now don't you worry yourself one bit. As I said, I'm Delia and I run the agency. It's always a bit awkward when you phone at first, I completely understand. So, why don't I explain exactly what services we provide, how it all works and what our charges are. Then we can discuss if we can be of any assistance to you. How does that sound?'

'Em...oh well, I suppose so...you sound so nice...'

She did! She smiled to herself.

'Right, my lovely, let's start with your name...'

*

Chief Inspector Sam Williams placed the phone back down and drummed his fingers on the desk. It could always be a bit awkward when retired cops phoned to ask a "wee favour" but, on this occasion, the request had seemed pretty harmless. A simple number-plate check would probably suffice, maybe followed by a few minutes of light investigative work. It was quite probably nothing anyway. He lifted the internal phone and dialled.

May as well pass the buck now...

Ten minutes later, and with a profound sense of relief, Constable Grace Lappin closed the door behind her as she left the Chief Inspector's office. The summons had caused her heart to leap into her mouth . She had only been at Partick Police Station for a few weeks and to be suddenly called to the Chief Inspector's office had immediately filled her with panic. But now she had been presented with a small task of her very own. A retired cop with a suspicious wife, a mysterious van that turned up regularly every four weeks, a widow and a young man...

She smiled. The implication was that there was "something going on" and, although obviously not a major crime, it all sounded rather interesting! All she had was a partial name —Domestic Service-something— and, of course, a vehicle registration. Grace was an enthusiastic recruit and was already planning the strategy for this somewhat minor investigation. She was about to step back into the main office when the door opened and Sergeant McIntosh came barging out.

'Oh, watch... right, Grace, we need to be off.'

'Eh, Sarge? Off where?'

Lola McIntosh rolled her eyes.

'Oh, there's going to be a bloody riot, apparently. Some Tory MP is turning up at Glasgow Uni and the left-wing students are out in force to protest. Now the right-wingers are there to lend support to the MP. Bloody students, you know what they're like. Well, you should, you were one until recently!'

Grace laughed.

'Aye, so I was Sarge. And what's your degree again?'

Lola grinned back.

'Bloody politics, should've stuck with it, better career prospects nowadays! Right, let's go before they start throwing meringues at each other. Grab a jacket, think there might be a storm coming.'

Chief Inspector William's request suddenly slid to the bottom of the priority list.

DCI Grant McVicar's first task of the morning had been to bring Superintendent Minto up to date with the murder enquiry, although there was little to add since he had spoken to her on Saturday. Once he had finished, she sat back in her chair.

'Hm. It's not much to go on, is it, Grant?'

'No, ma'am. I haven't spoken to any of the team yet but I'm hoping that there may have been a mis-per report overnight, that would be a start. Also, the post mortems are being carried out today and that should give us a more accurate time of death. Doctor Napier said she'd start first thing, so I'm hoping to hear late morning or early afternoon.'

'Good. Right, keep me informed if anything comes to light. This is a particularly unpleasant case, it would be good to get a quick result.'

'Yes, ma'am.'

He stood up and left the room, turning to say goodbye as he opened the door but Patricia Minto was already dialling a number on her phone.

He entered the office that served as the incident room for their investigation. The whole team was assembled, the ubiquitous white board taking centre stage, but they were obviously awaiting his arrival before defacing its pristine surface. There was a palpable sense of excitement in the room, like a charge of static electricity. Horrible the murders may have been but this was the job they were trained for and they were keen to start the investigation proper. Grant was sure that a thunderstorm was on its way and hoped that it would arrive soon. Tensions always seemed to run higher when the weather was muggy and oppressive. The situation wasn't helped by the inoperative air-conditioning system in the office. It was already hot and sticky.

Bloody cut-backs...

'Morning all. Glad you could join us, Sam.'

There was a mumbled chorus of greeting in response, although DC Samantha Tannahill's face reddened slightly. Briony glared at her boss but he didn't seem to notice.

'Right, let's get started. Bri, any news?'

'There is, actually.'

Grant's dark eyebrows shot up.

'There was a call from a Mrs Sheena Watt at eight forty-five this mornin'. Her son, Andrew, was expected for dinner last night but he didn't arrive. He's an outdoor activities instructor and an occasional mountaineer so she just assumed that he'd been workin' and hadn't had a chance to call her. She tried again this mornin' but when she couldn't get hold of him, she went round to his flat. His car was outside but there was no sign of him, or his car keys, for that matter. She couldn't be sure but she didn't think that he'd packed a case or a rucksack, apparently his stuff was all still there. She's worried that he's had an accident somewhere. You know, climbin' or somethin'...'

Grant frowned.

'Hm. May be a connection but more than likely she's correct...'

Briony hadn't finished.

'...aye, but not only that, Boss, he has a flatmate who seems to be missin' as well, although it's not been officially reported by anyone yet. He's not workin' at the moment so he should have been at the flat, apparently. Name of Chris Findlay.'

Grant was interested now.

'Okay, that *doesn't* sound like co-incidence, does it? Right, Cliff, you've got the best handwriting, grab a marker.'

'Sure, Boss!' The enthusiastic young detective constable sprang to his feet.

'So. Two victims, A and B, both young males. One longish blonde hair, the other cropped dark hair. Both bodies naked and hog-tied. That's hands and feet all tied together behind the back, for the uninitiated. Duct tape over their mouths, both show signs of having been assaulted prior to being placed in the water. That's pretty much all we know so far. Only other info is that one of the occupants of a camper van heard a vehicle leave the car park at three-seventeen a.m. on the Friday morning. Whether or not that's significant I don't know but it's another little piece of the jigsaw so you may as well put it down, Cliff.'

He paused to let the DC add all the relevant information.

'Right, for the moment, let's assume the victims' identities to be Andrew Watt and Chris Findlay with a big question mark...t hat's it. Location of bodies, Castle Semple Loch, of course, but place of assault probably elsewhere. Once we get the PM results we can maybe be a bit more specific. First body discovered Saturday at approximately seven forty-five a.m. by two female rowers. Second discovered approximately three hours later...'

He paused again, the silence broken by the squeaking of Cliff's marker pen.

'Location of both at the north end of the loch, approximately two kilometres from the jetties, or pontoons, as they're called. The weather was warm and calm but we're reliably informed that a wind usually gets up in the afternoon, apparently caused by hot air currents.'

'Who told you that, Boss? ' asked Faz.

Briony replied.

'I spoke to Tina Sturrock, the rowing club captain. As she put it, "it's a funny wee loch". Apparently they row early because it's nearly always calm but as the sun climbs, it heats up both the water and the air above the loch, drawing the cooler air in, almost invariably from the south end. She said that, as the day gets hotter, the wind tends to get up, blowin' to the north.'

'So that could have washed the bodies up the loch then?' asked Kiera.

'Well, she thinks it could have.'

'Right, Sarge; so, if a body *did* go in from the pontoon, how long would it take for it to get up to where they were found?'

'Tina wasn't exactly sure' replied Briony 'but she reckons that if a boat was left untethered, with an average breeze it could be ten feet out in maybe twenty or thirty seconds. The loch's about two kilometres long and she reckons a body dropped in the water at the pontoon could possibly end up at the head of the loch in about a day, dependin' on the exact...'

Grant interrupted and Briony gave him another cold stare, which he ignored.

'Which would, of course, tie in with the time estimated by the

German guy in the camper van.'

He paused again, aware that Cliff was struggling to get all the information down on the board.

'Now, we have two bodies, both well-built young men. It wouldn't have been easy to get these out of a vehicle and into the loch, if that's what happened.'

'Do you think that there might have been more than one murderer, Boss?' asked Sam.

'Maybe, I was wondering that myself. It would certainly make the disposal considerably easier. Now, the good Doctor Napier has given an initial estimate of twenty-four to forty-eight hours of immersion, although that'll be confirmed later, hopefully. And that's pretty much it. Any further evidence, anyone?'

He glanced over at Kiera, who had been co-ordinating the ground search by the uniforms.

'Nothing, Boss, and no tracks, the ground's like rock. You could drive a tank over it and you wouldn't know. No blood or any forensic evidence on the pontoons or on any of the small fishing jetties. There's a few of those further up the loch. Place is as clean as the proverbial whistle, I'm afraid. Well, apart from all the bird crap on the pontoons. I knelt in it and my jeans were disgusting!'

'Aye, I stood in some of it myself. Right, thanks Kiera. The divers didn't find anything either so, as I said, I think we can safely assume that the primary assaults weren't actually committed at the loch and it's likely that they were already naked and tied when they arrived. Once we get the results of the PM we'll have a bit more to go on. Right, anyone, any initial thoughts?'

Sam Tannahill made another suggestion.

'Is there a possibility that they could have been a couple, Boss? Would that have any bearing, do you think?'

'Hm, Bri had mentioned that.' Cliff, put it down with a question mark. If they were, could it be a jealous ex, maybe? Or two, for that matter? Put that down too until we investigate. Bri, can we speak to this Mrs Watt?'

'She said she'd wait at the flat in case her son came back. The poor woman's worried sick. I'll give her a call if you like.'

'Where is the flat?"

'Renfrew, well, up near Braehead, you know, that big new development that runs along the river front.'

'Right, we could be there in, say, half an hour. Can you give her a call and tell her we're on our way?'

He addressed the room.

'Has anyone seen the papers this morning?'

Kiera Fox replied

'Yes, Boss. It's on the front of most of them but the details are a bit sketchy.'

'Aye, much like ours, but if Mrs Watt's seen them she might well be putting two and two together herself. Right Bri, let's get up there. Sam, see if you can find out anything on this Chris Findlay, in case he's been reported missing elsewhere and we've not been notified. Once we speak to Mrs Watt we'll have more to go on. There's a good chance that she'll have an identification to make later today, poor woman. Can someone try and get hold of an Ordnance Survey map of the loch. Check all points of access, just in case we've missed any. Cliff, can you mark where you think the bodies were found. And can you also check in case we've missed any CCTV cameras round the village, or outside anyone's house. If anyone fancies a wee trip back down to the Loch, it wouldn't do any harm. Faz?'

DC Bajwa replied.

'How about Cliff and I head back down, Boss? We can check for security cameras then we can have another wee look about, see if there's anything we might have missed.'

'Okay, off you go. Right, Bri and I are heading up to Renfrew. Keep me posted if anything crops up.'

Briony stood up and they headed for the door. He looked at her and spoke quietly.

'If this *is* her son, then I'm afraid that's where you'll come in, Bri...especially as someone will need to identify the body. That's never pleasant...'

Aye, don't I know it. That's what I get for being trained in victim support...

*

Forty minutes later, Grant pulled his pick-up into a space outside the block in which Andrew Watt's flat was located. The street was quiet, with most occupants being at work. He hadn't taken this route to Braehead Shopping Centre for ages and was surprised at the level of development; where there had once been

acres of wasteland, there were now houses and roads, even a large
concrete block proclaiming itself to be a hotel. It was a whole
new community. They got out, walked over to the heavy entrance
door with its controlled entry panel and pressed the buzzer. It was
answered immediately and Grant gave Briony a knowing look; the
woman was obviously anxious.

'Hello, Mrs Watt? This is Det...'

'Yes, come on up.'

They could hear the worry in her voice; the door clicked as she
unlocked it. Grant spoke quietly.

'Christ, she's anxious...'

They climbed the stairs to the second floor where Sheena Watt
was standing in an open doorway. Grant reckoned her to be about
sixty, a kindly looking woman with black spectacles, short grey hair
and a very worried expression. They introduced themselves and
she ushered them in, closing the door behind her.

'He's a good boy, Chief Inspector. He always phones if he's not
coming, or even if he's just late. This isn't like him at all and I'm
worried he's away climbing and had an accident. Oh, just in here to
the left, that's the lounge. Can I get you a cup of tea or anything?'

'No, thanks very much, Mrs Watt. We're fine, but if you'd like
one...'

'No, no, I couldn't, not just now. I mean, we were so worried,
when I came over this morning and he wasn't here...and his car, I
mean, where would he be if his car's still here...'

Briony interrupted.

'Mrs Watt, you say his car's there but you think his keys are
missing?'

'Em, oh, yes. He always leaves them on the wee table in the hall.
I noticed his car but the keys aren't there, or in the drawer either.
That's odd, he always left them there, creature of habit, our Andy...'

Her voice tailed off.

'Could he have gone somewhere with his flat-mate? 'asked Grant,
as he and Briony sat down on the sofa. Sheena Watt perched
her petite frame on the arm of one of the chairs. She was clearly
fighting back tears.

'Well, that's the thing. Chris got rid of his car when he lost his job
and Andrew gives him a lift if he needs to go anywhere. He's such a
nice lad too...'

Briony interrupted.

'Mrs Watt, I'm sorry to have to ask but can you tell me the exact nature of the relationship between Chris and your son?'

The woman looked up, surprised at the question.

'The what...?'

The penny dropped. She smiled slightly and shook her head.

'They weren't a couple, if that's what you mean. Just very good friends. They'd known each other for years, Chris is a bit down on his luck and Andrew said he could stay with him. Well, actually, his dad and I own the flat, bought it as an investment. We might downsize when Tom retires, move here, it's nice… and, anyway, Chris has a girlfriend...'

'Have you checked with her?' Grant asked immediately.

'What? Oh, yes, I phoned her just before you arrived. She hasn't seen Chris since last week, she was away at a hen weekend. She'd tried to call him a few times but there was no answer and she just assumed he was busy. She's very worried too.'

Grant stood up.

'Could we have a look around, Mrs Watt, see if there's anything?'

'Oh, yes, certainly.'

She jumped up, eager to help. Grant continued.

'And do you have a photo of your son? Chris too, if you know of any lying about.'

'I've got loads at home, of course, but I think there's one in Chris's room, the two of them were away on a stag weekend a few weeks ago. The same wedding party as Judy, Chris's girlfriend. I'll fetch it...'

'It's okay Mrs Watt, if we could have a wee look first, just in case.'

'Oh...okay. Just through here.'

They entered Andrew Watt's room first. It was a reasonably spacious bedroom for a modern flat, with a large window making the room pleasantly bright. There was the usual clutter; a selection of deodorants and hair gel; an electric razor; some t-shirts lying on the bed; some letters, opened and casually thrown on the chest of drawers. There was a chair at the window and Briony crossed over to it, pointing to a pair of grey overalls that had been folded and placed over the back.

'Boss?'

Grant went over and looked at them.

'Domestic Services Agency? Mrs Watt, do you know anything about this?'

Sheena Watt was standing in the doorway; she crossed the room and looked at the overalls with a slight frown. She shook her head.

'No, I haven't a clue. Andrew is an outdoors instructor. He's a nice, hard-working boy but I wouldn't exactly say he's domesticated. Sorry, I've never seen those before'

Briony asked.

'Could I see Chris's room, please?'

'Yes, of course. Just through here.'

The second bedroom was slightly smaller but still bright. It was more cluttered and there was a quantity of dirty (and slightly odorous) washing lying in a corner. Mrs Watt smiled.

'He's just a big boy, really.'

Briony saw a photo frame sitting on the dresser and picked it up; six fresh-faced, handsome young men were smiling at the camera. Mrs Watt stood beside her.

'That's Chris, on the left. Andrew second from the right. Paul, the groom, is the one in the middle, the one that looks a bit worse for wear.'

Briony placed it back down, trying not to let Sheena Watt see her expression; they were a good-looking bunch of young men, carefree and happy, but she was pretty certain now... she opened the wardrobe and had a rummage; nothing. She crossed to the pile of dirty clothes and moved them carefully with the toe of her shoes. Underneath a couple of grubby t-shirts was a crumpled set of grey overalls identical to those in the other room. She put on a set of forensic gloves and carefully lifted them out – the same embroidered name adorned the pocket.

'You're quite sure you don't know anything about this Domestic Services Agency, Mrs Watt?'

'No, honestly, nothing at all, Sergeant. Unless Chris has picked up a job. He's been trying really hard, maybe something came up...'

'But it looks like your son has a pair too.'

'Well, the outdoor activities can sometimes be a bit unpredictable, I suppose. Andrew also did some acting, although I think that was a bit sporadic too. We didn't always collect rent from the boys, if they were a bit short... maybe Andrew was helping Chris out... honestly, Sergeant, I just don't know...'

They went back through to the other room, where Grant was having a look about. Briony had taken the photograph and showed it to him. They exchanged a look. Despite their immersion in the waters of Castle Semple loch, both were now certain of the identity of the two corpses. Grant spoke, his tone grave.

'Mrs Watt, could we go back through to the lounge please, I think we need to have a wee chat with you...'

*

They were driving back to Paisley, sitting in a despondent silence as Grant's pick-up sped westbound along the M8. After breaking the dreadful news, they had waited for Tom Watt to arrive. Briony had refused to leave Sheena Watt on her own and she had also arranged for a support officer to attend, insisting on waiting for their arrival before she and Grant finally left. Eventually Grant spoke, trying his utmost to sound sympathetic.

'It's never easy, Bri.'

She didn't respond at first; then she sniffed. Her voice was seething with suppressed rage.

'She's destroyed, Boss. Simple as that. He was the light of her fuckin' life and some bastard's taken that away.'

He had never before seen his sergeant this angry. He knew the feeling; if ever there was an incentive to find the killer, it was innocents such as Sheena and Tom Watt.

'We'll get him, Bri.'

She looked at him, her eyes moist.

'But how can you be so bloody sure, Boss. What if we don't?'

He smiled grimly.

'Don't know, but sometimes I can just feel it, in my bones, if you like. It's strange, but...we'll nail this bastard. Trust me! Remember that case, the young lassie up the Gleniffer Braes, when you...'

No, of course she doesn't fucking remember - it wasn't bloody her...

Grant had managed to find a space for the Hi-lux in the crammed car park and they were just about to enter Osprey House when his phone rang. He looked at the screen then put his hand on Briony's arm. She stopped, turning to face him as he spoke.

'Doctor Napier.'

He answered the phone as they stood on the steps, switching it to speaker so that Briony could hear.

'Morning, Doctor.'

'Good morning, Grant. I've just completed the first post mortem and I thought I'd better give you a call to update you with my findings. Normally I'd wait until I'd done them both but I'm presuming that the second will be more of the same.'

'Yes, so am I, unfortunately. What have you got?'

'Well, I carried out the examinations in the same order as the bodies were recovered, so this one is for the poor blond lad. Cause of death is drowning, I'm afraid, which, assuming they both met the same fate, means they entered the water still alive but completely unable to save themselves. As observed at the time of recovery, the wrists and ankles were tied together behind the victims' backs, with cheap, green nylon clothes rope. As this is available in almost any ironmonger, or discount store, it's virtually untraceable, alas.'

Grant and Briony exchanged a grim look; the pathologist continued, her tone matter-of-fact. Grant knew this was how she dealt with the horrors of her job, professional detachment. He usually managed to do the same. Usually...!

'Time of death pretty much as I indicated. Definitely not more than forty-eight hours and not less than twenty four. I would put it between twenty-seven and thirty-three so that would place time of death some time between about eleven on Thursday night and five a.m. on Friday morning. I can't really be more precise, I'm afraid, but hopefully that will be of use in your enquiries. As you saw, the victim's mouth was covered with silver duct tape, meaning he would only have been able to breathe through his nose. Obviously this stuff is readily available and completely untraceable. You can check it for prints but I doubt you'll find anything.. Still, you never know.'

She paused, as if to let it all sink in; or maybe just to collect her own thoughts.

'Now, as I mentioned, the victim showed signs of having been assaulted. The first body that I have examined. As I said, the first one that you discovered, the taller of the two, has extensive bruising on the body and arms, as well as considerable laceration inside the mouth and a couple of loosened teeth. There is also one cracked rib. All this, of course, is consistent with having been severely beaten.'

'How long before death, Doctor. Can you say?'

'Given the development of the bruising, I would say several hours prior to the time of death.'

'So this victim, at least, was assaulted before being tied and drowned?'

'Assaulted, certainly. Whether or not he was tied I couldn't say; this may have occurred before or after. There certainly isn't anything to indicate that he tried to defend himself which, again, may indicate being tied beforehand....'

She paused meaningfully. Grant knew she had something else of note to say.

'I see. Anything else, Doctor?'

'Yes, now that you ask. My analysis suggests that the victim had ingested flunitrazepam, somewhere between six and ten hours before death.'

Grant frowned – there was a familiar sound to the word.

'Fluni— what?'

'Better known as Rohypnol. The victim had, presumably, been incapacitated using the drug.'

Grant pursed his lips and let out a long sigh. Briony stared at him but remained silent.

'I see, Doctor. This puts a different slant on things.'

'Yes, indeed. I would say that this indicates a considerable degree of pre-meditation, Grant. Anyway, I'll examine the other body and I'll send you both reports by e-mail later today.' She paused, as if drawing breath. 'You know, he was a very fit and healthy young man, in his prime, you might say. Six feet two, weight ninety-three kilogrammes, well-developed muscles, minimal body fat, healthy organs. An absolute bloody shame!'

'Aye, Doctor, it is a bloody shame! Listen, I'll let you get on, can you please call me and let me know if the other victim displays similar injuries.'

'Certainly, Grant...'

She paused again, as if about to say something else.

'Grant?'

'Yes, Doctor?'

'Listen, it's not for me to tell you your job and I know you to be a highly competent detective....'

'Thank you, that's ki...'

'...but please, Grant, please catch the bastards that did this. Lock them up and throw the key as far away as you possibly can.'

He was taken aback. Dr Napier had never before spoken to him in this manner.

'Consider it done, Doctor.'

'Thank you. I'll be in touch later.'

He continued to stare at the screen as "Nippy" Napier ended the call, then looked up at Briony.

'Well, that's me told...!'

*

Once back inside the stuffy office (following a detour to pick up two coffees and a couple of doughnuts) Grant slumped into a chair. He took a sip of his drink, wincing slightly as he burned his mouth. He put down the mug and frowned.

'It doesn't get us much further does it?'

Briony was more pragmatic.

'Aye it does, Boss. We now know their identities, the time of death is pretty much set, we know that, technically, the loch is now officially the murder scene.'

'Aye, although the poor bastards were...well...'

She sighed.

'Yes, they were. The loch was just the final step, I suppose.'

They sat in silence for a few moments; the rest of the team were absent, being engaged on the various tasks set earlier. Grant took another careful sip of his coffee.

'This Domestic Services Agency. I think we need to follow that up, Bri. I mean, two young, healthy outdoor types. What the hell are they doing working in "Domestic Service"? Seems to be a connection, though. In fact, about the only one we have.'

'Aye, it almost sounds a bit Victorian, doesn't it? I'll get onto it, I'll have a look on-line and see if I can dig anythin' up.'

'Okay, I'll leave it with you. I'm going to take a run back down to the loch, see how Cliff and Faz are getting on. I'll let you know if I hear from Nippy, though I suspect it'll be more of the same. We need to try and get hold of Chris Findlay's family. You're sure there was nothing at the flat?'

'Couldn't find a thing, Boss, and Mrs Watt didn't have any contact details.'

'Bugger! Pity we couldn't find their phones, although presumably they were in their clothes, wherever they are. Wait... Sheena Watt said she'd phoned the girlfriend. Bri, could you give her a call and get the number, see if she has any details on Findlay's next-of-kin. Might be best to do it face-to-face if you can.'

Briony didn't look too happy at this suggestion.

'Should we tell her too, Boss? I mean, she was his girlfriend.'

He thought about it for a moment, then shook his head.

'No, not yet, not until the body has been positively identified; speaking of which, could you try and arrange that with Mrs Watt? Need to get it over with.'

'Hm, so I'm to be the bearer o' bad news again?'

He shrugged and made a conciliatory face.

'Sorry, Bri. The price of being trained for it, I'm afraid. Oh, and we'll need to organise a door-to-door up around the flat. Andrew Watt's car is outside but the keys are missing; Chris Findlay doesn't have a car and the girlfriend was away. There's no sign of any struggle in the flat so it's possible that someone might have taken them in or around the vicinity. Maybe a neighbour saw something.'

'What about public transport, Boss? Must be something running with all those houses?'

'Possibly. Worth seeing what buses are on that route and check if any of the drivers picked them up. Get Sam onto that. Of course, it could also have been a taxi. The problem is trying to pinpoint when anyone actually last saw them alive. Findlay wasn't working and his girlfriend was away. Find out exactly when she last spoke to him. Bri, that'll be something. Watt's employment seems to have been pretty sporadic so that's not much help either. No, I think this Agency may give us more of an idea. If we can track it down.'

He stood up.

'Thing is, they were fit, healthy lads. How in God's name did someone manage to give them Rohypnol? Weird... and, given Watt's body weight, how the hell did someone manage to carry them and dump them in the loch?'

'I was wonderin' that too. Do you think it might be more than one person?'

'I'm starting to wonder, Bri. It's a distinct possibility.'

'Right, Boss, I'll away and get on with it.'

'Good stuff; and I'll away and see how the boys are doing down the road.'

Chapter 4

Lunchtime. Delia stood up. She was starving, having somehow missed breakfast, and she had an interview scheduled for two o'clock. She grabbed her bag and, with a final check to make sure everything was in order, she left, closing and locking the door behind her. There was a secure entry at the door of the run-down office block but you couldn't be too careful these days. Three flights of stairs later, Delia Donald stepped out into the hot sunshine, walked a few hundred yards down the steep hill and on to a busy, bustling Dumbarton Road, the former main thoroughfare to its namesake. She continued along the hot, dusty pavement, her heart lifted by the benison of the sun, until she came to her most favourite shop, Matonti's delicatessen. As always, the welcome was profuse.

'Delia, mio amore. And how is my favourite lady today?'

She smiled. How could she resist his charms?

'Just dandy, Marco. All the better for seeing you, of course.'

The young Italian grinned, his beautiful white teeth gleaming in his dark, neatly trimmed beard. Her heart fluttered.

'And what can I get for my darling today? Wait, I have a beautiful, freshly baked ciabatta, simply bursting with sun-dried tomatoes, buffalo mozzarella and slices of Tuscan sausage in which the garlic positively sings to you like Caruso. How does that sound?'

She smiled. God, he was beautiful; she loved him dearly.

'That sounds absolutely fantastic, Marco, and a can of San Pellegrino, please.'

'Blood orange?'

'Ah, you know me so well, my man.'

'Oh, not nearly well enough, dearest. Listen, you have a seat and I'll get this prepared for you.'

He turned and shouted into the kitchen.

'Lena, your finest sausage ciabatta for our dearest Delia, please.'

A voice shouted through from the back shop.

'Okay. Hey Delia, how goes it?'

'Great thanks, Lena. You?'

'Yeah, good, thanks. Butter?'

'Please, probably shouldn't though...'

Marco grinned.

'Ah, you can't fatten a thoroughbred....'

The few tables in the deli were already taken so she perched herself on one of two high stools that sat beside a narrow counter, suddenly realising that this was the seat where she had first met Pam. She smiled at the memory...

*

It had been nearly six months ago; a "gey dreich" day, as her mother had been wont to say and that had summed it up perfectly. Overcast and grey, with sporadic sleet showers driven by a chill north wind, it was a Glasgow winter at its worst and Delia had sought comfort in her little haven that was Matonti's delicatessen. She had expected it to be quiet but she was wrong. It was full of people seeking similar sanctuary and, with a heavy heart, she realised that she would have to make do with a take-away and return to her rather dingy little office. Marco had smiled apologetically at her over the shoulder of a customer when, suddenly, she heard a soft, seductive and very feminine voice just behind her. It seemed vaguely familiar.

'You're welcome to join me, if you like.'

Delia turned to the source of the delicate tones and saw a woman sitting on one of the two tall stools, a coffee and a half eaten croissant in front of her. She was hard to age, possibly mid fifties, although she looked younger. She had beautiful ash-blonde hair, cut in a flattering, short style that framed what her mother would have described as a "handsome" face. Delia still wasn't sure if the term was entirely complimentary! The woman was tall and well-proportioned and she was dressed immaculately. In her brief appraisal, Delia noticed that she had very good legs and, somehow, she knew that the short boots she was wearing were one of those brands about which she could only dream. Jimmy Choo, or something of that sort. Although she couldn't quite place her, Delia had the impression that the woman might be a celebrity of some sort. There was definitely something familiar about her. She spoke again.

'Please? I could do with some company, actually.'

Delia smiled back and sat on the other stool beside the elegant, poised lady.

'So could I, if truth be told. It's one of my favourite places, especially on a gloomy day like this – I was surprised to see it so busy.'

'Yes, I was surprised myself, I think it's the miserable weather, people like to stay inside having that second coffee... and maybe another piece of cake!'

The woman smiled and, somehow, Delia felt she could trust her; she could certainly do with a friend...the woman continued.

'Yes, I must confess that I do rather like the cake in here. I shouldn't really' she patted her slightly round tummy 'but then, life's too bloody short...'

Delia saw the woman's smile falter and a hint of sorrow pass over her face, like a cloud fleetingly passing in front of the sun. Then the smile returned and the woman held out her hand.

'I'm Pam, by the way. Pam Lawson.'

Oh my God...

The woman looked at her, her hand still proffered. She gave Delia a questioning look.

'Are you all right? You look as if you've seen a ghost?'

Delia didn't know what to do. Of course, there had always been a faint chance that something like this could happen but...she swallowed hard; best to tell the truth! She took the woman's hand.

'Hello Pam. I'm Delia. Delia Donald.'

The two women stared at each other, their hands frozen in the handshake. Then Pam smiled and broke the silence.

'Well, that *is* a surprise!'

Delia smiled back as they released their handshake.

'Em, yes, it certainly is. Listen Pam, are you comfortable with this? I mean, I can always...'

'Och, don't be silly, Delia. I'm absolutely fine if you are. After all, I feel like I know you already and you certainly know enough about me! Right, let me buy you lunch then something delectable from the cake display – what do you fancy?'

And so, over a panini, a latte and a large slice of gooey, chocolate heaven, Delia Donald, owner of the Domestic Services Agency and Pam Lawson, one of her most recent clients, became friends.

*

'Hey, Delia, here's your lunch, baby.'

'What? Oh...oh, thanks Marco...'

'You were miles away there. Something on your mind?'

'Oh, no Marco, I was just remembering the day I met my friend Pam. I was sitting right here on this stool.'

Marco frowned very slightly.

'Ah si. Pam; the lady who rescued you...'

*

She finished her lunch and went over to the counter, taking her purse out of her bag.

'Can I have another San Pel to go please, Marco?'

'Sure, baby.'

As he placed the can into the bag, she saw him lift a small Italian sweetmeat from the counter and surreptitiously pop it into the bag beside the can of juice. She also saw the price – £2.95.

'Listen, thanks all the same, Marco, but I can't affo...'

'On the house, dearest Delia. You look hungry today. Better than a kiss. Well, of course, if you'd like to compare...'

Delia laughed. Oh, how she loved this, it was so often the highlight of her day. She placed a finger on her mouth, kissed it, then placed it on Marco's full lips.

'Away with you, Marco. I'm almost old enough to be your mother. Well, your big sister, at least!'

'Ah, mio cuore sanguinante, Delia! He groaned, holding his chest in mock pain. 'And what nonsense. You're hardly a day over twenty-five!'

Aye, and the rest, Marco...!

She took the bag and positively skipped out of the shop, smiling as she went.

'Enjoy, Delia!' he called after her, flashing the smile again. 'See you tomorrow!'

'Manyana!' She shouted over her shoulder. Marco's voice followed her out

'I think you'll find that's Spanish, mio caro...'

*

She rushed along the busy Dumbarton Road, anxious to get back, but the ascent of the steep side-street in which her office was situated seemed harder than normal in the airless, afternoon heat. By the time she arrived it was almost one-thirty and she still

38

needed to tidy herself up and prepare for the interview, which was at two; she got as far as the lobby when her downstairs neighbour accosted her.

'Good afternoon, my dear. There was a young man asking for you, said he had an interview?'

Duncan McGrory was an elderly, sad-faced accountant whose wife had died a number of years previously; he was also her landlord. Delia suspected he had nothing else to do with his life and she couldn't recall the last time she had seen a customer enter or leave his office. Actually, she couldn't recall seeing *him* arrive or leave and she had the suspicion that he slept there, although she had never liked to ask. He seemed to have a soft spot for her, however, and was always happy to provide her with tax and financial advice in return for what she considered to be a nominal sum – and, of course, the occasional smile, along with a few kind words! She smiled at him now, trying to ignore the ominous stains on his checked shirt and crumpled brown trousers.

'Oh, for goodness sake, Duncan, it's not 'til two o'clock! You know, I hate late but, sometimes, early is just as bad. Where is he?'

'Oh, I sent him packing. I'd noticed you going past...'

Oh did you now...!'

'...and I told him you'd gone for lunch. He said he'd come back at two.'

'Thanks a million, Duncan. Listen, I need to get upstairs and freshen up. I'd best hop off in case he turns up early again. Thanks so much.'

She turned to go but Duncan hadn't finished. He gave her a concerned and somewhat avuncular look, his watery blue eyes staring over the top of his ancient half-moon spectacles.

'Delia, I do worry about you sometimes. I mean, I've seen a few young men go up to your office, occasionally there's more than one. Are you sure you're quite...well, safe?'

'Och, yes, Duncan, thanks for asking though. These are the boys who work for me, my tradesmen, if you like. I know them all pretty well...'

'But you don't know this one, though. Big chap he was, too. You're sure you wouldn't like me to...sit in, perhaps?'

She smiled and touched his arm. It was as if the sun briefly shone on his face and she felt a twinge of what— sadness? Pity? Guilt?

'Duncan, you're such a sweetheart, that's really kind. No, I'll be absolutely fine, he comes with references so there'll be no problem. But it's so nice of you to think of me, really.'

He sighed.

'Well, if you're sure...but if you need me, just call and I'll come right up.'

Aye, tomorrow morning by the time you manage the stairs, you old darling!

'Will do, Duncan. Now, I must go and freshen up. Bye.'

A few minutes later, she closed the door behind her. She was safe.

*

Delia was vaguely regretting the garlic-laden sausage she had eaten at lunchtime. Apart from the certainty that it would repeat on her for the rest of the day, she was sure that her breath reeked of it. She entered the little toilet behind the desk, cleaned her teeth, washed her hands then had a quick look in the mirror. It was a most peculiar thing. The face that she saw was a very different one from that seen by others...

What Delia saw looking back at her was a small, slightly rounded face with quite large and close-set dark-hazel eyes (actually she would have loved green). She had once been told her that there was mischief in them but, no matter how hard she tried, she was never able to see it. Fortunately her lashes were quite long and dark, as was her slightly unruly hair that refused to do what was asked of it and persisted in forming large, random curls. She usually tied it back rather severely in an attempt to exercise a degree of control, as she had done today. She wasn't tall, about five-five (she would really have liked to be taller and usually wore high heels as compensation) and although her figure wasn't bad. She worked out when time permitted. She wasn't exactly what could be called voluptuous. In her favour, she didn't think she looked her thirty-five years. Most people (Marco Matonti included, apparently) took her to be in her late twenties. She didn't usually bother with a lot of make up; people could take her as they found her, but now she applied a small amount of dark red lipstick to emphasise what she considered a slightly thin top lip. That would do. A quick spray of "Insolence" and she was ready to face the world. A world that saw a very different lady...

*

Two o'clock, on the dot, the buzzer sounded; Delia pressed the intercom button.

'Hello, Domestic Services Agency.'

The voice was soft, quite high and polite, a good start.

'Hi, It's Aidan, Aidan Coulson. I've got an interview.'

'Hi Aidan. Come on up, I'm on the top floor, left-hand door, but you already know that, don't you...'

Oh now, Dee, don't be sarcastic...

She pressed the button to open the door downstairs, then crossed to her office door at which, a minute at the most later, there was a firm knock. She opened it and, despite her heels, found Aidan Coulson towering over her. She reckoned he was six-two easily. She held out her hand and he shook it firmly. He had a charming smile, she noticed.

'Come on in, Aidan.'

She closed the door and crossed back to her chair, a bit of an indulgence with a variety of levers and adjustments. She spent a lot of time sitting and she was damned sure she was going to be comfortable! Aidan stood in front of the desk, looking rather awkward, as if he couldn't decide whether he should just sit or wait to be invited.

'Right, Aidan, let me have a look at you. Could you take off your jacket, please?'

He gave her a sheepish grin as he removed his faded denim jacket, placing it over the back of the visitor's chair. He was wearing tight black jeans and a pale yellow linen shirt with short sleeves. She could see why. His muscles were beautifully defined, not the steroid-pumped monstrosities of a body-builder but more rounded and powerful like those of a true athlete. He had short dark hair and was clean shaven, with broad shoulders tapering to a neat waist and unfeasibly long legs.

'So, you say you're an outdoor sports coach. What does that involve, exactly? Oh, please, take a seat, sorry.'

Aidan sat down, smiling over at her.

Oh, he's a looker, this one...

'Well, I work up in Perthshire and the North-West mostly, doing a bit of orienteering, rafting, rock climbing, that sort of stuff. I also lead some minor mountaineering trips, you know, with all the fancy kit, ropes, pitons... it's pretty exciting but, to be honest, the work can be a bit sporadic.'

He certainly looked the part – the lyrics of a long-forgotten song suddenly sprang into her mind, "tall and tanned and young and lovely..." he was all that and more. She smiled sweetly across at him. He seemed nervous and she wanted to put him at his ease.

'I see. That sounds really interesting, Aidan; and it says here that you're a friend of Simon Hope...'

Simon bloody Hope...

Even after all these years, the mention of his name caused her stomach to churn very slightly, not to mention the vague feeling like a pulse of electricity in her...

No, Delia, don't...

She had been an innocent young student of English Literature at Glasgow University, not long arrived from the little provincial southern Scottish town of Dumfries. Everything was new; new city, new classmates, new seat of learning... and she was utterly miserable. Homesick, lonely, lost, until she had met Simon Hope.

She had been in the University library, desperately seeking inspiration for a critical essay on Gerard Manley Hopkins' epic poem "The Wreck of the Deutschland." She was also reluctant to return to her dingy student accommodation, where Tara, her tattooed and pierced flatmate, reeked of stale tobacco and chewed gum endlessly. She was staring at the pages, nervously gnawing at the end of her pen when, suddenly, a voice spoke softly, as if just behind her head.

'Hello, I presume you must be one of the new students. I'm sure I'd have remembered seeing you otherwise... settling in okay?

Simon Hope.

She recognised the soft, Aberdeenshire accent and turned, prepared to admonish him for making her jump; but, in that one lengthy second, she was lost. She opened and closed her mouth several times, like a goldfish blowing bubbles, before managing to blurt out

'Em...yeah, just started first year... a few weeks ago...I think.'

Oh God...

He smiled. It was the most beautiful thing she had ever seen.

'Well, whichever week it was, welcome. I'm Simon Hope,

currently doing a bit of research here— oh, and doing some lecturing as well. Can't keep away from the place, it seems. A man's got to do, and all that nonsense.'

He extended his hand and she took it. His grip was firm, his palm warm and she tried very hard not to imagine it touching her...

Nooo...

'Hello, I'm Delia... Abercrombie. Nice to meet you, Simon.'

She could feel the colour rise in her cheeks and she didn't know why she had struggled to tell him such a simple thing as her surname.

'Well, it's very nice to meet you too, Delia Em-Abercrombie...'

And so it began; he just happened to be one of her tutors...

*

'Excuse me Delia, but are you okay?'

'What? Oh, I'm so sorry, Aidan, I was miles away. It's just that Simon and I go back quite a way. How is he?'

'Well, if you know Simon, you hardly need to ask. He's the proverbial guy who fell in the Clyde and came out with a salmon in his mouth. He lives in a beautiful country house up in deepest Perthshire, sitting in about fifty acres! Spends most of his time writing, of course. I think he's on his ninth novel now. Making a bloody fortune, especially since his "Saint Mungo - Sinner" series got snapped up by Netflix.'

Oh yes, she knew alright. It was one of Delia's great indulgences! With considerable difficulty she had persuaded her (hopefully-soon-to-be ex) husband, Danny, that they needed Netflix purely so that she could watch Simon's brutal but compelling tale about Mungo Harris, the violent, maverick Glasgow private investigator unfold. And she was sure that she recognised herself in one of his characters. Maybe one day she'd ask him...

'Yes, he has done rather well' she replied.

'That was how we met, actually,' continued Aidan.

'Really?' She was very interested now.

'Yes, as well as the outdoor stuff, I also have an equity card. You know Andrew Watt, of course?'

Andy was also one of Delia's "boys", another tall and well-built specimen. She rather liked him, although he was a good deal younger than she was.

'Oh yes, I know Andrew well. He works for me.'

Aidan grinned.

'Yes, he told me. Actually, if you don't mind me saying so, I think he's... well, let's just say he's fond of you.'

She could feel the colour rise in her cheeks.

'Och, away, Aidan. Anyway, I know that Andrew has a minor part in the series. I've been following it faithfully.'

Aidan sat back in his chair and put his hands behind his head, his muscles rippling as he did so.

'Well, Andy and I were doing a bit of climbing up in Skye last year and he mentioned that they were looking for some new cast members for the next series. He knew Simon, of course, said he'd put in a word; before I knew it, I was having dinner with the man himself, we had a good chat, he pulled a few strings and managed to get me cast in a small, but fairly crucial, part. I start filming in a couple of weeks.'

'Really? What part's that?'

'Sorry, Delia, if I let anything slip they'd sue the pants off me, but if you watch the next series, you can't miss me...'

Yes, you'd be hard to miss...and as for the pants being off...

'Oh, you meanie!' she laughed.

'...oh, and it was Simon who suggested that, if I needed some extra income in the meantime, you might be interested!'

'Yes, good old Simon. Anyway, down to business, then. I take it Simon has explained what we do here?'

'Oh, he certainly has...'

Chapter 5

By the time Grant arrived back at Castle Semple loch, the haze had burned off and it was another glorious late-summer day. There was still a uniformed cop at the entrance but, as before, he was waved through and he parked in the still-deserted car park next to what he assumed to be DC Cliff Ford's car.

Seriously...a bloody Ford...!

He allowed himself a smile. He realised he was warming to the enthusiastic young detective. He found Cliff and Faz searching round the pontoons and they came over to meet him. He knew by the expression on the faces that their trip hadn't turned up anything remotely significant. Cliff shook his head.

'Nothin', Boss. The uniforms an' the SOCOs have been pretty thorough anyway but we've had a good snoop about an' there's no' a single thing to indicate any suspicious activity here. Gound's just too dry and dusty.'

'Ok Cliff, it was worth a try. Listen, let's go and grab a bite. There's a decent wee cafe up in the village. You never know, some of the locals may have seen something suspicious.'

The two detective constables looked surprised at this slightly uncharacteristic show of generosity, friendship, even!

'Em, yeah, that'd be great, Boss, cheers.' replied Faz.

'Right, let's just walk up the road, get more of a feel. Mind you, I already know it reasonably well.'

'Aye, you live down here, don't you, Boss? 'asked Cliff.

'Not far, up the hill, just outside Howwood. Sometimes cycle down here, I can do most of the loop on the cycle track and I usually stop here for a coffee...'

He stopped, realising once again that he hadn't for months...

*

Over the excellent soup and sandwiches in The Junction Cafe, Grant brought them up to date with the latest developments on the case, including his theory that there might be more than one person involved. They were about to leave when his phone rang . It was Dr Napier again, with the results of the second post-mortem.

'Grant.'

'Hello Doctor. You've finished the second one?'

'Yes, and it's more of the same. Well, except for one aspect.'

'What's that?'

'This poor chap was dead prior to being placed in the water. However he did in fact, drown, but in his own blood.'

Grant squeezed his eyes shut as if trying to block out the image. Dr Napier continued.

'The beating was brutal and I would imagine that the victim was probably unconscious following it. He had considerable laceration to his gums, including three missing teeth, and he continued to bleed after the duct tape was applied. His airways became blocked with blood and he suffocated. As I said, my suspicion is that he was probably unconscious, which is a small mercy.'

Again, he could hear the suppressed anger in the Doctor's voice

– this case seemed to have really upset her. He thanked her and ended the call, then turned to Faz and Cliff.

'Well, same MO as the first, as expected, although this poor bastard was dead before he was thrown in the loch.'

'Dead?' asked Cliff in surprise.

'Aye. Choked on his own blood, apparently...'

He paused, his brows furrowed in thought.

'I think this has to be significant. And I think that we need to have a good look round their flat, just in case they were involved in something. It's starting to show the hallmarks of a gangland-style killing.'

'I get what you mean, Boss' replied Faz. 'Dealers, maybe? It's not just murder, it's like, well, a message, isn't it?

'Aye, exactly. Warning people not to cross a line. Maybe they were branching out on their own. I'll call Bri, get Mrs Watt's number and arrange for you to carry out another search of their flat. But go easy, the poor woman's distraught, naturally. Could be wrong, of course, but we need to check all avenues. Have another look for the car keys too. His car's still outside so where the hell did they go – and how? Right, let's get on...'

*

Once he was back at Osprey House, Grant phoned Andrew Watt's parents. It was his father who answered the phone and Grant could clearly detect the emotion in the man's voice. He asked if he could arrange for Cliff and Faz to return to the flat and carry out a more thorough search. Although obviously distraught, the significance of Grant's request wasn't lost on Tony Watt.

'And what, exactly, are you looking for, Chief Inspector?'

'I'm not sure, Mr Watt. Anything that might cast some light on why your son and his friend were murdered.'

Mr Watt wasn't convinced.

'Really. Well, I can tell you right now that Andy wasn't involved in anything criminal, if that's what you're thinking.'

'Mr Watt, I'm not thinking or suggesting anything. We simply want...'

'And what, exactly, *do* you "simply want," Chief Inspector?" Listen, my son was a good, hard working young man and if you think he had any involvement in anything like...well, drugs or something criminal, then you're wrong.'

Although sympathetic, Grant was wearying of Tom Watt's remonstrations.

'Mr Watt, we're simply carry...'

'I don't suppose you're aware of his charity work, Chief Inspector?'

'Em, no, what charity work?'

'Andy lost a good friend to heroin a number of years ago. Since then, he's become very involved in a Charity called Scottish Families Against Drugs...'

He paused.

'...or was, now, I suppose...'

'Mr Watt, I appreciate your sentiments and I appreciate the information you've provided, but if we're to try and catch the murderer then we need to get as much background knowledge on your son as we can. So, please, can my officers come and have another look round the flat?'

Tom Watt sighed.

'Oh, I suppose so. Give me half an hour.'

*

It was later in the afternoon when Grant received the first snippet of information that made the hairs on the back of his neck tingle. Cliff and Faz had returned to Andrew Watt's flat where they had been met by Tom, Andrew's father.

As indicated by the father, they found absolutely nothing to indicate any criminal involvement of either young man; nor did they find the car keys. Briony and DC Sam Tannahill had organised some uniforms to carry out door-to-door enquiries, often a fruitless and disheartening task. However, eventually they tracked down two separate residents who reported that, early on the Thursday evening, they had noticed the victims, whom they recognised, getting into a white private-hire cab. As this was a fairly commonplace occurrence, they hadn't taken much notice and were unable to provide any further details on the cab. Still, it was a start...

It was about an hour later when Briony phoned back. The excitement in her voice was clear.

'Right Boss, we've got somethin'. I've just spoken to a young woman who was late home from work on Thursday. She saw the taxi too and recognised Andy. Apparently he's in some television series. From the description of the person with him, I'd be fairly certain that it's Andrew and Chris.'

'Good stuff, Bri. Don't suppose she got the registration, by any chance?'

There was a pause.

'Better than that, Boss! Her boyfriend bought her a dash-cam for her birthday! I've got it with me, just need to plug it into a computer and we should have the whole thing in glorious technicolour... well, you know what I mean!'

Grant hung up, a smile forming on his lips. He knew this might well prove to be the turning point that could break the case.

*

The team were assembled in the now uncomfortably hot meeting room; Cliff was updating the white board with all the latest information, having removed the question marks from the two young mens' identities.

'Right' said Grant, standing up. 'We've confirmed the victims' identities; we know that Chris Findlay's girl-friend spoke to him early on Thursday afternoon so, presumably, they were both still alive at that point. Anyway, Dr Napier has confirmed the time of death . Well, of the victim who drowned in the loch. As no earlier than say, eleven p.m. on Thursday. Now, there's no way that anyone could have disposed of two bodies in the loch with the chance of any cars still hanging about in the car park so, tying in with the report of a vehicle passing at about three a.m. on the Friday morning, I think we can safely assume that this was when they were placed in the water. It fits with everything else.'

Faz was sitting at a laptop loading the information from the dash-cam. Suddenly he looked up and grinned.

'Right, got it. Here we go...'

Grant continued.

'Now, our tech-genius here is about to show us dash-cam footage taken outside the victims' flat, early on Thursday evening. We've got witness reports of the two men getting into a white private-hire cab and now..'

They all crowded round the screen, watching in anticipation as the scene unfolded; Grant was at the front.

'Right, Faz, stop...okay...' he rubbed his hands together 'fan-bloody-tastic! There we go – the car's a Skoda. See the logo? And the men getting in certainly look like the two victims. Faz, is there any way you could enhance the images of the driver? And can you maybe enlarge the reg plates so we can track him down? See what magic you can work. Sam, once Faz has done his stuff, run a check on the registration.'

He rummaged in his trouser pocket and pulled out a couple of crumpled twenty-pound notes.

'Anyone fancy a take-away. It's on me...?'

Delia locked the office, checking it one final time before she turned for the stairs. It had been a pretty good day; a new member of her team recruited, calls from a couple of regular clients as well as that hesitant, first-approach earlier in the morning. Maybe that would be a suitable first client for Aidan...

As she drove home to the tidy little bungalow that she now called home, her mind strayed back to the saga that was Simon Hope. She sighed. It seemed so long ago but every time she thought that she was finally over him, somehow his name popped up, causing the bitter-sweet memories to flood back into her seemingly powerless mind...

It had been a Friday night, mid-way through her first term. Delia hadn't found it particularly easy to make new friends. A lot of her class-mates had formed early alliances from which she seemed to be excluded. Many of them came from Glasgow and, somehow, she still felt like an outsider, a gauche young woman from the provinces. She had been a bit of a late starter, her widowed mother lacking the financial resources to subsidise Delia's further education. In order to save sufficient funds, her working gap year had turned into three and, at twenty-one, she neither fitted with the late-teenagers nor the mature students. Rather than spend every weekend alone, she would occasionally make the long train journey home to Dumfries, but her mother's health had deteriorated in the last year and Delia always returned on a Monday feeling that University was actually a rest from her weekend of chores.

It had been about four o'clock and she had just seated herself at a corner table in the library, preparing for yet another essay.

'Hello, Delia Em-Abercrombie.'

It was his customary greeting.

'Oh, hello Simon. How's things?'

She had finally been able to hold a conversation with him without stumbling over her words, but she could feel the heat rise in her cheeks. Why on earth did this unbelievably beautiful and charismatic man seem interested in her? A few of her class-mates had made sarcastic comments about his attention . Presumably they were jealous...

'All the better for seeing you, Delia. So, what are you up to this weekend?'

'Oh, nothing much, really. A bit of studying, I'll maybe go for a walk in Kelvingrove Park tomorrow, do some washing, all the usual boring stuff.'

'Are you hungry?'

'Sorry?'

'Are you hungry, Delia? I take it you do like to eat sometimes, rather than burying your pert little nose in some mighty tome?'

She laughed. He had such a way with words.

'Well, I suppose a Pizza wouldn't go amiss...'

'Pizza! Don't be ridiculous. Right, away home and get yourself ready – glad rags and all that nonsense. I'll meet you outside at six o'clock.'

'But...'

'No! Not a single "but", Delia. It's Friday night. Time to let our hair down; I'll pick you up at six!'

She glanced at her watch; she had two hours...

*

The evening in Rogano, Glasgow's famous Art-Deco restaurant, had passed in a haze of wondrous food, copious quantities of fine champagne and stimulating, entertaining conversation. In fact, it was one of the best evenings of her life but, all too soon, it was over; once Simon had paid the bill (ensuring that she didn't get a sniff of the final total) she was courteously helped into her coat and they were walking back towards Central Station and the taxi rank. Simon opened the door of the nearest cab then stepped in after her. The cabbie turned round.

'Where to, Sir?'

'West End. Wilton Street, please.'

'Sure thing! He replied, switching off the "For Hire" sign before indicating and pulling out onto Gordon Street.

Surprised, Delia turned and looked at Simon.

'Wilton Street? I don't live in Wilton Street, Simon.'

'I know, but I do...'

*

Twenty minutes later, they were climbing the stairs to his flat, Simon having asked her in for coffee and, maybe, a nightcap. The journey had been made mostly in a companionable silence; she had leaned against him, feeling his masculine warmth permeate through her thin coat and she realised that she was now in a wonderful, slightly euphoric state induced by champagne, fine food and attractive male company; what she was beginning to think of as "the danger zone..." She was young and inexperienced . He seemed so confident, so elegant and poised, and he was with her... she sighed, knowing what would happen, knowing that she was powerless, knowing that she didn't care...

They reached his landing, Simon unlocked the heavy wooden door and they entered his flat. The hall was bigger than her own bedroom, tastefully decorated and softly lit with a beautiful Tiffany lamp, its multi-coloured glass shade casting rainbow colours on the clean, elaborately-corniced white ceiling. Delia's eyes widened as she smiled.

'Oh Simon, it's gorgeous.'

He turned to face her.

'And so are you, Delia...'

The hall was deliciously warm and cosy, mainly due to the presence of an old-fashioned cast iron radiator on one wall, above which was a large mirror with an ornately carved gold frame. Simon gently guided her across, his hands still exploring, until her bottom was almost resting against the hot metal. The feeling of the warm air drifting up between her thighs was glorious. Simon mumbled into her neck.

'I adore the feel of warm flesh, especially a delicious round, soft arse such as yours.'

Oh my God..

His hands were caressing her, stroking the exposed skin of her thighs and her near-naked buttocks. After a few minutes he pulled away slightly and turned her round until she was facing the mirror. He smiled at her over her shoulder.

'It's those eyes, Darling Dee, especially now that you're aroused. They're so full of mischief...'

And so it happened, right there, in the beautiful, warm hallway...

Delia had had a few brief encounters, of course. There wasn't a lot for teenagers to do in Dumfries of a weekend, after all! These tended to take place in a friend's flat, or in a house when someone's parents were away. What her fellow students referred to as an "empty." They invariably involved a half bottle of something cheap and nasty to drink, sometimes a few puffs of a somewhat soggy and disgusting joint. They had been both unfulfilling and unsatisfactory and Delia had been left wondering why there was such a bloody fuss about sex. Until that moment...

It was everything that sex in her previous encounters hadn't been. Intense, electric, wonderful...and now she was sitting near-naked on the polished wooden floor beside this beautiful, sexy man, his arm resting protectively around her shoulder, her head nestled in the dark hairs of his chest. He leaned down and kissed her neck gently as he whispered

'Oh, but you're a dark horse, Delia Em-Abercrombie . A tigress in disguise.'

She smiled and stroked his hair. She had realised that she loved those curls. She had never felt so grown-up, so fulfilled, so confident, in her entire life.

'Well, if I'm a tigress then you're a lion, Simon Hope. Take me to your lair...'

The table was littered with near-empty food containers and a half-full bag of prawn crackers. There would be time to clear it all up later. At the moment, Grant's team of detectives were like hounds on the scent. There was no way they were going home!

They had quickly traced ownership of the Skoda to a Paisley taxi firm, Cliff and Kiera having been despatched to track down and interview the driver. They had returned after an hour, having found out that Andy and Chris were regular customers of the firm and that the driver had dropped them at the Cartbridge pub in Paisley.

'The taxi firm said that they always took the boys home' said

Kiera 'but, on the Thursday in question, no taxi was ordered. I suppose they could have used a different company but they seemed to be creatures of habit so I kinda doubt it.'

Grant considered this.

'Right, that might be significant. Either they used a different company or someone else offered them a lift. Or...'

'They might have been abducted' Sam spoke timidly. DCI McVicar made her slightly nervous.

He looked at her.

'Hm...'

'Remember that Dr Napier said they were drugged, Boss' interjected Briony. 'If they *were* in the pub then surely that would have been the perfect opportunity to spike their drink?'

Grant looked at his watch.

'Aye, and there's still time to go and check. Bri, we'll head across to the Cartbridge and see what they have to say. You too, Faz, just in case there's any tech involved, CCTV or the like. Listen, the rest of you get off home. We'll start afresh in the morning. Good job, guys, we're making progress.'

He stood up and Briony followed suit, realising that in the months she had known DCI Grant McVicar, she had never seen him so animated, so engaged.

Strange that it should take a couple of murders...

Chapter 6

Delia Donald swallowed the last mouthful of Glayva, sat back on the tweed couch and closed her eyes. She should really go to bed but the mention of Simon Hope had badly unsettled her – more than usual, for some reason. Briefly she toyed with the idea of phoning him but she knew it would serve little purpose He would ask to see her, she would refuse, the conversation would become awkward, and they would part on a harsh word...

No, Delia, just leave it... unless you're really desperate...

She got up and went into the kitchen, where she poured herself another hefty measure of the sweet, comforting liqueur, popping in a couple of ice cubes. She may as well. She certainly wouldn't sleep tonight...

*

Simon Hope had a lot to answer for. Apart from everything else, he had broken Delia's heart; but he was also responsible for the idea that became the Domestic Services Agency.

It had come about completely by accident. Delia had nearly finished her third year, having metamorphosed from a rather gauche country girl into a more mature, poised (and slightly self-satisfied) young woman-about-town. After an evening celebrating Simon's recent appointment as assistant head of department (involving copious amounts of champagne and followed by some intense love-making) they were lying in his warm, soft bed, casually discussing one of the senior University professors, an attractive lady in her sixties whose husband had died a number of years previously. Delia knew she was lonely and, on several occasions, the woman had expressed considerable envy at Delia's relationship with the gorgeous Simon. It was supposed to be a secret but in the cloistered environment of Glasgow University, secrets didn't keep particularly well!

'You're so lucky, Delia, you know. Simon is...well, he's bloody gorgeous, if truth be told. God, just to have an hour with him. I'd pay a bloody king's ransom!'

Delia had felt her face redden at this rather vulgar statement from a respected member of the University staff.

'But surely there are eligible men out there, Dr Fisher. I mean, you're an attractive woman...'

Dr Fisher smiled at the compliment.

'Thanks, Delia, but I'm not interested in a relationship, my dear. I just want sex.'

Delia laughed as she related the tale to Simon.

'I mean, I went totally scarlet, I couldn't believe what she had just said...'

'She's got a point, though' said Simon, with a mischievous smile.

'What? No, don't say that...'

'Think about it, Dee. She's been happily married for years, her poor husband pops his clogs, she's left on her own. She doesn't want a replacement but she still has physical needs. What does she do? Young folk...well, they head to a pub or a club, pick someone up, have a wee fling. That doesn't happen when you're sixty-ish, fifty-ish even. You still have needs, you can't be bothered with all the faff of a relationship, what the hell do you do? No, I reckon there's a market there. She said it herself. She'd pay a king's ransom!'

Delia was aghast.

'Simon! That's awful. It's... it's... well, I don't know but it's not right.'

'Why not? Recruit a few young guys – there's plenty who fancy the older ladies and would be more than happy giving them some satisfaction in return for a small fee...'

'But that's prostitution, Simon, you can't...'

'I'm just saying. I bet if you put the proposition to Dr Fisher she'd jump at the chance. And I know a couple of guys who would probably be totally up for it!'

He chuckled wickedly but Delia was horrified.

'No, Simon, you can't, it's just wrong. What about the young men, paying them to have sex with older women... it's exploitation, that's what it is. Plain and simple.'

'No it's not! You're not forcing them to do anything they don't want to do, just rewarding them for keeping a lonely old woman happy, and maybe having a bit of fun along the way! Winners all round – and you could keep an administration fee. Christ, what a great idea, I don't know why I didn't think of it before!'

They had argued for ages but, as usual, Simon's persuasive nature (and the champagne, of course) had prevailed and the seeds were sown. Of course it wouldn't be prostitution, exploitation, any of the things that had seemed so rational to Delia. No, it would be a kindly, sympathetic service, offering pleasure with no commitment to lonely older ladies.

'But surely you'd risk getting caught!?' she had asked, still doubtful.

'Not if you were careful. You could give the guys a uniform. The clients would love that. A van, call it something innocuous like... well, the Domestic Services Agency, or something of the sort. Work on the premise that they're visiting to repair something, unblock the sink, fix the dishwasher.; maybe even some gardening. There's loads of excuses for them to be there. Keep regular accounts that show legitimate services. As I said, repairs, gardening, all these things would normally attract a fee, wouldn't they? You could even develop a code of some sort for their real activities, one that only you know. Then, if anyone looked at the books, all they'd see would be normal, everyday tasks— simple! Pay the guys in cash, they'd be more than happy with that – straight in the back pocket! It needn't be suspicious at all. After all, no-one's going to blow the whistle, are they? They'd be too embarrassed. No, I think it could work. In fact, I'm going to have a wee look at this, come up with a business plan of some sort... and, as I said, I know a couple of guys...'

As usual, the conversation had developed into an intense physical interlude. Somewhere, deep down, Delia found the idea rather exciting and her mind had started to race with the numerous erotic fantasies that could ensue. Maybe she'd write a book...thus, the concept of the Domestic Services Agency was born and it would quite probably have remained as just that, if it hadn't been for the phone call.

She had been in that delicious hazy state that came the morning after a night of champagne and sex. She had heard Simon's phone ringing but had chosen to ignore it, until she heard the words

'... okay, love, I'll be up as soon as I can. Tell mum I'm coming. I'll meet you at the hospital.'

Suddenly, she was wide awake.

'Who was that, Simon?'

He sat up, swinging his legs out of the bed.

'Em...no-one...listen, I'll get us a coffee...'

She grabbed his arm.

'No! No coffee, Simon. Who were you calling "love?"'

He turned and stared at her, a distant and slightly furtive look in his eyes.

'Actually, Dee, I should probably have told you before. You see, I'm married...'

She had stormed down the stairs five minutes later, dishevelled, distressed and with tears stinging her eyes.

You stupid bitch, Delia Abercrombie! You fucking stupid bitch...

Monday night was seldom a busy night in Paisley's well-established Cartbridge pub. A few regulars, a few strangers...

four young men were chatting and guffawing in the far corner, celebrating an eighteenth birthday (with at least one fake ID having been shown)

Meg McCorquidale ran a tidy shop, apart from the doubtfully-aged lad, nervously sipping his pint, she tolerated no nonsense, the pub was spotless, the brass taps gleamed and her staff were reasonably honest and friendly. She was standing behind the bar, polishing some new wine glasses that she had just unwrapped, when they walked in; her instinct told her immediately that they were police, CID judging by their plain clothes. Fortunately, she had a clear conscience and, placing the glass on the counter, she smiled.

'Evenin', officers, an' what can I do fur you the night?'

Briony smiled back at the woman.

'Are we that obvious?'

Meg grinned.

'Listen, hen, when you've been in this game as long as I have, you can place folk within seconds. police, drug dealers, Jehova's Witnesses...need to be on the ball! Anyway, the name's Meg, Meg McCorquidale. How can I help you?'

'Right, Meg, I'm Detective Sergeant Quinn, this is my boss D.I. Grant and that's D.C Bajwa. I'll tell you what it is – you have a quiz night on a Thursday, I believe?

'Aye, an' very popular it is too. Got five regular teams on the go.'

'Right, can you think back to last Thursday...' she reached into her bag and took out a copy of the photo of the stag weekend attended by Andy and Chris '...do you recognise any of these young men?'

Meg McCorquidale smiled and pointed at one of the figures.

'Och, aye, of course I do. That's big Andy...and there's his mate Chris – they come along most Thursdays for the quiz; they're pretty good, actually. Nice lads – I take it you know about Andy?'

Grant frowned, and took over the questioning.

'No, Meg. What do you mean, exactly?'

'Oh, he's a bit of a local celebrity. He's in that series on the telly... what's it called...oh aye, Saint Mungo-something. Not a huge part but he's been in a good few episodes. Mind you, he's a good lookin' big lump of a laddie, an' the lassies love him...'

A frown creased her freckled face.

'...now you come to mention it, Thursday just there was a bit strange.'

Grant furrowed his brows.

'Strange? In what way?'

'Well, they came in as usual, full o' the joys. They always seem to have a bit o' ready cash on them. About seven, I'd say, they usually have a couple of pints before eight . That's when the quiz starts. These two guys came in not long after and they immediately recognised Andy. I remember one saying that his wife really fancied him; that really appeals to the big lad an' Chris just basks in the reflected glory. He's an awfy nice boy too. Anyway, next thing it was autographs, an' I think they stood Andy and Chris a couple of pints.'

'Does that happen often, Meg?' asked Briony.

'Aye, maybe every couple o' weeks, someone comes up and talks to Andy. Men occasionally but more often women, wantin' a selfie... sometimes a bit more, if you know what I mean...'

She gave a suggestive wink and Grant responded immediately.

'And does he ever oblige, do you know?'

Meg shook her head.

'Och, no, he's decent enough, is Andy. Sometimes they get a wee kiss but I've never seen him follow up on the offer – well, not so far as I know, anyway.'

She stopped and frowned.

'The thing is, it's always a busy night an' I didn't really notice them after that, I don't think they took part in the quiz, though. Normally they say cheerio when they head off. Here, I'll ask my barman, he was on last Thursday. Cal!'

A slightly overweight man with an earring and slicked-back black hair sauntered over and stood beside Meg – his expression was a bit less welcoming and Grant got the feeling the man had something to hide. He spoke in a broad West of Scotland accent.

'Aye, Mrs M. Whit's up?'

'D'you remember last Thursday, when Big Andy and Chris were in. Those two that bought them a pint? What happened after? I don't remember the boys at the quiz.'

'Naw, they left.'

'They left? Where did they go?' asked Grant.

'Dunno. They seemed a bit worse fur wear an' the two men took them outside, think they said somethin' aboot gettin' them some fresh air.'

'Did they have much to drink?'

Cal frowned.

'Hm, now you come to mention it, I think they only had a couple o' pints, the other two guys wis buyin'.'

He looked down at Meg, whose expression had become more sombre. She looked up at Grant.

'Here, has somethin' happened to them?'

'I'm afraid so, Meg' replied Grant 'but I can't go into details at the moment. Listen, I don't suppose you know these other two men, by any chance?'

Meg shook her head and looked at her barman.

'Naw, Mrs M. Never seen them before. They acted like they knew the boys but maybe that was just 'cos they recognised Andy. Aye, it *wis* a bit odd, now I come tae think aboot it...'

Faz interrupted

'Can I ask, do you have CCTV in here, Meg?'

'Aye, we do. Mind you, I haven't checked it for ages. Listen, you'd better come through to the office. Cal, keep an eye on those lads in the corner...'

Fifteen minutes later, Faz had located the recording.

'Look, that's them, Boss . And there's the other two guys. It's not that clear but I could probably clean it up... right, let's have a look at the one outside...'

They gazed silently at the grainy images showing on the small flat-screen television screen. It showed Andy and Chris staggering as they exited the pub, then Chris stumbling slightly and being supported by one of the two unidentified men. They walked a few unsteady paces then the men helped them into the rear side door of what looked like a white Ford Transit-style crew bus. Once all four men were inside, the van drove off.

'Any chance you could get the number from that, Faz?' asked Grant.

'Not here, Boss, but if I could take it into the office I should be able to clean it up.'

Grant looked at Meg and raised an eyebrow.

'Aye, go on then. As long as you bring it back in one piece.'

'Don't worry, Meg, Faz here is an absolute wizard with these things. We'll get it back as soon as we've got the necessary images. I'll give you a receipt.'

Briony gave him a look of surprise and surreptitiously patted Faz on the shoulder. Their boss wasn't in the habit of dishing out such praise!

Chapter 7

It was just after eight-thirty when Grant keyed his security code into the panel at Osprey House and, already, it was shaping up to be another hot, sticky day. A couple of minutes later, he entered the office, surprised to see the whole team already assembled and busy working on laptops or reports. Briony smiled at him and glanced at her watch. She decided to risk it...

'What time d'you call this, Boss, eh? She quipped.

Despite himself he smiled back as he mumbled.

'So it needs a Chinese takeaway to get you lot in on time...'

Briony chuckled.

That's more like it...

'Okay, what have we got?'

Faz flashed his customary grin.

'Plenty, Boss. Have a look.'

Grant crossed over and looked at Faz's laptop screen.

'I cleaned it up, got the van registration and a reasonable look at their faces. It's a crew-bus type van, with a rear cab. Andy and Chris got in the back.'

Faz played the slightly grainy footage; Grant could see the strangers helping the victims into the van. There didn't seem to be any sign of force being used.

'Good lad, Faz, good lad. Right, let's run...'

'Done, Boss' said Sam with a smile. It's registered to...'

She looked at her own screen.

'... "Bin there, Done that" They're a wheelie-bin cleaning company, it seems. I did a bit more digging; turns out they're a minor subsidiary of a company called Paton Transport which, in turn, is a subsidiary of a firm known as EnviCon Ltd. Their details are a bit more, em, hazy, shall we say, but they seem to own a raft of other businesses including numerous East-end pubs, a couple of small taxi firms and a chain of tanning salons going by the name of "Tan-Tan".'

Grant stood up and smiled.

'Great work, Sam...'

'Ah, but I'm not done, yet, Boss. I managed to track down the directors...'

Grant crossed over and looked down at the list, his eyes widening in astonishment.

'Well-bloody-well...'
Michael John Pettigrew
Veronica Ann Pettigrew
Helena Joy Pettigrew.
'...got you, you bastards.'

He patted Sam on the shoulder then straightened up and clapped his hands. The room seemed to be supercharged, all his team were smiling, except Briony, who looked puzzled. Grant turned to her.

'I take it you're not yet familiar with the delightful Pettigrew family, Bri?'

She shook her head.

'No, Boss. Anyone care to enlighten me?'

Grant looked across at Cliff Ford.

'Cliff, would you care to bring the sergeant up to speed regarding the Pettigrews' pedigree? Briony's from the East, after all.'

'Aye, sure thing, Boss. Well, Sarge, Pettigrew senior... jeez, where do Ah start? He must be, what, mid to late sixties now an' never successfully prosecuted. My old man used to say —he was a sergeant in the East End— "Son, there's bad, there's worse, then there's the Pettigrews." Said he never met such evil people in all his time on the force. Stopped at nothin' to get their way, apparently. Mainly thievin', re-set an' protection in those day, drugs came later on but now, well, anythin' that'll make money, ah suppose. But then there wis Ricky; that changed a lot things...'

Cliff looked over at Grant; his smile had faded and he was now staring at the floor. He seemed reluctant to continue the story.

'Boss?'

There was silence; then Grant took up the narrative.

Richard 'Ricky' Pettigrew had been the eldest child of the notorious Michael, groomed from an early age to take over and run the family business. Like his father, a combination of luck, intimidation and the best QC that money could buy managed to keep Ricky out of jail. Then, one day, about ten years previously, he had been murdered. Not a quick kill, though; ankles, knees, elbows, a point-blank shot to each and, as Ricky lay writhing in agony, his trousers were unceremoniously pulled down, the barrel stuffed up his rectum and a final two shots were fired. He died in Glasgow's Royal Infirmary a few hours later, his family at his bedside. Despite vowing vengeance on the perpetrators, Michael

Pettigrew was a broken man and shortly afterwards, the running of their crime empire was passed to Ronnie, Ricky's junior by four years. It was now said that there was a fourth level of evil added to the three mentioned by Cliff's father.

Grant stopped speaking and the occupants of the room stared at him. Some knew the story already. He started again, his gaze still fixed firmly on the floor as he spoke.

'Ronnie Pettigrew. There was never a more evil, vicious piece of work walked the streets of Glasgow...'

Another pause. He took a deep breath.

'Anyway, to cut a long story...I was a detective sergeant at the time, my boss was DI Jacky Winters. A bloody good cop, straight as they come. Problem was, he got too close to Pettigrew's operations and Pettigrew took him out.'

Briony looked at him, her mouth open.

'Took him out? Surely no...'

'Aye! He just disappeared one Friday night, then his body turned up a few days later, floating in the Clyde just next to the Renfrew Ferry. You know, the night club. The PM said he'd been drinking heavily and it was assumed he either fell, or was pushed, off one of the bridges...'

Briony continued to stare at her Boss.

'...only thing was, Jacky Winters was teetotal. Couple of days after that, I got a card personally addressed from Pettigrew junior. Sending me her deepest condolences, the bitch, plus a wee note warning me of the perils of drinking too much, a nicely veiled threat. But there was no doubt; they simply pumped him full of booze and threw him in the fucking river...'

There was now a profound silence in the room. Briony looked astonished.

'Wait... Ronnie Pettigrew's a woman?'

Grant lifted his head and looked at her; he had a strange expression on his face, she thought, a mixture of anger, sorrow... and something unfathomable.

'Aye. Veronica's her given name, she's Ronnie to all and sundry.'

Grant then looked back at the other faces staring at him.

'Anyway, moving on, this is a major breakthrough. Even if we can't directly link the Pettigrews to the murders, if her employees are responsible then it'll give us an excuse to go and rattle her cage at the very least. But we'll have to play this very carefully, just like her scum-ball of a brother, Ronnie Pettigrew has already managed to wriggle out of a number of very tricky situations, leaving Prosecuting Counsel wondering just what the hell happened and the Procurator Fiscal baying for blood, as often as not mine.'

'So what now, Boss?' asked Briony. 'I mean, surely this puts a different slant on the case, eh? Do we go after this Ronnie Pettigrew, do you think?'

Grant scowled and rubbed sweat from his forehead.

'I'll have a word with The Mint – thing is, technically Pettigrew isn't on our patch so we might have to liaise with the lads up in Glasgow. I'll check it out with her...at some point.' He turned back to Briony. There was a strange, almost maniacal, gleam in his eyes.

'Right, we need to play this very carefully. First, we need to get hold of that van – I don't think for a minute that these two unidentified men were acting in the victims' best interests. We'll need evidence – prints, hair, blood, anything; even if they weren't assaulted in the vehicle, there should be prints in the rear cab at the very least. We still don't know who these guys were but we've certainly got enough evidence to interview the Pettigrews. Right, Bri, we'll head across and catch them un-awares. Time for your initiation...'

As she drove to work, Delia Donald wondered just how long this good weather could continue. The forecast was full of ominous warnings of impending severe electrical storms but she had wakened to yet another beautiful morning – and a vague sense of suffocation, which had immediately been followed by a deep pang of guilt. In many ways, Pam Lawson had been her saviour. God knows what her brute of a husband, Danny, might have ended up doing to her. Although the physical scars had long since healed, the very thought of him, touching her, forcing himself...

She closed her eyes briefly, then opened them in alarm as her car nudged the kerb.

Careful, girl...!

She shook her head violently. It was over now, that chapter of her life was closed. Thanks to Pam Lawson, of course...

*

A few weeks after their chance meeting in Matonti's Deli, Pam had phoned and invited Delia to lunch, this time in an expensive Italian restaurant in Glasgow's West End. Pam had insisted that it was her treat and Delia felt it would have been churlish to refuse.

It was over the second glass of wine that the question came. It was both expected and dreaded, if Delia was being honest with herself.

'So, Delia, tell me, how on earth did you get into this line of work? I mean... well, the old cliché "what's a nice girl like you..." etcetera; but, seriously, you do seem to be a sweet girl, how did you end up running the Agency?'

Delia took a long sip of her chilled Sauvignon Blanc, placed the glass on the table and sighed.

She brought Pam up to date with the saga that was Simon Hope, to the point where they had split up. Pam gave her a sympathetic smile.

'That must have been hard, Delia. I mean, seeing him nearly every day, how on earth did you cope?'

' Actually, I'm not sure that I did – I wonder if I had some sort of breakdown, when I think about it. To make matters worse, he kept trying to win me back, telling me I was the true love of his life, how he was going to get a divorce as soon as he could, how he couldn't live without me. The usual crap that married men come away with, of course, but it made the situation even harder. I even considered dropping out of Uni but what else could I do...?'

She stopped and took another sip of wine – well, more a large mouthful...

'Then, one day, Professor Fisher took me aside. "Delia" she'd said. "I don't mean to be crude, but I know you and Simon aren't... well, you know. Anyway, I don't suppose there's any way you could... och, no, it's ridiculous, sorry I asked..."'

'And what did you say?'

'Well, it was a bit of a shock but, oddly enough, it seemed to confirm what Simon had already suspected. So I gritted my teeth and said "No, I'll ask, Professor, and I'll let you know." And I did. I thought that it would just really embarrass him and, at least, I would get a bit of revenge. After all, she was a lot older than him and I honestly didn't think he'd be the least bit interested.'

'Good for you, Delia, that was very brave; and the rest, as they say, is history, I suppose?'

'Well, yes and no. To my great surprise, and to add insult to injury, Simon actually did the deed, the professor paid him the agreed amount and, give the rotten sod his due, he gave me half. I wasn't going to take it at first but I realised that I could actually do with the money. The truth is, Simon had been supporting me for three years, wining and dining me, buying me clothes, taking me away for weekends... I wasn't sure that I could actually survive without him but the problem was I couldn't bear the thought of anyone else having him, even though I wasn't,– if you see what I mean?'

'Hmm, yes, I understand. That must have been ghastly, Delia. But how on earth did that lead you to setting up the Agency?'

'Actually, a lot of it was down to this professor. Surprisingly, she turned out to be a bit of a sex addict . After all, she was an attractive enough woman who had been widowed for years. She had a great social life, went loads of holidays – she was really well off. But it seemed that she didn't want a relationship, just a quick shag...oops, sorry, Pam... with a younger man. Sorry, I didn't mean to offend...'

Pam laughed.

'Don't worry, my dear, I'm a big girl and I know fine well what I'm doing. No offence taken, really. Go on.'

'Well, over the next few months, the professor had a good few "dates" with Simon. Then she introduced him to a couple of her friends and, although the good Mister Hope always gave the impression that he was having fun, I suppose there was only so much that even he could physically manage and it was only a matter of time before he started to introduce a few of his own friends, although just what his relationship with these men was, I'm still not entirely sure. Anyway, within six months it had grown into a reasonable business and we were making a good bit of money. I suppose I felt slightly guilty but I was pretty desperate; most of the other students had jobs or supportive families. All I'd had was Simon and now he was out of the picture.'

Their desserts arrived, two delicious helpings of a rich, alcohol-soaked tiramisu. The ambience, the wine and the food were making Delia somewhat garrulous. She went on.

'So, in the end, it was actually Simon who made the break.'

'Really?'

'Well, in a way. One day, he just came up to me and said he wasn't doing it anymore, he wasn't interested. Just like that. Of course, he was the star of the show, Simon always had to have the lead part. But by that time I had another ten guys on the books, so I told him it was fine by me. Give him his due, he gave me the final encouragement I needed to actually turn the agency into a viable business.'

'What, just by walking away from it? '

Delia paused and stared at the table.

'Em... no. He'd started seeing someone else; yet another affair behind his wife's back.'

'God, the conniving bastard! Poor woman. Did she know, do you think?'

Delia shook her head.

'I haven't a clue, Pam; although I wouldn't go quite so far as to refer to her as a "poor woman"'

Pam looked somewhat taken aback.

'Oh, but why not?'

'Well, I suppose I should take what he said with a big grain of salt but, by all accounts, she was a pretty difficult creature to live with.'

Pam gave a slightly sarcastic smile.

'But that's the standard tack, of course; blame the wife! I suppose she "didn't understand him."'

Delia smiled back.

'Sort of— Simon said she was very involved in the church. She'd had a pretty strict religious upbringing, apparently, and she did a lot of missionary work overseas, usually Africa; water projects, orphanages, all that kind of stuff – that was how he had all the time to... well, you know. He said that he could never live up to her expectations of him...'

She paused for a moment, a distant look in her eyes.

'...and she never really wanted to have what he called "proper" sex with him... mind you, I'm still not exactly sure what Simon's definition of "proper sex" was!'

Pam sat back and laughed.

'Hah! And there it is, the root of evil in all men! If only they thought with their brains rather than their balls...'

Delia blushed slightly at Pam's sudden, surprising coarseness and the conversation lulled; they finished their desserts in a very slightly embarrassed silence, then Delia continued.

'So, I kept up the Agency throughout my final year, just in a low-key kind of way. To be honest, a lot of my clients just wanted company, it wasn't necessarily about the physical side of things. Then, when I graduated, I had a choice to make, go into something safe like teaching or turn the agency into a proper business. Somehow, I felt I wasn't cut out to work at the so-called "chalk-face" so, that summer, I spent my spare time finding a wee office and setting myself up. All according to Simon's original and detailed business plan, of course. And here I am. Proprietrix of the Domestic Services Agency.'

'Yes, Delia, here you are.' Pam smiled and raised her glass towards her new friend. 'And very glad I am, too.'

'Really?' Delia's smile returned. 'I often wonder. I try not to think about the morality of it too much and I keep hearing Simon's voice saying "You're providing a kindly, sympathetic service, offering pleasure with no commitment to lonely older ladies." I suppose I am but...'

Pam put down her glass.

'So, tell me, where does your husband, Danny, fit into all this?'

'Danny? Oh well...'

Delia's smile vanished. She took another slug of the delicious, chilled wine, the attentive waiter having re-filled her glass.

'It was on one of many post-graduation nights. I had become quite friendly with Jenny, another slightly older student and she had organised it. We were all in a pub in Byres road and I have to confess I was pretty much hell-bent on having a good time and finding a decent man. I was really missing Simon and... well, the sex-life, I suppose. It was Jenny who noticed Danny. He was at the bar with a few friends, they were all pretty drunk. "Dee, there's a reasonably good-looking bloke over there and he's definitely giving you the eye." she'd said. I had a quick look and I didn't particularly fancy him but, after a few minutes, he came over and started to chat me up. By that time I was drunk and I suppose I was at a pretty low ebb since my split with Simon because, after a few weeks, we were going steady, in a few months we were engaged and within a year we were married. Bliss! Also, the Agency really was an enormous risk; to be perfectly honest, I really hadn't a clue what I was doing and I realised that I needed some kind of anchor, some stability in my life. I moved in to the family farm that he had inherited when his father died, with great hopes of a lovely old farmhouse, an Aga and the stable full of horses that I would undoubtedly have.'

'And did you get them?'

'I certainly got an old farmhouse but it needed a huge amount of work, much more than we could afford. He'd just set up a business erecting agricultural buildings, cow sheds and the like. The house is still a work in progress, according to Danny. As to the horses, well, that never happened either. All I got was...'

Her voice tailed off and she gazed sadly into her wine glass.

'What, Delia? I have the feeling that you're not too happy. What's wrong?'

'Och, it's just married life. Pam. We all get in a rut...we're probably not the people we were...'

Pam smiled and took her hand. Delia was surprised at the rather intimate gesture.

'You remember I said yesterday about life being too bloody short?'

'Yes Pam. I thought you looked a wee bit sad when you said it.'

Pam paused, taking a large slug of her own wine. She put down the glass and sighed heavily.

'I was married to the most wonderful man, Bill Lawson. Coincidentally, like your Simon, he was a handsome Aberdonian and a few years older... anyway, he had started a wee marine engineering business, pretty much from nothing; he was a smart, intelligent and friendly man, everyone liked him. But he worked hard, he gained a good reputation and, suddenly, he found himself with one of the major companies involved in the North Sea oil boom. Made a bloody fortune, retired and sold the business for an even bigger one. We were married for nearly...'

Her voice tailed off and Delia could see the tears welling up in her new friend's eyes.

'Yesterday was the third anniversary of Billy's death. Cancer, just six weeks after diagnosis. Gone, just like that. And all the bloody money, the house, the car, I'd give it all to have one more day with him.'

Pam reached for her napkin and dabbed at the tears that were now running down her cheeks. Delia squeezed her hand.

'Oh Pam, I'm so sorry. I had no idea...'

'Och, Delia, how could you possibly have known? When I phoned you...well, a friend had suggested it might do me good. I was lonely, I just needed some male company. I didn't want a replacement for Billy, I just wanted...well, a man, I suppose. After much soul-searching I phoned you and here we are.'

Delia smiled and, reaching back across the table, gave Pam's hand another squeeze. She lifted her glass and Pam did the same.

'Indeed Pam. Here we are. To us!'

*

They had coffee and a liqueur then, just after three-fifteen, Pam asked for the bill. The waiter brought it on a small silver tray, along with some expensive looking chocolates and Pam grabbed it before Delia could see the amount.

'My treat, Delia.'

'Oh no, Pam, please...'

'No, absolutely not. I asked you, it's on me.'

'But...'

'No "buts", Delia. Indulge me – after all, what else have I got to spend it on...except enjoying myself...'

She gave Delia a knowing wink.

'...and I most certainly have enjoyed myself.'

'So have I, Pam, very much indeed. Thanks a million, it was a wonderful lunch.'

It was only as they were leaving the warmth of the restaurant that she suddenly put her hand to her mouth and gasped.

'Oh my God!'

Pam stopped and turned, a look of alarm on her face.

'What, Delia? What is it?'

'My car! I've had half a bottle of wine and a Glayva – there's no way I can drive. Oh shit...'

'Oh, don't worry, dear. I know the manager. You can leave the car here and get Danny to come for you, surely?'

'I can't, he's away down to Northumberland for a couple of days to see some farmers he's been talking to. He landed a new contract yesterday and he's better placed to tender for new work... oh shit...'

Pam paused for a moment, thinking; she seemed to reach a decision.

'Listen, Delia, have you anything else to do today?'

'No, nothing. I pretty much tied everything up this morning. Why?'

'Well, as I said, I've really enjoyed today, so why end it now? Let's get a taxi back to mine and you can stay over? I'm sure I'll have something that'll fit you, unless you sleep in the altogether...?'

Delia looked slightly taken aback and Pam laughed.

'Oh, goodness, I'm not propositioning you, my dear, although, I must say, you are a very pretty wee thing... no, we can have a snooze, watch a film, have some supper and crack open another bottle of wine. I've a nice spare bedroom just waiting for you . It'd be fun and it's been years since I've had a real "girlie" night.'

Delia thought for all of a nanosecond; her own house would be cold and empty, all she had to look forward to was a ready meal from the freezer and the small consolation of having the bed to herself... She smiled.

'Why the hell not? Lay on, Macduff...'

Pam looked at her curiously.

'Most folk say it wrong. They usually say "lead on"'

Delia laughed

'I'm an English graduate... remember?'

✳

Delia was now driving along Dumbarton road, wondering just how on earth she had got there. The memory had been so powerful that she must have been driving on auto-pilot.

Get a bloody grip, girl. You need to keep your senses about you...

Eventually she found a parking space and headed towards her office. Well, with a detour to Matonti's, of course. The sun was shining, life was good and, as Marco flashed his charming smile at her, her heart sang. Things were on the up...

Chapter 8

DCI Grant McVicar and DS Briony Quinn were heading eastbound on the M8, their final destination being the Pettigrew residence in Glasgow's East End. Driving behind them were DC Cliff Ford and DC Kiera Fox. Grant wasn't sure how this meeting would pan out and he wanted backup, just in case; Ronnie Pettigrew wasn't a woman to be underestimated.

Half an hour later, they pulled up outside a property in Glasgow's Mount Vernon area. Cliff and Kiera had parked a couple of hundred yards down the road, with instructions to remain in their car. Bidewell Crescent was a quiet location, with numerous Victorian red-sandstone villas set back from the road and lining both sides of the street. Most had been sub-divided but number seventeen was clearly still one house; surrounded by a neatly-trimmed beech hedge. Just visible behind the shimmering green foliage was a sturdy chain-link fence, as well as numerous security cameras. They got out of the car and Briony looked curiously at the Pettigrew family home.

'Not takin' any chances, eh Boss?'

He shrugged.

'More afraid of their enemies than they are of us. Come on...'

They walked over to the solid, electrically-powered gate that guarded a cobblestoned driveway, behind which sat a black, top-of-the-range Audi sports car, "RAP 1". As they approached, the gate swung open and, as they passed through, Grant mumbled.

'Aye, thought they'd clocked us...'

As they walked up the drive, he turned to Briony.

'Welcome to Fort Apache, Mount Vernon. Home of the Pettigrew clan.'

'Pretty fancy. There's money here, right enough, Boss.'

He sneered.

'Dirty money, though... right, let's see who's at home. Her car's here, anyway.'

As they climbed up the steps, the solid, polished-wood front door opened to reveal the formidable Pettigrew matriarch, Helena.

'Ah don't need tae ask whit youse lot are. Whit are you wantin'? Someone got an unpaid parkin' ticket?'

She cackled at her own joke. Grant and Delia didn't crack a smile.

'We'd like a word with your daughter, Veronica, and also with you, Mrs Pettigrew.

Grant had used "Veronica" deliberately, he suspected that it's use would irritate the woman.

'Me? Whit the fuck do youse want wi' me? Ah'm just an innocent housewife.'

'All the same, we'd like a chat, if that's all right.'

She glowered at them for a moment before replying; Grant thought she was going to refuse them entry.

'Ronnie's here, though whether she'll want a word wi' you is another matter. You'd better come in.'

They entered the house and the woman closed the door behind them. It was an odd mix, some obviously expensive pieces of furniture were dotted about, with a variety of brash and inelegant ornaments adorning them. The artwork, too, looked expensive but was entirely random and tasteless, with no common theme. They could hear the sound of a radio playing somewhere but they were ushered into a small bay-windowed lounge with a comfortable leather suite and an enormous plasma television.

'Sit doon. Ah'll see if she's busy.'

They took a seat and waited...after about fifteen minutes, Grant stood up, muttering.

'I've had enough of this, I'm...'

The door opened and Ronnie Pettigrew walked in to the room. Briony had never encountered the woman and it seemed that she carried about her a tangible aura of evil. It made the hairs on the back of her neck stand up. Probably in her late thirties, she was very attractive, if slightly hard-faced, with full lips and a mane of thick, dark hair cascading over her shoulders. She smiled, a cold smile that didn't reach her cruel grey eyes.

'Officers. Sorry to keep you, was just concludin' a little bit of business.' She looked directly at Grant.

'Nice to see you again, Serg.. .oh, now wait, did I not hear you've moved a few rungs up the ladder? Congratulations.'

How the fuck does she know...?

Grant scowled but said nothing. Whilst Ronnie Pettigrew was well-spoken, hinting at an expensive education, she was unable to keep the Glasgow twang completely subdued. She sat down on one of the leather armchairs, ostentatiously hitching up her tight-fitting and smartly-pressed navy trousers as she did so, revealing shapely ankles and expensive-looking black patent shoes. Grant found the mannerism exceedingly irritating. But also slightly...

No...

She sat back, gracefully crossed one leg over the other and smiled again.

'So, what can I do for you? What brings you over to the East End?'

She spoke casually and easily but there was hidden menace in her tone. Fortunately, Grant wasn't easily intimidated.

'Miss Pettigrew... Mrs Pettigrew, are you familiar with a company called "Bin there – Done that?'

Ronnie Pettigrew laughed.

'Well, that's an imaginative name, is it not? But, no, not specifically. Why?'

'It appears to be part of a larger company called EnviCon Limited...'

She smiled. Again, it didn't reach her eyes.

'Yes, well, of course we've heard of *that*. Our main business, as I'm sure you know, is public houses and tanning salons...'

'Yes, I'm well aware of that, Miss Pettigrew. However, 'Bin there" is owned by EnviCon. You're sure you've never heard of it...?'

He looked pointedly at Mrs Pettigrew

'Or you, Mrs Pettigrew?'

She scowled at him.

'Ah might, I think it wis wan we took over wi' a couple o' other concerns. Clean and service wheelie bins, dae they no'?'

Ronnie Pettigrew responded.

'Och, yes, Mum, I remember now. I thought that daft name was familiar. Aye, I know the one. So what's happened, Grant, are you investigating wheelie bin fraud now?'

Briony raised an eyebrow at this lapse into familiarity, but Grant didn't seem to notice. Despite the disparaging jibe there was a faint brittleness to her tone. Grant suspected they were hitting closer to home.

'No, Ronnie, we're investigating a double murder.'

He paused to let the statement sink in. The response wasn't exactly what he expected. He could see a look of surprise pass fleetingly over Ronnie Pettigrew's face, although she recovered quickly. Her mother's mouth dropped open in shock. The daughter spoke.

'What? Murder? What the hell's that got to do with us, or wheelie bins, Grant?'

She seemed genuinely taken aback, although it could have been an act. Grant ignored the question.

'How many vans do you operate in connection with this business, Miss Pettigrew?'

This time it was Helena who responded, the shocked expression still on her face.

'Ji...jist the wan.' she looked at her daughter 'It's Shug and Ta...'

'Shut up, Mum!' snapped Ronnie. 'Grant, obviously we want to help you with your enquiries, but...'

'Miss Pettigrew, a vicious double murder has taken place. If you withhold any evidence then you may be held as an accessory. Now, we have both the vehicle registration and the registered address of the Company, which is here, this being EnviCon's registered head office. Can you tell me where this vehicle is normally kept? Your mother has indicated that the two men who use this vehicle are named 'Shug", or presumably Hugh and, what, "Tam?"is it?'

Mrs Pettigrew turned to her daughter.

'Ronnie, jist tell them. We've nothin' really to do with them an' if they've done...'

'For fuck sake, Mum, will you shut it...'

Ronnie Pettigrew stopped suddenly, realising that her thin veneer of respectability had split wide open. She smiled ingratiatingly, obviously marshalling her thoughts, but Grant could see her face redden; whether from temper or embarrassment, he couldn't tell.

'I'm sorry, perhaps my mum's right. The men who run the company are Hugh Dougall and Thomas Molloy. They operate from a compound that's next to Paton Transport, just off Kenmuirhill Road.'

'Thank you, Miss Pettigrew, I'm glad you managed to remember that information.'

She ignored Grant's sarcasm. Briony spoke for the first time and Ronnie Pettigrew turned her cold stare towards the sergeant.

'I don't suppose you can account for their movements at any point last week?'

Ronnie Pettigrew snorted derisively.

'Of course not, Sergeant, they're just a wee subsidiary business, how would I know what they do on a day-to-day basis? They were part of the transport group that we took over a few years back, seemed a shame to deprive them of their livelihood so we let them carry on, they pay us a minimal rent and a small percentage of profits but, other than that, we have nothing to do wi' them.'

'Very magnanimous of you, ma'am, I'm sure' she replied. 'And it's surprising what you can remember when you put your mind to it...'

Grant stood up before Ronnie Pettigrew could respond. He could see the conversation starting to descend into an unproductive spat.

'Right, Miss Pettigrew... Mrs Pettigrew, thank you for your time... and, of course, your assistance. We'll go and have a word with Messrs Dougall and Molloy.'

Helena Pettigrew escorted them to the front door, closing it behind them without a word. Just before it slammed shut, they heard an older, slightly frail voice call out from the depths of the house. Grant and Briony remained silent as they walked out of the gate and got back in the car. As they drove off, Briony spoke.

'Well, that was interestin', Boss. Sid you see the mother's face, eh?'

'I did indeed, Bri. She was shocked. Whatever the Pettigrews' involvement, I don't think she knew anything about a murder.'

'No, an' I'm not even sure about junior either. She seemed pretty surprised too. Strange.'

'Aye, it is. If they *were* involved then I'd have expected them to be better prepared for us. But they both seemed a bit taken aback and I don't know what the hell to make of it. Right, let's go and see what these two scumballs have to say for themselves. Give Kiera a buzz and tell her where we're headed.'

*

Kenmuirhill Road wasn't far from the Pettigrews' house and they arrived within minutes. They pulled into the dilapidated, but securely-fenced, compound that contained a large industrial warehouse, the logo "Paton Transport" emblazoned across the front in black letters; a variety of similarly-embellished HGVs were parked in the pot-holed yard. Grant stopped the pick-up and Briony looked about.

'Over there, Boss, that portakabin - it's got a "Bin There" sign on it.'

Grant drove slowly over, parking a bit away. They both got out, Cliff and Kiera doing likewise. Grant crossed over to the two constables.

'Kiera, you get back in the car in case they try to do a runner. Cliff, you go round the back in case there's another door. Bri, you're with me. Right, let's go.'

They strode purposefully across the intervening space and up the three steps leading to the door. He pushed the handle. It was locked. He banged his fist on the door.

'Police. Open the door.'

Nothing.

He banged again, harder this time.

'Police. Open up.'

A gravelly voice called out from behind them.

'Can Ah help youse?'

Grant turned, A swarthy, middle-aged man, fag in hand, was ambling across towards them. Despite his girth, he looked surprisingly fit and tough, like a wrestler gone to seed.

'I'm looking for Hugh Dougall and Thomas Molloy.'

'Aye, weel, ye've found wan. Ah'm Tam Molloy. Whit ur ye after?'

Grant pulled out his warrant card and held it up.

'Mr Molloy, we're investigating two murders and believe you may have information. I must caution you that anything you say may be used in evidence against you and that you need not answer any of our questions.'

'Aye, aye, Ah've heard aw' that rubbish afore. Whit the fuck's it got tae dae wi' me?'

'You *and* Mr Dougall. Do you know his whereabouts?'

'Aye, last time ah seen him he wis takin' a shite across there' He indicated the adjacent warehouse. 'Oor toilet's buggert an' he wis needin' tae drop wan. Here he's comin' noo.'

A slightly younger man was approaching, his dark hair tied in a short pony-tail; however, his grubby t-shirt showed sinewy arms and he appeared broad shouldered and powerful looking. Grant realised that they could easily have been a match for the two murder victims, especially given their background and their apparent association with the violent Pettigrew family.

'Whit's up, Tam? Who's this lot?'

'Cops, Shug. Accusin' us o' murder, if ye like.'

Hugh Dougall laughed, although there was little humour in it.

'Whit? You an' me, Tam? Ach, we're jist a couple o' simple souls, officers, mindin' oor ain business...'

Grant had had enough.

'Cut the crap! You were both seen with the victims at a pub in

Paisley and you were seen to make contact with them. We have CCTV footage that shows the victims entering your van. We need to have a look at your vehicle. Now!'

Hugh Dougall smirked, revealing several stumps of rotten, broken teeth.

'Aye, weel, that'll no' be so easy, Ah'm afraid.'

'Why? What do you mean?'

'Weel, it wis stolen, see. Jist last night.'

Grant was speechless for a moment.

'Stolen. Aye, that's fucking convenient, I must say.'

Tam Molloy pulled a shocked face.

'Here, watch yer language, Shug here's awfy easily offended...'

'Aye, I'm bloody sure he is – right, we're taking you two in for questioning, and there's a lot of questions that need answering; for a start, why didn't you report the theft of your vehicle?'

'Och, we were jist aboot to...'

Grant called to Cliff, who was walking across the yard towards them. He strode over to meet him, making sure he was out of earshot of Dougall and Molloy. He spoke quietly and concisely.

'Cliff, caution them and detain them, I've had enough of their nonsense. Get them over to Helen Street and safely locked up then come back here and carry out a thorough search. Bring some uniforms too, if you can get any. We're looking for bloodstained clothes, duct tape, rope, basically anything that'll tie these two arseholes to the assault and the murder. I'll get in touch with The Mint and get warrants for their houses, Sam and Faz can take charge of that. We'll stay here and have a sniff round.'

He strode back across to the two truculent-looking individuals who were lounging, hands in pockets, under the watchful eyes of Briony and Kiera.

' Molloy, before we take you in, get that fucking office opened. I want a look inside.'

Molloy sneered.

'Dae ye no' need a warrant fur that, officer...?'

Delia wiped her face with the napkin, picked up her can of San Pellegrino and drained it – it was warm in the small office, even with the window wide open. She sat back in her chair, placed her hands behind her head and let her mind wander. It was cathartic and, anyway, she had nothing else to occupy her at present...

*

The evening with Pam had been superb – the promised (and welcome) snooze, a couple of "girlie films", then cheese on toast washed down with a bottle of decent red wine. Finally, Pam had showed Delia to the small but well-appointed spare bedroom.

'Oh, it's lovely!' exclaimed Delia.

Pam smiled indulgently.

'I'm glad you like it, Delia. Actually, this was my Aunt's house. She died a few years ago and I was her only relative, so it came to me. It was on a long-term let until a few months ago.'

'So you don't actually live here, then?

'No, my main house is still up north. I decided to keep this one, partly as an investment and partly as a wee base. I've still got a few friends down this way and, to be honest, I've been coming down a bit more recently since... well, you know. But I don't get many visitors, I'm afraid...'

The shadow passed across her face again. Pam sat on the bed and Delia sat beside her, holding the older woman's hand.

Pam explained that, despite her beloved Billy's apparent sexual prowess, and despite repeated visits to a variety of clinics and specialists, they had never managed to have any family and, somehow, adoption had never been an option for either of them. Delia had vaguely wondered if Pam was subconsciously "mothering" her and, if she was, she certainly wasn't going to object.

Pam stood up and smiled; the dark moment seemed to have passed.

'Right, I'll go and see if I can find something that fits you. I'm afraid I'm a bit bigger than you are, though!'

Delia had gone into the small en-suite toilet and had a quick wash. Pam returned with a camisole top and a pair of silky pyjama bottoms.

'I found these. Must have had them for ages. They might do the job...'

Pam busied herself turning down the bed as Delia stripped off and slid into the soft, pink pyjama top. It was a bit big but it would be fine. Pam turned round and smiled.

'Oh my, you do look pretty!'

Delia put on a saucy pose and, as she did so, the slightly-large garment slid off her shoulder, exposing her right breast. With a small, embarrassed giggle she reached to pull it back up but Pam grabbed her hand.

'Delia, what the hell's that?'

'Wh...nothing, it...it's nothing, Pam.'

'It doesn't look like nothing to me.'

Delia tried to free her hand but Pam wouldn't let it go.

'Those are bruises, Delia. Let me see. Take that camisole off, come on, let me have a look. Please, Delia.'

Somehow she hadn't the energy to resist. Like a child, she raised her arms and allowed Pam to slide the garment off, revealing Delia's soft, pale skin, her delicate square shoulders and pert, well-formed breasts. The latter were covered in dark bruises and a few angry red weals; there were several more bruises on her side. Delia lowered her head and closed her eyes as Pam stared at her in horror.

'Delia, who in God's name did that to you? Was it Danny? Tell me, please Delia. Tell me...'

Pam reached forward and pulled her friend against her, stroking her hair gently.

'Tell me, Delia.'

Delia's eyes started to lose focus...

*

Someone was shaking her; gently, but firmly.

'Delia, Delia, are you okay? Delia, talk to me. Delia...'

Finally she opened her eyes; Pam was sitting beside her on the bed, staring at her with an expression of deep concern.

'Thank God. Oh Delia, my dear, what the hell's going on?

Delia buried her head in her friend's soft, comforting shoulder... and told her.

It had started not long after they were married. Danny had been drinking and had decided that they were having what he called "rumpy-pumpy."

"Don't call it that, Danny, please; you know I hate it! Anyway, I'm not feeling particularly great tonight, and..."

"I don't give a fuck. You're my wife and I'm having you, whether you like it or not..."

And he had. Painfully, brutally and entirely against her will. She was sore for days. He had been apologetic, of course. It had been the drink, he was stressed with the business, all the usual excuses. But it had happened again...and again...then, when finally she *had* tried to resist him, he had started to hit her, to punish her; again... and again... and always where it wasn't visible...

'So I learned to shut it all out; I just closed my eyes, let it happen and waited for it to be over. Eventually I became numb, it was the only way I could survive. And that's what happened to me there, Pam. I shut it all out again, I went into my own little world and let it happen, although it was only the memories this time. But it hurts, it hurts all the time...'

She started to sob, almost hysterically. Pam could feel the hot tears soaking into the shoulder of her blouse. Gently, she stroked Delia's soft, curly hair.

'But why, for the love of God, did you put up with it, Delia? You should have left. The bastard could have killed you...'

'What could I do, Pam?' wailed Delia. 'Run back home to my mother with a failed marriage behind me? My mother's very old-fashioned about divorce and she's pretty frail. If I'd told her even a fraction of what had happened... ' She shook her head violently. 'I had no-one to turn to, Pam, I had no-one...'

She broke down in more floods of tears. As Pam continued to stroke her friend's dark curls she, too, was weeping; partly with sorrow but mostly with sheer, naked fury at the brute who had done this to Delia.

*

Pam had run a bath and eventually persuaded her friend to undress fully and step in to the hot, scented water. She sat down on the toilet, gently stroking Delia's hand and talking in soothing tones. She had decided not to ask about the numerous marks on the girl's soft, round behind but she was certain that they, too, had been caused by Danny Donald. An hour or so later, Delia had almost returned to her former self. Pam briefly left her alone to get dressed and, fifteen minutes later, they were sitting on the bed, drinking jasmine tea and eating chocolate biscuits. Once again, Pam's brows were furrowed as if deep in thought; finally she seemed to reach her decision.

'Delia...'

Delia turned towards her and smiled.

'Yes, Pam?'

'How long is Danny away for, did you say?'

A brief shadow seemed to pass across Delia's face, but she smiled back and answered.

'Oh, until Friday, I think he said. Probably later in the evening as he's in Northumberland. Why?'

Pam stood up.

'Why, Delia? I'll tell you bloody why, my darling. First thing tomorrow, we are going over to that farmhouse of yours, we are packing every single thing that belongs to you and you are moving in with me, immediately! The spare room isn't a spare room any more, it's your room.'

Delia looked at her, uncomprehending.

'Wh... I don't understand, what do you mean?'

'I mean you're coming to live here, Delia Donald. You're leaving that piece of shit who calls himself your husband, who drinks, who assaults you, bruises you...from what you've told me he bloody well rapes you – it's criminal and God have mercy on him if I ever get my hands on him, I'll... I' ll.'

Delia could feel her focus slipping again but, this time, she managed to control it.

'Y-you mean it, Pam. You really mean it? But why, why on earth would you take me...'

Pam smiled.

'Because, Delia, you're one of the most warm and lovable people I've ever met. If I'd ever been blessed with a daughter, I'd have wanted her to be just like you.'

*

Delia gave a small shiver – the very thought of Danny Donald made her feel dirty, used, frightened even. She daren't think what might have become of her if it hadn't been for Pam...

Wonderful, kind, loving, generous Pam; there was just one problem – she was, indeed, treating Delia like the child she never had and it was starting to wear thin; sometimes she struggled to hide her irritation. Despite the unpredictability of living with Danny, for the most part she had been free to come and go as she liked, as long as she had a cold beer and a hot meal ready for his arrival from work; and, as long as she plied him with sufficient alcohol, he usually ended up apologising for his "calling off the rumpy-pumpy", as if it was something that she actually wanted! She screwed her face up in disgust – how she hated that term for sex...

As to other events...well, she didn't need to think about those, because she was safe now, living in a nice little bungalow outside Milton of Campsie. Pam still travelled up North to visit friends but, when she was at home, she had hot, home cooked meals on the table, (Delia was very slightly concerned that her waistline was expanding) there were regular trips to the cinema, shopping excursions and dining out at the weekend. It all sounded idyllic, it was what she had dreamed of, but somehow...

And then there was the car.

*

Pam had advised her to get rid of her ageing and decrepit BMW.

'It's for your own safety, my dear. For a start, it's unreliable and winter will be here before you know it. But more to the point, Danny knows both the car and your registration. What if he saw you?'

'But he hasn't a clue where I am, Pam. Anyway, he took no interest in the agency, I don't think he even knows what I actually do or where my office is.'

'Well, there, you see "you don't think" but you also don't know. No, you should get rid of it, Delia. Listen, my aunt's car is still in the garage and I never use it. Why don't you take it?'

Delia had drawn the line at this. Pam had allowed her to escape from her abusive husband and his dreary farmhouse but she wasn't going to accept any more charity. However, Pam's concerns about Danny had slightly unsettled her and, after all, there was no harm in having a look...

She duly headed to the dealership in Yoker that normally serviced her trusty old runabout, where they had made her a reasonably generous trade-in offer then shown her the car that she instantly fell in love with, a second-hand, low mileage, alpine-white BMW sports hatchback. A great deal for only £19,650, less her trade-in. She had thought about it for a few seconds...and said "yes please!"

It took just under half an hour for the pleasant, but slightly embarrassed-looking, salesman to return and politely inform her that they were unable to arrange the finance for her purchase. She had left the dealership, her cheeks burning and her eyes stinging with a combination of disappointment and humiliation. She climbed into her aged BMW and returned to the comforting embrace of her friend.

'I mean, I should be good for it, Pam. There's a bit of cash in the bank, more than enough to cover the deposit. I don't understand it. They just said that, unfortunately, they weren't able to obtain the necessary credit.'

She detached herself from Pam and sat down, staring despondently at the floor.

'Delia, I'm sure it's just a misunderstanding. Have you checked your credit score recently?'

Delia looked up.

'My what?'

Pam's eyebrows rose in surprise.

'Your credit score, dear. Surely you check it regularly?'

'Em...no, I don't know how.'

'Goodness, you really should. Any sudden change in your credit score is usually the first sign of identity theft. Well, we can soon change that...'

And they soon did. Twenty minutes later, they were sitting in front of Delia's laptop, Pam having signed her up with an Experian credit-check account; they were staring at the screen in silence. Finally, Pam spoke.

'That's not good, Delia. Not good at all, I'm afraid.'

Of a possible, top-rating score of 999, Delia Donald's was registering the meagre amount of 115. Even she could see that this was very bad indeed.

'But I don't understand, Pam. I've got a couple of store cards, with virtually nothing on them, and a credit card, but I don't have any loans, I pay my bills at the office, how...'

Pam was scrolling down the account history. Delia looked on in horror.

'What are those? I don't have a loan for ten thousand. Or a credit card sitting at...'

As Pam continued to scroll, Delia's debts continued to mount. She stared at the screen in horror.

'Pam, what the hell's happened...'

Delia closed her eyes in an attempt to stem the tears; Pam put a comforting arm around her shoulders.

'I'm afraid that Danny, bastard that he is, seems to have screwed you in more ways than one...oh, sorry, that didn't come out the way I meant it, Delia. But he has – he's taken out loans in your name, he's signed you up to a mortgage on the farm, as well as the land, by the looks of the amount. But what the hell's he doing with all the money?'

Delia opened her eyes again and looked at her friend.

'I don't know, Pam. I mean, he kept asking me to transfer money from the Agency. It was always until the cash came in for a job, or to buy new equipment, or steel for a building. He always meant to pay it back...'

'Yes, they always do. But, obviously, he didn't. It's a small fortune. He could have a drug habit. I suppose he could even be a gambler, or be using prosti...'

'Oh no, Pam, don't say that, please, it's too close to home.'

'Oh, I'm sorry...well, it's just that he does seem to have been going through money like water. Up until recently, though. He's obviously in dire straits now, I'd imagine.'

'And so am I, by the looks of it. Oh God, what now, what on earth do I do...'

She closed her eyes again but this time two tears ran down her pale cheeks. Pam thought for a few moments.

'Well, for a start I think you need to have a word with an accountant and a solicitor. I'll arrange that, but I suspect the best course of action will be to declare yourself bankrupt.'

Delia looked at her in horror.

'Bankrupt! Oh no, Pam, I couldn't, the shame...'

'Delia, there's no shame, especially when it isn't your fault. It would mean you could walk away from all this, leave that pig to wallow in his own shit.'

'But if I was...bankrupt, I couldn't get a mortgage, buy a house...'

'You don't need a house, dear. I told you, this is your home now. Look, you go and make us a coffee, I'll make a few calls and we'll get this mess sorted out...'

Pam, of course, *had* sorted it out, ably and efficiently; Delia was declared bankrupt. Pam set up a new current account for the Agency, with Delia having full access. She would effectively continue as before. Business was on the increase and it would give her a level of independence. It would also continue to keep Pam satisfied. Free of charge, of course. Reluctantly Delia went along with it all, it seemed the most sensible option; but she was upset, angry, shocked and, finally, numb. Pam assured her she would get over it. She told her not to worry, only the two of them would know. But it was still profoundly humiliating.

A few days later, she had returned home from work to find the aunt's white BMW sitting in the driveway, freshly-valeted and with a tank of fuel. She had determined to refuse it – unfortunately she made the cardinal error of taking it for a test drive...

Her reverie was broken by the ringing of her phone. She sat forward, ran her hands through her unruly dark curls and swiped the screen.

'Good afternoon, Domestic Services Agency, how may I help you today?'

Chapter 9

Eventually Molloy had relented. Despite his bluster he was well aware that Grant could get a warrant if necessary. Unfortunately, the hot, grubby and odorous "Bin there – Done that" portakabin had yielded no evidence. Some decidedly haphazard paperwork, a couple of hi-vis jackets and hard hats (why the hell did a wheelie bin company need hard hats?) three pressure-washers and a quantity of industrial cleaning and disinfecting products. Grant decided to call it a day. Cliff would be back soon for a more thorough search. They walked towards the pick-up, having decided to head to the detention centre at Govan's Helen Street HQ where they would interview Dougall and Molloy.

'Sod all here, Bri. But if their van *was* stolen, as they claim, where are the keys? There's no sign of forced entry, so how did the alleged thieves drive it away without them. It's bollocks, if you ask me.'

'Of course it is, Boss. I don't think there's any doubt that they've got rid of it themselves, pretty suspicious if you ask me, eh. Anyway, they'll just say they left the keys in it by mistake.'

'Aye, you're probably right. Listen, check if the yard's open at night . If it is, there might be a security guard; if it's locked, then someone would've had to open the gate. Mind you, if it's owned by the Pettigrews, then it's unlikely that anyone would risk breaking in... I take it you put out a search request for the van?'

'I did and no doubt it'll turn up sooner or later; probably havin' been torched, which means forensics will have a bugger of a job gettin' anythin' from it.'

'Hm, you're probably right there too, Bri. Okay, let's get back and see what these two idiots have to say for themselves; see if we can wipe those smug smiles off their ugly faces!'

They were just about to enter the pick-up when Grant's phone rang. He stared at the screen, his dark brows furrowing as he saw who was calling..

'Bri, you go on in, I need to take this...'

She watched him pacing back and forth in the dusty yard as he spoke. When he finished the call, his expression told her that something was amiss and, when he entered the vehicle, her suspicion was confirmed; his face registered no emotion, his eyes were blank.

'Everything okay, Boss?' she asked, trying to keep her tone light.

'Fine.'

Aye, right...

*

He didn't say a word on the journey back to the Helen Street police headquarters, where Molloy and Dougall had been detained. Briony knew when to keep silent. He would come out of it eventually. As they pulled in to the car park outside the detention centre, she decided to ask again.

'So what was the call about, Boss?'

'Nothing' he replied, wrenching on the handbrake; she placed her hand gently on his arm.

'Boss, come on – I know you well enough to know when it's something. Tell me... please?'

He sat in silence for a few minutes, Briony's hand still resting on his sleeve. Finally, with his head down, he spoke.

'It was Louise.'

'Louise?'

'Brian's widow.'

'Oh. '

She paused, then, in a quieter voice, she asked.

'And?'

'It's Finn's birthday on Thursday...he's my godson...'

He paused and sighed

'...and she's having a wee party, just family and a few friends from school. At her house...'

Briony could see how painful this was for him.

'And she wants you to go?'

Grant didn't reply immediately then, fighting his emotions, he murmured

'She wants me to...to say something...'

Briony frowned.

'I'm sorry, Boss. Say something?'

'Aye...'

He hesitated. Briony knew the big man was struggling. Finally he managed to speak.

'The thing is, the family are putting a memorial bench in the local swing-park, where the boys play. The council have approved it, the local press are coming and they want a wee dedication ceremony after the party. They want me to say a few words... actually, the whole thing was Finn's suggestion...'

He turned and looked at her, suddenly grasping her arm.

'Christ, Bri, how the hell can I? I mean, I can't just stand up in front of all those people and... fuck, I don't know how I can...'

She looked straight at him.

'Because Louise has asked you to. Because Finn needs you to, Grant. I know it's hard, really, I do. But you need to do this, you need to move on, for your sake and for theirs. You can do it, I know you can...'

'How do you know, Bri? How the fuck can I possibly...'

She interrupted and gave him a small smile

'Because you were his best friend, Grant McVicar. He'd have wanted you to...'

*

After passing through the numerous levels of security at Helen Street, they had just entered the building when they bumped into an angry-looking DC Cliff Ford. Grant had recovered somewhat and sensed that something had happened.

'Everything okay, Cliff?'

Cliff shook his head.

'Aye, until Bryce bloody Turnbull appeared, here to represent "his clients"'

Bryce Turnbull was one of Glasgow's top QCs and his presence came at a price, a great price; one that only the likes of the Pettigrews could afford. Grant scowled at the news.

'Shit— there's no way those two half-wits can pay for him.'

'No' replied Cliff. 'But you know who can, Boss. I'll bet you a pound to a penny it's bloody Michael Pettigrew, or that daughter o' his, that's financin' it. But, anyway, there he is, large as bloody life with the two o' them sittin' lookin' as smug as you like, waitin' for you to appear.'

'Okay, Cliff, we'll deal with it. You get back over to that yard and have a good look about. See if there's any trace of bloodstained clothing hidden away somewhere, anything that might connect them. Get some uniforms to help you.'

'Aye, will do Boss. Cheers. An' good luck!'

As Cliff stormed out, Grant turned to Briony and sighed.

'Best get it over with, then...'

*

There really wasn't much to get over; the two men stuck resolutely to their story. The van had been stolen the previous night and they were just about to report it; yes, they had been at the pub in Paisley; yes they had chatted to the two men and asked for Andy's autograph. Andy and his friend appeared to have had a bit too much to drink and they had given them a lift to Renfrew, dropping them off near the old Ferry from where they had intended to walk home in an attempt to clear their heads. All very neat, all very tidy. They claimed they were completely innocent, at which point Bryce Turnbull indicated that they should say no more. He gave Grant and Briony a smarmy smile.

'As you can see, officers, my clients are innocent of any wrongdoing. In fact, the theft of their van, which has serious implications for their livelihood, renders them as victims and I would have hoped that you would treat them as such.'

Grant spoke with barely controlled anger.

'Mr Turnbull, your clients are being questioned as part of a double murder enquiry. We have CCTV footage, as well as their admission, that suggests they may well have been the last people to see the victims alive, having taken them in the van that was conveniently stolen from their yard. We will continue to hold them for the maximum period until our investigations prove their innocence, or guilt.'

They had terminated the interview and the two men remained in custody, despite Turnbull's protests. As they walked back to the office, Briony turned to Grant.

'He's a bloody menace, that man, eh. Worse than the criminals, if you ask me.'

'Aye, you should hear Sheena McPartland talk about him.'

'What, the Fiscal?'

'Yup. Went to Uni with him, apparently. Hates him with a passion. She'll be absolutely delighted when she hears that he's on the case!'

They had just got back into his office when the phone rang. From his terse reply of 'Yes ma'am', Briony knew exactly who it was from...

*

Grant closed the door behind him and walked away from the gruelling meeting with Superintendent Minto. Naturally she was under pressure from her own superiors. A murder was always bad news, a sadistic double one considerably more so, although the public had, until now, been spared the nastier details. She had left Grant in no doubt that she wanted a fast result and he had struggled to re-assure her that one would be forthcoming. He had told her that two potential suspects were now in custody, although the evidence was circumstantial (and pretty thin on the ground). He also advised that they were employees of the Pettigrew's Company, EnviCon, which had elicited a thin smile. Patricia Minto shared his feelings about the notorious crime dynasty. Finally he had told her that their investigations were continuing and he was reasonably confident that he had identified the killers. As he had left, she had given him a frosty stare, stating, 'I'm meeting the Fiscal later today and I'd like to be able to give her some good news. You know what she's like. Remember, I'm counting on you, Grant. I'm afraid you need to consider this case as a test of your fitness for duty.'

Aye, thanks a bunch...

*

As he arrived back at the meeting room he met Briony coming out. His face was like thunder.

'I take it it didn't go well, Boss?'

'No, it bloody didn't!'

'Oh well, maybe this'll cheer you up – they've found the van.'

He pursed his lips and exhaled in relief.

'Great. Where?'

'North Ayrshire. Back road from Dalry to West Kilbride. It's been rolled down a bank and torched but I've arranged for some SOCOs to attend and see what they can dig up for us.'

'Good. Come on, let's go and have a look for ourselves. I've got the Mint breathing down my bloody neck and I need to give her something to soothe her troubled brow.'

Forty-five minutes later they were standing on the twisting country road that runs over the hill from Dalry to the little Ayrshire town of West Kilbride. The pleasant little valley was lush but airless, with a heavy, oppressive feel in the atmosphere. There was a sharp turn with a steep drop away to the left-hand side and Grant had stopped the pick-up about a hundred yards further up the road, which was currently closed in each direction by a couple of marked cars. The van had been located about twenty feet below road level and, as Briony had predicted, it was a burnt out shell. One of the SOCOs was climbing back up as Grant and Briony arrived. Grant knew him from numerous previous cases.

'Gordon, how's it going? Anything?'

Gordon Harris, a competent and highly respected forensic scientist, grinned as he clambered through the hole that the van had left in the rather flimsy-looking crash barrier.

'Aye, Grant, and I reckon it might just be your lucky day!'

Grant and Briony exchanged an optimistic look.

'Go on.'

'Well, as you can see, the van's completely burnt-out but, judging by the widespread burning of the surrounding vegetation, I'd say that the subsequent fire was definitely started deliberately, most likely using cans of petrol or a similar accelerant; plenty of it too, given the extent of the damage. We'll have a look along the road and the valley later and see if we can find any containers kicking about. Most of the vehicle has been completely gutted, along with the fittings and, of course, most of the evidence.'

'So where does the luck come into it, Gordon?' asked Grant somewhat impatiently.

'Well, the van's lying on its right-hand side; now, the floor in the rear of the vehicle was lined wi' three-quarter inch marine ply and as the van rolled, the flooring must have dislodged and landed on said right-hand side, which then effectively became the base. So, although the wood is pretty charred, the side of the van underneath is relatively undamaged, as is the face of the ply that was originally uppermost on the floor, if you see what I mean.'

'Aye, I get you. So what you're saying is that you have a viable van side and a partly viable floor?'

'Exactly; and, from what we have so far, there's fingerprints and even some strands of hair and other fibres, clothing possibly. As I said, your lucky day, Grant. Here, is this to do with those two guys that were found up at Castle Semple, by any chance?'

Grant nodded.

'Aye, it is. Listen, Gordon, can you get everything you possibly can and get it along to us as soon as? The two clowns who own it are claiming it was stolen last night but if we can prove that they had previously been in the rear, along with the victims, then that should be all the evidence we need to link them with this case. By the way, was there any trace of blood?'

Gordon nodded his head.

'Just a few splashes here an' there, consistent wi' someone gettin' a good going over. Certainly not. A great deal, but we'll get samples, don't you worry. Listen I'll get back down and get on wi' things I'll keep you posted. Any chance we could get some more uniforms to help if we're goin' to search for petrol containers?'

'I'll see what I can do. Problem is, there must have been another vehicle present so there's a good chance they took them away with them.'

'You might be surprised though, Grant. It often amazes me the stupid mistakes these idiots sometimes make. Worth lookin' anyway.'

'Aye, it is, Gordon. Bri, can you see if you can rustle up a few more troops?'

She took out her phone.

'On it, Boss.'

Gordon Harris grinned again.

'Cheers Grant, an' make sure you catch this bastard...'

He scrambled away back down the overgrown bank as Grant and Briony turned and walked back along the road. She ended her call.

'Right, they should get another four uniforms down in the next half hour or so.'

'Good stuff.' he paused and frowned 'Certainly seems to have caught the imagination, this case.'

'Sure has, Boss. And no wonder, it's pretty horrible. Just so long as the bloody press don't get hold of it. That'd be all we'd need, eh.'

'Aye, this is exactly the kind of gruesome sensationalism that sells copy. I hope no stupid bugger decides to make a few quid by passing on anything...'

'God help them if they do, Boss. They'll have me to deal with!'

He looked sideways at her and raised an eyebrow.

'Aye, that might be scary right enough, Sergeant Quinn!'

*

It was nearly five o'clock when the preliminary forensic reports came through. Grant and his team were assembled in their meeting room, going over what information they had to date. He ended the call on his mobile and smiled at the officers assembled in front of him.

'Right, we've got a load of positive prints from the rear of the van. Those of Molloy and Dougall, as we'd expect, but also Andrew Watt and Chris Findlay. This proves that they were in the back of the van and that the assault probably took place there. Easy enough if they were under the influence of Rohypnol, I'd imagine. We've also got a few hairs from both victims as well as partials on a few footprints which might identify the two accused. No results from the blood as yet, that'll take a wee bit more time, but I we've got enough to definitely connect Molloy, Dougal and their van to the victims. You're sure there was nothing at the yard, Cliff?'

'Nope, Boss. There were a few skips about but they were emptied on Friday afternoon, apparently, so unless we go searching the landfill sites, I doubt we'll get anythin.'

'Hm, don't want to go down that route just yet. Right, I'll speak to The Mint, we'll get a warrant to search "M and D's" respective houses. We might manage to get some further evidence from their clothes, but the chances are they've been destroyed after they carried out the assaults.'

He paused and Briony asked

'What about this Domestic Services Agency, Boss? Do you still want me to chase it up?'

'Definitely, Bri. I've got a feeling it ties in with all this somehow.'

He turned back to the occupants of the room.

'Right Cliff, get all this down.'

Cliff eagerly lifted the marker and stood beside the white board, hand poised.

'So, we have a definite link between the Pettigrews, Molloy and Dougall, whom we will call the suspects for the time being, plus another between said suspects and the victims. We have the van, allegedly stolen but hopefully about to provide considerable evidence, despite having been torched. As yet we have no motive and no specific evidence of any of them having committed murder, only of what we'll refer to as the abduction and assault.'

Kiera Fox asked.

'So what now, Boss. Are we ready to charge them?'

'No, not yet, Kiera, unfortunately at the moment there's not enough evidence to charge them with the murder, but we've got until tomorrow and I can easily justify an extension if we need it, although hopefully we won't. We've got absolute proof that they had contact with the victims in the Cartbridge and we know the victims were in the van, where we can justifiably assume the assaults took place. What we need to find is a motive and I have a funny feeling that Ronnie Pettigrew is involved somewhere. Let's call it a day, guys. Sleep on it, come back refreshed and we'll tackle it in the morning.'

Part Two

I tell myself that I shouldn't go but, as always, I don't care to listen. As the song goes, "I just can't fight this feeling anymore". I can't even remember who sang it, but it's true, it's true...

I need to see her, I need to see what she's doing... but not face to face, no, that would never do! Just a glimpse, from a safe distance, just to keep the memory fresh, no matter how painful. Of course, I really need more than a glimpse. I need to... God, I don't know what I need...

But I need to go. I tell myself I shouldn't...but I know I will. I'm just waiting, watching the clock, I can't sleep anyway. It's nearly midnight, the death of another day's life...

FOh sleep, why dost thou leave me, Why thy visionary Joys remove...

Anyway, where the hell did that come from? Must look it up. Not now, though, there's more important work to be done...

Chapter 10

Grant swore under his breath, wishing he had remembered to have the air-conditioning in his pick-up re-charged. As always, it was one of those things that was ignored during the winter months then eventually remembered when the weather suddenly became unbearably hot; the temperature dial was optimistically turned to "low" but the vents obstinately continued to expel hot, dusty air. This had gone on all summer and, somehow, there had never been time...

The story of my bloody life...

He opened the window in an attempt to cool the interior as he headed up the A737 to the office, hoping that today would be the turning point in the case that had become known in the press as "the bodies in the loch".

Twenty minutes later, he turned off Inchinnan road and into the car park for Osprey House. His car was no cooler. And neither was he...

*

He opened the door to the meeting room to find it warmer than ever, with his team already at work. Briony was studying her laptop, a mug of coffee in her hand. Faz, the constable whom he now considered to be his "techie" was already at work checking HOLMES, the police database on to which all relevant information was uploaded. He appeared to be scrolling through numerous pages, searching for something... anything...

'Morning troops. What's new?'

Briony put down her coffee.

'Nothing yet, Boss. Faz is checking for any info on this Agency. Seems to be below the radar, whatever it is.'

Grant sat down in a chair and closed his eyes. He wished the storm would come, it was too bloody hot...

*

Delia Donald was also sitting in the stifling heat of her little office where she, too, was wishing the storm would come. Fortunately her windows faced over the back courts of the surrounding tenements and she could open them without having to suffer the worst of the noise and exhaust fumes that invariably wafted up from nearby Dumbarton Road. However, the day was airless and there was no cooling draught to lower the temperature of the small, stuffy room. She had dressed accordingly and was wearing a pale blue sleeveless top above a pair of cream linen shorts which, although rather crushed, showed off her shapely legs, now nicely tanned from her days spent in Pam's small but well-tended south-facing garden. She fanned herself with a magazine and decided to open the iced latte she had purchased from her dearest Marco; she had just removed the lid when the phone rang.

'Good morning, Domestic Services Agency, Delia speaking, how may I help you...'

       *

Ten minutes and one new hesitant but rather demanding client later, she sat back and took her first sip of the delicious, chilled coffee. Miriam Oliphant had described herself as a lonely, "sixty-ish" widow, although in Delia's experience, this usually meant she was probably just on the right side of seventy. The agency had been recommended, of course; she didn't usually do this sort of thing, of course, but she wanted/needed a man, of course! However, as the conversation had progressed, her initial hesitancy was replaced by a somewhat precise set of requirements; it wasn't just any man that she needed! No, Miriam wanted a strong powerful type; handsome, with big muscles, no body hair and "well endowed" (well, she hadn't actually put it quite like that, but Delia had known what she meant when she had said "I want a *big* man, if you know what I mean..." She imagined Miriam winking lewdly as she said it!). Delia took another sip of her rapidly-warming latte and smiled. She placed the cup down and picked up her phone. She knew exactly who to send to the up-market address in the leafy Renfrewshire suburb of Kilmacolm: Euan Johnstone.

       *

'Delia! how's it goin'?'

'Just dandy, Euan! You?'

'Aye, well, apart from bein' far too hot to work out, I'm fine thanks. You know, I hate to say it but I'm gettin' right fed up with this weather.'

Delia laughed as Euan continued.

'Anyway, Delia, I take it you've got a gig for me?'

'Indeed I do. A new client too, looking for a big, strong boy so, naturally, you were my first call. There's only one thing...'

'Oh, what's that?'

'Well, she wants you this Saturday and I know you often have shows or competitions on at the weekend. I said I'd ask if you were free.'

Euan Johnstone was a fanatical body-builder, competing nationally and, on occasions, internationally. He was fit, tanned and from what she could gather, he had an almost insatiable sexual appetite; the women who liked muscles (and not all did) loved him!

'I am actually. My next competition isn't for a few weeks, down in Birmingham. So, aye, I'd be delighted... as always...'

So will Miriam Oliphant, hopefully...!

*

Constable Grace Lappin pulled the ring on her can of chilled Diet Coke and took a welcome sip. It was already hot inside the West End police station and she looked longingly across at the people happily sunning themselves in Thornwood Park, the little patch of green on the other side of Dumbarton Road. Maybe she'd nip over at lunchtime and catch a few rays herself...

She turned back to her computer. It had been a busy couple of days and she had only just remembered on her way to work that morning the task set her by Chief Inspector Sam Williams. She ran a quick search of the van registration that she had been given and was surprised to find it registered to an address just off Dumbarton road, eastwards towards Partick Cross. She also now had the full name, Domestic Services Agency.

Well, that's a start...

Out of curiosity, she accessed the HOLMES system and typed in the new-found phrase. To her amazement, it appeared to be tagged to another investigation in Paisley. There was a contact number for a DC Fazil Bajwa.

Odd...

She decided that she'd better give him a call and lifted her mobile. Faz answered after the third ring.

'DC Bajwa.'

'Oh, hello, it's a Constable Grace Lappin here, I'm phoning from Glasgow West End... well, Partick, really!'

'Oh! Right,, hello Grace, I'm Faz, so what can I do for you?'

'Well, em, Faz, on Monday my Chief Inspector asked me to look into a wee matter, apparently an old colleague had called in asking for a favour...'

*

Faz ended the call, jumped to his feet and ran out of the meeting room; a few seconds later he was in Grant's office.

'Got it, Boss!'

'Got what, exactly, Faz? Money to fix the air-conditioning?'

The enthusiastic DC paused briefly but he was getting used to his boss's cynical comments.

'No, the Domestic Services Agency! I just had a call from a beat cop over in Partick. Apparently she was following up some minor enquiry from a retired inspector. Seems his wife was convinced there was something funny going on with the woman across the road, it's a bit of a long story...'

'Aye, well, save the story for later. This Agency?'

Faz continued.

'Okay, well, it seems this retired cop witnessed a rather passionate exchange between his neighbour, who's in her seventies, by the way, and the guy from this Agency. He managed to get a partial name on the guy's overalls but he also got the van plate. It's registered to a Delia Donald, apparently she's the proprietor of this agency, at an address somewhere off Dumbarton Road – just along from the cop shop, in fact. PC Lappin asked if we wanted her to go along and speak to this Donald woman so I...'

Grant leaned forward and raised his voice, glaring at the constable.

'What? You didn't bloody tell her to...'

Faz tried unsuccessfully not to look hurt as he interrupted his Boss's tirade

'No, of course I didn't Boss. I'm not daft. I told her to leave it as it was part of our investigation. Give me some credit.'

Grant leaned back and rubbed his neatly-trimmed beard.

'Sorry, Faz, that was good work; and of course you're not daft— well, most of the time. I'm a bit crabbit today, didn't sleep well last night. Too bloody hot.'

Faz forced a smile. His boss's moods could be wearing.

'It's fine, Boss, but you're right, it is too hot, even for a bloke like me!'

Grant stood up, relieved that his constable seemed to have

accepted his apology. The last thing he wanted was to alienate his team, although it occurred to him he may already be too late.

Need to watch my bloody mouth...

'Right, where's Bri, is she still in the office?'

'Aye, she was when I left.'

'Good. Guess where we're headed, and you may as well come too, Faz. Although, having said that, the air-con in my pick-up's buggered as well so it'll be like a bloody oven.'

' I'll survive. Be nice to get a trip to Partick, almost like a holiday!'

Grant raised an eyebrow at him.

'You're easy pleased, sunshine...'

*

Delia had spent the rest of her morning bringing her book-keeping up to date. With a little help from Duncan, her tame accountant, she kept a tidy (if un-submitted) set of accounts that specified the various "jobs" that her boys were sent to carry out; all according to the detailed instructions given by Simon Hope, all legitimate household tasks, all noted in her journal and on her computer. A simple fee (albeit rather high) paid to her personal account (well, to an account in Pam's name now, to which she had full access, of course) and fifty pounds cash paid in person to her employees, again all correctly recorded. The fees for any other "services" were paid directly to her boys by the clients and, to date, there had never been a problem with this arrangement. In fact, many of her clients had paid bonuses for the services they received, and it was testament to Delia's relationship with them that her boys usually told her; a couple had even offered to share it with her but she had declined, remaining content to take the booking fee. All in all, it equated to a reasonably respectable gross income of just over forty thousand a year. Unfortunately, until recently, the bulk of this had gone to shore up her estranged husband's ailing business; as the thought of Danny entered her head, she could feel the panic rise...

No, don't, Delia. That's all over now...

Despite her accountant's avuncular and benign persona, he was still a shrewd and astute financial manipulator with a serious hatred of the Inland Revenue. He had managed to keep her operation completely off the radar somehow (she wasn't quite sure how) and, as a result, the Agency was almost untraceable and completely untaxed. This was fortunate indeed, given that she was now, technically, declared bankrupt! Still, that, too, would pass...

She decided it was lunchtime but, as she stood up, ready to head to Matonti's Deli, the door buzzer sounded. She sighed; it was probably Andy and Chris. They still hadn't come in for their payment for the previous week and, although they would have been paid by the client, they had never been known to refuse their fee from the Agency. Then she had a thought. Maybe they could all go for lunch. She smiled, walked to the door and pressed the intercom.

'Domestic Services Agency!' she trilled into the mouthpiece.

'Hello, this is Detective Chief Inspector McVicar and Detective Sergeant Quinn. Could we have a word with you please?'

Oh fuck, fuck, fuck...

*

Delia had recently heard an item on the radio about "square breathing" a relaxation technique apparently carried out by US Navy Seals prior to an operation. Breathe in for five seconds... hold for five, out for five, rest for five... No, the Seals' missions obviously couldn't have been as dangerous as the situation she was currently facing. She heard the footsteps on the landing outside; she took a final deep breath and held it, hoping she wasn't shaking too badly. She remembered Simon's words...

"If they ever come knocking at your door, whatever you do, don't panic. As long as your books are all correct and show nice innocent tasks for your employees, the worst that can happen is you'll get a tax investigation and a hefty tax bill. Plead ignorance and flutter your eyelids, Dee. They're your biggest asset, eyes full of innocence..."

As she opened the door, she doubted that it would work. Still, she'd give it a try...

*

The door opened and Grant and Briony found themselves staring down at Delia Donald. She wasn't at all what either of them had expected. The vague suggestion that this Agency may be providing some kind of escort services had immediately conjured up a stereotypical image of a middle-aged and blowsy type, fag in mouth and a low-cut top revealing a large and slightly sagging bosom. Instead, they were faced with a petite, smartly dressed and extremely pretty dark-haired woman who was looking nervously up at them through long dark eyelashes. Grant had long since learned never to rely on first impressions but, somehow, he got the feeling that there was nothing particularly evil about this girl. As if sensing his scrutiny, she looked directly at him and smiled; for the first time in years, he felt the faintest twinge of that that strange, undefinable feeling in the pit of his stomach...

For fuck sake, Grant McVicar, get a bloody grip...

It was Briony who spoke first; she glanced briefly at her Boss, wondering why he hadn't taken the lead, then she showed Delia her warrant card.

'Mrs Donald, can we come in please?'

'Oh...oh yes, of course, I'm so sorry. It's just...well, you know...I'm not used to being visited by the police...'

She gave a nervous giggle and moved aside, allowing them to enter the small, stuffy office and, as Grant stepped past her, he caught the faint whiff of some extremely expensive fragrance. Delia moved a side chair across to the desk and placed it next to the one that was already there.

'Please, have a seat. Sorry, was it Inspector McIver?'

'McVicar' he corrected. 'DCI Grant McVicar and DS Briony Quinn.'

'Oh, sorry. Well, I'm Delia Donald. But of course, you seem to know that already. What can I do for you?'

Briony's scrutiny was less sympathetic than Grant's. She wasn't at all sure about this woman and, already, she could tell that she was one of those females who had a "way" with men. The effect was already apparent with her Boss. Again she took the lead.

'Mrs Donald, could you tell us exactly what services your Agency provides?'

Delia smiled – her heart was pounding and she was sure they would notice. She didn't warm to this woman and it had nothing to do with her dark skin; no, DS Quinn made her feel decidedly uneasy, the way she was looking at her. It was as if she could see into her very soul.

'Yes, certainly, Sergeant. You see, my clients are mostly older ladies living on their own. They need help with all sorts of things that their husbands used to do; you know, gardening, a bit of decorating, lifting stuff into lofts. Anything of that sort really. My boys can also carry out minor repairs on a variety of household appliances. They're all well-trained and handy and I vet them myself to make sure that they are honest and trustworthy. Oh, and sometimes my clients want a man to accompany them to the theatre, or even just to go for dinner; it's not much fun going out for a nice meal on your own, you know...'

Grant knew.

'...and in all the time that I've been in business I've never had a single complaint.'

'I see. And that's it, eh?'

Delia frowned slightly.

'Yes, that's it. Why, what else would it be?'

Finally Grant spoke, his voice uncharacteristically gentle. Again, Briony gave him a questioning glance.

'Well, Mrs Donald, the thing is, we had a report that one of your clients, as you call them, seemed to be a bit... amorous, shall we say, with one of your boys as he left her house. How would you explain that?'

Delia felt as if her heart was about to stop, but she laughed lightly, desperately hoping it didn't come across as nervous.

'Inspector, you need to remember that a lot of these ladies have been on their own for some time and they're bound to be lonely. Now, I certainly don't encourage my boys to become too attached to the clients but, occasionally, one or two of them have had to... well, let's just say fend off some slightly amorous advances, if you know what I mean. But they're very diplomatic. After all, no woman likes to feel rejected, no matter how old or unattractive they are.' She glanced at Briony and Grant could sense his sergeant bristling. Delia continued.

'But my boys are good at letting them down gently, if you know what I mean.'

Grant decided that this line of questioning was getting them nowhere. Even if Delia Donald *was* running some sort of escort agency, she was hardly likely to openly admit it. He decided to change tack.

'Mrs Donald, do you have an Andrew Watt and a Chris Findlay on your books?'

He detected a faint flicker of concern on her face.

'Yes, I do. They're very nice young men, share a flat, I believe. Why, is anything wrong?'

She looked at Grant then Briony. Their expressions were grim. It was Grant who replied.

'Mrs Donald, I'm very sorry to have to tell you this, but their names will be in the papers today anyway. I'm afraid that Andrew Watt and Chris Findlay were murdered last week. You may have seen reference to what the Press are calling "the bodies in the loch." Unfortunately, that was Andrew and Chris and I'm leading the investigation into their deaths.'

He waited for a response but none came. Delia Donald just stared at the space between them, her pupils widening. She seemed to be muttering something Grant couldn't make out.

Briony immediately sprang out of her chair and ran around the desk, kneeling beside Delia. She looked across at Grant, her expression having changed to one of concern.

'I think she's going into shock, Boss. I've seen behaviour like this occasionally, although more usually when someone's been abused. It's like they close down... give me a minute.'

She took Delia's hand and stroked it, speaking softly.

'Delia, Delia, can you hear me? Delia, it's okay, it's Briony. You're goin' to be okay, eh.'

She continued to stroke Delia's hand and, gradually, Grant could see the woman's focus return very slightly and the tears start to well up in her eyes. She turned and looked at Briony, shaking her head as she did so.

'Please, no, please say that's not true...not my boys, not Andy...'

She fell forward on to Briony's shoulder. With a worried look the sergeant glanced over at Grant, who was sitting with his mouth open. The interview wasn't exactly going to plan.

*

It had taken nearly ten minutes for Delia to calm down sufficiently to talk. Grant was mightily impressed with Briony's skills. She had moved her chair round and was now sitting beside Delia, still holding her hand and talking gently to her. Finally, she lifted her head and looked across at him, her eyes red and puffy.

'I'm really sorry, it's just so... so awful. I mean, who would do something horrible like that?'

Grant attempted a smile and, to his surprise, there was a flicker of one in response.

'Well, that's what we're here to try and find out. Mrs Donald.'

'Delia, please. My husb...well, I've been separated for a few months. You see, he wasn't exactly a nice man...'

Briony glanced meaningfully over at Grant.

'It's okay, Delia. Now, I need you to tell us everything you can about Andrew and Chris; when you last saw them, which of your clients they'd been working for, anything at all.'

'Oh... well, that'll be easy. Actually, I had been wondering why they hadn't come in for their pay, it wasn't like them. Now I know...'

Her voice tailed off and Grant thought she was going to break down again. But she sat up in her chair, squared her slight shoulders and started to rattle the keys of her laptop, speaking softly as she did so.

'Right, let's see. Their last job was for a lady called Ellie Braid. She lives in a flat in Queen Margaret Drive. She had some furniture arriving and needed help to move it up the stairs, then move stuff about inside the flat. That was last Thursday. They picked up the van about ten-thirty.'

'You have a van?' asked Grant.

'Oh yes. The boys pick it up before a job so that they can carry tools and stuff, or in case they have to move anything. The office comes with a single parking space, it's out the back if you want a look.'

Grant nodded across at Briony, who was still holding Delia's hand.

'We'll get some SOCOs over to have a look, get some prints.'

He turned back to Delia.

'Do you have a time, Delia? And when did you last see them?'

'Em, yes, they were booked from eleven o'clock. She said an hour should do it and I was out when they handed the van keys in. Well, they put them through the letterbox downstairs. I wasn't back 'til the next day so I haven't seen them since...'

She looked down at the computer and shook her head sadly. Grant interrupted before she lost focus again.

'Delia, what do you know about this Ellie Braid? Have you met her?'

Delia looked back up.

'Oh, no, all our dealings have been by phone. She just calls as and when she needs the boys to do any work for her. I've got her address and a contact number though, if that's any help. She was a regular client, often needed wee jobs done in her flat.'

She accessed the laptop again, picked up a pen and scribbled on a piece of paper, handing it to Briony. The sergeant looked at it.

'Don't you have a mobile number for her, Delia?'

'No, that's all she gave me. Some older clients don't like mobile phones. I just presumed Ellie preferred to use her landline.'

'Anything else?' asked Grant.

Delia thought then shook her head.

'No, I don't think so. That was it. Ellie booked them last Monday and paid the fee. The boys picked up the van keys on the Thursday morning then dropped them off some time in the afternoon when I was out. I've a few sets of keys, they could have held on to them, but they'd parked their car here anyway. That's the last I saw of...'

'Right, Delia. We'll get all your personal details in case we need to get in touch with you again. I really appreciate your help. I know this must be very difficult for you but every little bit of information can hopefully help us find the murderer so, if you think of anything else, please let us know.'

As he stood she smiled up at him again, triggering the same response as earlier.

Shit...I don't need this...

*

Delia gave them a final watery smile, closed the door behind them then turned and leaned her back against it, trying not to cry. Once she heard the outer door bang shut, she rushed over to her desk and picked up her mobile, scrolling through the contacts list. There was only one person that she wanted to speak to now. She opened the contact, her thumb hovering over the "dial" symbol as she looked at the name.

William U.

Chapter 11

Grant and Briony were heading back along the hot, dusty and fume-laden Dumbarton Road towards Partick Police Station, having decided it would be easier to park there and walk to Delia's office. They had left Faz talking to Grace Lappin. Grant wanted to find out as much as he could regarding the complaint the retired cop had made. Briony turned to Grant.

'Well, Boss, thoughts?'

He didn't respond at first. He hadn't entirely made up his mind about Delia Donald. Briony spoke again.

'What d'you reckon, villain or victim, eh?'

He turned and looked at her, raised a dark eyebrow and shrugged his broad shoulders.

'Bit of both...!'

Slightly taken aback, Briony laughed.

'Well, that's certainly sitting on the fence!'

'And what about you, Bri? You seemed to change your point of view somewhere along the way!'

Briony looked serious again as she replied.

'Hm, well, I'm still pretty undecided about Mrs Donald but I don't think there's any doubt that she was in an abusive relationship, although to what extent I couldn't say. When you told her about Andrew and Chris... that's sometimes how abuse victims respond when you start askin' what happened to them. It's how they behave when the actual abuse is takin' place, whether it's sexual or physical, or even just emotional; a kind of self-preservation mechanism. They just want to block everything out.'

'Do you think she might have had something to do with the murders?'

Briony considered this for a moment then shook her head.

'If you pushed me, I'd say probably not. I was more meanin' that the news came as an enormous shock to her; but I'm keepin' an open mind...'

She gave him an odd look.

'... and so should you, Boss, eh?'

He stopped and turned to face her.

'And what the hell is that supposed to mean, Briony?'

Shit...maybe that was a bit harsh...

'Sorry, Boss, it's just... och, nothing...'

'Aye, exactly that. Nothing.'

'Sorry' she mumbled again. He could be so bloody touchy sometimes! They walked for a few paces in silence, then she continued

'Anyway, Delia Donald?'

She paused again, thinking.

'I do think the news was a complete shock. She did genuinely seem to be fond of them. I still can't decide exactly what her agency is up to, though. Can you?'

He shook his head.

'No. It all sounds plausible enough, I suppose. Anyway, that's low priority at the moment. Right, let's see if Faz has found out anything, then we'll head up to Queen Margaret Drive and see if we can have a word with Ellie Braid, whoever the hell she may be.'

*

They entered the main office and found Faz, coffee in hand, chatting animatedly to Grace Lappin. He saw them and smiled over, his white teeth flashing through his black beard.

'Just finishing here, Boss.'

He turned and handed Grace his mug. As he did so, Grant was sure he heard him say that he'd call her. Judging by the smile on the young female constable's face, she was rather enthusiastic about this suggestion. In a few minutes they were back in the uncomfortable warmth of the pick-up and, once he had turned right on to Dumbarton road, Grant turned and spoke over his shoulder to Faz.

'Anything we should know about there, Faz?'

The DC looked very slightly embarrassed.

'Och, turns out she's a big fan of Indian food, Boss and I said I'd take her for a proper curry some night, that's all!'

Briony gave him a quizzical look. She knew a lot about mixed-race relationships.

'That was quick work, Faz. Em... will your family be okay with that, though?'

Faz grinned back.

'It'll be on a need-to-know basis, Sarge... anyway, I phoned Jim Nugent, the retired cop who made the complaint, seems his wife had been pestering him for ages. Apparently this white van turns up every four weeks, regular as clockwork, always on a Monday at ten in the morning. It stays one hour then leaves. That's it, well, apart from the fact that he saw the woman, Reeny Dalrymple, snogging the workman, or whatever he is, just before he left. He managed to get the registration and a partial of the logo on the guy's overalls.'

'It kind of ties in with what Delia Donald told us, Boss' said Briony. 'Maybe she did just get amorous and tried it on with him. Worth pursuin', d'you think?'

'To be honest, probably not at the moment; I doubt it's relevant at this stage.' replied Grant. He was now heading up Byres Road towards its intersection with Great Western Road, after which it would become Queen Margaret Drive, the location of Ellie Braid's flat. As he drove, he filled Faz in on what they had found out from Delia. The young DC replied.

'So this Ellie Braid might have been the last person to see them alive, well, other than their killer, of course. Unless she was involved in some other way.'

'Aye, but to prove that we'll need to see if there's any link with Dougall and Molloy. Of course, she might well just have been another client, as Delia Donald refers to them. Right, here we are and, guess what, there's no bloody place to park. Just need to chance it...'

Grant parked on a double yellow line, hazards flashing and the mileage log sitting on the dashboard. Hopefully it would deter any over-zealous wardens! They crossed the road to the close leading to Ellie Braid's flat; the controlled entry had a handwritten label simply stating "Braid." He pressed it. Nothing. He tried again. Still no response.

'Well, so much for that plan. Bri, try giving her a call in case the buzzer's not working.'

Briony took out her mobile and dialled the number that Delia Donald had given them. It rang four times then a generic answering message cut in; she tried again but there was still no answer. She frowned as she put her phone away.

'Who the hell doesn't have a mobile these days? So what now, Boss?'

'We'll try one of the other flats and see if they can let us in. They may know something about her.'

On the fourth attempt, Grant got an answer from an Anthony Higgins, Esq.

'Hello, Higgins here!'

'Mr Higgins, this is a DCI McVicar. I need to speak to one of your neighbours, an Ellie Braid, but she doesn't seem to be at home. I wonder if you can give me any information about her?'

There was silence for a moment, then Mr Higgin's cultured, plummy tone asked.

'I take it you have your warrant card, Mr McVicar?'

'Of course, and I have two colleagues with me, DS Quinn and DC Bajwa.'

There was another pause.

'Bajwa, eh? That's not a common name. Well, not in these parts.'

Grant looked at his constable and raised an eyebrow. The plummy voice continued.

'Used to work with a Primodray Bajwa at the Western Infirmary. Any relation?'

Faz's eyes widened as he looked at Grant.

'Em, aye, actually that was my dad.'

'Come on up!'

The buzzer sounded and they entered the tiled splendour of the close.

*

Fifteen minutes later they were having tea and scones in the beautifully furnished and comfortable flat that belonged to retired paediatric surgeon, Anthony Higgins (Esq!) The immaculately dressed gentleman (complete with crimson bow tie) put down his cup and smiled across at Faz.

'Yes, he was a wonderful man, your father. A great friend and a skilful surgeon. I was so sad when he passed. Bloody cancer! Still, he'd have been proud of you, I'm sure, Fazil.'

Before the DC could reply, Mr Higgins turned to Briony and beamed.

'And what's your background, my dear?'

Briony was surprised at the rather forthright question.

'Em, it's a long story, Mr Higgins . My father was US Navy, based at the Holy Loch, you know, near Dunoon?'

'Oh, I knew it well, used to go down to Sandbank every year with my brother – we were keen yachtsmen in our day...'

Before Briony could continue, he turned back to face Grant.

'...so, you'd like to know about the elusive Ellie Braid, I believe.'

'Yes, if you don't mind, sir.' replied Grant.

'Well, I think the word "character" would best describe her – with the possible prefix of "colourful" or even "slightly dodgy", if you'll excuse the vernacular.'

'In what way, Mr Higgins?'

'Oh, Anthony, please, although I insist on "th" rather than "t".
Well, for a start, Ellie Braid doesn't actually live here.'

The statement hung in the air as Anthony smiled. He was
obviously enjoying the effect it had caused. Grant broke the silence.

'But her name's on the buzzer; and we have information that this
is her address.'

'Oh yes, indeed it is. But she doesn't actually *live* here, you
see. She uses it for...well, I don't really know, exactly; nefarious
purposes, or dirty deeds, I'd say if you pushed me.'

'What sort of dirty deeds, Anthony?'

'Well, she frequently entertains young gentlemen, for a start.
Then there are the "oddities", as I call them. Ne'er-do-weels, as my
mother used to say. I suspect she's providing them with some illicit
substance or other, although I have no proof, of course.'

'And have you not reported this, sir? asked Briony, unsure if the
familiarity had extended to her.

'Oh yes, my dear, I did once or twice. Some very nice officers
came round and interviewed me but, of course, she was long gone
and there's no pattern to it. Eventually I gave up.'

Aye, the usual story, not enough time, not enough resources...
Briony spoke again.

'Can you describe her... Anthony?'

'Indeed I can! Again, what my mother would have described as
a "bit of a hard ticket". She was from Dennistoun, you know, my
mother. Ms Braid has the face and complexion of a heavy smoker,
but was probably good-looking once. I would say she's comfortably
in her sixties. Well-made woman, dresses expensively but hasn't the
class to go with it, if you know what I mean. A thick mane of dark
hair, but I'd imagine it's probably dyed nowadays. About five foot
nine in her stocking soles, although I've neither measured her nor
seen her in said soles, before you ask!'

Grant smiled. The description of "character" could equally be
applied to Anthony Higgins!

'Can you remember when you last saw her, by any chance?'

'Certainly! She arrived here last Wednesday night and stayed
over. Next morning, two good-looking young men arrived and
stayed for an hour or so before leaving. Ellie left about an hour

later. I met her on the stairs as I was leaving. We usually say hello and have the obligatory chat about the weather, as you do. Doesn't do any harm to keep on good terms with the neighbours!'

Briony took out her phone and showed it to Anthony. She had taken a photo of the one she had found in the boys' flat.

'Are these the young men in question, Anthony?'

He pulled an expensive-looking pair of tortoiseshell reading glasses from a leather case and perched them on his nose.

'Yes, I'd be pretty certain that those are the men in question.'

He looked up and slid the specs down his nose, peering over them at his audience.

'Are these, by any chance, the two unfortunate chaps who were found in that loch?'

Oh, he's sharp...

'Actually, yes, Anthony, they are' replied Grant 'and we think they were murdered later that day.'

'Can I ask who did the post mortem?'

'Yes, it was Doctor Margo Napier.'

'Ah. Nippy! How is she. Haven't seen her for ages.'

Grant laughed.

'I thought it was just us who called her that. She's fine, I'll tell her you were asking for her next time I see her.'

'Please do. Damned good pathologist but a temper like a bloody Tartar. I've seen strong men quail!'

Grant could have stayed talking to Anthony Higgins all day. The flat was comfortable, the tea and scones most welcome and Anthony... well... but they now needed to pursue this fresh and interesting line of enquiry.

'Well, many thanks, Anthony, but we must be getting on. You've been a great help but could you possibly do me a favour, please?'

Anthony Higgins peered over his spectacles again and smiled.

'Call you immediately if she turns up, by any chance?'

'Got it in one!'

He handed Anthony a card with his number and they took their leave. As the door closed behind them, Briony turned to Grant.

'Worth having a look upstairs, just in case?'

'Aye, why not.'

It proved fruitless and, after getting no response from the other flat on Ellie Braid's landing, they made their way back out. As they crossed Queen Margaret Drive, Grant glanced back up at the solid, sandstone building and saw Anthony Higgins looking out of his window. He gave them a cheery wave as they climbed back in to the car. Grant laughed.

'Doesn't miss a bloody trick, that man. Christ, what a guy! Right, back to base and see what we can find out about this woman.'

He had just started the engine when Briony put her hand on his arm.

'Boss, something's just come to me.'

He turned and looked at her, raising his eyebrows.

'What, Bri?'

'Remember the last time we were at the Pettigrews' house?'

As if I'd bloody forget...

'Aye. What about it?'

'As we were leaving, someone called out from inside the house. Sounded a bit frail.'

'It would probably have been Pettigrew senior. Guy's a bit of a wreck, by all accounts, never seen outside these days. What of it, Bri?'

'Well, I didn't pay much attention at the time but, thinking back, it sounded like he called "Ella" or "Ellie, maybe? Just a thought. It just came to me there.'

Grant considered this.

'Hm, her name's Helena, I know that much. Don't know if "Ellie" is a corruption, usually it's "Helen" or "Lena." But from Anthony Higgins' description it could be her, if you think about it. Faz, give Cliff a call and see if either he or his old man know of any other name Mrs Pettigrew goes by. And while he's at it, get him to pull up their marriage certificate. Might be worth finding out her maiden name.'

'On it, Boss 'replied Faz, pulling out his phone. Grant turned and winked at Briony.

'Nice work, Briony. If, by some stroke of good fortune, Ellie Braid *is* Michael Pettigrew's wife, well then...!'

Delia Donald switched off her laptop and stood up. She couldn't get away quickly enough now that she had derived a modicum of re-assurance from the phone call. She managed a faint smile. You couldn't fault him for trying...! She replayed the call as she closed the door and walked down the stairs.

*

'Well, well, if it's not my mischievous little Dee. How the devil are you, my darling?'

Oh God...

Despite their history, Simon had insisted that, in the case of a dire emergency (and what had happened earlier had definitely fallen into that category) she was to phone him. However, they had agreed to keep his name anonymous on her phone directory, hence the acronym "William U" - "When It Looks Like It's All Messed Up." And now it looked as if it was.

'Not so good, Simon. Terrible, in fact...'

Somehow she had managed to keep her composure as she told him the story, although her voice quavered as she mentioned Andy and Chris's names. As always, he remained calm, his soft, Aberdeenshire accent acting as a balm on her troubled psyche.

'Oh, my poor Delia, how awful. Christ, I knew them both. Well, Andy, mostly, I'd just met Chris a couple of times when they were up on some expedition or other. But surely the police don't suspect you...'

'No, no I don't think so, Simon. But they were my boys, I'm responsible...' Her voice tailed off as she bit her lip. She *wouldn't* cry...

'No, Delia, you are *not* responsible. What happened is nothing to do with you, it's to do with some bloody psychopath who, for some unknown reason, has decided to... well, you know...' he paused, as if thinking. 'What about a jealous husband, maybe?'

'Simon, honestly, I don't know. I don't really know anything about my clients, if truth be told.'

Well, except for Pam...

'Hm. Listen Delia, I'm going to come down...'

She raised her voice in alarm.

'No Simon, please don't. I'm getting my life sorted, I've left Danny...'

'You've what? Christ, about bloody time. Why didn't you tell me? And where are you staying?'

'With a friend, Simon, and that's all I'm saying. Please, just be at the end of the phone if I need you but I beg you, don't come down looking for me, I don't think I could face you at the moment. And anyway...'

Or resist you, for that matter...and, anyway, presumably you're still married...

They had spoken for another fifteen minutes or so, his soft, sweet voice washing gently over her. He had tried to persuade her to change her mind about meeting but she had remained resolute – she knew that if he appeared when she was at such a low ebb then it would be all too easy to fall back into the honey trap that was Simon Hope!

*

She stepped out into the hot afternoon and headed towards her car. Soon she would be in the sanctuary of Pam Lawson's house. She would be safe there.

Chapter 12

The pick-up had exited the south side of the Clyde Tunnel and was heading towards the westbound M8 slip road when Faz's phone rang; it was Cliff. Faz answered and put his phone on speaker.

'Right, ah didn't even need to check the marriage certificate, although I'm gettin' a copy just to be sure. Ah phoned my old man an' he told me all we needed to know. Helena Pettigrew's maiden name *was* Braid. Came from a decent enough family, she'd started a college course but somewhere along the line she met Michael Pettigrew and that was it. Her family was devastated. Even then he had a bad reputation but Helena wouldn'ae listen tae reason an' her old man died not long after. My Dad says Pettigrew senior was a good lookin' guy when he was younger, well-built and always with a pocket full o' money. Had a way with the ladies too, apparently.'

'Did your Dad say anything about her being called "Ellie" by any chance?' asked Grant, his excitement rising.

'Aye, that's the thing, Ellie wis her old man's pet name for her when she wis a wee lassie. Apparently Michael Pettigrew liked it an' it stuck; that's what he's always called her.'

Grant glanced at Briony and raised an eyebrow, lowering his voice.

'So Ellie Braid and Helena Pettigrew are one and the same person.'

He raised his voice again for the benefit of the phone.

'Good job, Cliff, we'll come back to the office and I'll have a chat with The Mint, work out what our next step's going to be; she'll want to have a chat with the Fiscal, I'd imagine. Then I think we'll head out and have another wee word with Mrs Pettigrew, aka Ellie Braid. This casts a whole new light on things.'

Faz ended the call and Grant spoke.

'Right, we'll have a quick meeting and bring everyone up to speed, then we'll head up and speak to Helena Pettigrew. I'll get some uniforms to come as backup in case we decide to take her into custody. Don't imagine that'll go down particularly well with junior. Bri, can you and Faz head up to Helen Street and have another go at Molloy and Dougall? Let them think the net's closing and see if we can't frighten them into confirming our suspicions about the Pettigrews involvement. Don't mention the van just yet, let's keep that up our sleeve. They probably think that, having torched it, they'll be safe. Oh, and best phone ahead so they have their solicitor present, otherwise they're unlikely to say a bloody word. And we'll need to have another chat with Delia Donald. I'm beginning to think there's a lot more to this Agency of hers than she's letting on. We're getting closer, guys, we're getting closer...'

*

The team was assembled and a second white board was standing next to the first. Cliff was poised, marker in hand and there was a palpable sense of excitement in the stuffy room. The temperature seemed to have risen another degree and they were all showing the signs, sleeves rolled up, hair lank (well. where hair was present), foreheads moist with perspiration. Not one of them seemed to notice. They were waiting. Finally Grant, who had been scribbling on a notepad, stood up, frowning as he struggled to read his hieroglyphics.

'Right, here's where we're at. Two victims, Watt and Findlay, who worked for what we'll call the Agency. They had an appointment with Ellie Braid, aka Helena Pettigrew, wife of Michael and mother of Ronnie, at eleven on Thursday morning, in her flat in Queen Margaret Drive. Finished whatever they were doing at twelve, then they returned to Partick and put the keys to the van back through the Agency letterbox some time after one. That's when Delia Donald, the proprietor, left the office; presumably they stopped for something to eat en-route. After that, there's a gap until they were caught on dash-cam outside their flat in Renfrew about seven on the Thursday evening, getting a taxi to the Cartbridge pub in Paisley.'

He paused to let Cliff catch up.

'Okay... right. Not long after they entered the pub, two men, who we now know to be Molloy and Dougall, entered and bought the victims a drink, into which they presumably placed the Rohypnol. All four left some time later and the CCTV shows the victims entering Molloy and Dougall's white van. We know that Molloy and Dougall are employees, albeit indirectly, of the Pettigrews but they claim total innocence, saying that they dropped the victims off in the vicinity of the old Renfrew Ferry... got all that, Cliff?'

Cliff had moved to the second white-board.

'Right, the van was allegedly stolen on Monday night, although this was not reported, and subsequently found burned out, having been deliberately set alight. However, forensics have identified fingerprints and hair belonging to the victims, as well as prints belonging to Molloy and Dougall. This places them all in the rear of the van. Remember that the CCTV shows the victims getting into the cab so they must have been taken in to the back at some later point. The pathologist puts time of death between eleven p.m. on the Thursday and five a.m. on the Friday. We have a German camper van driver who heard a vehicle at three a.m. which would tie in with the time-slot that the victims were placed in Castle Semple loch. Tina Sturrock estimates that the bodies could have reached the other end of the loch by the Saturday morning.'

There was silence, broken only by the frantic movement of Cliff's marker pen as he annotated the information his Boss had fired at him. Grant looked round the room.

'Right, we need to establish motive. Were Molloy and Dougall acting on behalf of Pettigrew, senior, junior or both? If so, why? Was something going on with these young guys – were they involved with the Pettigrews in a criminal capacity? Mr Watt senior is adamant that his boy was both honest and extremely anti-drugs but that's not to say there wasn't some tie-in of which he's unaware. Thoughts, anyone?'

Sam Tannahill spoke first.

'There's got to be a connection with this Agency, surely? If these boys were... well, "doing the business" with Ma Pettigrew and either her husband or her daughter found out..?'

She paused for a moment.

'Wait, we're making the assumption that, if there is a sexual aspect to this, it's with the mother. What about with the daughter? Either way, by all accounts they're a pretty nasty lot. Sounds like an assault like this would be well within the Pettigrews' capacity. What do you think, Boss?'

It was as if a cloud had passed over Grant's face, although only Briony seemed to notice. He waited a few seconds until it passed.

'Aye, thanks for reminding me, Sam, they're certainly about as nasty as you'll get; and that's a fair point. We'll check with Anthony Higgins and see if he's been aware of anyone else using Ellie Braid's flat, although he's stated that the most recent visit was by the mother. That's not to say there haven't been other visitors with Ronnie Pettigrew, of course.'

Faz looked up from his laptop.

'I suppose that would tie in with them being naked, wouldn't it? I mean, if they were shagg... em, well, you know... but if that's what they were doing with either of the women then the assault would kinda make more sense if they'd been stripped, if you see what I mean. Making a point, maybe?'

'I'd already thought of that, Faz' said Grant 'Yes, it could be an act of retribution, either injured pride, jealousy or a combination of both; in which case, having provided the, well, manpower, so to speak, is Delia Donald also in danger, we have to ask?'

Sam spoke again, her brows furrowed in thought.

'So let's assume that Molloy and Dougall were instructed by one of the Pettigrews to abduct the boys, tie them up, assault them then dump them in the loch, knowing they'd drown?'

Grant turned to her.

'Right, we know that Rohypnol was used to incapacitate them. After all, they were fit, healthy and well-built young men and, even given the violent nature of Molloy and Dougall, you would have expected them to have put up a pretty reasonable fight. The drug would explain their lack of resistance. Neither of our two potential suspects show any signs of injury resulting from a fight so the use of this "date-rape" drug would certainly explain a great deal.'

Cliff spoke next.

'We'd wondered how they got the bodies in the loch, Boss. If it was Molloy and Dougall, then that would also make sense, wouldn't it? I mean, being two of them an' pretty strong buggers, by the looks o' it.'

'Aye, Cliff, it certainly would. But let's get back to motive.'

He looked at his attentive audience.

'So we've got a lot of evidence, but we need to find out what was going on with these boys and Ellie Braid, or maybe Ronnie Pettigrew. Why would either of the Pettigrews have them killed? Is this Agency really just what Delia Donald claims it to be, providing older ladies with help around the house, or is it really a fancy escort service, providing young men for sex? Or possibly even something else? And is Delia Donald involved in any way other than merely supplying the, em...manpower? '

'Villain or victim? '

Grant glanced at Briony as she spoke. He wasn't so sure now...he continued.

'Right, so let's assume these boys *were* having sexual relations with Ellie Braid, or Helena Pettigrew. Did the family find out? Were Molloy and Dougall sent to get rid of them? Although Pettigrew senior is a shadow of his former self, he'll still be a proud man, he won't like "losing face", if you know what I mean. Or was it Ronnie who found out and decided that no-one was going to get frisky with her dear old mum? Or did she find out her mum had stolen her man, or men, and was taking revenge?'

'So we need to find out exactly what was happening in that flat, don't we, Boss?' asked Kiera.

'Aye, Kiera, and with whom, if possible. Right, let's get moving. Cliff and I are off to see Mama Pettigrew. Bri and Faz, you're heading up to Helen Street, have another go at Dougall and Molloy. Sam, you and Kiera give Delia Donald a call and see if you can have a wee chat. She might be at her office in Partick, but she's staying with a woman called Pam Lawson, who seems to have taken her in...'

He glanced across at Briony, who raised an eyebrow.

'em...listen, we think she's had a pretty rough time with her estranged husband, badly abused, by the sound of it, so don't be too heavy-handed. But see if you can get her to open up a wee bit on what, exactly, her boys got up to. As far as I'm concerned, even if she *is* running an escort agency, at this point in time our main concern is the murder enquiry; we'll hang fire on any other transgressions for the time being. Try and get that across to her, she's a bit fragile at the moment.'

He looked over at Briony, who rewarded him with a slight nod. She would have a word with him about his treatment of Sam later...

*

Grant and Cliff duly arrived at the Pettigrew residence in Mount Vernon. Cliff seemed strangely excited, almost as if he was heading to visit a celebrity of some sort. He had spent most of the journey trying to suppress a grin. Grant had turned to him and raised a dark eyebrow.

'You're looking awfy happy about this, Cliff.'

'Och well, it's just my da's told me so much about the Pettigrews that ah am kinda excited about finally gettin' close to them... silly, ah know, but they're kinda legendary. But in a weird way, if you see whit ah mean...'

Grant understood. Vile as they were, the Pettigrews were effectively a Glasgow Criminal Institution and it wouldn't do Cliff any harm to familiarise himself with what Grant considered to be "The Enemy"; anyway, he was quite sure that his DC would have a somewhat different perspective once the visit was over. At least he hoped so!

He pulled the pick-up in to the kerb outside the Pettigrews' impressive Victorian mansion. A glance showed that Ronnie Pettigrew's Audi was absent. This would certainly make the forthcoming interview slightly easier. A marked police Shogun pulled in behind them, manned by four uniformed officers; two male and two female. Grant wasn't taking any chances. He walked back to the van and Scott Conville, the capable and tough-looking sergeant in the driver's seat, lowered the window.

'Right, Scott, just stay put until we've conduct the interview. I suspect we'll be taking Mrs Pettigrew away for further questioning and that's unlikely to go down too well!'

He glanced along the street, past the van. As he had been speaking, two men had exited a vehicle parked a few hundred yards further down and were leaning against the wall, arms folded, their scowling faces turned towards the police presence. The sergeant looked in his mirror then looked back at Grant.

'Okay...and there's another couple behind you, sir.'

Grant turned and saw another pair adopting a similar and equally menacing stance about fifty yards further up Bidewell Crescent.

'Problem, Scott?'

The burly cop grinned and winked.

'Nope!'

*

'Ma daughter's no' here.'

'Actually, it's you we want to speak to, Mrs Pettigrew. Or should that be Miss Braid, perhaps...?'

The expression on her heavy-featured face changed instantly from one of belligerence to one of alarm. She stood aside.

'Youse had better come in.'

*

Grant and Cliff were seated once again on the leather couch. Grant felt that the small TV room was becoming unpleasantly familiar but Cliff was looking around, taking it all in. Helena Pettigrew was sitting opposite; she was obviously nervous and was picking at a rag-nail on the thumb of her left hand with a distinctly worried expression on her face. Finally she spoke.

'Ah wondered if ye'd make the connection.'

Grant didn't reply and he could sense Cliff fidgeting beside him. Like her daughter, Helena Pettigrew seemed to exude a vague aura of evil, presumably acquired from years of marriage to the family patriarch. The awkward silence continued, during which Grant sat and looked at the woman. He sensed that she was considering very carefully what to say next. Finally, she spoke.

'Aye, Braid. That *wis* a long while ago.'

She looked questioningly at Grant.

'How did youse find oot?'

'My constable here, his father used to work the East End.'

She frowned across at Cliff.

'Funny, Ah thought you looked a wee bit familiar, son. Ford, did you say?'

'Em, aye, Cliff.'

'Mm. Cliff, eh? Whit wis yer auld man's name?'

Grant interrupted.

'We don't need to go into that, Mrs Pettigrew. We have a few questions for you; and I must advise you that you needn't answer these but, if you do, then the information you give us may be used as evidence in a court of law....'

She glared at Grant and interrupted.

'Should ah have ma solicitor present then?'

Grant matched her glare with one of his own.

'If you feel it necessary, in which case we'll continue our interview in Helen Street.'

She considered this.

'Aye, whitever; go on then, ask.'

'First of all, do you own a flat in Queen Margaret Drive, under the name of Ellie Braid?'

'Aye, ah do, Why?'

'Just establishing that it *is* your flat, Mrs Pettigrew. Now, are you familiar with a company called the Domestic Services Agency, run by a lady called Delia Donald?'

There was a longer pause this time. Grant wondered if she was going to refuse to answer but, finally, she did.'

'Aye, they do a bit o' work for me from time tae time.'

'I see. What kind of work, exactly?'

She looked down and away from his scrutinising gaze and, when she answered, Grant was certain she was lying.

'Em, just bits an' pieces, you know, fixin' stuff, carryin' stuff aboot...'

'Did you, at any time, engage in any physical, or sexual activity with these men?'

Unfortunately this question pushed her over the edge. She seemed to reach a decision.

'Ah'm no' answerin' any more questions. No' without ma solicitor present.'

She sat back in her chair and folded her arms purposefully across her substantial bosom.

'Fine, Mrs Pettigrew. In that case, I must ask you to accompany us for questioning. You may be detained pending further investigation...'

The woman laughed bitterly.

'Whit? You're arrrestin' me? Aye right, on whit charge, may ah ask?'

'We're just detaining you, Mrs Pettigrew. We're investigating the murders of the two young men I mentioned, who were seen at your flat in Queen Margaret drive on the morning that they died.'

He could see her eyes widen in alarm.

'Whit? Ah had nothin' tae dae wi'...'

She shut up like a clam, her thin, smoker's lips set in a firm line. Grant stood up, Cliff following suit.

'Right, Mrs Pettigrew, you need to come with us...'

'But ah cann'ae leave Michael, Ronnie's oot an'...'

'I'm sorry, but that's not our concern. If you'd like to phone your daughter then by all means do so but we must ask you to accompany us.'

She stood up quickly, leaning towards him and glaring at him; Grant recoiled slightly, sensing that she may have been about to hit him. Instead, she reached into the back pocket of her tightly-fitting jeans and pulled out her phone. She dialled a number and was answered almost instantly.

'Ronnie? Aye, oor friend McVicar is aboot to *detain* me...'

Grant could hear the expletive-laden shouting on the other end of the phone.

'Ronnie, Ah'm fine. Just get Turnbull to come over to...'

She looked at Grant.

'Where am ah bein' taken, exactly?'

'Helen Street, Govan. I'd imagine Mr Turnbull will...'

She had turned away.

'Helen Street, Ronnie. Get Bryce there as soon as...'

More shouting.

'Listen, don't you worry aboot me, hen, just get yersel' back as soon as an' see to yer father. Ah dinn'ae want him here on his own, you know what he's like.'

Ronnie Pettigrew's voice quietened and Grant could see that Mrs Pettigrew was listening attentively. She smiled; a cold, evil smile, similar to her daughter's, he thought.

'Aye, cheerio hen, luv ye too.'

She finished the call and looked up, narrowing her eyes. It was a look of pure hatred.

'Ronnie wis askin' for you, Mr McVicar. Says you've no' to go oot celebratin' just yet. Says she wouldn'ae want you getting drunk an' havin' an accident. Says you'd know whit she meant...'

Grant turned his back on the woman, stormed out of the room and out of the house. He beckoned to the four uniform cops, who immediately exited the police Shogun.

'Right guys, we're taking her in. Ladies, can you see to her. You know what these people are like, don't want the slightest hint of impropriety.'

The two WPCs walked briskly through the gate and, as they did so, Grant could see the two groups of men that had been loitering starting to move closer to the police van. The sergeant and the constable placed their hands on their short batons and stood their ground on either side of the gate. A few minutes later, Mrs Pettigrew came out, flanked by the two WPCs, with Cliff bringing up the rear. She had put on a light coat and her handbag was over her shoulder; she carried her head high, smiling at the hard-looking men who were now standing beside the two uniformed cops. One of them spoke.

'You awright, Mrs P? Needin' any help?'

She sneered.

'Naw, Duggie, Ah'm fine. Jist answerin' a few questions fur these clowns. Ah'll be back soon. Could you go in an' keep a wee eye on Mr P? Just until Ronnie gets back?'

Duggie smiled.

'A pleasure, Mrs P., a pleasure.'

The sergeant stepped aside and allowed Duggie to pass through the gate and enter the house. Mrs Pettigrew walked over to the police vehicle and stepped inside, one of the WPCs following her in and closing the door behind her. The other uniformed cops also entered the Shogun and, as Grant and Cliff headed back towards the pick-up, he heard one of the remaining gang speak in a low, menacing voice.

'Big mistake, filth. Bi-ig mistake...'

As he closed the pick-up door and drove off, Grant hoped it wasn't...

'Hey sweetheart, everything okay?'

'No Simon, everything is very far from okay!'

Delia was struggling to maintain her composure, although Simon's soft, soothing Aberdonian voice was already helping.

'That doesn't sound so good. What's the matter.

'It's the police. They want to come and speak to me again.'

'I see. Right, don't panic...'

It was too late. She was already panicking!

'Oh Simon, I'm so afraid. I don't know what they want and I don't know if I can...'

'Listen Dee. I'll be down in about four hours. Hold them off...'

'No Simon. Please, don't come, it'll just make things more difficult. Please!'

'But for God's sake why not, Delia? Just tell them I'm a friend who wants to make sure you're okay! Listen, I'm going to leave and...'

'NO!'

There was a pause before Simon Hope responded, a slightly bitter and harsh tone to his voice.

'Oh my, you *really* don't want me down, do you?'

And, with that sentence, Delia realised that she had made the correct decision.

'Simon, it's not the interview, it's what might happen afterwards. I can't go back there, really...'

'...and, anyway, what would Francesca say?'

There was a stony silence; then

'She's away.'

'I see! The cat's away so the mouse...'

Simon raised his voice. There was anger in it now.

'That was low, Delia. You have no idea what it's like...'

'Then why don't you leave her, like you always promised you would?'

He was almost shouting down the phone now.

'I probably would have if you had given me the slightest bit of encouragement. The woman's become a bloody religious fanatic. She's away to Africa again, for six weeks this time, some fresh crisis or another...'

Probably would have...?

'Oh yes, it's always her fault, isn't it? She's off doing good work somewhere while you...'

'Don't bloody start, Delia. She may be well-intentioned but it's at the expense of our relationship, always has been. We pretty much lead separate lives...'

'But you *are* still married, aren't you?'

Silence.

'Aren't you, Simon?'

'Yes' he mumbled.

'Why? *Why* don't you divorce her?'

'You know why. It would destroy her; she'd never agree; I owe her; choose whichever one you like. After all, she supported me...'

There was another, longer pause; Delia knew exactly what he meant. Simon had eventually been sacked from his position at Glasgow University after one affair too many. Virtually unemployable (his reputation as a serial womaniser having preceded him) he had struggled as an aspiring author whilst his long-suffering wife worked to support him and helped to look after his aged and ailing mother. Now that he had finally achieved considerable success, his warped conscience somehow wouldn't allow him to abandon her completely.

Strange that it didn't stop him from playing around, though...

Finally he gave a casual laugh.

'Delia, it was all so long ago, surely you can think of me as just a friend now? Come on, nothing's going to happen.'

Oh, you think, Simon Hope...?

'Please, Simon. I'll be totally honest, the state I'm in I don't think....'

She halted, afraid that the quaver in her voice would betray her feelings. She waited with bated breath for his reply, hoping he would back down. Despite everything, she really needed his advice. He sighed heavily.

'Well, okay. But I *do* think you're being a bit silly, Delia. Anyway, have they said what they want?'

She breathed an inner sigh of relief.

'No, just that they want to ask a few further questions.'

'Okay, then let's work on the basis that it's the murders they're interested in, not the doings of a suspected small-time escort agency. Now, as I said before, you need to keep your head – stick to the plan and...

*

After she had ended the call to Simon, Delia Donald's next call had been to Pam Lawson, who was now standing behind her in the small, hot and stuffy office, one hand laid protectively on Delia's shoulder; the open window allowed a steady drone of traffic noise to form a soundtrack to the tense atmosphere. DC Kiera Fox and DC Sam Tannahill were sitting opposite but it was Pam who spoke first.

'Is this really necessary, officers? After all, Delia has suffered an enormous shock with the deaths of her employees. I'm at a loss to understand what more you're wanting from her?'

Kiera Fox shrewdly regarded the two women opposite her, in no doubt as to where the power lay. She had a great instinct for human relationships and spoke in a forthright, slightly abrupt manner when interviewing anyone that she considered to be potentially on the wrong side of the law. She completely ignored Pam Lawson. It wasn't her that they were here to interview, after all.

'Mrs Donald, we understand that you sent Andrew Watt and Chris Findlay to carry out some work for a Miss Ellie Braid on the day of their murder. Is that correct?'

Pam answered before Delia could speak.

'We've already confi...'

Kiera interrupted and gave Pam Lawson a decidedly frosty look.

'Mrs Lawson, whilst I appreciate your concern for your friend, I must remind you that we *are* investigating a double murder. Can I please ask that you remain silent whilst I carry out the interview?'

Pam Lawson looked furious but remained silent.

'Mrs Donald?'

'Em, yes, that's correct.'

'And can I ask, what exactly was it the the two men were required to do for Miss Braid?'

'Em, well, I don't know exactly, she just said she needed two men for...well...'

Sam interjected, her tone softer and more sympathetic.

'Mrs Donald, I'm sorry to have to ask, but were you aware of any sexual relationship that may have occurred between your client, Miss Braid, and these two men?

Pam Lawson couldn't contain herself any longer.

'Really, Constable, that's a ridiculous suggestion.'

Kiera glared up at Pam and raised her voice a notch. She wasn't about to allow this woman to take control of the interview.

'Mrs Lawson, this is your last warning, I must...'

'No, this is *your* last warning, Constable. First of all, I, myself, am a customer of the Domestic Services Agency; that is how I came to meet my friend Delia. And, in fact, how I came to discover that she had suffered years of abuse at the hands of the... the... well, I hesitate to use the term "man", that was her husband. And I can assure you, in all that time, her young men have behaved with perfect decorum and good manners and have carried out a number of household tasks over the last few years, tasks that I have been unable to carry out since the death of my dear husband. These allegations of yours are complete and utter nonsense. Now, that is quite enough. I am advising Delia to say nothing more to you. If you want to talk to this poor young woman again then I will ensure that my solicitor is present, and let me assure you that he is the best that money can buy so I suggest you tread very carefully indeed. This conversation is over.'

'Mrs Pettigrew, I need you to tell me what, exactly, was the nature of your relationship with Andrew Watt and Chris Findlay.'

'You don't need to answer that, Helena.' interjected Bryce Turnbull.

Grant glared at the QC.

'Mister Turnbull, may I remind you that we are investigating a brutal double murder and if your client has any evidence that can lead to the conviction of the killers, then she needs to inform us.'

'My client is completely innocent, Chief Inspector, how many times do I...'

'Bryce, it's awright, Ah've nothin' to hide.'

'Helena, please...'

Helena Pettigrew glared at Grant.

'They were a pair o' lookers, Andy an' Chris...'

'Helena, I must warn you...' said Bryce Turnbull, placing his hand gently on her arm.

'Naw, Bryce, this isn'ae right. Ah liked those boys an' now they're dead.'

'But Helena...'

Grant interrupted.

'Mrs Pettigrew, I don't need details, but were you intimate with these two men?'

Turnbull raised his voice menacingly.

'Chief Inspector, I must warn you...'

'We were close.' murmured Helena Pettigrew.

'Close?' asked Grant.

Bryce Turnbull gave his client a warning look.

'Aye, close. That's all Ah'm sayin'.'

'And what exactly am I to take from that, Mrs Pettigrew?'

She glared at him.

'For fuck sake, Ah said we were close, take whit the fuck ye want, Mr Clever-dick.'

She turned her glare towards Cliff, who had been sitting quietly throughout the verbal sparring.

'An' you can wipe that smug look aff yer face, Mister Ford junior. Ah ken fine well who yer father is! Oh aye, an' where the bastard stays...'

Bryce Turnbull grabbed Helena Pettigrew's arm, barking at her as he did so.

'Helena! Enough. No more!'

She subsided, although her normally cold grey eyes seemed to smoulder like burning coals through her half-shut eyelids. When she spoke again, her voice was laden with malice.

'Aye, whitever. But Ah'm tellin' you, McVicar, Ah had fuck all tae dae wi' their deaths. They were lovely young guys, well put together an' each one a damn sight more o' a man than you, ya big, baldy-heided bastard!'

Grant rose to his feet and glared down at Bryce Turnbull, whose face bore an expression somewhere between horror and amusement.

'Mr Turnbull' he hissed 'I'd strongly advise you to keep your client in check and to advise her to watch her mouth. Interview terminated.'

He stormed out of the room, followed by a slightly shell-shocked Cliff Ford.

*

The team were assembled in the meeting room. It was late but they were well aware that, during an investigation such as this, there was no such thing as "regular hours". Grant's face was still scarlet from a mixture of rage and embarrassment. At the insistence of Bryce Turnbull, he had released Helena Pettigrew, having little reason to detain her any longer. He stood up, almost knocking his chair over as he did so.

'Right, following on from our recent interviews, Helena Pettigrew has admitted, to all intents and purposes, that Watt and Findlay were more than workmen. She has said that they were "close" as she put it and from that I take it they had a physical relationship of some sort. Cliff, would you agree?'

Cliff had been mulling over the heated interview, torn between loyalty to his boss and the mileage (not to mention the free pints) that the story would earn him down the pub!

'Aye Boss. Defi-nately! Ah don't think there's any doubt she was up to somethin' naughty wi' them.'

'So let's work on that basis. Right, unfortunately Sam and Kiera have had less luck with Mrs Donald. Kiera?'

'No, sorry Boss. God, that woman, Pam Lawson. From what I hear she'd give Bryce Turnbull a run for his money. Even threatened us with the best legal advice that money can buy! The only thing she's confirmed is that she was a customer of the agency and she claims that everything was above board, so no-one's admitting anything there, I'm afraid.'

Sam Tannahill seemed reluctant to answer.

'Em...pretty much the same as Kiera, Boss. Lawson and Donald are obviously very tight and I doubt if we'll shift them from their story now. As Kiera said, Pam Lawson is a force to be reckoned with and I doubt that we'll get much more from Delia Donald now that she's on the case. To be honest, she's a pain in the bloody arse!'

There was a ripple of laughter amongst the others. Grant managed a slight smile.

'Okay. Well, whether this apparent "physical" arrangement is between Mrs Pettigrew and the boys directly or through the Agency is probably immaterial, but at least we've established a connection that could give us a motive. Bri, can you update us with the suspects?'

'Still stickin' to their story, Boss. Just happened to be in Paisley, went in to the Cartbridge for a drink, didn't know the boys would be there, it was a total co-incidence. Oh, an' they said that they'd never heard of Rohypnol, far less havin' given it to the victims. All very slick and rehearsed. The two of them were just sittin' there, smug and self-satisfied, with one o' Bryce Turnbull's minions by their side.'

Grant frowned.

'Bugger. I thought the evidence might have scared them a bit. Right, Cliff, the board, if you please. And, in case anyone hadn't realised, it's going to be a late night...'

Chapter 13

Detective Sergeant Briony Quinn was worried.

In the months that she had worked with Grant McVicar, she had developed a great respect for his methods and his incisive, enquiring nature. Despite his moods he was, in general, a fair-minded and reasonable superior officer. She had worked with considerably worse and, if truth be told, she was starting to like the man, well, with reservations. However, this case seemed to be affecting him differently from anything that had gone before.

She knew, of course, about the history between Grant and the Pettigrew family. The death of his former boss, DI Jacky Winters had, in Grant's mind at least, been laid firmly at the door of Ronnie Pettigrew. But there was something else, something that she couldn't quite put her finger on. There was an almost unhealthy aspect to his hatred for the Pettigrews, Ronnie in particular, something that seemed to go further than a mere professional dislike; worse, it seemed to be affecting his relationship with his junior officers.

As she turned her Volkswagen off Inchinnan Road and keyed her pass-code into the barrier for Osprey House, she tried to put it out of her mind. Unsuccessfully...

*

Before heading for the meeting room, Briony went into the adjacent smaller room that served as a kitchen and made herself a coffee. She opened the fridge in the hope of finding fresh milk when someone entered behind her; it was Sam Tannahill.

'Morning Sarge.' she said, her voice flat and emotionless.

'Morning, Sam. Everythin' okay?'

There was a telling pause. Briony looked at the face of the DC and could see her troubled expression.

'Sam, what's the matter.'

'Och, nothing Sarge. Has the kettle just boiled?'

'Sam, what's goin' on? You've got a face like a wet weekend in Portobello, eh!'

Sam managed a slight smile.

'We usually say Dunoon...em, well, I don't know if...listen, Sarge, can I speak to you in confidence?'

'Aye, of course, Sam, unless it's related to our enquiries.'

Sam shook her head.

'No, no, it's nothing like that...it's...well, it's the boss.'

'What, DCI McVicar?'

Sam cast her eyes down to the floor.

'Yes.'

Briony felt a sudden twinge of alarm. He wouldn't, surely...

'He hasn't...well...tried anythin'?'

Sam looked up aghast, shaking her blonde curls.

'Oh no, Sarge, nothing like that! No, it's just, well...'

Her voice tailed off. Briony knew how difficult it was to discuss the behaviour of a senior officer. God knows she had had her share of similar woes. She decided to finish the sentence for the troubled DC.

'He's a crabbit sod and you don't think he values you, is that it, eh?'

Sam looked up in surprise at this forthright statement.

'What? Em, well, yes, that's about it, Sarge.'

She hesitated.

'Actually, I was thinking of giving up as a detective and going back to uniform.'

Briony was horrified.

'Oh Sam don't, please, you're doin' great here. Listen, obviously I can't say too much but there's a lot goin' on with the boss that you don't necessarily know about. He puts a brave face on things but, well, after all that happened...'

'I know, Sarge, and I know how terrible that must have been but he makes me feel so, well, worthless, I suppose.

It's horrible. I do my best, but...'

Briony was furious. Grant had a great wee team and this was how he made them feel.

'Listen Sam, I'll have a word...'

'No, please, don't, it'll just make it worse...'

'No, it won't. I can handle him, Sam, leave him to me. Grant McVicar needs to get a bloody grip and I'll make sure that he does.'

*

'Aye, come in.'

Briony pushed open the door to Grant's stuffy office, manoeuvred herself and the two mugs of coffee through the opening then pushed the door shut with her foot. She placed the mugs on the desk and, without invitation, sat down.

'We need to talk, Boss.'

*

Twenty minutes later, Grant was still sitting at his desk staring at the space recently occupied by his sergeant, his coffee untouched. He was stunned; he was also hurt and slightly angry – she had no right to speak to him the way she had.

Or had she? Aw fuck...

It hadn't always been this way. Having always been well treated by his old boss, friend and mentor, the late DI Jacky Winters, he had tried to behave likewise towards those below him. He thought it had worked. Well, up until...

No...no...

He leaned his elbows on the desk and dropped his head onto his hands, wondering for the umpteenth time if he had made a mistake in returning to front-line policing. He had been offered other positions, office based, that would have spared him all this grief, but, no, he had specifically requested that he return to his old position of DCI at Paisley. "Confronting his demons" was how he had thought of it. Unfortunately they seemed to be gaining the upper hand. One in particular...

On top of all that, he still had to keep his promise and speak at Finn Thackray's party later that day, as if he didn't have enough on his plate. He groaned and rubbed his hand across his bald head, wiping away the beads of sweat. Maybe Briony Quinn was right.

After a few minutes, he stood up, strode purposefully across his office and along to the meeting room. He was going to sort this . Now!

*

'Sam. A word in my office, please. Now!'

He stormed out, leaving Sam Tannahill staring helplessly at Briony, the latter looking aghast at Grant's terse command. As Sam stood up, she seemed to be on the verge of tears; she walked out and along the corridor, then knocked on her boss's door.

'Come in, Sam.'

She stepped in and closed the door – she didn't want anyone else to hear whatever was coming; her shoulders were slumped and her head hung down. It was like being back at Park Mains High School, on the single occasion that she had been called to the headmaster's office. She felt physically sick.

'Sit down, please.'

She obeyed, looking up at him.

'Listen, Boss...'

He looked across at her, his dark brows furrowed. To her surprise, he tried to smile but it seemed to be a struggle.

'No, Sam, you're doing the listening. Briony told me you're thinking of quitting as a detective.'

'Em, well, I...'

'Right, I have just one thing to say to you. Don't you bloody dare!'

'Sorry?'

'You heard, Samantha Tannahill. I said "don't you bloody dare". You're already a first-class detective constable with the makings of an even better sergeant in a year or two. You're smart, you're a grafter, you have courage and spirit, you're a great team player. Exactly what the force needs. So I don't want to hear another word on the subject. Just because you get landed with a bad-tempered, grumpy so-and-so like me doesn't mean you've to go off handing in your resignation. Honestly, I have no excuse; reasons, maybe, but we shouldn't let our personal lives get in the way of our professional one. But believe me, Sam, it's bloody hard... so, I'm really sorry. I can understand why you feel the way you do but it's me, not you and if I've upset you, or put you down, then I apologise. You're a highly valued member of this team, we all like you and respect you, so don't you forget it.'

Two tears ran down the DC's freckled cheeks.

'And don't start bloody greetin' Sam, or you'll have me at it too.'

She retrieved a tissue from the pocket of her jeans and dabbed her eyes, laughing through her tears.

'Okay, Boss, sorry.'

'Right, bugger off and sort yourself out.'

She stood up.

'Oh, and just one more thing, Sam.'

'Yes, Boss?'

'If, by any chance, you decide to give Briony Quinn a hug, add an extra squeeze from me. But don't you dare tell her or you'll be handing out parking tickets faster than you can say '"McVicar"!'

*

The minor emotional trauma over, the team were assembled once more in the hot, stuffy atmosphere of their meeting room. The outside temperature seemed to have notched up yet another degree and everyone was decidedly uncomfortable. Grant stood up and ran a square of kitchen roll over his head, cursing again the lack of budget that prevented the repair of the air-conditioning.

'Right, two things. We need to prove conclusively that Molloy and Dougall carried out the assault because, at the moment, it's mostly circumstantial. We also need to properly establish the motive, because, at the moment, it could be one of several. Faz, could you go and see Anthony Higgins again and see if he's been aware of anyone else using the flat. In particular Ronnie Pettigrew. Take Sam with you, I think she'll like Anthony!'

They stood up and left, Sam giving her Boss a somewhat less frosty glance as she passed.

Grant turned and looked out of the window, marshalling his thoughts. There was a distinct heat haze forming over the adjacent buildings and he was sure the spell of hot weather must surely break soon; just as he wanted the case to break, preferably implicating the Pettigrew family. He also wished the day was over as he was dreading the evening's event. Briony cleared her throat and he turned back to face the remainder of his team.

'Sorry, was miles away.'

Briony gave him a re-assuring smile.

'Anyway, on to the assaults. So far, we've not found enough evidence to prove beyond reasonable doubt that it was Dougall and Molloy. Bri, let's go back over to their offices, have another wee rake about...'

He caught Cliff's eye.

'...no disrespect, Cliff, I just want to make absolutely sure. Check, double-check then check again. Listen, you and Kiera come with us, we'll give it a final going over, maybe have a look in that transport company's warehouse as well. Whoever did the deed must have had at least some blood on their clothes. Remember one of the boys bled so badly that he choked to death. Nothing's turned up from the search of their houses so there's a reasonable chance that they disposed of their stuff somewhere back at their offices. Right, come on, let's see if we can wrap this up today; I've had enough...'

*

An hour later, they had arrived at the scruffy portakabin that served as the headquarters of "Bin there. Done that" and, as before, it was locked. Fortunately Grant knew that the key had been given to the depot manager at the adjacent Paton Transport warehouse. Surely that would count as implied permission?

'Right, have a sniff about, I'll go and get the keys.'

It took only a few minutes to locate the manager, who was sitting having a coffee and a cigarette in the office. With a grunt he produced them from a drawer in his untidy desk.

Aye, so much for no smoking in the workplace...

Leaving Briony and Kiera to search the warehouse, Grant walked back across the dusty yard; as he did so, he recalled his first meeting with the suspects. They had claimed to have been been using the transport company's toilet, stating that their own was broken; the memory raised a tiny niggle in Grant's mind. He approached the portakabin, unlocked it and opened the door. The smell that emanated wasn't pleasant, a mixture of stale smoke, sweat and general filth, greatly exacerbated by the relentless heat. He called to Cliff, who was poking about amongst a pile of old tyres.

'Cliff, come on and have another look inside.'

'Aye, sure thing, Boss.'

They walked through the cramped and untidy space, looking for anything that might offer a clue; there was nothing.

'Remember they said their toilet was broken, Cliff?'

'Aye, "buggert" wis the term he used, ah recall.'

'Indeed. Let's have a wee look.'

Grant opened the door to the tiny toilet, almost gagging on the vile smell. He lifted the lid of the pan to reveal a filthy, brown interior and he quickly shut it again. The window was open slightly and the cramped space was filled with noisy bluebottles, attracted to the stench. He was about to leave when he looked at the cistern; it was the usual, cheap plastic affair, stained and faded but what caught his eye were a couple of scratch marks at the edges, as if something had been driven under the lid.

'Did you check inside the cistern, Cliff?'

There was a pause before the DC answered.

'Em, no... no, ah didn'ae, Boss. Here, ah'll have a look now...'

Cliff reached forward to grab the plastic lid but Grant put his hand on the DCs arm.

'Gloves, sunshine!'

'Oh, aye, right enough, Boss, sorry.'

Grant pulled a couple of pairs of thin latex gloves from his trouser pocket, handed a pair to Cliff and they both pulled them on. The DC reached for the lid again and tried to raise it.

'It's stuck, Boss. Need somethin' tae prise it open.'

'Aye, that's what I thought. Look at the sides.'

Cliff looked at the scratches then turned and looked at his Boss. Grant could see the colour rising in the DC's cheeks at having missed a potential clue.

'Ah'll away an' see if ah can find a screwdriver.'

Grant tried the lid again but it was tightly jammed down. Cliff quickly returned with a rusty screwdriver and pushed it into the tiny gap, levering the top up slowly and twisting the blade as he did so. Finally it popped off and Grant lifted it away. They looked inside but there was no water; instead, the space was filled with a plastic Aldi shopping bag; Cliff lifted it out and opened the top. They looked inside the bag then Grant looked up at his DC.

'Well, well, well...'

*

There was a distinct air of expectancy in the hot, stuffy room; as usual, Grant took the floor.

'Right, our good friend, Anthony Higgins, says that no-one other than Ellie Braid, aka Helena Pettigrew, has used the flat in Queen Margaret Drive. At least, as far as he is aware, but I'm inclined to believe him; our friend Anthony is a one-man neighbourhood watch! This indicates that any relationship with the victims involved only Ellie Braid, although we can't rule out the possibility of other locations being used, I suppose. But we'll stick with Mrs Pettigrew, or Braid, for the moment.'

He paused and wiped the sweat from his forehead.

'However, our search of the "Bin There" premises was much more productive and has turned up a hitherto undiscovered couple of t-shirts and a pair of trainers, all considerably blood-spattered.'

Cliff avoided his boss's gaze. He was angry at himself and felt he had let Grant down. His boss continued, 'Now I don't think there's any doubt that these items belong to Molloy and Dougall, although forensics are still to confirm this. We've got SOCOs over there as we speak, checking for prints and anything else they can find, but we now have absolute proof that they assaulted the victims then presumably dumped them in the loch. Right Bri, let's head up to Helen Street and have a final go at Messrs M and D, let them know just how much evidence we have and see what they have to say for themselves. Cliff, you phone ahead and let them know we're coming. No doubt they'll want Bryce bloody Turnbull present.'

*

Hugh Dougall was sitting opposite Grant and Briony in the windowless and stuffy interview room, the immaculately turned-out Bryce Turnbull sitting next to him with an ill-concealed expression of disgust on his face. It was quite obvious to Grant that he was in attendance at the request of the Pettigrews.

Which means they've got something to hide...

'Right, Mr Dougall. I have just one question; answer it and we can save ourselves a lot of time, effort...'

He cast a meaningful glance at Turnbull, who studiously ignored it.

'...and money!'

Dougall frowned nervously at them across the table but remained silent. Grant leaned forwards.

'Why did you do it, Shug? Why did you kill them?'

Hugh Dougall sat up in his chair, his mouth agape as he turned to Bryce Turnbull, who had the good grace to look surprised.

'Chief Inspector, I have no idea to what you are alluding, but I can assure you...'

Dougall interrupted, ignoring the lawyer's glare of annoyance.

'Here, whit are ye on aboot? Ah never murdered nobody! That's pure shite, that is...'

'Hugh, leave this to me, please. As I said, Chief Inspector...'

This time it was Briony who interrupted.

'Mr Dougall, we have evidence linking you to the abduction of Andrew Watt and Chris Findlay. Fingerprints belonging to you, Mr Molloy and the deceased were found in the back of your van, which had conveniently been stolen and set on fire. Unfortunately for you, the evidence wasn't completely destroyed as intended. We have now found clothing and a pair of trainers in your offices which also have blood on them and it is only a matter of time before that is also matched to the deceased...'

The barrage of evidence left Dougall looking stunned; Turnbull interrupted again, obviously agitated.

'One moment, Sergeant, you're telling me that you searched Mr Dougall's premises without a warrant. I don't think that...

Briony glared at him and continued.

'Mr Dougall had already kindly allowed us to search his premises without a warrant; presumably he didn't think we'd look in the toilet cistern. He had left the key available at the adjacent Paton Transport in case we needed further access. That was a mistake, Mr Dougall. It could prove to be a very big mistake...'

'It wisn'ae ma trainers, it wis Tam's...'

Dougall stopped mid-sentence and his eyes widened, as he realised what he'd said. Turnbull turned and glared at his client, raising his voice as he spoke.

'For God sake, will you be quiet and leave this to me? Now look, officers...'

'No, you look, Mr Turnbull.' interrupted Grant, the anger rising in his chest. He stabbed his finger towards the lawyer as he continued. 'Two young men have been brutally murdered. For your information, and I may add that this isn't in the public domain, one of them was still alive when he was unceremoniously dumped in Castle Semple loch and left to drown. The other one was already dead as a result of choking on his own blood. We can prove that your client and his associate, Mr Molloy, were seen with the victims that evening. We know that, earlier in the day, the victims were at Helena Pettigrew's flat or Ellie Braid, which is her maiden name, as I'm sure you are well aware. We know that it's EnviCon, the Pettigrews' company, that employs your clients, albeit indirectly.

We have forensic evidence confirming that the two young men were disabled using Rohypnol and, by their own admission, your clients were with the victims in the Cartbridge pub, where they bought them drinks, the perfect opportunity to administer the drug. Your clients claim that they subsequently gave the victims a lift to the Renfrew Ferry area. We can prove that the young men were, at some point, in the back of your client's van before it was allegedly stolen. All that remains is for us to find out why this vicious and brutal act took place. However, we have enough to be going on with. Mr Dougall, you may as well tell us . You're going to be done for murder anyway, telling us the truth now might just get you a few years off...'

Hugh Dougall jumped to his feet. Grant yelled *Officers!* at which the two uniformed policemen outside the door immediately entered the interview room and strode across to Dougall, who had a manic expression on his face. He sat back down and the officers retreated.

'Here, haud on, there's no fuckin' way ah'm takin' the rap for murder. We wis just tae give them a doin', that wis aw. Ah never killed naebody, that's a load of shite...'

Turnbull had also risen to his feet and had his hand on Dougall's shoulder. He practically screamed in his client's face.

'Will you shut your stupid mouth, Dougall? I told you. Let me handle this, you bloody idiot!'

He turned and forced an insincere smile towards Grant and Briony.

'Officers, could I have a few minutes alone with my client please?'

*

The few minutes turned into almost an hour and Grant was becoming increasingly impatient, despite Briony's best attempts to keep him calm. Finally, they were called back to the interview room, where Bryce Turnbull was sitting next to Hugh Dougall, the smug expression now conspicuously absent from the latter's surly face. The interview was recommenced.

'Well?' snapped Grant.

Turnbull immediately replied.

'Having discussed the matter with Mr Dougall and Mr Molloy, we have decided that it would be in Mr Molloy's best interests to appoint another solicitor. From here on in I will be representing

Mr Dougall exclusively. I believe Mr Molloy now intends that Miss Valerie Traynor of Kirkbride Traynor will be his legal representative. You may wish to discuss and confirm this with him, of course.'

Grant scowled at the smarmy, immaculately-dressed solicitor. Of course, he knew that, under the circumstances, it was highly likely that each man would eventually choose to have a different lawyer; the problem was that it meant they could then accuse each other of the crime, making the truth even more elusive. But there was absolutely nothing he could do about it.

'Fine, I'll do just that. With regards to our previous conversation, which you so abruptly terminated, has your client anything further to say?'

'My client has prepared a short statement.'

'And?'

Turnbull cleared his throat.

'My client, Mr Hugh Dougall, is prepared to admit that there may have been a misunderstanding and an altercation between himself and the two victims. However, he denies any subsequent involvement in the abduction, assault and, in particular, the murder of the said victims. Instead, he names Mr Thomas Molloy as the individual responsible for the first two alleged crimes, although he does not name Mr Molloy as having committed the murders.'

'And that's it?

'Yes.'

'Bollocks.'

'What? Now, Mr McVicar, there's no need...'

'Yes, there is, Mr Turnbull. This whole story is a load of complete and utter bollocks. Your client has already admitted on the recording that he was responsible...'

'My client was being pressurised by yourself, Mr McVicar. He was scared that he was being accused of murder, an accusation that he strenuously denies, I may add.'

'Well, he can deny it all he likes.'

Grant glared across at Dougall, who was now squirming in his chair. Before Turnbull could continue, Grant asked.

'Did you strip them?'

'Eh? Whit...?'

'Did you strip them? Did you strip the victims before you tied them up and assaulted them, Mr Dougall? Did you like seeing them naked, Mr Dougall. Did it give you a thrill...?'

Bryce Turnbull was on his feet.

'That's it . This interview is over...'

Grant had also jumped to his feet and was leaning menacingly across the table. Briony grabbed his arm as she hissed 'For God's sake, Boss...' He ignored her.

'No, it is *not* over, Mr Turnbull. Your client is a filthy, lying bastard, acting for reasons unknown on behalf of a family of filthy, lying bastards...'

'BOSS. For God's sake, STOP!'

Grant turned and stared at her, a manic gleam in his eyes. He dropped himself heavily back into the chair. Dougall was looking across at him with the expression of a terrified rabbit facing a shotgun. Bryce Turnbull looked as if he was about to explode.

'Chief Inspector, this is completely unacceptable...'

Dougall interrupted. He was almost babbling.

'Ah never stripped naebody. Are ye sayin, whit... ah'm some kind o' fuckin' pervert?... Mr Turnbull, tell him...'

The lawyer lifted his briefcase.

'This interview is over, Chief Inspector. I'm not having these ridiculous allegations and insinuations bandied about, upsetting my client. I'll be making a complaint to your superiors...'

Grant stood up again, shoving his chair back noisily; he towered over the lawyer.

'This interview is over when *I* say it is, Mr Turnbull and you can complain to whoever you bloody well like. Now, unless your client can give me any further information that can prove his innocence, he's about to be charged with murder.'

He glared down at Dougall.

'Did you hear that, Mr Dougall. M-U-R-D-E-R. You and your buddy killed these men and you are going to be put away for a long time...'

Dougal now jumped up. Briony was the only one remaining seated. The accused's glance darted between Grant and Bryce Turnbull.

"For fuck sake, Turnbull, just do whit ah asked. Tell him!'

'Dougall, if you don't shut up right now then I walk – do you understand?'

Dougall closed his mouth but before any of them could sit back down, Grant leaned over menacingly.

'Why did you do it, Dougall? Was it Ronnie Pettigrew that told you to do it - was it? Tell me - now, Dougall. We'll find out eventually. Save yourself any more grief.'

Dougall stared at the table and mumbled.

'It wis just a doin'. We never killed them... we just left them, we knew someone wid find them...'

He looked up at Grant, the fear clearly visible in his eyes.

'Honest, Sir, we just gave them a doin', we...'

'Dougall!' screamed Turnbull; the man, who was now mumbling incoherently, ignored him.

'Enough!' snapped Turnbull, slapping his hand hard on the table as his face turned purple with suppressed rage. 'Right, officers, you have my client's statement. We're done here.'

Grant glared at him.

'Aye, so we do, as well as some pretty damning evidence. Dougall will be held here until we decide what action we're taking next. We'll see what Mr Molloy has to say, shall we?'

Before Grant could say "interview terminated", Bryce Turnbull leaned down and whispered in his client's ear. Grant couldn't hear everything that was said, but the words "fucking moron" and "speak to Miss Pettigrew" were just audible. He smiled grimly as he and Briony left the room.

*

They had to wait for another twenty minutes before Valerie Traynor arrived. Grant had encountered her before and knew her to be a clever and capable defence lawyer – the firm of Kirkbride Traynor were only one step down the ladder from the Turnbull operation. However, she was more business-like and less ingratiating than Bryce Turnbull and Grant held her in slightly higher regard. Slightly...

Thomas Molloy was considerably less volatile than his associate, remaining almost completely silent throughout the interview. Val Traynor had read her client's statement and, as expected, Molloy now blamed Dougall for the assault. Of course he, too, strenuously denied murdering the victims. Despite Grant's goading, Molloy absolutely refused to rise to the bait; even the mention of stripping the victims elicited only a slight twitch of the accused's right eye. The interview was concluded with little further information having been gleaned, very much to Grant's annoyance. As they left the room, Briony looked at him; she didn't like the expression on his face. Had she been asked to define it, well...

Murderous, perhaps...

'So that's their game. Lay the blame on each other, eh?'

Grant stared at the ground as they walked.

'Aye. To be expected. I suppose it was too much to hope for that they'd stick together, but at he end of the day all they care about is their own slimy skin. Bastards.'

'Aye, bastards...'

*

They were driving back to Osprey House in a rather strained silence. The interviews seemed to have drained Grant and Briony thought he looked absolutely exhausted. He let out a long sigh. They were very nearly at the end of the investigation, he was sure.

But am I sure...really...?

And, as the tiny voice of doubt was running through his mind the same whisper was echoing in DS Briony Quinn's head. She said nothing; after all, he *was* the boss. But as she watched the expression on his face, the frown, the pursing of the full lips, she knew that he was lost in his troubled thoughts. She fervently hoped he would come to the correct conclusion. Suddenly, he seemed to reach a decision and he turned his gaze on her.

'I'll see what The Mint has to say.'

He had then telephoned Superintendent Minto and brought her up to date with the enquiry. The call was on speaker.

'Are you quite sure, Grant?'

'Yes ma'am. I don't have any doubt. We've got all we need to charge them.'

There was a pause before Superintendent Minto responded.

'And what about you, Sergeant? Do you agree with The Chief Inspector?'

Briony looked at Grant. Did she?

'Em, yes, ma'am. I'd go along with DCI McVicar. I think we've got enough evidence now.'

'Good, I'll speak to the Fiscal and give you a call back.'

She ended the call. Grant looked sideways at Briony – somehow his eyes seemed distant.

'Thanks, I appreciate your support. Right, we're nearly there. Christ, Bri, I need a coffee.'

*

It was nearly forty minutes before Grant's phone rang again. He answered it almost immediately, putting it on speaker. Patricia Minto's voice was characteristically unemotional.

'Grant'

'ma'am.'

'Right, I've spoken to Sheena McPartland and she's happy for you to go ahead and charge Dougall and Molloy. But for God's sake make sure you've got enough evidence to support the charges, Grant. I don't want this back-firing. Remember who you're up against. You need to be absolutely sure.'

'Yes ma'am, don't worry, I am, thanks.'

Grant nodded to Briony as he terminated the call.

'Right, the Fiscal's given us the go ahead, Bri, let's go.'

She hesitated and he frowned at her.

'What?'

'Would we no' be best to wait until tomorrow, eh Boss? Remember what the Super said, we need to be sure.'

'I think we've got more than enough to go on, don't you?'

'Aye, but if we leave chargin' them until Friday it would give us the weekend, just in case. If we charge them today, then...'

'Yes, the hearing'll be tomorrow; I'm well aware of that, Bri. But I don't think we need to delay it until Monday. I mean, what more do we need? No, let's get it over with, sooner the better as far as I'm concerned, then we can all bugger off home for the weekend.'

He turned and walked away, leaving Briony staring at his back and wondering why he was in such a hurry and just what the hell was going on in the big man's mind. Then it dawned on her; Finn Thackray's birthday party...

*

They entered the stuffy interview room once more, the first of the accused having been brought back in. The smell of stale sweat was almost overpowering and Bryce Turnbull was sitting beside Dougall, his nose wrinkled in disgust and looking as if he'd rather be anywhere else than in the company of his client. Grant and Briony took their seats, remaining silent for a few moments, whilst

Dougall sat, shoulders hunched and staring despondently at the scratched surface of the table. Finally Grant looked up at the two sharply contrasting figures opposite him and took a deep breath...

'On the night of Tuesday 27th August at Castle Semple Loch, Lochwinnoch, you, Hugh Dougall, whilst acting with Thomas Ninian Molloy, or others as yet unknown, having previously incapacitated, assaulted and tied Andrew Graeme Watt, did place him in the water of Castle Semple Loch, as a result of which he drowned and you did murder him...'

Chapter 14

It had been an absolute nightmare.

He had nearly been late; once Molloy and Dougall had been formally charged and dispatched to HM Prison Barlinnie, there had been the usual administrative processes to go through, after which Superintendent Minto had insisted on a meeting with the Fiscal to discuss the case. Grant had the suspicion that neither woman was entirely happy with the situation but it was agreed that the two accused would attend a hearing the following morning where they would enter a plea. Not guilty to all charges and accusing each other of the assault, judging by the noisy remonstrations of Bryce Turnbull and the restrained protestations of Valerie Traynor. Finally, to cap it all, there had been a minor accident on the A737, causing further delay. Grant usually felt a sense of elation when a charge of murder had finally been brought, especially in a case such as this. Today he felt physically sick.

When he finally arrived at the party, he had done his utmost to remain upbeat and cheerful. After all, Finn Thackray was his godson and this year's birthday was taking Brian's eldest boy into double figures. But when Louise had opened the door, with Finn at her side, the shock must have been visible on his face; the boy was the image of his father. Louise had smiled ruefully.

'I know, Grant, just like his dad, the wee rascal!'

She had rubbed her son's mop of dark hair affectionately but Grant could see the pain in her eyes. He had hugged her then, the two of them clinging to, and trying to find strength from, each other. Finally he entered the crowded lounge. The atmosphere seemed false, with everyone putting on a brave face; all kind, decent people, their lives ripped apart by the terrible tragedy. There were a few smiles, a few looks...

Christ, don't fucking start, Grant, not now...

Mercifully, Louise served the food – she had always been a superb cook and tonight she had made a special effort. He was filled with admiration for the woman – if he was struggling then God only knew what kind of hell she went through every day and night, every morning when she awoke in the empty bed. Once everyone had been fed (although the quantity of un-eaten food indicated a distinct lack of appetite) the little group made their way along to the nearby swing park, where a few local dignitaries, as well as a photographer from the local paper, had assembled. A few words were said, the bench was unveiled... and then it was his turn.

The small assembly had fallen respectfully silent as Grant stood before them, his eyes blurred with un-shed tears and hands shaking very slightly. He looked down at the hollow, meaningless phrases he had scribbled down earlier; all he really wanted to say was "Brian, I'm so, so sorry..."

Finally, it was over. The group applauded but Louise left and ran back towards the house. Finn came over and gave him a hug.

'Thanks, Uncle Grant. That was really nice.'

Grant ruffled the boy's hair, just as Louise had done earlier.

'Aye, no problem, wee man. It was my pleasure.'

Finn looked up at him; his heart lurched.

'Oh, and thanks for the money, that was really nice.'

'You're welcome lad.. See and use it for something nice!'

'I'm wanting a new game for the x-box. I'll maybe put it towards that.'

'Good plan, Finn.'

Finn looked up at him. Grant felt his heart was about to stop, the boy was so like his friend.

'You could come up to Braehead with me if you like and we could have a wee look? I'm trying to get mum to take me on Saturday but she said she won't have time. Could you take me, Uncle Grant? Please?'

Fuck...!

'Aye, maybe, Finn. I've got a lot on but I'll see what I can do...

listen, I'd better away and see how your mum's getting on. She looked a bit upset.'

Finn looked up at him again, his eyes wide and dark, just like Brian's.

'She'll probably be crying. She does that a lot.'

Grant patted the boy's hair then trotted ahead of the sombre little assemblage and into the house – he entered the kitchen where Louise was standing at the sink. He could see her shoulders shaking and he went over and put his arms round her. She turned around and collapsed against him. They stood in silence for a few minutes; they could hear the guests returning but it seemed that, somehow, they realised that Grant and Louise needed their space. Finally Grant broke the silence.

'It'll pass, Louise, eventually. The first time of everything is the worst then, next time, it won't be the first.'

She nodded, sobbing into his chest.

'You're probably right, Grant. But it's... Christ, I miss him so bloody much. That silly, lop-sided grin of his, the daft exaggerated Yorkshire accent he put on. And it's the stupid wee things, like his shaving stuff in the bathroom, I can't bear to throw it out... oh Grant, I feel so... so...'

He held her tighter.

'I know, Louise, I know... so do I...'

'What are we going to do?'

She started sobbing again. He didn't have an answer. He couldn't even answer it for himself...

*

Finally his ordeal was over. He left the house, promising to call Louise in a few days to see how she was, promising Finn a trip to Braehead, promises he was unlikely, or unwilling, to keep. He climbed in to the sanctuary of his pick-up and pulled away, barely noticing the ominous dark sky that was rolling over from the west. But, as he pulled into the drive of Bluebell Cottage, he immediately sensed the muggy, oppressive atmosphere. There was an odd, greenish-tinged light that made the late summer leaves stand out vividly against the branches of the trees. No birds sang, no cows lowed, nothing broke the eerie, brooding silence. Somehow, though, he couldn't bear the idea of sitting in the house, alone with only the company of his thoughts. He knew exactly what he needed, thunderstorm or no thunderstorm! He entered the house, took a small bunch of keys from the drawer in the hall table then walked over to the garage and opened the door. After scrambling through an assortment of sundry building materials, he managed to recover his ageing but trusty mountain bike; it was covered in cement dust and the tyres were a bit flat but a wipe of the frame and saddle and five minutes with the pump rendered it roadworthy. He went back to the house, then changed into cycling shorts, a vest top and a pair of light Nike trainers. Hopefully he could do the loop before the storm came; down through Howwood, on to the cycle track, back off at the loch then back up the hill. An hour should do it, a burst of intense physical effort that might help to clear his grief-stricken mind...

*

He was just approaching the ruin of the ancient Collegiate Church when he heard the first rumble of thunder and he realised that he had miscalculated, badly; he obviously wasn't as fit as he had thought! Grant pushed harder, grunting with the physical effort involved, then suddenly there was an intense blue flash of lightning and an almost instantaneous crack of thunder. It seemed to be almost overhead. Another flash, another crack...

Holy shit...

And then the heavens opened.

Grant felt as if someone was hosing him with lukewarm water. He had never been caught in rain like this, it seemed almost like a solid entity. His legs pounded the pedals, driving him on. More lightning, more thunder. It seemed to be all around him now and he was starting to feel decidedly uneasy. Grant realised that he may actually be in considerable danger. He came to where the main track was crossed by a path leading down from Parkhill woods, the police tape still fluttering in the strange wind that had risen, and leading down to the loch itself. He decided that it might be safer to head downwards and along the loch path so he turned left and free-wheeled down what had become a brown, frothing stream. Another flash, another crack. He could smell the ozone in the air and, although it was terrifying, it was also incredibly exhilarating. As he splashed his way down towards the loch he realised he was grinning from ear to ear.

Christ, maybe I've got a bloody death wish...

He reached the loch, barely visible in the uncanny deluge, and turned right, pedalling furiously along the slightly rougher track. Once he reached the visitor centre he could at least shelter safely until the storm passed over. He passed one of the small fishing jetties that jutted out into the dark water. Something caught his eye.

What the...?

Through the rain and the gloom he could just make out that someone was sitting hunched over at the end of the narrow wooden structure. He stopped as a spiked, violet fork flashed across the sky. His spine seemed to tingle with the static as the rumble of thunder sounded, almost deafening him. He dropped the bike and ran down the jetty, stopping a few feet behind the small figure; the last thing he wanted was to scare them into jumping into the loch. He bent down.

'Hey? Hey, are you okay?'

There was no response; he edged a bit closer.

'Can you hear me? Are you all right?'

The figure turned and stared at him with wide, expressionless eyes. Her dark hair was soaked, plastered to her skull; she was hugging her knees and rocking back and forth, as if in a trance. There was another brilliant flash of lightning, illuminating her face in its unnatural violet-blue light.

It was Delia Donald.

*

He was kneeling in front of her, his hands gently shaking her shoulders. She was wearing jeans, a white t-shirt and light trainers and was completely saturated and shivering, despite the near-tropical humidity of the storm. The last crack of thunder had been almost overhead and their exposed position made them extremely vulnerable.

'Delia! Delia, it's me, DCI Grant McVicar. Delia, can you hear me?'

She looked at him uncomprehendingly just as another near-blinding flash bathed them in its eerie light. Her face suddenly changed as she finally recognised him and she started to sob.

'Delia, are you okay? We need to get away from here, now!'

He stood up and held out his hands but she just looked at him, mumbling something that he couldn't make it out over the deafening rumble of the thunder, which was now almost continuous.

'Delia, we need to go. Can you walk? We need to get away from here.'

She shook her head and looked at him.

'No...no, let me stay, let me stay with my poor boys...'

'Delia, they're not here, they're gone. Come on...'

Flash! Crack!

Shit...

He bent down; putting one arm under her shoulders and the other under her knees, then lifted her up. She offered no resistance and he was surprised at how light she was. Grant carried her back to the path where he had abandoned his bike and he put her down, grabbing her again as she almost collapsed.

Fuck...

He lifted up the bike with one hand, supporting her with the other then, with a bit of a struggle; managed to lift her on to the saddle, although her feet were nowhere near the pedals.

'Right, you hang on to the handlebars and I'll push you along.'

She managed to lean forward and grasp them as he put one hand behind her back and the other in the middle of the bars between hers. He started to propel her along the track which, by now, was a sea of muddy water. Grant bent his head and pushed on as the storm continued to rage about them until, finally, the rowing club and the visitor centre loomed into sight through the seemingly interminable torrential rain. He pushed the bike up the small ramp and under the meagre shelter offered by the entrance canopy of the centre, then helped her off. She grasped his arm, her fingers biting into his flesh; he realised that she was in shock of some sort.

'Delia, how did you get here? Did you drive?'

She nodded and murmured.

'M… my car... it's over there...'

He looked across. The white BMW was the only car left in the car park, which was now almost completely underwater.

'Delia, are you able to drive?'

She shook her head and he realised that it was probably a stupid question. He frowned; the bike certainly wouldn't fit in the car but he could leave it at the loch. No-one was going to steal it this evening! But should he be alone with a potential suspect, especially in the state she was in? He shook his head, knowing the answer;

he decided he would phone Briony. If they could shelter until she arrived, then she could arrange to take Delia home or wherever she was staying. Then, as clear as the last lightning flash, his mind saw his phone sitting on his bedside table where he had placed it whilst changing.

Fuck...

'Delia, do you have your phone with you?'

She looked up at him and nodded, then reached into the back pocket of her sodden jeans and pulled out an iPhone. She pressed it; the screen was totally blank. She stared at it.

'It's not working, sorry...'

Shit...

He had run out of options.

'Never mind, have you got your car keys?'

She fumbled in her other back pocket then handed them to him. He pressed the button and, to his profound relief, the lights on the BMW flashed welcomingly. His plan now was to phone Briony as soon as he got home and get her to meet him at his house

'Right, come on, let's get out of here.'

Leaving his bike propped against the wall under the canopy, they got into Delia's car, although Grant was now seriously worried about her mental state. Having pushed the seat back as far as it could go, he started the car, relieved to hear the engine burst into life. He reversed and turned. The car park was now an almost-continuous sheet of water and he was concerned about the depth, worried it might flood the engine. Driving slowly, keeping the gear low and the revs high.

Thank God it's a manual box...

Finally they made it out of the car park, turning right and up into the village; the frequency of the lightning flashes and the rumbles of thunder started to diminish as the dark clouds finally passed over; Grant couldn't recall ever having experienced such a violent electrical storm and, strangely, there was now a slight feeling of anti-climax. He realised that it had, in fact, been extremely exciting!

Fifteen minutes later he arrived at Bluebell Cottage and turned left into the remains of his drive. The torrential rain appeared to have washed most of the gravel onto the road. Delia seemed to have recovered slightly although she hadn't spoken a word on the journey. As he got out, he realised that the rain was finally easing off to a desultory drizzle and the sky above was starting to lighten considerably; down the Garnock valley he could see patches of blue peeping through the thinning clouds and he realised that there might even be a spectacular sunset to cap off the evening's storm. Delia had managed to get herself out of the car and was standing up, albeit somewhat shakily; he helped her to the front door and finally got her inside.

'Right, come in, let's get the kettle on and I'll phone Briony...'

She grabbed his arm again.

'No, no, please, just phone Pam. I want to go home.'

'Wha... oh, Pam Lawson? Aye, you stay with her, don't you?'

Delia nodded her affirmative.

'Actually, she probably saved my life.'

He looked at her, suddenly on the alert.

'What do you mean, Delia?'

She looked away.

'My husband was... he was...'

He could see her start to lose focus again and remembering Briony's suspicions, he decided now was not the time to push it. He took her gently by the shoulders.

'It's okay, Delia, You don't need to say anything, you're safe here. Come on, I'll phone your friend and we can have a cuppa while we're waiting for her to get here.'

She had followed him into the kitchen and he switched on the kettle.

'Right, I'll get you a towel and see if I can rustle up something dry, though I doubt if there's anything of mine that won't drown you!'

He smiled briefly at his unintended pun, went into the bathroom and grabbed a fresh towel. Grant returned to the kitchen where Delia was sitting on a stool, the water dripping off her and forming a puddle on the wooden floor. She was soaked, bedraggled and looked utterly miserable; his heart went out to her. He knew exactly how she felt.

*

Ten minutes later, she was holding a mug of steaming coffee in her hands, the towel wrapped round her hair and draped over her shoulders. Grant having provided her with a clean t-shirt and a short, pale-blue terry-towelling bathrobe that he had won in some daft raffle down in Howwood's Station Inn. He leaned against the worktop and regarded her curiously. She certainly was an enigma. As Briony had asked, villain or victim? At the moment, he was leaning heavily towards the latter; and what had Briony meant with that stupid comment about keeping an open mind. Of course he was! He had, indeed, phoned Pam Lawson, as asked; but he had also phoned Briony and asked her to come down. She had still been at Osprey House and should hopefully be arriving in about fifteen minutes. He hadn't been able to contact Pam immediately and it would be at least another forty minutes or so before she arrived. He took a sip of his coffee, looking over the rim of his mug at his unexpected guest. Delia Donald looked understandably vulnerable, hurt and lost; he realised, however, that she also looked incredibly cute, sitting there wrapped up in the silly dressing gown and the white towelling turban, wisps of dark curls peeping out from underneath. And those eyes... as soon as he thought it, she looked up under her long lashes as she caught his gaze.

'What?' she asked, with a small smile.

'Eh... oh, nothing, Delia. Just wondering if you're okay.'

Her smile widened very slightly but there was still pain in her expression.

'Well, I am, sort of...thanks to you, Inspector.'

'Grant, please.'

'Oh, is that okay? I mean, am I not still a suspect or something...?'

'No, Delia, I don't think you are, well...'

Open mind, Grant, open mind...

She didn't let him finish.

'Okay, Grant it is, but really, I can't thank you enough. I don't know what came over me. I just wanted, needed, to see where... well, you know. Then the storm came and, somehow, I couldn't leave. It's like I was in shock or something...'

Her voice tailed off at the memory.

'I think you were, Delia. You were in a hell of a state and, to be honest, I think we were both in a fair bit of danger. I've never seen such a violent thunderstorm before.'

She looked up, her face suddenly more animated.

'Yes, wasn't it amazing? The strange thing is, it was kind of exciting, if you know what I mean.'

He smiled back. He had suddenly realised that, since the storm had started, he hadn't given a thought to the pain of the evening's earlier events.

'I do. When I was cycling down to the loch I realised that I was grinning from ear to ear. It was totally wild...'

Suddenly they ran out of things to say. After an awkward pause, her smile faded.

'They were such nice boys. I still can't believe it...'

A tear ran down her cheek and he realised that, really, she was nowhere near being "okay".

'Delia, please, don't dwell on it, it won't help.'

'Won't it?'

'No, it won't. Actually, I'm speaking from experience here.'

She looked up, curiously raising an eyebrow, but remained silent.

Oh Christ...!

He sighed, furrowing his brows in thought; should he?

Aw, what the hell...

'See, the thing is... well...'

She looked at him questioningly.

He changed his mind and shook his head.

'Aw, never mind, you don't want to hear about my woes, Delia. Let's just say you've got to move on. I only wish I bloody could...'

She smiled again and, somehow, it lifted his heart slightly.

God, she's a strange wee thing...

'You know, my friend Brian used to say "just get...'

Before he could finish, the doorbell rang.

'That'll be Pam, hopefully' she chirped, putting down her mug.

'Em, it might not be. You see, I called Briony as well, she...'

Delia's expression changed instantly. She glared across at him.

'What? I asked you not to, Grant, I wanted...'

'Delia, listen to me, please. Briony was in victim support before she joined me. She's been terrific, putting up with all my crappy moods, listening to my depressed rambling. I wanted her to have a wee chat with you. Please, Delia, it'll help, I promise.'

She gave him a suspicious look as he left the kitchen.

'Well, I suppose it can't do too much harm...'

*

Grant heard the growl of a powerful engine approaching and immediately went to the front door. A black Range Rover scrunched over the piles of gravel that had once been his drive and stopped; Pam Lawson turned off the engine and climbed elegantly out of the door. He had to admit that she was a tall, striking woman, dressed in tight jeans and a lightweight waterproof jacket, hardly necessary now as the anticipated sunset was casting a beautiful orange glow over the pristine, rain-washed foliage. The birds were in full evensong, as if celebrating the passing of the storm. She walked purposefully up his house, where he was waiting in the open doorway. She wore a thunderous expression.

'This is a bloody disgrace, Chief Inspector— how dare you!'

He held up his hand.

'Mrs Lawson, let me explain...'

'Explain?' she barked. 'Explain how Delia finds herself alone with you in your house? Believe me, you'll be hearing from my sol...'

'She was down at the loch, Mrs Lawson. Sitting on a jetty, in the middle of a raging thunderstorm. She was in shock, she couldn't drive, her phone was saturated. That's why she's here. I bloody rescued her, if you must know.'

Pam gave him a searching look.

'You had better be telling the truth, Chief Inspector... anyway, where is she?'

'She's in with my sergeant.'

Paw Lawson looked as if she was about to explode.

'Your sergeant! Oh really, this is totally unacceptable. You *are* going to be hearing from my solicitor first thing, I can ass...'

He held up his hand, trying to stem the outburst.

Christ, it's worse than trying to stop the bloody rain...

'Mrs Lawson, will you please stop jumping to conclusions. For a start and, as I am sure you are only too well aware, anything Delia may say would be completely inadmissible as there is only one officer present, no solicitor, your friend isn't under caution and the conversation isn't being taped. But they're not discussing the case, be certain of that.'

'So what the hell are they discussing, Inspector, the bloody weather?'

'Quite possibly! Listen, please, come in, let me get you a coffee and I'll tell you exactly what's been happening.'

Pam Lawson grunted but entered the house and followed him into the kitchen, currently aglow with the light of the setting sun.

She looked out of the window, down over the glistening valley.

'Hm, well, I must say this is rather nice, Inspector.'

'Thanks; and Grant, please.'

She gave him a look.

'Hm.'

'Can I get you a coffee, Mrs Lawson?'

She paused.

'Well, okay, white, no sugar; and you may as well call me Pam, I suppose.'

He decided to try and call a truce and extended his hand. She hesitated then took it, shaking it briefly; her grip was surprisingly firm. It was a start...

'Right, Pam, please let me explain. Briony Quinn was in victim support before she came to work as my DS...'

He paused, choosing his words carefully.

'Em...let's just say I have my own demons and she's helped me deal with them. Briony was suspicious that Delia had been abused by her estranged husband...'

Pam interrupted, the anger returning to her face.

'Abused! The bastard nearly killed her! You should have seen her, Grant, bruises all over her breasts. By all accounts he frequently raped her, taking her completely against her will. He beat her, hurt her. Do you know, he even burnt her with an iron when she refused him... the man was an absolute monster. Goodness knows what would have happened if I hadn't taken her in... men are such bloody animals sometimes...'

The fury subsided momentarily but Grant was taken aback at her tirade and her vicious generalisation. He interjected.

'That's a bit harsh, Pam. Not all men are like that, I can assure you. Anyway, that's pretty much what I suspected. Delia made a comment to that effect tonight and I thought Briony might be able to help.'

He handed Pam the coffee and she smiled slightly in thanks before continuing with her rant.

'You're right. I'm sorry, Grant. You know, I've tried to get her to press charges but she refuses. The man should be locked up but, to be honest, I don't think she could cope with it all being brought out in court; it would destroy her, she's still very fragile; and now these bloody murders...'

Aye, now these bloody murders...

She sipped her coffee and he explained in more detail what had happened at the loch, how Delia had ended up at his house. Pam listened and he could see her harsh expression soften slightly.

'Hm, well, I suppose that does cast a slightly different light on things, Grant. Fair enough, I'm sorry if I jumped to conclusions. I've become rather protective of little Dee and I'm sure you can understand why.'

'I do, Pam, and I'm thankful that you got to her in time. It's often difficult to get victims of domestic abuse to come forward, you know. After all, it's usually just one partner's word against the other's and it's never an easy case to pursue. Anyway, we'll see what she has to say to Briony.'

They made small talk for another ten minutes or so then they heard the lounge door open. Briony peeked out.

'Oh, hi, Mrs Lawson. Could you both come through please?

They put down their empty mugs and walked into the lounge that was bathed in the fading glow of the spectacular sunset. Delia was sitting on the couch, still in the turban and the dressing gown. She had obviously been crying. Pam immediately sat beside her and put her arm round her shoulder.

'Oh Delia, sweetheart, are you okay? Grant's been telling me what happened, you poor little poppet...'

Grant looked at Briony, who raised an eyebrow but remained silent. It was Delia who spoke.

'I'm okay now, Pam, thanks to these two...'

She smiled up at Grant and Briony.

'...if it wasn't for Grant I'd probably have been hit by lightning. As for Briony, well...'

Pam also smiled up at the two officers.

'I really can't thank you both enough. You've been extremely kind, but I think we should be getting this one home and in to her bed. Quite enough adventures for one day!'

She ushered Delia to her feet.

'Now, dear, I've brought your jammies, so if you can get changed I'll get you back and safely tucked up. A good night's sleep will do wonders...won't it, Sergeant?'

Briony gave Pam a brief nod; Delia looked up at Grant and smiled. He felt his stomach clench slightly.

'Thanks again, Grant.

He stared at her, unsure of what to say; fortunately Briony came to his aid.

'Listen, Delia, you've got my number, just call if you'd like to chat some more, eh?'

To the surprise of both Grant and Pam, Delia walked over to Briony and gabbed her in a tight, almost passionate embrace, which Briony returned. They heard Delia whisper.

'Thanks Briony. I don't know what I'd have done without you tonight...'

Grant glanced at Pam Lawson and saw a strange expression flicker across her handsome features. Jealousy, perhaps; he wasn't altogether sure...

*

Grant closed the door behind his visitors and gave his sergeant a rare smile.

'Coffee?'

Briony sighed.

'Bloody shame I'm drivin', I could do with somethin' a lot stronger.'

'That bad?'

'Oh aye! And worse; an' that bloody woman...'

'What, Pam Lawson?'

'Aye, her. Fair do's, by all accounts she saved Delia but did you see their relationship. Delia's become the daughter Pam never had. She thinks she's motherin' the lassie when in fact she's smotherin' her. God, she's jumped from one controlling, manipulative relationship straight into another, albeit without the violence; which, by the way, was pretty extreme and absolutely vile. There's no doubt that he's raped her on a number of occasions and some of the other stuff... he really should be locked away...'

She looked down, lowering her voice.

'...you know, what happened to those poor boys, no-one deserves that, it's inexcusable but, if anyone came close, it would be that bastard Danny Donald...'

Grant grabbed her arms, staring down into her face. It was filled with hatred and loathing.

'Come on, you know you're not supposed to become personally involved, Bri. You've done your best to help Delia, don't get so angry...'

'But it's bloody hard when you've heard the things I just have, Boss. Really, I feel so, so sorry for her, she's like a poor lost kid with no-one to turn to. Pam Lawson will destroy her in the end, I'm sure of that. She's so beholdin' to the woman that I can't see a way out for her... aw fuck it...'

Suddenly Briony pulled away from Grant and punched her fist into her other palm with considerable violence; Grant didn't know what to say. His sergeant had always been so strong and supportive for him, but now she was angry, hurt and filled with spite and he didn't know how to deal with it.

Christ, sometimes I fucking hate this job...

He knew that there was an unopened bottle of Glenmorangie stashed safely in a cupboard. For a moment, he was tempted. One wouldn't do either of them any harm, surely?

'Listen Bri, em...'

She looked up, the anger subsiding.

'Aye?'

'Em...come on, let's have a quick coffee then call it a night; listen, I really appreciate you coming over, I think it was a big help for Delia.'

She smiled.

'No problem, Boss. The poor girl's in a really bad place just now, well, emotionally, anyway.'

She paused and gave him a searching look.

' Anythin' you want to talk about while I'm here?'

Is now the time...?

'No, you're alright, Bri. Just been a hard day, that's all. Come on...'

Chapter 15

As he drove up the A737 the next morning, Grant was mulling over the previous evening's events. Taking Delia back to his house had probably placed him at risk of a variety of accusations. Fortunately, that scenario seemed to have been avoided. Why hadn't he taken her to the nearest police station or back to Pam's, for that matter? He could easily have taken a taxi back home, or got

Briony to come and collect him. In retrospect, it had been a foolish action and he was lucky that Pam Lawson hadn't decided to take the matter further. He smiled and shook his head.

Don't be a bloody fool, Grant McVicar...she's still a potential suspect, for fuck sake...

As for the Glenmorangie, as Briony had left he had insisted that she take it; it turned out to be her favourite. But it had been a close call, very close...

Aye, better out of temptation's way...!

*

Grant pulled into the parking compound outside Osprey House, surprised to find a number of spaces available. A few minutes later, he stood in front of his team in the meeting room, now a good few degrees cooler. There was an air of expectancy and also of slight satisfaction – they knew that the case was finally drawing to a conclusion. Grant stood up, looked at them and gave them the benison of a broad smile.

'Okay, first up, well done everyone; as you all know, we've now charged Dougall and Molloy and they will undoubtedly be remanded pending trial in an hour or so. Personally I think it highly unlikely that they'll get bail. However...'

He paused and looked at them.

'...we aren't done yet, I'm afraid. Cliff, where are we with the SOCOs?'

'Well Boss, they're still up at the "Bin there" Portakabin, the clothes are away tae get checked for DNA an' stuff...'

Cliff was obviously still feeling guilty at having missed the hidden clothing. Grant reckoned it wouldn't do him any harm; he'd try harder next time...

Briony spoke.

'Would it be worth checkin' where the accused claim they dropped the victims off, Boss, eh? Just in case...'

'Fair point, Bri. Okay, Faz, you and Kiera get yourselves over to Renfrew, near the Ferry, they said. I'd presume it's where the road to Braehead turns off. I think there's a few tenement flats and a pub on the corner so we might be lucky if they have CCTV; check that out, see if anyone was out walking a dog, anything. Have you got the van registration and description?'

Faz and Kiera were already on their feet; Kiera patted her bag.

'Yup, Boss, all here. We'll keep you posted.'

'Right. I'll maybe take a run over after the hearing, just to see for myself.'

He sat down, clasped his hands and stared at the floor; it was as if he had suddenly run out of steam.

'Boss?' said Briony. 'You okay?'

He looked up at her.

'What? Aye, I'm fine. Thing is, I really wanted to try and prove the connection to the Pettigrews; I'm sure they're behind this in some way. I don't really think those two clowns set out to do this on their own. They've hardly a brain between them.'

'You need to try and let it go, Boss. I know how badly you want them but I don't think it's goin' to happen this time.'

Grant looked as if he was about to snap back at her but, fortunately, Sam spoke first.

'But won't it all come out at the trial, Boss? I mean, surely those two aren't just going to stand there and take the blame for everything?'

Grant looked at her, his expression grim.

'Sam, you don't know these people. You know, a friend of mine once described what he called the "might" of the police. He said that trouble seldom came to the door of an officer because, as he put it "our gang is always bigger than their gang". Unfortunately that doesn't apply to the Pettigrews— I mean, take Jacky Winters...'

His eyes seemed to lose focus for a moment before he continued.

'...they had no qualms then about killing a serving officer; a bloody Inspector at that! If low-lifes such as Molloy and Dougall dared to open their mouths then they'd be as well asking for a solitary cell and a length of rope. Twenty years inside, looking over your shoulder every minute, every day, wondering when it's going to come... not to mention what would happen to their families! No, they'll take the rap; their sort always do.'

'Like Omerta?' asked Sam.

Grant pulled a face.

'Aye, something like that, only without the honour! Right, Bri and I need to be off to court. Sam, can you have another look at this EnviCon company, see if you can come up with anything that we could use? There'll probably be nothing but it's worth looking into. Could you also start getting everything properly collated so its ready for the fiscal; look through it all, make sure we haven't missed anything obvious. Have a think about any other possible links we could explore that might pull the Pettigrews further into the case.'

He stood up and pulled a face.

'I know she's on the same side but Sheena McPartland always manages to make me feel inadequate. Let's bloody show her we know what we're doing this time.'

*

As they left Osprey House, Grant asked.

'Bri, would you mind if we take your car? I want to give Pam Lawson a call and see how Delia is after last night's excitement.'

Briony raised her eyebrows.

'Aye, sure, no problem, Boss.'

They pulled out of the car park as Grant dialled Pam's number. It was answered after a few rings.

'Good morning, Grant.'

'Good morning, Pam. Sorry to disturb you, I just wanted to know how Delia was this morning.'

'That's kind of you. I took her in some breakfast a while ago and she's just finished. I think she's okay. Well, as okay as she'll ever be, of course...'

Grant interrupted. He could do without another tirade on the subject of Danny Donald.

'Well, let's hope things continue to improve. I was pretty worried about her last night. Listen, could I possibly have a wee word...'

He was aware of Briony giving him a sideways glance; there was a brief pause before Pam Lawson answered.

'Is it necessary, Grant?'

'Em, well, no, I just wanted to ask her how she was.'

Pam's tone hardened very slightly.

'I think it would be best if you just let her be, Grant, she's very delicate just now, what with...well, you know what I mean. Why not phone later and see how she's doing? I'll tell her you called, though.'

'Em, well, okay, I'll do that, Pam. Oh, and listen, could you also say to her that...'

But Pam Lawson had ended the call; Grant glared at his phone.

'Madam hung up on you, then?' asked Briony.

'Aye. She's a bloody menace, that woman.

'She is that!'

They drove on in silence for a few moments, then Briony cast another sideways glance at her Boss.

'You like her, don't you?'

'What? Pam Lawson? No, I bloody well do not...'

Briony laughed.

'I'm no' talkin' about Pam Lawson and well you know it, Boss.'

Try as he might, he was unable to suppress a slight smile.

'Och away and don't be bloody daft, Bri. Anyway, what would she be doing with a big, baldy-heided, gloomy lump like me?'

'Ah, methinks the man doth protest too much...anyway, I've seen the way she looks at you...'

'Right, we're nearly there. Let's get our professional faces on and forget about it. Ye're talkin' mince withoot the gravy, as my granny used to say!'

*

It was over. At Paisley Sheriff Court, under the cynical eye of Sheriff Susan Young, Messrs Hugh Dougall and Thomas Ninian Molloy had, as expected, pleaded not guilty to the charges of the abduction and assault of Andrew Watt and Chris Findlay, each accusing the other of the crime. They had both pleaded not guilty to the murders. Bail had been refused and they had been duly despatched to Barlinnie Prison, where they would most probably continue to be held until their trial commenced. Sheena McPartland, the fiscal, had made a point of speaking to Grant after the hearing.

'Well, so far so good, Grant. I trust that you're investigations are continuing, though? I don't want the defence coming out with any surprises, especially Bryce...'

Grant interrupted the tirade before it started.

'Aye, of course, Sheena. Just a matter of confirming a few details... there's no real doubt that they're guilty, despite their pleas.'

'Hmm, well, as I said, unfortunately one of them has that pompous and self-important prick Turnbull fighting his corner. Val Traynor I can handle but Turnbull...' She practically spat out the name of Dougall's expensive defence lawyer. Grant sympathised. After all, he too had a nemesis...

'Don't worry, Sheena, we'll have all the confirmation we need next week. Just wish I could have got the Pettigrews as well . There's no doubt that they're implicated in some way. Just can't bloody prove it, as always.'

'Yes, that would have been a real feather in our cap. I take it there isn't enough evidence to tie them in?'

'Only that Helena Pettigrew had some kind of dalliance with the victims but, as they were seen later I don't think she's personally responsible. No, it's Pettigrew Junior that I suspect is behind it all. I think she found out that something was happening between the victims and her mum and she probably had them "taken out" as a matter of family honour, if you get my drift.'

Sheena McPartland pursed her lips.

'Hm, I know what you're getting at but I think it's too tenuous a connection to proceed with a prosecution. We'll certainly be calling Mrs Pettigrew as a witness though and I don't imagine she'll be too happy about that. Listen, do you think it's worth calling Ronnie Pettigrew as well. See if we can't trip her up somehow?'

Grant shook his head.

'Without testimony from the two accused, I think it'd just be a waste of time, to be honest. The woman's too smart and they're not daft. A wrong word and their lives won't be worth the proverbial button.'

'No, I suppose you're right. Okay, I'll let you get off, keep at it, Grant, we don't want these two slipping out of our grasp. Well done.'

Well done! Bloody hell...

*

There was an all round sense of relief back at Osprey House now that Dougall and Molloy were safely locked away pending their trial. Grant knew it should feel like a result but, somehow, it was a bit of an anti-climax. He knew the case wasn't over, of course; there was still plenty of work to do, collating results, and working on making the case for the prosecution as watertight as they possibly could. Normally by this stage he would have been on a bit of a "high". He always got a buzz from hearing the Sheriff remanding those he had placed in the dock. Watching their faces as the reality of a trip to the notorious Victorian edifice that was Glasgow's Barlinnie Prison loomed before them.

Faz and Sam's trip to Renfrew had, as expected, neither proved nor disproved Dougall and Molloy's claim that they had dropped the victims off.

'Nothing, Boss, sorry.' said Faz, his customary grin absent. He didn't like being beaten! 'The CCTV in the pub is ancient, uses old video cassettes that are completely worn out. No-one saw anything. At least, they're not admitting to it. Waste of time, really.'

'Aye, well, thank's for trying anyway, guys.'

He gave a heavy sigh. Why was today so different? It suddenly dawned on him

Brian's not here...

Briony immediately saw the cloud pass across his face; she casually walked across and spoke softly as the others chatted about the case.

'You're missin' him, eh?'

Christ, how does she know...?

'Em, listen Bri...'

'Grant, it's absolutely fine. Brian was your partner for years, you shared so much, you can't just forget about him, especially at times like this. But don't forget about the rest of us either...'

She smiled; and he found himself smiling back..

'Couldn't have done it without you, my friend.'

Briony quickly turned away. Once again he had taken her completely by surprise. Sam Tannahill, who was staring at them, raised her eyebrows questioningly and Briony briefly wondered if the DC suspected that there was something going on between them. She shook her head very slightly; the last thing they needed were rumours of an office romance...

Chapter 16

Euan Johnstone heard the heavy oak door close behind him with a solid thump and, as he scrunched across the gravel drive towards his black SUV (parked adjacent to a beautiful, silver seven-series BMW) he breathed a deep sigh of relief.

He had always accepted that his work with the Domestic Services Agency was simply a means to an end. Of course, he enjoyed sex as much as the next guy (more, perhaps) and, sure, mature women were often more fun, especially when they were paying for the privilege! But sometimes...well, today had most definitely been one of those times. Miriam Oliphant had been extremely demanding, asking him to perform a variety of sexual acts. Normally he derived varying amounts of pleasure from these (depending on the client) but today he had thought he was going to suffocate. Then, when she finally, and thankfully, reached her orgasm...

Jesus...

He rubbed his neck. It was still sore and he hoped that the woman hadn't done him any permanent damage. Still, she had been generous, a fifty-quid bonus on top of his fee and he was still to get his retainer from Delia. He liked Delia, actually he liked her very much; he would go and see her on Monday and they would have a good laugh about his experience; maybe he'd ask her out for lunch.

Now, that would *be fun...*

He turned the van out of the gravel drive that led away from the solid, blonde-sandstone detached villa, then made his way along the tree-lined street in the sedate little Renfrewshire town of Kilmacolm. It was almost deserted, save for a lone delivery van that had pulled out behind him.

*

Half an hour later, Euan arrived at Glasgow's Braehead Shopping Centre, having decided that, following his morning's exploits, he deserved a Big Mac, large fries, a full-sugar cola, a chocolate milkshake and a McFlurry. En route he had received a text from a friend (well, from the message it looked as if the "friendship" may be moving up a few notches...) asking him to meet later for "a few drinks then, maybe, a bit of fun..." He grinned. He'd drive home, leave his car and get a train. If there was one thing Euan Johnstone liked, it was that sort of "fun"...

As expected, the car park was busy but he found a space easily enough and was soon standing in the usual Saturday melee at McDonald's. On this occasion (actually, on quite a few occasions) he hadn't bothered to wear the Agency overalls. It was always a bit of a pain having to change afterwards and anyway, Delia was unlikely to find out. His mouth was already watering and he wished the queue would move a bit quicker. As he waited, he looked around, hoping to find a free table, preferably across from a single, attractive woman, although he knew this was unlikely;

there were kids everywhere! He noticed a man, accompanied by a youngish boy, who seemed to be about to leave; if the bloody queue would get moving he might just time it nicely and get their table. The man stood up. He was tall, well-built and bald, with a neatly trimmed beard. The boy looked nothing like him and Euan assumed it was probably the acquired son of a "partner". A relationship with baggage, as he thought of it.

Aye, no' for me, that; can't be doin' with baggage...

The boy was a good looking youngster but wore a very serious, almost sombre expression. The two were speaking and, suddenly, the man made as if to grab and hug the boy but, at the last minute, he seemed to stop himself, following which the boy turned and stormed off. Euan was intrigued, it was a slightly unusual little scenario and he felt a brief pang of sympathy for the tall, shaven-headed man. He shuffled forward a few steps as the queue finally moved and, as he did so, the man caught his eye; he looked utterly miserable!

*

Grant had received the phone call from Louise Thackray on the Friday evening. They had chatted for a short while then Louise had asked

'Grant, at the party, did you say you'd take Finn up to Braehead to buy a game for his x-box?'

Did I...?

'Aye, I think I might have.'

'Oh, great. He's been going on about it ever since and he's desperate to spend the money you gave him. Listen, I don't suppose you could do it this Saturday? I've got to take his brother to rugby training at Birkmyre Park, up in Kilmacolm. I can't leave Finn and he'd just be standing about anyway. He's not really sporty.'

Grant hated Braehead; in fact he hated shopping in general. An idea jumped into his head.

'Listen, why don't I take Callum to the rugby. After all, I played a bit when I was younger...'

Louise interrupted.

'I know, Grant, but Finn's desperate for you to take him shopping. He's really fond of you and he's going through a bit of a bad patch at the moment...'

Aye, aren't we bloody all...

'...but you could take Callum another time, if you like. I think it would be really good for Finn, and you, for that matter.'

Reluctantly, Grant had agreed and now, here he was, desperately trying to put a brave face on things. This, apparently, included lunch in McDonald's!

'Right, is that you done, Finn?'

Grant stood up, psyching himself up for the continuation of the shopping expedition. Finn dipped his last chip in the ketchup, popped it in his mouth then jumped to his feet, somewhat more enthusiastically than Grant.

'Yes, Uncle Grant, thanks, that was brilliant. I love chicken nuggets. Mum always cooks us posh stuff and I never get nuggets at home.'

'Aw, you're lucky, Finn, Your mum's a great cook, always was. She doesn't need to give you processed food like that.'

Finn sighed.

'I know, Uncle Grant, but I get fed up with the fancy stuff she makes. Sometimes I just want chicken nuggets, or fish fingers even.'

Grant managed a slight smile.

'Och well, once in a while won't do you any harm, I suppose. But don't you dare complain about her cooking. You're lucky to have a mum who cares enough to feed you properly. I wish I had someone to feed me!'

Finn Thackray looked up at Grant with his big, serious eyes; Brian's eyes.

'Do you like Mum?'

'Of course I do, son. She's lovely.'

Finn paused and Grant realised the boy was struggling to hold back his tears.

'W...w...well, could the two of you not get married? I mean, I know she likes you, Uncle Grant, and you like her, and you're on your own...'

'Finn, it's not as simple as that. We're great friends, but we're not...'

'But why not?' wailed the boy, his tears now streaming down his cheeks. Please, will you think about it, Uncle Grant. Please? I'll say to Mum...'

Grant crouched down and grabbed the boy's shoulders, gazing into his moist eyes.

'No, Finn, you will *not* say to your mother. Please, you need to understand, people don't just get married because...because, well...'

'Because you don't love her?'

For fuck sake...

Grant stood back up, looking down at the boy who so resembled his friend.

'Of course I love your mum, Finn, but not like that. I'm there as a friend whenever she needs me, whenever you need me, but...aw shit.'

'It's okay, Uncle Grant, I understand.'

The boy looked dejectedly at the floor, kicking at a chicken nugget that had fallen. Grant stepped forward as if to hug him, then stopped. Finn looked up at him expectantly. When nothing happened he turned and stamped away, leaving Grant staring around helplessly and wondering just what the hell to do.

You understand, Finn? I wish I fucking did..

*

Having safely deposited Finn back at his house, and having elicited a firm assurance that nothing of their conversation would be mentioned to his mum, Grant headed home. Louise had tried to persuade him to stay for dinner but he felt that it might give Finn false hope and that was the last thing he wanted. As he drove up the narrow Belltrees Road, he wondered once again if he should go and see his friends, who would undoubtedly be quaffing a pint or two in Howwood's cosy Railway Inn. Maybe they would understand. He shook his head sadly.

Aye, and maybe they wouldn't...

Bobby Urquart rolled over in his bed and groaned. He reached for his phone and checked the time: eleven-thirty.

Wee buggers...

He had been working the Saturday night shift at Bridge of Weir's Baltic Leather Works and had crawled into his bed at eight-thirty that Sunday morning. His wife, Sheila, usually managed to keep the kids quiet, a task recently made easier by the long, hot summer; fortunately his nine and twelve year-olds, Sophie and Paul, seemed to prefer being outdoors to sitting in front of a screen or a device, much to their parents' surprise! He sat up, feeling increasingly irritated; the kids were shouting and screaming now and there was no way he'd get back to sleep with that noise going on.

'Sheila! Sheila, are ye there?'

A voice replied from downstairs.

'Aye, Bobby, whit is it? How're you no' sleepin?'

'How do ye think? Those bloody kids are makin' one hell o' a racket. Whit are they doin?'

He heard footsteps on the stairs and the door opened.

'Ah sent them ootside to play, Bobby. It's a nice enough mornin' an' they seem to love the fresh air.'

'Aye, well, can ye get them to keep it doon a wee bit. Ah'm on again tonight an' Ah'll be bloody knackered.'

'An' you're rememberin' yer mother's comin' over at three for her dinner?'

'Aye, ah'm no' likely to forget that wee treat! Christ, it's gettin' louder. Is somethin' wrong?'

'Oh dear God, Ah hope they've no' been down at that bloody loch again.'

Robert and Sheila Urquhart lived in a semi-detached ex-council house located at the end of the little cul-de-sac of Loch road, the last row of houses in the village of Bridge of Weir. Across the adjacent field lay the small Houstonhead Dam, a relic from the long-disappeared Laigh Mill. It was mostly used by fishermen nowadays but, like all small areas of water, it was a magnet for the local children, especially during the recent warm weather. Sheila's heart started to race. The kids were well warned to keep away (an instruction they generally chose to ignore) and, as it had been pretty wet on Thursday during the thunderstorm, she knew that the water level would have risen.

'Ah'd better go an see whit's up. Ah hope to God nothin's happened!'

She left Bobby lying in bed, an angry expression on his face as he reached for his cigarettes, and ran down the stairs. She went out of the back door, walked across the patchy grass to the fence to find seven or eight children, of assorted age and gender, running across the field towards her; two of the girls were clearly upset. Sophie was at the front and she rushed up to her mother; she was so out of breath that she could hardly speak.

'Oh...oh...mum...'

The girl started to cry and Sheila Urquhart reached over the fence, lifting her daughter up as the others arrived and crowded round, talking and shouting in a rising cacophony of sound. Sheila raised her voice.

'Will you aw' shut up! Paul, what in the name o' God are you yellin' aboot?'

Paul drew himself up importantly.

'It's the loch, Maw. There's a dead body in it...'

For once, Grant had had a reasonable night's sleep and he awoke more refreshed than he had felt for ages. He lifted his phone, surprised to see that it was nearly nine-thirty; he seldom slept this late and he afforded himself the luxury of lying back on his bed, gazing at the ceiling and letting his mind wander; it was filled with an almost incoherent jumble of thoughts. The investigation of the brutal murders, one of the worst cases that he had encountered; his complex relationship with Louise and Finn Thackray; the bond that seemed to be forming between himself and Briony Quinn surprised him and he smiled. Although no-one could ever replace Brian, that didn't mean he couldn't go on to form another excellent working relationship. The Pettigrews; maybe Briony was right, maybe he needed to back off and bide his time, but it was hard, after everything...

He tried to resist the next thought but it edged it's way insidiously into his brain; Delia Donald... before it could fully develop, he sat up and swung his long legs out of the bed.

Time for a coffee...

*

Grant was sitting in his lounge, head back against the leather settee . He had almost forgotten what it felt like to relax. He was contemplating his lunch; there was bound to be something in the freezer that he could defrost but it could wait a wee bit longer. His eyes started to close...

He jumped up as the harsh ring of his phone intruded on the soft, gentle wave of sleep that was engulfing him. It was an unknown mobile number and he gritted his teeth as he answered it.

If this is about the bloody car accident I might have been involved in...

'McVicar.'

'Hello, is that DCI McVicar?'

'Yes, who is this?'

'Sorry to disturb you on your day off, Chief Inspector, it's Inspector Tommy Wylie, K division, think we've bumped into each other a few times.'

Grant had a vague recollection of a small, sandy-haired uniformed officer with prominent teeth.

'Oh, aye, got you now. So what can I do for you, Tommy.'

'Well, I'm up at Houstonhead Dam. You know, the wee loch just outside Bridge of Weir, heading towards Houston...'

'Aye, I know where you are. Go on...'

'Well, I'm aware, of course, that you were heading the enquiry into the bodies found in Castle Semple loch. I believe you charged a couple of guys on Friday...'

God, get to the bloody point, will you...

'Aye that's right.'

'Well, the thing is, a bunch of kids were playing down at this wee loch and they've found a body. We're in attendance and, by all accounts, it's the same MO. Naked, hands tied, tape over the mouth. I thought you should be made aware.'

There was a long pause

Oh Jesus fucking Christ...

Chapter 17

The first signs of an early Autumn had begun. The sky had shed its beautiful azure blue and was now a dull, leaden grey; a fine, West of Scotland drizzle was falling, the kind that seeps into everything; clothing, hair, the soul... The temperature had dropped a good ten degrees and DCI Grant McVicar shivered as he nodded to the uniformed constable, lifted the blue and white tape and strode purposefully across the damp grass towards Houstonhead Dam.

Briony was there already, with Cliff and Sam busy organising the uniformed constables and making sure the locus was secure. His sergeant gave him a concerned look and shook her head.

'Not good, Boss.'

'Bloody understatement; have you called the pathologist? Is it Doc Napier again?

'Yes to both. As usual, she was none too pleased but she's beaten you to it. She's down at the loch already carryin' out a preliminary examination.'

Grant peered towards the water and saw the slight figure of Nippy Napier, wearing a pair of fishermens' waders and standing in the water.

'Hm, okay. Right, what's the story? All I got from Tommy Wylie, after he'd finished bloody waffling, was that another body had turned up and he thought it looked like the same MO. Please tell me he got it wrong?'

'Afraid not, Boss. We had a quick look, although we didn't want to get too close until the SOCOs had a good look about. But again the body seems to be naked, hog-tied and with duct tape over the mouth. From what I could see, he was a pretty muscular young lad, maybe even a body-builder. Blonde, with one of those funny haircuts, dead short at the sides— oh, and a tattoo on his chest, think it was the Scottish lion rampant; poor bugger...'

Her voice tailed off as she gazed down at the small hive of activity at the water's edge.

'...and, unfortunately, it was a bunch o' kids that found it this time. In fact, I think that's a couple of them over there, eh.'

She pointed towards a group of children that were gathered behind the police line, where several uniformed officers were preventing them from getting too close. Crowded around them were about thirty curious adults, craning their necks and obviously desperate to find out what had happened, although it was highly likely that the local grapevine had already done its worst! Parked in the little cul-de-sac, almost hidden amongst the numerous police vehicles, was an ambulance, its blue lights flashing. Briony continued.

'A youngster called Paul Urquhart seems to be their self-appointed spokesman; the wee lad feels pretty important about it all. I've had a chat, I think he's okay but a couple o' the wee lassies are pretty traumatised. They're in the house with Paul's mum, she seems to be a bit o' a mother hen and she's lookin' after them 'til their parents get here. There's a paramedic with them as we speak.

Do you want to have a word with them, Boss?'

He shook his head.

'Could you do it, Bri; you'll be better than me, the mood I'm in. Take Kiera as well and see if there's a child protection officer coming, poor wee buggers are going to need help with this.'

'Och, you'd be surprised, Boss, they're generally more resilient than you'd give them credit for. Right, I'll grab Kiera and try to take a few statements.'

'Oh, have you called Fire and Rescue, just in case...?'

She gave him a look.

'...in case there's another one?

Aye, of course I have, Boss. They're on their way.'

He should have given her credit.

'Em, sorry' he mumbled.

She gave him a brief smile that he felt was undeserved. As she turned to leave she paused, staring down at the group of figures at the side of the small loch.

'Hang on Boss, somethin's happenin'...'

Grant followed her gaze. As they watched, the pathologist stood up and turned towards them, even from where they stood, they could see the expression of shock on her face; one of the uniformed cops turned away and vomited heavily into the long grass. The other officer in attendance took a couple of steps backwards before stumbling and landing with a splash in the shallow water.

'What the fuck..?'

Grant and Briony walked quickly towards the loch, although Margo Napier was now striding across the wet grass, her face white and her features set in a shocked but angry scowl under her bright red Nike skip-cap. She was pulling off a pair of rubber gloves and she shoved them into the pocket of the pristine white overalls she was wearing, glaring up at Grant as she approached. He managed to speak first.

'What the hell is it, Doctor?'

She shook her head.

'Same as the other two, except for one minor detail.'

They waited for her to continue.

'This one's had his genitals cut off and stuffed in his mouth...'

Grant and Briony stared at Doctor Napier in a stunned silence. She continued.

'But, that aside, the MO seems identical. This time, however, there's duct tape and some crude wadding over where...well, where the emasculation took place.'

Grant was struggling to assimilate this new information. He tried to remain calm but this fresh piece of information, coming on top of the discovery of a third murder victim, had severely shaken him.

'Uh...do you think he drowned, Doctor?'

She gave him a stony look.

'Oh, for God's sake, I can't answer that at the moment. I won't know until I get him on the table...'

Her shoulders slumped and she let out a long sigh. It was if all the fight had suddenly left her.

'My understanding was that you'd caught the bastards who were responsible, Grant. Now we've got another bloody swimmer, this time with his genitals cut off. What the hell's going on?'

He shook his head.

'I wish I knew, Doctor, I wish I bloody knew... by any chance can you give me an indication of how long the body's been in the water?'

She took a deep breath and let it out slowly between her pursed, smoker's lips; her life had been spent dealing with death and decay and she was weary. She really should retire...

'I can't be precise, of course, but preliminary examination would indicate less that twenty four hours.'

Grant's heart plummeted. He had clung to the hope that the time of death might have pre-dated Molloy and Dougall's arrest.

'Okay, thanks Doctor. When can you do the PM?'

'First thing tomorrow. I'll let you know immediately.'

She drew herself back up and gave Grant and Briony a curt nod.

'Right, I'm away home to check that my roast beef hasn't been burned to a bloody crisp.'

She strode purposefully away across the field, lighting a cigarette as she went. Grant wondered how she could examine a brutally mutilated and murdered body then head home to eat a lump of roasted meat; he suddenly remembered Briony's explanation of how Delia coped: "compartmentalisation".

Wish I could bloody do that...

The two officers stood in silence for a moment, then Grant turned to Briony.

'For fuck sake.'

She looked at him.

' Aye, for fuck sake indeed, Boss.'

'Right, we'd best get started. Bri, you away and speak to those kids now.'

He paused then lowered his voice.

'You know what this means, of course?'

She gave him a sympathetic look as she nodded.

'Aye, Boss, I know. Sorry.'

'Aye, but it's not your bloody fault, is it...?

As she walked away to find Kiera, he looked around, taking in the scene. The little loch lay a couple of hundred yards from the main Bridge of Weir to Houston road, at the bottom of a gentle slope. It was surrounded by fields, populated by a number of rather damp-looking black-and-white cows, lazily chewing the grass and entirely unaware of the tragedy unfolding around them. There seemed to be a rough track leading down to the loch and a couple of old-fashioned wooden rowing boats were tied to a post, presumably for the use of the fishermen. The uniformed police were swarming around the edge of the field, cordoning it off with blue tape. A second ambulance had arrived, parking at the side of the main road and, as the paramedics walked across the field towards him, Grant recognised one of them from Castle Semple. The man nodded as he approached.

'Mornin'.'

Grant mumbled his reply. The man's expression was stony.

'Well, we could certainly be doin' without another bloody body turnin' up in a loch. What the hell's goin' on?'

It was the second time in ten minutes that he had been asked this question. Again, he shook his head, his brows set in a deep frown.

'That's what I'm here to find out... em...'

The paramedic frowned back.

'What?'

'Just to warn you, this one's not pleasant.'

'Huh— When's a dead body ever pleasant? Anyway, best go an' have a shufti.'

They walked away but Grant remained, staring at the small loch, now sullied like it's larger counterpart just a few miles away. At this particular point in time, he needed to be by himself.

*

What had he missed? He had been absolutely convinced that it was Molloy and Dougall. All the evidence suggested it was them, right down to their partial admission; but they had been in custody since the previous Tuesday. He had initially hoped that the body might have been in the loch since before then but, even before Dr Napier's initial findings, he had doubted it. It was a small stretch of water, there were fishermen, kids, surely someone would have noticed it? Also, if the victim *had* been missing since last week, would someone not have reported it? And why, in God's name, had this other brutal mutilation been carried out? It didn't make any sense; or was he so blinkered, so desperate to find anything that might lead to the downfall of the Pettigrews that his judgement had been impaired? He just didn't know anymore.

Christ, Brian, what the hell do we do now...?

He started walking towards the water. He was already soaked; he had put on a jacket but hadn't brought a hat and although he knew there was a hood rolled up inside the collar he couldn't have cared less. At least the feel of the cool rain trickling down his neck made him feel alive, not like the poor bastard floating in the loch with his private parts stuffed in his mouth; he shuddered, this time not from the cold. Suddenly, he jumped as the strident ringing of his phone interrupted his dark, despondent thoughts and, in a temper, he wrenched it from his pocket. He looked at the screen and groaned; it was Superintendent Patricia Minto. He briefly considered not answering it but knowing it would only have been delaying the inevitable, he slid his thumb across the rain-spattered screen and lifted the phone to his ear.

'Super.'

'Grant, I've just heard. What the hell is going on?'

Christ, not again...

'Well, it seems that another body has been found, Super and...'
She shouted into the phone.

'Grant, please don't state the bloody obvious. I am well aware that another body has been found. I am also well aware that this is another murder. Is that correct?'

'Well, I haven't actually seen the body yet...'

'Oh for God sake, Chief Inspector, just give me a straight answer for once. The grapevine's been buzzing and I've already had Sheena

McPartland ranting at me and calling you for everything under the sun. She's suggesting that I remove you from the case, so I need you to give me a reason not to do so. I'll ask you again: is it the same MO?'

He considered hurling his phone down the field and into the loch, but managed to control the urge.

'Yes, ma'am, it is, by all accounts.'

'Has Doctor Napier had a look?'

'Yes.'

'And...?'

'She thinks it's not been in the water any longer than twenty four hours. ma'am.'

'In which case, it can't have been the two men that you've charged?'

'Em, no, ma'am, probably not.'

'Probably!' She screamed. 'You arrested these two idiots last Tuesday. Less than twenty-four hours takes us to lunchtime Saturday, if my arithmetic is correct. There's no bloody "probably" about it, Grant.'

'No ma'am, sorry.'

'Yes and you bloody should be. Right, I've got the Divisional Commander to phone next, he's going to be dead chuffed about all this, I don't think. You get on with it and get me a result; the correct one! Remember what I said.'

'Yes M...'

She had hung up before Grant realised that he hadn't had the chance to inform her about the emasculation.

Shit...!

The team had been waiting for Grant to arrive for some time. He had taken a detour back home to change out of his saturated clothes, as a result of which he arrived about forty minutes after everyone else. The room smelled strongly of curry.

'Help yourself, Boss' said Cliff as he finished off a poppadum. 'There's loads, ordered too bloody much, as usual.'

'Aye, thanks' mumbled Grant, spooning some lamb bhoona onto a piece of cold, stodgy naan. It would undoubtedly give him heartburn but what the hell; wasn't that what Rennies were for...?

Once he had cleared the plate (after a second helping) he pulled off a few sheets of kitchen roll and wiped his hands and mouth, ignoring the trail of curry sauce that had dribbled down the front of his grey t-shirt.

'Right. First, I owe you all an apology.'

'Boss. there's...'

'No Briony, let me finish. I'm the DCI, the senior investigating officer, I took the decision to charge Molloy and Dougall. I was wrong. Despite that, you are all implicated to an extent, so I apologise wholeheartedly. You deserve better.'

There was silence. No-one knew quite what to say. He looked up at them, his eyes making contact with each and every one of them.

'So, we can sit here all night, feeling angry, pissed-off, sorry for ourselves, whatever; or we can sort it and find the bastard responsible for these murders. What's it to be?'

Immediately Sam Tannahill replied.

'You know the answer Boss. We're right behind you, just tell us what the plan is and we're on it.'

There was a general murmur of assent. It was obvious to Grant that Sam spoke for each member of his team. He could feel his eyes pricking slightly; they did, indeed, deserve better. And he deserved much worse...

*

It was well after eight o'clock; they had checked for missing persons, they had scrutinised all the statements taken earlier that day, they had re-examined every aspect of the previous murders. The white boards were set up once more, with all the relevant information carefully set down once again by Cliff. Grant stared at it for a few minutes as Faz uploaded the fresh information on to Holmes.

'Right. I think the first port of call has to be Delia Donald. We don't have any missing persons reported, we have no identity, the only possible lead at the moment is that he's another one of her "boys". It's a long shot but I think we need to pursue it.'

He took out his phone.

'I'll call Pam Lawson and see if Delia's available.'

'She'll no' be happy, Boss.' said Briony. 'You know how protective she is.'

'Well, she'll just need to be happy, otherwise we'll bring Mrs

Donald in for questioning. To be honest, the way I'm feeling I'd be quite prepared to do that, just to show Pam Lawson who's running this bloody investigation. '

He dialled the number and Pam Lawson answered.

'Grant, I didn't expect to be hearing from you at this hour on a Sunday. Is everything okay?'

The hostility in her voice was obvious.

'No Pam, I'm afraid it's not. There's been another murder, same method as the first two, We have no report of anyone missing and no means of identification and I wondered if there was any possibility that it could be another of Delia's boys.'

There was a long pause. When Pam finally spoke, her voice sounded strained.

'And why on earth should you think that, Grant?'

'Well, as I said, the same method was used and he appeared to be a fit, muscular young man, in a similar mould to Andrew Watt and Chris Findlay...'

He avoided mention of the emasculation, that could could come later, if necessary.

'...look, would it be all right if we came over and...'

'No, actually, it wouldn't Chief Inspector. I have a few friends round for dinner and it would be most inconvenient if you were to...'

Grant interrupted. His patience with the woman was exhausted.

'Pam, when I ask if it would be all right, I'm really just being polite. We intend to be at your house within the hour; if you refuse then I will have a warrant issued, we will take Delia in for questioning and there will be nothing you can do to stop us. Now, I don't believe for one minute that's what you want so surely it's better if we keep it informal at the moment?'

'Really, Chief Inspector, this is most...'

He softened his tone very slightly.

'Pam, I understand. However, *you* need to understand that I'm now investigating a third murder; and, without going into detail, this one is considerably more brutal. Believe me, I'd much rather be at home with a coffee and a good book than standing in Osprey House, tired, with indigestion and trying to make sure we don't have to deal with any more of these hideous crimes. So, please, don't stand in my way. We're the good guys, remember...'

Briony smiled. She was impressed!

'Oh, very well, then. But please go easy on poor wee Delia, she's still fragile, as I'm sure you can imagine. Will your sergeant be accompanying you?'

Grant looked over at Briony and mouthed "are you coming?", to which she nodded an affirmative.

'Yes, Sergeant Quinn will be there. She seems to have struck up a rapport with Delia so I think it'll be helpful.'

'Very well, I'll see you in about an hour. You have the postcode?'

'Yes, we should have all your details on file.'

'Good. It's just on the edge of Milton of Campsie, off Antermony Road. That's the A891, I believe. Call if you get lost.'

'Okay, thanks Pam, I really do appreciate it. We'll try not to keep you too long. Bye.'

He ended the call and smiled at Briony.

'Sorted. Come on, let's be heading.'

He grabbed his jacket.

'Right all, let's wrap it up for the night. We'll go and see Delia, then let's all get a good night's sleep and come back fresh tomorrow. We should get the PM from Doc Napier early doors, see if that gets us any further forward. Might be worth going out to Barlinnie and having a word with Dougall and Molloy, although it's now pretty unlikely that they're implicated in this one. I suppose we'll need to tell them the news at some point. Shame. Anyway, 'night, all, and thanks again, I really appreciate your help...and your loyalty. You're a damned good bunch.'

As they left, Briony caught Sam's eye; the latter raised her eyebrows and smiled, telling Briony that Grant's words had hit the mark.

About bloody time too...

*

By the time Grant and Briony reached Milton of Campsie, it was dark and the drizzle had turned to a fine mist, making visibility extremely challenging. They drove slowly along the main road, Briony keeping watch on the sat-nav as Grant peered through the gloom.

'Right, it's just coming up on the left, Boss.'

Grant slowed the pick-up and turned sharply into a short gravel driveway. There was a security camera clearly visible above it and he turned to Briony

'Fancy. She's not taking any chances.'

'Aye, well, it is a bit out o' the way, I suppose. Better to be safe.'

'I suppose.'

Grant eased his vehicle up the driveway, which was illuminated by short silver post lights. They arrived outside the neat, tidy bungalow, where Pam's Black Range Rover and Delia's white BMW were parked.

'Looks like she got rid of the guests, Bri.'

'Aye, well, I suppose a couple o' cops turnin' up at your door late on a Sunday night is a bit o' a dampener, eh?'

'Aye, you're probably right. Unless, of course, there weren't actually any guests to start with. Okay, let's see what they have to say for themselves. At least she's opened the door. Good start!'

Pam Lawson ushered Grant and Briony through the outer porch and into a small but tastefully furnished hallway. The few pieces of artwork adorning the walls were beautiful and understated but, before Grant could either admire or comment on it, she had opened a polished, oak door.

'In here, officers. I've got the fire on. Quite a change in the weather tonight.'

The room was spacious but cosy . Again, it was tastefully furnished, with a luxurious tweed-covered couch and two matching armchairs. A few expensive-looking side lamps gave a welcoming glow and an oak coffee-table sat in front of the open fire, in which a few logs were crackling. It was almost uncomfortably hot and Grant could feel beads of perspiration break out on his forehead. Sitting in one of the chairs, her slender legs curled up under her and wearing a white towelling bathrobe was Delia Donald. Her dark, shiny curls spilled over the high collar and there were dark circles under her eyes. She looked up at him and treated him to a small, timid smile. Despite his best attempts, Grant felt as if his heart fluttered briefly and, as he smiled back, he was painfully aware of Briony giving him a look. Pam spoke, seemingly unaware of the brief exchange.

'Have a seat, please. Can I get you a coffee, tea, or something stronger, perhaps?'

'Em, no th...'

'Actually, I'd love a coffee, Mrs Lawson' interrupted Briony. Here,

I'll come and give you a hand.'

The sergeant practically bundled Pam Lawson out of the room. *'What the...?'*

Grant sat down on the empty chair; it was too close to the fire for comfort but he didn't want to push it back and further away from Delia. He smiled at her and she dropped her head slightly, looking over at him through her long eyelashes. She looked...

No, Grant, no...

'How are you, Delia?'

She sighed.

'Honestly?

'Aye, honestly, please.'

'Absolutely awful.'

He shook his head.

'I'm so sorry, Delia, and the last thing I want to do is upset you any more. Has Pam said...?'

'Yes, yes she has. It's so...oh, Grant, I can't believe it. I thought you'd caught the people who...well, Andy and Chris, you know...'

Grant could see she was struggling.

'Okay, Delia, just take it easy. I know how hard this must be for you. All we need to know is if there's any possibility that this new victim could be one...'

'Oh, please, Grant, please, don't say it, don't...'

He stopped. Although he now realised that Briony had managed the situation superbly, allowing him a few minutes alone with Delia (for whatever reason), they would be back at any moment and Pam would immediately form a defensive shield round her "little one", making questioning her extremely difficult. However, he didn't want to push her too hard in case she withdrew into herself, as she had done before. He chose his words carefully, aware of the clinking of dishes nearby.

'Delia, just let me run this description past you and see if it rings any bells. Male, blonde hair, almost razor cut at the sides but a bit longer on top. About five-eleven with a very muscular build, possibly a body-builder. Light blue eyes.'

Delia was staring at him, her own dark eyes widening.

'...and a tattoo of the Scottish lion over his upper left chest... Delia! Delia!... shit! Briony, Pam, can you come here. Now!'

*

Despite the repeated interventions of Pam Lawson, it was Briony who eventually managed to calm Delia down and return her to a state where she could speak semi-coherently. She bit her lip, fighting back the tears.

'I'm so, so sorry, I'm such a nuisance. What must you think of me...?'

Briony was holding Delia's hand and Pam was standing behind her, gently stroking her hair. Grant was still sitting opposite, feeling slightly guilty, totally helpless and filled with admiration for his sergeant, who was still speaking to the traumatised woman. She spoke softly and gently, her Fife lilt emphasised almost as if she were crooning to a baby. It was mesmerising.

'Delia, you're fine, ma lovely, you're fine. Dinn'a you worry about us, it's you we need to worry about. I know this is just awful for you but you need to try and put it out o' your mind. Now, breathe deeply. That's it, in, out, in, out. Good girl, that's the stuff, eh. Now, close your eyes again, go back to that safe place...'

'What safe place?' snapped Pam, frowning. 'What do you mean...'

'Ssshh, Pam, please. Just let her be for a moment, eh. It's just a wee place where Dee feels safe.'

'She's safe here, for goodness sa...'

Briony glared up at the woman; she spoke not a word but the expression on her face was enough to silence Pam Lawson, no mean feat in itself; the scowl remained, however. Briony turned her attention back to Delia.

'Okay, that's ma girlie. Sshh, now, breathe, in, out, in...'

Briony was still stroking the back of Delia's hand and Grant could see the distressed girl's features gradually relax.

'That's it. That's ma lassie.'

Delia's eyelids started to twitch and her head fell forward slightly. Briony caught her Boss's glance and he mouthed

'Is she sleeping?'

Briony nodded and, very slowly, stood up and released Delia's hand, beckoning them to leave the room. Once outside, she spoke in a low voice.

'Right, let her sleep there for a wee while, maybe half an hour or so. If you sit wi' her, Mrs Lawson, and be there when she wakes up. Don't talk about it, try and get her straight to bed. Maybe sit wi' her again until she gets to sleep. A good night's rest should make a big difference.'

Grant spoke trying to keep his voice low.

'But what about...'

Briony treated him to a glare, albeit somewhat milder than the one used earlier on Pam.

'Don't even think about it Boss! You're no' speakin' to her until tomorrow afternoon at the earliest.'

*

As they left the secluded bungalow that Pam and Delia now called home, he sensed a faint thawing of the older woman's icy attitude towards his sergeant; he was beginning to realise just what a great asset Briony was. And what a good friend she was becoming!

Chapter 18

Pam Lawson sat in her bright little conservatory, nursing her third coffee of the morning and listening to the rain drumming relentlessly on the roof. Despite having quit nearly twenty years previously, she was desperate for a cigarette; fortunately there were no shops in the vicinity, otherwise she may have been tempted to nip out and buy a packet. She briefly considered driving into the nearby village of Milton of Campsie but she daren't leave the house in case Delia came round and found her gone! She sipped the steaming liquid, screwing her face up slightly as the shot of vodka that she had poured in hit the back of her throat. She suspected it was going to be a difficult morning.

Delia! Pam was torn in her feelings about the child; no, she wasn't a child, of course but, despite everything, she couldn't resist the urge to mother her, to care for her; especially now, when things seemed to be going from bad to worse.

Why does life have to be so bloody complicated...?

Understandably, Delia hadn't been back at her office since that bloody Inspector had told her that two of her beloved "boys" had been murdered. Pam knew that he was only doing his job but...and the way he had looked at her, it was quite clear that the man was keen on her.

Well, he'll have to go through me first...

She allowed herself a wry smile at the thought. After all, he *was* a tall, well-built and reasonably handsome man...

But as for his sergeant; well, of course she wasn't racist in any way, but the woman was pushy to the point of being rude and seemed intent on taking on the responsibility for Delia's emotional and mental well-being. She had no right; after all, Delia was hers...

For goodness sake, Pam, what are you saying, of course she's not yours...

A sudden noise behind her made her jump, knocking her coffee mug off the table and onto the tiled floor, where it smashed into fragments amongst the brown liquid. She turned to find Delia standing ghost-like in the doorway.

'Delia, you gave me such a fright!'

'Sorry' Delia mumbled.

'Dee, are you okay?'

Delia just stared back at Pam, her tousled hair and the dark circles under her red-rimmed eyes contriving to make her appear more vulnerable than ever. Pam's maternal instinct went into overdrive; ignoring the mess on the floor she jumped to her feet and swept Delia into a warm embrace. To Pam's surprise, Delia pulled away ever so slightly.

'I'll survive, Pam, but I just can't believe it, though. I mean, what did Euan ever do to hurt anyone. He was so sweet...'

Tears started to well up again but Delia managed to stem them. She walked over and sat on the wicker couch, drawing her white towelling robe tightly around her slight frame and daintily tucking her slim legs underneath her.

'I'll get you a coffee, dear. Would you like some toast?'

'No, I'm fine, thanks. Just a coffee please, Pam.'

'Okay, two ticks.'

Pam returned a few minutes later, carrying a tray laden with two mugs of steaming coffee, a jug of cream and a plate of mini-muffins. She placed it on the glass-topped table then reaching into her pocket, she took out a mobile phone and handed it to Delia.

'Your phone was in the kitchen, Dee; I see you've had a couple of missed calls from someone called William U. Who exactly is William U?

Delia lifted a mug, studiously avoiding Pam's gaze.

'Em, it's a sort of... it's... well, it's Simon.'

'What? Simon bloody Hope? Delia, what are you playing at? After the way that bastard treated you? What the hell is he phoning you for?'

'Actually, I phoned him, last night.'

Pam's voice rose a notch.

'Last night? But you were sound asleep, Delia, how could you..?'

'I woke up, about three I think. I just needed to talk...'

'But you could have talked to me, sweetheart. You could have wakened me, you know that.'

'I know that, Pam, but you'd had a difficult day yourself and I didn't like to waken you. I just needed to talk to Simon, but his phone must have been switched off.'

'No bloody wonder, at three in the morning; and, anyway, what was yours doing in the kitchen?'

'It was nearly out of charge so I took it through to plug it in. Are you checking up on me now, Pam?

Pam Lawson was taken aback; Delia had never before shown any sign of dissent or resentment but there was a tone in her voice that she hadn't heard before. It was slightly disconcerting.

'No, no of course I'm not, Dee, I'm just concerned. You really should have wakened me, you know. I'm there for you any time of the day or...'

Delia's phone started to vibrate, the ringer still switched off. As she lifted it, Pam managed a quick glance at the caller ID: William U. Before Delia swiped the screen to answer she looked over at Pam.

'Could I take this in private, Pam, if that's okay?'

Pam glared at her and stood up.

Actually, it's not bloody okay, you ungrateful little bitch...

*

'Darling Dee, what's the matter? You don't normally call me in the middle of the night and my phone was off. Has something happened?'

'Simon, it's awful... they've found another body and they think it's another one of my boys, Euan Johnstone.

'What? The body builder guy? Jesus, Delia, you're not serious?'

'I am, Simon.'

She paused, struggling to maintain her composure.

'What's happening? Who's doing this to my poor boys. I mean, what harm have they done to anyone? All they've done is... well, you know what they've done. It's surely not that wrong, is it? They don't deserve...'

She gave up and broke down completely.

'Delia, Delia, calm yourself, my sweet. Of course they don't deserve it. No-one deserves that— well, except maybe the person who did it... but you can't blame yourself for this. What are the police saying to it? They said on the news that two men had been charged.'

Delia managed to regain her composure slightly.

'I know, but they've been in jail since last Tuesday, I think, so it couldn't have been them. '

'Really! So is this a copycat murder?'

'No, I don't think so, Simon. I think they arrested the wrong people. Grant said that this one's worse than the others.'

Simon's tone changed slightly.

'Grant? Who, exactly, is Grant, Dee?'

'Grant McVicar. he's the chief inspector that's carrying out the investigation.'

'Oh, so you're on first name terms now, that's nice.'

There was a hint of sarcasm —or was it jealousy— in his tone but Delia ignored it. When she didn't respond he continued.

'The bloody fools, though! That's the police for you; break a speed limit, drive home after a pint and they're all over you like a rash. Commit a couple of murders and they arrest the wrong bloody people. Jesus...'

'Simon, what am I going to do...'

'Well, I'll tell you what *I'm* going to do: I'm going to come down right now...'

'No, Simon, I told you, please don't, I've got enough on my plate...'

'No, my poor Dee, I insist; you need me now, more than ever and I promise that I'll be the perfect gentleman. Now, just tell me where you're staying.'

Delia was starting to lose control.

'Please Simon, don't, I beg you...'

Without warning, the conservatory door flew open and, almost before Delia could turn round, Pam Lawson had grabbed the phone out of her hand and lifted it to her mouth. Her voice was different, it had a cold, harsh edge to it; Delia barely recognised her friend.

'Now just you listen to me, Mister Simon bloody-break-poor-Delia's-heart Hope. Don't you *dare* come down here pestering this poor girl. She's been through enough and the last thing she needs is you turning up on the doorstep and taking advantage of her. I've heard all about you and let me tell you I don't like any of it! I know about your philandering, I know about your poor wife. God knows how she puts up with it, I'd have been out the door long ago so I suggest you bugger off and stop chasing after women entirely ...'

She paused for breath, allowing Simon to interject.

'If I could just point out that it was Delia who phoned me, Mrs whoever-you-may-be. Actually, I don't believe we've been introd—'

'And we're never going to be. I'm blocking this number right now...'

'Oh, don't be so bloody stupid, woman, Delia can easily unblock it...'

'Stupid!' screamed Pam. 'Now you listen to me, you arrogant prick. Phone Delia again or come near here and I'll serve a fucking injunction on you so fast you won't know what's hit you, you piece of shit...'

Simon Hope laughed.

'Hah, brilliant. I do love a woman with spirit, and a colourful vocabulary! But I'll tell you what, Mrs whoever-you-are, you're going to make a superb character in my next novel...'

'Fuck off, wanker!' screamed Pam, ending the call and slamming the phone down on the table. Delia sat gaping at her, all her worries and fears temporarily forgotten. She had never seen this side of Pam before and she didn't know whether to laugh or cry; it really was most impressive!

Grant and Briony were heading through the Clyde Tunnel, having ascertained that Delia Donald was in a fit state to talk to them. Grant had phoned earlier and suggested that they meet in Delia's office at two-thirty, as all the details of her "boys" were kept there. Pam had reluctantly agreed, on the condition that, once again, she would also be present. Finally, she had told Grant that

Delia believed the victim to be Euan Johnstone, another of her "boys" hence Delia's "upset" the previous evening. It was as if Pam Lawson had kept this vital piece of information until last and, once again, her slightly obstructive behaviour had infuriated him. He was still ranting about it as they joined the Clydeside Expressway. Briony finally managed to interject.

'Listen, I know she's pretty over-the-top, Boss, but on this occasion I think it's best for her to be there to be honest, I don't think Delia's in any condition to drive at the moment anyway.'

Grant had bowed to his sergeant's opinion, although he wasn't prepared to put up with any nonsense. They needed to press on with this investigation; he had already received another call from Patricia Minto, reminding him of his precarious position and informing him that the Press were having a field day at police Scotland's expense. Doctor Napier had also called just before lunchtime, confirming that, as with the others, the latest victim had been drowned, although he had probably been unconscious when placed in the loch due to the considerable bleeding following the emasculation. The other main difference, however, was that this time there was no evidence of a physical beating having taken place. As with the previous victims, he had been a fit, healthy and powerfully built young man; and, as was customary with the pathologist, there was a postscript.

'So, on this occasion, I have found traces of Ketamine in the victim's blood.'

'Ketamine?'

The name sounded vaguely familiar.

'Yes. It's similar in effect to Rohypnol, although it's unrelated. It's carried by GPs and paramedics. It's frequently used for pain management in cases of severe injury.'

Grant considered this.

'So it wouldn't be too hard to get hold of, then?'

'Well, it certainly wouldn't be easy. Any drug of this sort is very closely controlled. But, in the right circumstances, I suppose... oh, and you might also find vets carrying it, for anaesthesia in animals. I don't know if that's much help but there it is...'

Grant had ended the call with more questions than answers.

There was still no report of a missing person fitting the victim's description, but no doubt it would come in time; once they had spoken to Delia Donald, they should at least have an address. They drove in silence, each lost in their own thoughts until, finally, they reached Dumbarton Road. Grant turned right into the steep side-street, scanning the roadside for a parking space. To his surprise there was one almost opposite Delia's office building; further up the street, Briony noticed Pam's Range Rover.

'I see her ladyship's here already!'

He grunted.

'Aye, well, let's get this over with.'

*

'So, Grant, what do you want to know?'

Already Pam seemed to have taken over the role of spokesperson. Grant thought the woman looked strained, older almost. Presumably the case was taking its toll on her, just as it was with everyone else concerned. She was standing protectively behind Delia, who was sitting across the desk from Grant and Briony, her laptop open in front of her; although Delia had obviously made an effort, she had been unable to conceal the puffy eyes and the dark circles under them. Grant couldn't help but feel sorry for the poor woman. She inspired a desire to protect her from the evils that seemed to be heaping themselves upon her slight frame. He was beginning to understand why Pam Lawson acted the way she did.

He replied, in a gentle voice.

'Well, assuming that the victim is Euan Johnstone...'

He saw Delia wince at the mention of the name but she managed to control her emotions.

'...then we need an address, a vehicle registration if you have it and a contact number, although if it's a mobile then I doubt that'll be of any use. We also need to know if he visited any...'

Delia gave him a wan smile.

'Clients? Yes, he was out on Saturday, in Kilmacolm. I'd completely forgotten about the booking, with everything...'

Grant gave Briony a look . This wasn't too far from where the body had been found.

'Right, we'll need details and we'll most definitely need to talk to this...client. Okay, about Euan. Do you know where he lived and if he lived alone?

She nodded.

'Yes, he has...sorry, he had a wee house down in Port Glasgow, I think. Euan is… was… well, what you'd call a "ladies' man". He had a real eye for the girls and liked living on his own so that he could… em, entertain, if you know what I mean.'

She tapped her keyboard, managing to switch into a more business-like mode.

'Right, let's see, yes, here's the address. Orchard Crescent, I think it's quite a new development down near the front.'

She wrote it on a sheet of paper, along with Euan's mobile number. Grant tried calling but it immediately switched to voicemail. It was eerie hearing the sound of a dead man's voice. He saw Delia squeeze her eyes shut and he ended the call.

'Any idea what his vehicle registration was, Delia?' asked Briony.

'No, sorry, I don't. I know it was a Kia, I think; black, that's all I know.'

'Okay, that's a help, we'll need to try and find it…'

'But he would have been in the van.'

Grant had forgotten that the Domestic Services Agency owned a van. The SOCOs had checked it over but, as it had yielded no significant evidence it had remained at Delia's office.

'Did your boys always use the van?'

'Yes… well, nearly always. They sometimes changed in the back, after…well…'

She looked slightly embarrassed.

'But Euan definitely took it. He'd taken the train up to Glasgow on Friday and he said he was coming to collect it.'

'But what about the keys? I thought you hadn't been in your office?'

Delia shook her head sadly.

'I hadn't. I thought I'd mentioned that I'd ordered a few spare keys so that my boys could pick the van up whenever it suited them. It seemed easier, you see, especially if we were busy…'

'Okay, if he took the train, presumably his own vehicle is still at his house. So where the hell is the van? We'll already have the details from last…'

He stopped, not wishing to rake up any more unpleasantness for the girl. There was an awkward silence; Grant took a deep breath. He was dreading the next part.

'Delia, I'm sorry but I have to ask you something else. We know that the two guys we have in custody assaulted Andrew and Chris.

They've admitted as much, although they've now retracted their initial confession. The thing is, in light of what's happened, it now seems possible that they're innocent of the first two murders, well, one of them, at least...'

Delia gave him a worried glance but he decided not to go into detail.

'However, this latest death casts a whole new light on things. As you probably know, we don't usually release all the details of a murder. Once we charge someone, there's no need and it'll usually all come out at the trial anyway. But this third murder was considerably more brutal than the first two, although we suspect that it was carried out by the same person, or persons. Now, what I need to know, is there anyone that you can think of who might have reason to carry out these crimes? Someone with a grudge against you or your boys, or anything, really; can you think?'

Delia looked both shocked and terrified.

'You mean you think someone is targeting my boys? But why? Why would anyone do that?'

Briony smiled re-assuringly.

'We're not sayin' that just yet, Delia. But there's obviously some sort o' a link. Look, can I ask you somethin' entirely off the record...'

Grant frowned at her. This wasn't in the script! She ignored him and carried on speaking.

'...as I said, *entirely* off the record. Delia, will you please tell me *exactly* what your boys were up to? Are you runnin' an escort agency?'

'Yes.'

Grant's eyebrows shot up.

'What did you say?'

Briony spoke before Delia could respond.

'That's all we need to know, Delia, let's leave it at that, eh Boss? But this casts a somewhat different light on things. Now Delia, the next thing we need is a list of everyone on your books, just in case; your boys and your clients. Can you give me that?'

Grant could see Delia's face redden. She looked absolutely mortified. He waited for an outburst from Pam but, when none came, he glanced up at the woman. He found her expression difficult to read; surprise, anger, relief? He wasn't sure... Delia mumbled, 'It wasn't what you think, Briony, it was, it was... well...'

'Delia, don't worry, it's okay, you're not being judged here. As I said, it's entirely off the record and, to be brutally honest, I think it's goin' to be all over now, don't you?'

Delia stared at the desk and silently nodded her assent.

'Good. Enough said. Right, a list if you can, Delia. Oh, and mark the one that Euan visited on Saturday.'

Grant turned to Briony but his sergeant just mouthed "later." Delia pressed a few keys and the adjacent printer spewed out four A4 sheets. She took them, underlined one name, then handed them to Briony.

'Great, thanks. Now...'

Delia looked up.

'Can I ask, do you have any more assignments booked?'

Delia shook her head.

'No, after...well, you know, I didn't take any more calls, there's nothing in the diary. I'd forgotten about poor Euan...'

'Good, that's a relief. Okay, last thing, and this is very important, Delia. Does anyone else have access to your computer or your database?'

Delia shook her head forcefully.

'No, absolutely not! Anyway, I have a good, long password and I don't take the computer home.'

'So it stays here all the time?'

'Yes.'

'How secure is your office? Does anyone else have a key?'

'Em, yes, the accountant down the stairs, just in case there's an emergency. He's my landlord, actually. But Duncan's quite old and he's a lovely wee man...'

Grant interrupted

'We'll still need to talk to him, Delia. If he had access to your office then he may have been able to access your database.'

'But Duncan wouldn't hurt a fly! Anyway, I think he's very fond of me; he's very protective, even though he's quite old...'she smiled at the thought '...in fact he's often expressed concern for me when any of the boys came up. He always said "just call and I'll come up right away". He's such a dear!'

Grant and Briony exchanged a look; Delia's portrayal of Duncan's innocence was only serving to increase their suspicions.

'Is he in just now?' asked Grant.

'I think so. Actually, I sometimes wonder if he stays here all the time. His wife died years ago and he's such a poor, lonely soul. I think he drinks a bit too...'

'Okay, we'll have a wee chat with him once we leave.' said Grant. 'And you're absolutely sure that no-one has had access to your computer, either recently or in the past.'

'No, absolutely not. I never...'

She put her hand to her mouth, her eyes widening in horror.

'Oh my God!'

'What, Delia?' asked Briony. 'What is it?

'Danny.'

'What, your ex?'

Pam replied on Delia's behalf.

'Technically the vile Mr Donald isn't Delia's "ex" just yet, although my solicitors are working on it. Are you aware of what the bastard did to her?'

'Yes, she told me' replied Briony.

'Hm. But apart from the physical abuse?'

Briony looked surprised.

'What do you mean, Mrs Lawson?'

'She didn't mention the financial side of things at all?'

'Oh please, Pam, don't, it's so embarrassing.' Briony spoke in her gentlest tone.

'Dee, we need to know. We need to know everythin' so we can catch whoever did this. Tell us, please?'

Delia looked up at Pam.

'Can you, Pam? I can't bring myself...'

Pam Lawson took a deep breath; they could see the undisguised rage on the woman's face as she spoke.

'After Dee came to stay with me, I set her up with an Experian credit check account. It turns out that as well as propping up his own ailing business with the earnings Delia made from the agency, this piece of garbage had also taken out several loans in her name, including credit cards and a re-mortgage of his decrepit farm. The sums ran well into six figures and we had to declare Delia bankrupt in order to safeguard her. Goodness knows what he's doing now, since the proverbial goose has fled the nest along with the golden egg. I hope the bastard's fucking struggling...oh, excuse me.'

'But what in God's name was he doing with that amount of

money?' asked Grant, ignoring Pam's lapse into profanity.

'I don't know' replied Delia. 'I didn't know about any of this until Pam found out. I just thought his business needed propping up a bit, that's all.'

'And now that this extra source of income has dried up, I wouldn't imagine that Mr Donald is too happy.' Grant continued. He gave Briony a questioning look, which she immediately returned.

'Exactly' stated Pam. 'That's why we've been really careful to make sure he doesn't find out that Delia is staying with me. Mind you, God help him if he came calling at my door!'

Aye, God help him indeed...

There was silence for a few moments then Grant could see the look of comprehension form on Pam Lawson's face.

'Oh my... that could be the motive, couldn't it! Revenge for what she's done to him! The bastard. The man's capable of anything!'

'What? Oh no, surely not, Pam. I know Danny's bad but...'

Briony was beside her in an instant, gently stroking her hand. She caught her just in time.

'Delia, listen, keep calm, breathe, that's it, good girl, good girl. Now, can you give us your husband's address, eh? And a description. I think we need to talk to Mr Donald, urgently.'

*

Pam had made them all coffee; Delia was sitting in her large, complex-looking office chair, her shoulders slumped and a miserable expression on her face. Briony was crouching on the floor beside her, holding her hand and, once again, Grant was aware of Pam's slightly jealous expression at the ministrations of his sergeant.

'Okay Delia, that's it, just relax. Now, can you give us the address and put it out of your mind.'

Delia gave Briony a blank stare.

'The what? Oh, yes, of course, the address. Em, but he won't be home.'

'What? How do you know that?' asked Grant.

'Well, Danny travels about a lot. His company make agricultural buildings, you know, cow sheds and things and he covers the whole of south west Scotland and sometimes the North of England. Earlier this year he started going down south on business every

Monday and he always stays over. Actually...'

She paused, staring down at the floor, then swallowed back the tears... well, I'm pretty sure he was having an affair. Although, to be honest, that suited me fine, other than being cheated on, of course. But he never came home on a Monday, always later on the Tuesday.'

'Okay, but we'll need the address anyway, Delia. We'll nip over and have a look, just in case; he may have changed his routine now that you've left.'

Delia looked across at him from under her long eyelashes; once again he felt that slight, unsettling sensation...

Get a bloody grip, Grant...

She nodded her head.

'I suppose. Okay, it's past Blanefield, heading out on the Glasgow Road, the A81, I think. A couple of miles along there's a private road off to the left with a sign for Mid Blane farm; that's us...well, him, really, I suppose.'

'Great. Now, Delia, I need a description— Actually, I don't suppose you'd have a photo...'

Pam Lawson gave him a disparaging look.

'...no, probably not...a description will be fine, if that's okay.'

Delia sighed.

'Well, he's about six feet one, sandy-fair hair, thinning on top. He's a bit touchy about that. And a moustache.'

'Just a moustache. No beard?'

'No. Oh, and he's quite well-built, you know, drinks too much, eats rubbish when he's away...he's got blue eyes and he's a bit freckly. Pretty ordinary, really.'

Briony looked up at Grant and he nodded. She released Delia's hand and stood up, giving her shoulder an affectionate pat.

'Good job, Dee. You're done now, that's all we need.'

She looked at Pam Lawson.

'Get her away home now, Pam, she should be okay. Just let her rest, maybe stay with her until she gets to sleep.'

She looked back at Delia.

'You've got my number, Delia. Just call me if you need to talk.'

'She'll be fine with me, Sergeant' stated Pam. 'I'll get her safely tucked up and make sure she gets a good night's sleep.'

Briony gave the woman a stony look.

'Aye, whatever, Mrs Lawson.'

Sensing the tension in the air, Grant also stood up.

'Right, Bri, let's get going and let Pam take care of Delia. We'll head out to Mid Blane farm and see what's what. Many thanks once again for your time, ladies.'

As they headed to the door, Delia jumped up, ran across to Briony and gave her another fierce hug. Grant looked over at Pam Lawson; as his mother used to say, she "wore a face like thunder..."

Chapter 19

The attractive little village of Blanefield lay tucked away under the shadow of Dumgoyne, at the western end of the Campsie Fells. Grant and Briony had just arrived, Faz and Cliff having been summoned and currently en route. Grant had messaged Sam and Kiera, who had been at Barlinnie breaking the news to Molloy and Dougall, giving them the details for Miriam Oliphant. Grant had already phoned and spoken to the woman and, from her tone, he suspected that it might be a more unpleasant interview than the one at Barlinnie...

Do them good, though...

A couple of uniformed police were also on their way as backup, although from what Delia had told them Grant didn't hold out much hope of finding Danny Donald at home. He pulled in to the side of the road, switched off the engine, leaned his head back and closed his eyes. Briony sat in silence. Her Boss obviously wasn't in a mood for conversation and, if truth be told, she could do with a rest herself...

He woke with a start at the sound of someone rapping on the window. Cliff's Ford had pulled in behind them and Faz was standing beside Grant's pick-up, grinning in at them. He wound down the window.

'Sleeping on the job, Boss?'

'Aye been a long week...'

Briony rubbed her eyes.

'Sorry, Boss...right, what now?'

'We'll head up to this farm, get the lie of the land' replied Grant.' Seems unlikely that Donald will be at home but we can have a look about, familiarise ourselves with the layout for next time. Delia says he usually gets home later on a Tuesday so let's hope he keeps to form. What about the uniforms, Faz?'

'Coming from the local constabulary, Boss, although I'm not sure which office. Suppose it just depends who's available, although it'd be good if we got some locals. Might have better info. Anyway, I told them to wait at the road-end until we get there.'

'Good stuff. By the way, how did Sam and Kiera fare on their excursion to the "Big Hoose"?'

Faz pulled another face.

'Well, needless to say Turnbull and Traynor turned up, screaming blue murder and demanding that their clients be released; of course, the girls reminded them that they're still being charged with abduction and assault and probably the manslaughter of Chris Findlay. Still, at least that's it done and they're on their way to see this Oliphant woman as we speak; think they're a bit traumatised, to be honest.'

'Aye, well, it won't do them any harm to be exposed to the wrath of a couple of indignant defence lawyers and their self-righteous clients; and by the sounds of it, Ms Oliphant won't be any better. Right, let's make a move.'

Faz returned to Cliff's car; Grant indicated to pull out and the small convoy headed towards Danny Donald's farm.

*

They had only driven for a couple of minutes when they saw the patrol car sitting at the side of the road, its blue lights flashing. A farm road led off to the left; a decrepit sign, its corner missing, hung from a rusty post. It bore the legend "Mid Blane F..." They had arrived. Grant pulled in behind the patrol car and got out, approaching the driver of the vehicle. He shivered. The temperature seemed to have dropped again and there was the hint of further rain in the brisk wind that was blowing up from the Old Kilpatrick Hills.

'Afternoon, lads. DCI McVicar, DS Quinn. Right, we'll go first, you follow us up just in case. Our info suggests that there'll be no-one at home but we'll have a wee look around anyway.'

'No problem, Sir.' replied the uniformed sergeant.

'Listen, are you locals, by any chance?'

The sergeant smiled.

'Fraid so, Sir, born and bred in Milngavie, came out here on my bike as a laddie. I'm Sergeant Craig Morton, by the way. Lookin' for insider information, I take it?'

'Aye, if you have it. Do you happen to know anything about the occupants of the farm?'

'Not personally but I had a wee look when we got the shout. Nothing untoward, only thing of note is that Mr Donald has a shotgun licence, although most of the farmers round here tend to keep a couple o' licenced guns.'

'Hm. Don't think he's actually a farmer, though, as far as I know he sells agricultural buildings. Anyway, thanks, it's certainly worth noting.'

The constable sitting in the passenger seat leaned over and spoke.

'My uncle farms a couple o' miles along the road, sir, and I gave him a call. He doesn't know much about this guy other than he seems to be a bit o' a loner; inherited the farm when his father died but, like you said, he doesn't actually farm it anymore. He quoted my uncle for a tractor shed a couple o' years back, apparently his price was way over the odds. Uncle Alec chased him and apparently Mr Donald was none too happy, lost his temper and stormed off in his pick-up, taking a wooden fence post with him. Mind you, Uncle Alec can be a bit of an awkward bugger himself, typical farmer, you know...'

'Aye, I know the type! Right, let's head up and have a look.'

The convoy drove slowly up the rutted farm road for about half a mile until they came to the huddle of buildings that comprised Mid Blane farm. They entered the farmyard, in the centre of which stood a large, two storey farmhouse. It was surrounded by an assortment of buildings in varying states of decay.

'Hm, not much of a place, is it?' said Grant.

'No, it's no', Boss. Pretty damned bleak. Look at the state o' those old sheds!'

There were a couple of dilapidated barns on the left as they drove in, their red corrugated-iron roofs collapsed and the supporting columns standing in redundant rows like some ancient Greek temple. Amongst the ruins were a variety of old, rusty farm implements, as well as piles of tyres and rusting oil drums. Grant frowned.

'Doesn't look like the place has been used as a farm for years.

What a bloody mess.'

They parked in front of the farmhouse, exited the pick-up and Grant stood, hands on his hips, looking around and taking in his surroundings. He was used to farms; he liked them, the activity, the smell, the sounds; but here, all of these were absent. No cattle lowed, there was no distant bleating of sheep, no smell of silage or slurry. No dogs barked and there was no sound of any tractors trundling about; it was eerily silent, apart from the breeze soughing in the few surrounding trees. Cliff and Faz were standing alongside the two uniformed officers and it was the constable who broke the silence.

'Bloody funny farm this, if you ask me, Sir. Hasn't been worked for ages, by the looks o' it. What a waste.'

Grant was thinking exactly the same thing.

'Sorry, constable, I didn't get your name.'

'Oh, it's Pete Fleming, sir.'

'Right, Pete, could you call your Uncle Alec again, see if he knows what the score is here. There's no beasts, no cultivation and I'm wondering what the hell's going on.'

'Aye, no bother Sir.'

The constable pulled out his phone.

'Right, Faz, Cliff, check out that building in front of the farmhouse. It seems to be the only one that's in reasonable condition. We'll see if anyone's at home, although there's no vehicles about.'

Cliff and Faz walked across to the large, stone building that sat across from the farmhouse. It appeared window-less, although there were a couple of Velux skylights set in the slated roof. Grant and Briony walked across to the front door of the farmhouse and climbed up the worn stone steps. There was no bell and the dark blue paint was flaking off the surface, leaving the wood exposed in places. He banged his fist against it.

'Police! Open up, please.'

Nothing, The sound seemed to echo around the outbuildings. He tried again, slightly harder.

'Police.'

Again there was no response. He tried the handle but, finding it locked, he turned and they stepped back down to the muddy farmyard.

'Let's have a look about.'

They walked round to the right of the building, where a conservatory jutted out of the gable wall. The inside looked a mess. There were old newspapers strewn on the dilapidated cane furniture and a number of empty beer bottles scattered about the floor. As well as a liberal scattering of dead flies, the windowsills were adorned with a selection of dead plants that looked as if they hadn't been watered since Delia had left. Grant found it extremely depressing and tried not to think of Delia having to return here every night, having to...

No...!

He stood back from the dirty window and tried the door; as expected, it, too, was locked.

'Nothing here. Let's try round the back.'

They walked round the whole building, looking in the various windows; like the conservatory, the interior had a neglected and dirty appearance. Eventually, they arrived back at the stone steps, having found nothing of note and seen no sign of occupancy.

'Well, it looks like Delia was right, Bri. No sign of anyone and the place looks like a bloody midden inside. Christ, poor girl, having to put up with this, not to mention...'

His voice tailed off and Briony turned to look at him. She spoke gently.

'What was it you were sayin' earlier, Boss? About no' becomin' involved...'

He reacted just a bit too quickly.

'I'm not bloody involved, Bri, I just feel heart-sorry for her.'

She knew he wasn't being totally honest, but she chose to ignore the fact.

'Aye, fair enough Boss; and so do I. What a bloody miserable existence it must have been.'

'Right, there's no point in staying any longer if she thinks he's away 'til tomorrow, let's...'

'Boss' shouted Cliff, as he and Faz walked across the yard.

'Aye, Cliff, anything of interest?'

'No, but the place is pretty well secured. There's no windows, only a couple o' double-glazed skylights. Didn't think it was worth takin' the risk an' climbin' on the roof, in case it gave way. The door seems to be covered wi' a metal sheet an' it has one o' those steel covers that goes over the padlock; wonder if he's hidin' somethin' in it?

'Maybe. Mind you, it's pretty remote out here, especially if they were both out during the day.' he looked about the derelict farm. 'That's pretty much it, I think; there's no other buildings intact as far as I can see. Right, I'm going to phone The Mint.'

He pulled out his phone and dialled his Superintendent's number as his colleagues stamped their feet, trying to ward off the chill of the damp mist that was starting to form. After a brief conversation, he put his phone away.

'Okay, that's sorted. She's going to arrange a warrant and we'll come back later tomorrow. Hopefully Danny Donald will be back by then and we can have a proper look round. At the moment this is all conjecture but, by all accounts, he's a right violent bastard and I'd imagine he's harbouring a pretty serious grievance against his wife, now that she's left and taken away his source of income. Right, let's get back to base and get warm.'

*

Grant had asked the uniformed cops if they, or some of their colleagues, could take a run past Mid Blane farm every so often, just in case Danny Donald returned early. They were on the way back through the Glasgow suburb of Milngavie when his phone rang; he put it on speaker.

'Kiera. How's things? Did you get anything useful from Miriam Oliphant?'

Kiera let out a cackle.

'Oh help. She's a character, if ever there was one! Mind you, she seemed genuinely upset at poor Euan's demise, to give her due. She says that he was only there to do some work in the garden. That's a bloody joke. She has about half an acre that looks like the bloody Botanic Gardens, must keep someone busy for about two days a week. But I'd say she's well out of the frame for the murder, though! Just a scary woman with a healthy appetite for men.'

'Good, I'll trust your judgement. Anything else on the victim?'

'Aye, Boss, the local boys down in Port Glasgow tracked down Euan Johnstone's old man, lives in Wemyss Bay. Seems he's divorced and his ex is down south somewhere. One of the victim's neighbours had a key for Euan's house and let them in. They found a Domestic Services overall just like the other two, looked almost brand new, as if it had hardly been worn. As expected, his vehicle was parked outside, no sign of the Agency van. They're sending a car for the dad so he can go and make a formal identification, but I think it's pretty certain.'

'Aye, sounds like it. Listen, could you ask Sam to go up, just to be there at the formal ID.'

'Aye, will do, Boss.'

'And I heard you had fun up at Barlinnie.'

Kiera let out another chuckle.

'Aye, they weren't happy, Boss! Wanted their clients released on bail but I reminded them, in no uncertain terms, that Messrs Molloy and Dougall were still suspects and, anyway, they had accused each other of the assault so they haven't a hope of getting out!'

'Good for you, Kiera. Good experience for you and Sam too.'

'And worth it just to see their smarmy faces. Turnbull looked like he was having apoplexy!'

'Hah! I like that. Bryce Turnbull having apoplexy! Okay, Kiera, we'll be back soon. There's no sign of Donald so we're getting a warrant and we'll head back over tomorrow. I'd say he's now what's called a "person of interest". See you in a bit.'

*

Back at Osprey House, they were having their usual daily de-briefing session. Sam was at the QEU hospital where Euan Johnstone's dad would have the painful experience of identifying his son's body. At least it was done by video link these days, sparing the families the distress of seeing their loved ones "in the flesh". Still, it would be an ordeal for the young constable.

Briony was going through the list of names, with Faz and Kiera phoning each of Delia's "boys".

They had discussed carefully what needed to be said to the young men. Even if they had no further assignations, they were still potentially at risk until the murderer was apprehended and they needed to be vigilant. Kiera was just finishing a call to a Ross Hendry.

'No, Mr Hendry, I'm sorry, but we can't provide someone to watch your house. Honestly, I don't think there's anything specific to worry about, we're just being...no, Mr Hendry, no, I'm sorry, but we...Mr Hendry, please, there's no need to take that tone... Mr

Hendry? Hello?'

She put down her phone and looked over at Grant.

'Expects a policeman outside his door. Says if he gets murdered next then it'll be our fault and he'll make sure his family know so they can sue the pants off us. I suggested he go and stay with them but that doesn't suit him, apparently, as they live in Inverness. I said he might be safer if he felt that worried but, well, you heard the outcome.'

'At least we're giving them the heads-up, Kiera. Any more?'

Faz put down his phone.

'Last one, Boss. Lad called Aidan Coulson, seemed nice enough and very grateful.'

'Right, job done. Okay, let's get a coffee and...'

He was interrupted as Sam entered the room, her expression grave; Briony immediately went across to her.

'Everythin' okay, Sam?'

Two tears ran down Sam's cheeks as she shook her head.

'Och, it's just that poor man. When he saw Euan he completely fell apart. It was just so, so sad.'

Briony put her arm round Sam's shoulders and guided her to a seat.

'Right, sit down an' let's get you a wee cuppa. You'll feel better in a minute.'

Five minutes later Cliff re-appeared with a tray containing six steaming mugs and a packet of chocolate biscuits. As the team ate and drank, they discussed their plans for the next day and their impending visit to Mid Blane farm. Grant wondered just what the hell they might find.; whatever it may be, there was no room for any further mistakes. His career now depended on it...

Part Three

I must do something. I can't continue with this half-life. Actually, that could be an interesting quasi-scientific topic:- "the half-life of man".

I digress. I have to take action. But what action to take? When it comes down to it, do I actually still want...no, it's still too raw. But if the opportunity happened to present itself? Wrong? Maybe... especially if I were to engineer the opportunity. And, let's face, it, I'm ideally placed...

No, no, you mustn't think like that!

Oh, if only I could sleep, but why dost thou leave me???

"Sleepers, wake"...thank you, Johannes...!

Chapter 20

Delia Donald woke from the nightmare in a blind panic; she sat up and looked around the room in sheer terror but there was no one there. She turned on the bedside light, illuminating the soft, pastel décor and the tasteful furniture; she was safe.

She pulled the covers down and lay back on her pillows, breathing deeply and trying to find her safe place, just as Briony had told her to do. She realised that she was becoming rather fond of Briony Quinn; her initial impression of an officious and unsympathetic police officer had been replaced with the realisation that Briony was actually a very capable, caring and warm individual, one of the few who seemed to be able to help her make any sense of her feelings and her fears. She was also becoming rather fond of...

No, Delia, not again, you've had enough of men to last you a lifetime...

She was filled with a desperate need to talk to someone and she briefly considered waking up Pam. After Grant and Briony had left in search of her estranged husband, they had closed up the Domestic Services office and returned to Pam's house, collecting a take-away Chinese meal on the way. This had been washed down by at least a bottle and a half of Sauvignon; well, she had probably only had the half. Pam certainly liked her wine! She decided against it; despite what her friend might say, Pam really wasn't too keen on being disturbed in the middle of the night.

But Delia knew that there was one person whom she could call, any time of the day or night. He seemed to keep odd hours; after all, he *was* an author! Yes, there was always Simon bloody Hope... she reached for her phone; it wasn't there.

Damn...

She swung her legs out of the bed and looked on the floor; no phone. She knelt down and looked under the bed. It wasn't there either. She crossed to the small couch and rummaged through her handbag but there was still no sign of it. She definitely hadn't taken it out elsewhere in Pam's house, she knew that much. As she stood looking intently around the room, willing it to appear, she remembered that she had last checked the screen in her office, before placing it on the desk. She realised that she hadn't lifted it again before she left and she groaned; she really needed to talk to Simon and now that she didn't have her phone, the desire seemed stronger than ever. There was only one thing for it...

Fifteen minutes later, dressed in jeans, a sweater and a pair of trainers, Delia crept out of her bedroom, listening at Pam's door as she passed; as expected, she could hear her friend snoring loudly. She crossed the hall, lifting a light rain-jacket from the coat-hook then, crossing to the door, she gently unlocked it and eased it open, praying it wouldn't suddenly decide to develop a creak. Fortunately it remained silent and she closed it with great care, locking it behind her. Pam's bedroom was at the back of the house but, even so, Delia thought that the sound of her car starting might waken her, so she slipped in to the driver's seat, turned on the ignition and let off the handbrake. With a slight crunch of tyres, her BMW rolled down the gentle slope of the gravelled drive and onto the deserted road, where she turned the ignition, started the engine and drove slowly out of earshot before accelerating. She looked at the clock on the dashboard: 2.47 a.m. and she was free!

The road was deserted at that ungodly hour and Delia arrived at Partick just before three-thirty. It was still dark, the fine drizzle having turned to a heavier precipitation and she knew that parking would be at a premium, all the local residents being at home. Suddenly, she gave an involuntary shudder as she remembered that the van was missing. There would be a space at the back of the office.

Still, at least I won't get soaked...

She drove through the entrance to the office car park and pulled into the narrow space; five minutes later, she quietly closed the outer security door behind her before creeping up the stairs to the little office that had, for so many years, been her sanctuary. Now it just seemed to be full of dark, sinister memories and she knew that this would be her final visit.

*

Duncan McGrory stirred and opened an eye, aware that the beginnings of a severe headache were lurking somewhere in the recesses of his cranium. He grunted and sat up, his stockinged foot colliding with something solid and knocking it over with a clatter, sending it rolling beneath the faded brown couch on which he had been sleeping. He bent down, wincing with the pain in his head and his neck, and retrieved the object. It was an empty bottle of Co-op own-brand blended scotch whisky. He held it, staring at it and considering it absent-mindedly. Had he really drunk all that? He supposed he must have...

His thoughts were interrupted by another sound. Footsteps in the hallway; was it perhaps the opening of the main door that had wakened him? He hadn't the faintest idea of the time but he knew it was somewhere in the middle of the night. With a struggle he stood up and crossed to the door, where a small CCTV system had been installed; it allowed him to check on whoever may be calling, or just on whoever may be passing. He peered at it as the slight figure disappeared from view, the dark curly hair immediately revealing her identity.

What on earth is Delia doing here at this time of night...?

His first instinct was to open the door but he stopped himself, his hand still on the handle. He was very fond of Delia. Actually, he had been in love with her for years; just paternally, of course, but if only he had been twenty years younger... Anyway, the last thing he wanted was for her to see him like this, half-drunk, dishevelled, his clothes crushed and soiled and, from what he could tell, rather odorous. No, he would clean himself up a bit; if she came back down later he would open the door and see if she was all right. He padded back through to the room that served as office, lounge and occasional bedroom; there was a bookcase on one wall, filled with box-files and paperwork and he was sure that one of the files contained...

Ah yes, here it is...

He twisted the cap of a full bottle of The Famous Grouse and went in search of his tumbler.

*

Delia sat at her desk, tired, lonely and almost unbearably sad. This little room had meant so much to her, it had been the one place that she had felt safe, secure. When Briony said "go to your safe place" it was here...well, as it had once been; but not now; not since...

She let the tears fall, unashamedly, unfettered. She let them run down her cheeks, on to the desk, until there were no more. She sniffed and pulled a tissue out of her jeans, dabbing her eyes and wiping her cheeks; this wouldn't do! There was a half-full pack of

A4 printer paper on the desk and she moved it to reveal her phone. No wonder she had missed it. She lifted it up and sat back, her thumb hesitantly hovering over the entry "William U".

Should she?

*

'Hello Dee. Another late night call . And to what do I owe the pleasure this time?'

His husky, Aberdonian tones washed over her like a balm, soothing her troubled mind, igniting her...

No...no...no...!

'Oh Simon, I'm so sorry...'

'Don't be sorry, Dee. Never be sorry for phoning me. Actually, I always live in the hope you will, even if it's only when things are going wrong. But aren't you worried you'll waken up Madam? I don't want another ear-bashing!'

'Don't be like that, Simon, Pam's been my saviour. Anyway, believe it or not, I'm at the office.'

He sounded genuinely surprised.

'What! What on earth are you doing at the office? Wait, you've not moved out, have you?'

'No, no of course not. I left my phone here earlier and I wanted to...'

She paused, listening.

'Are you driving, Simon?'

Was that a slight hesitation...?

'Em, yes. Why?'

At this time of night...?

'Oh, I just wondered, it's pretty late or early, oh I don't know...so where have you been?'

There was a definite pause this time.

'Oh, just out, you know. Like you!'

Touche!

She gave a small laugh.

'Out where, Simon? Hot date, in Francesca's absence...'

Oh, that was low, Delia...!

But why did the thought make her stomach churn? He gave a wry chuckle.

'Ouch! But a man's got to get on with his life, you know; anyway, say the word and I'll be high-tailing it down to you, dearest Dee.

You know that.'

She did. "Yes" was on the tip of her tongue, but she resisted.

'It wouldn't work, Simon, it's been too long...'

'No it hasn't. Just a matter of a few years. Anyway, it only serves to increase the desire...

Oh yes...

'No Simon. At least, not yet...'

Oh God, why did I say that...?

He laughed again.

'Oh my goodness Dee, finally, a ray of hope...'

*

She woke to find herself slumped forward in her chair, her arms on the desk and her head resting on them. She sat up, rubbing the back of her neck, which was stiff and uncomfortable. She shivered. The heating was off and she was freezing. The sky was light but overcast and, as well as the drizzle, there was a slight mist dulling the view from the window. She looked at her watch. It was nearly eight o'clock and she smiled; she knew exactly what she needed!

*

Ten minutes later she arrived at Matonti's Delicatessen, where a few folk were already awaiting their early morning fix of fine Italian coffee. She opened the door and Marco looked up, grinning as soon as he realised who had just entered.

'Ciao, stranger!'

He came out from behind the counter and, in six quick strides, he had grabbed her in a warm and extremely welcome bear-hug, leaving the other customers staring in bewilderment. The expression on one girl's face leaving no doubt that she would have liked the same treatment!

'Oh Marco, it's great to see you' she mumbled, into his garlic-scented apron.

'You too, Delia baby, you too. I thought you'd left us. What's been happening?'

She sighed as he released her, then sat on one of the stools. Lena Matonti had come out of the back shop and was attending to the customers and shaking her head in mock annoyance, mumbling something to the effect of not being able to get the staff these days. When the customers had left, she, too, came across.

'Hey, Delia. You okay?'

Delia shook her head and proceeded to blurt out her sad tale (well, most of it), Marco and Lena staring at her in astonishment. Somehow, Delia managed to get to the end without breaking down in floods of tears. She finished speaking and stared at the floor; Lena took her hand, concern showing on her face.

'My God, Delia, that's awful. Oh, your poor boys... I'm so, so sorry.'

Another couple of customers came through the door and Marco left to attend to them. Lena was stroking the back of Delia's hand. She realised how comforting it was and it reminded her of Briony. They sat in silence then, once Marco had finished, he came back over with a steaming mug of hot chocolate and an almond croissant.

'Here, baby, drink this. Chocolate always helps. Especially in liquid form.'

Delia took the mug, cradling it in her hands and gazing at her friends over the rim. She took a sip of the delicious, viscous liquid.

'Oh, that's so good, Marco, grazie.'

'Prego, Delia, prego. So what now, dearest?'

She took another sip before replying.

'Now? Well, that's it. I'm closing the agency, this'll be my last day. Then...well, who knows; at least I've got Pam.'

She took a bite of the delicious croissant, leaving a slight dusting of icing sugar on her top lip. Marco leaned forward with a napkin and gently wiped it off.

'Delia, I'm so sorry, we'll miss you, won't we Lena?'

. She smiled, trying her best to sound cheerful.

'No we won't. You'll be back, Delia, I know you will. You'll miss the coffee, the cake; and him.' she gestured at her gorgeous brother. 'You'll miss this daft lump of Italian manhood. Charms the women and chases the men!'

Marco laughed, a wonderful deep rumble and gave an expressive shrug.

'Hey, Sis, maybe I like both, eh?'

Lena chuckled and Delia joined in. Yes, she would be back. There was no way she could leave this place behind! She was feeling better already. Had Marco put something extra in that hot chocolate?

Grant had just arrived at Osprey House and he wasn't in a good mood. He went straight to his office and sat down at his desk, glaring at the mountain of paperwork that seemed to have accrued over the last week. A couple of minutes later, Briony knocked then stepped in.

'Mornin' Boss. what's up?'

He grunted.

'Didn't sleep well.'

She knew better than to ask. She had heard the phrase so many times before. He stood up and headed for the door

'Right, let's get on, work to do... let's have a chat with the troops.'

*

Faz had called the uniformed cops that had been keeping an eye on Mid Blane farm but it remained unoccupied. Sam Tannahill had just brought in the warrant to search the property and its surrounding buildings.

'So when do we carry out the search, Boss? Do we go now?'

'No, Sam, I think we'd be best to wait 'till Donald gets back. If he turns up and the place is crawling with cops, he's hardly likely to walk up and introduce himself. No, we'll hold off until he makes an appearance, whenever that may be. Need to get the SOCOs over, plus a few uniforms...'

His mobile rang. It was a Glasgow number that he didn't recognise.

'Excuse me a minute, guys.'

He swiped the screen.

'McVicar.'

A woman answered. He recognised the voice but couldn't quite place it.

'Hello, Grant?'

'Aye. Who's this?'

'Hi, it's Lauren Porterfield here.'

His voice softened.

'Oh, hello Lauren. How's it going?'

Chief Inspector Lauren Porterfield worked out of London Road police Station in the East End of Glasgow. Grant had met her on a few occasions; training events...funerals...

'Aye, fine thanks, Grant. You?'

Aye, where do I start...?

'Och, just getting on with it, like the rest of us.'

'Yes, you're investigating those loch murders, aren't you?'

'Aye, for my sins.'

'Terrible thing. How's the case progressing?'

'Well, I take it you heard...?'

She interrupted.

'Yes, I did, but from what I can gather it looked pretty cut and dried, until...'

She paused tactfully.

'Aye, well, fortunately we've got someone else in the frame now. Shouldn't be long 'til we wrap it up, hopefully.'

'Good, good. Listen, Grant, that's why I'm phoning, in connection with the case. Well, apparently...'

His curiosity was aroused.

'Apparently? What's that mean, Lauren?'

'Well, the thing is, I had a rather unexpected visitor a few minutes ago. A certain Miss Veronica Pettigrew.'

His heart stopped for a second.

What the fuck...?

'Pettigrew? What in God's name was she wanting, Lauren? I'm assuming she wasn't handing herself in and confessing to her crimes?

Lauren Porterfield laughed.

'Oh, I wish, Grant. No, all she wanted was to give me her number and ask that you phone her. Said it was in connection with your current case. She didn't know how to contact you and I certainly wasn't handing out your number to her without checking with you first; I seem to recall that there's a history between you two...'

You could say that...

'Aye, kind of. Don't suppose she said anything else?'

'Nope. Just said it was in relation to the case. I'll give you the number...'

Grant ended the call and looked at his team. They were trying not to stare at their Boss. The suppressed anger in his voice had been painfully apparent. He stood up.

'Got a call to make'

He stormed out of the room.

*

Forty-five minutes later Grant was driving his pick-up slowly along the side of Glasgow Green, scanning for a parking space. In a terse phone call, he had arranged to meet Ronnie Pettigrew in the Winter Gardens, the large cast-iron framed glasshouse attached to the rear of Glasgow's beautiful Victorian People's Palace. Luckily, a van pulled out just as he was about to give up and he manoeuvred his pick-up into the vacant gap. He sat for a few moments trying to marshal his thoughts; the problem was, he wasn't exactly sure what they were...

He walked up the steps and through the foyer of the museum. pausing before he entered the lofty glass building at the rear, bright and humid despite the miserable weather. He was confronted with an open area filled with tables and chairs, behind which rose a dazzling array of tropical foliage and plants. It was magnificent. He looked over to his left and there she was. Ronnie Pettigrew. She was wearing a tight cream sweater, probably cashmere, and her shapely legs were crossed under a fashionable, green sunray-pleated skirt. She turned towards him and smiled. He took a deep breath and walked over. She should have looked somewhat out of place in the austere Victorian setting of the People's Palace but there she sat, cool, calm and confident... and...

'Grant.'

'Miss Pettigrew.'

'Oh, for God's sake, Grant, we're off the record here. Don't be such an arse, just call me Ronnie.'

'Fine. Ronnie then. So what do you want?'

'Aye, straight to business, as usual. Wasn't always like that, was it...?'

No, it wasn't...

'Listen Ronnie, I don't know what the hell you're wanting but there's absolutely nothing that I'm going to give you. If you have any information relating to this case then tell me now or else I walk away. End of story.'

She regarded him coolly across the table for a few moments, then replied in a softer voice.

'I don't suppose you'd let me buy you a coffee?"

He sighed.
Oh, what the hell...
'Go on then.'

*

They sipped their drinks in silence for a few minutes then Ronnie Pettigrew put down her cup.

'Right, Grant. Just hear me out, will you?

He looked across at her and nodded.

'Right. First of all, despite what you may think, I respect you. You are what you are, you're a decent enough guy and, as far as I know, you're straight. Not all of you lot are, you know.'

Unfortunately, he knew...

'Me? Well, I am what I am too, rightly or wrongly; I've learned to accept it, I don't judge myself, I just get on with it. But it might have been very different, if...'

Her voice tailed off and her face took on a pained expression. Somehow Grant knew it wasn't feigned and he finished the sentence for her.

'If Ricky hadn't died?'

She nodded.

'Yes. Well, obviously you know what happened.'

She sighed, then continued.

'So, I'd been to university, I had a degree, I could have had a career but, well, after what happened my dad was never the same. Ricky was gone...'

Again she paused; this time Grant couldn't quite decide if it was genuine or merely for effect.

'So you took over the family business.'

She nodded.

'No choice, really. Anyway, that's history and I'm no' here to give you a history lesson, especially one with which you're already familiar.'

'So what *are* you here for, Ronnie? To buy me off?'

She sneered at him and shook her head.

'You see, you immediately jump to conclusions, Grant McVicar, and not always the right ones.'

'No? Well, what then?'

'My Mum.'

'What, Helena? Or is it Ellie? Never quite know these days...'

'Helena. You know damned fine that's her name.'

'Maybe, but not when she was cavorting...'

Ronnie Pettigrew leaned forward, her hard, attractive face angry.

'Just shut the fuck up, will you?' she hissed. Grant smiled cynically.

'Oh, here we go. What's next, going to force a bottle of whisky down my throat and throw me in the river?'

She sat back.

'Let's not go over all that again. It's a figment of your imagination.'

'Really! Jacky Winters never touched a drop...'

'Hah! You think? Jacky Winters was an alcoholic; had been for years, just hid it very well. So much for you being the smart detective, Grant. If you'd asked at a few pubs in the area, they'd have told you. Always had a nip of vodka ready at the back door when he came calling; on the house, no questions asked, no smell on the breath... I'm not saying he was on the take, just liked his dram and looked after those who provided it.'

Grant stared at her, unable to decide if she was telling the truth or if this was just more of her lies. He would find out, though...

'Anyway, you said you're not here to discuss history. So, your mum. What about her?'

Ronnie sighed and crossed her legs. Her pleated skirt rippled and there was a faint swish as her nylon-clad legs rubbed against each other. She was wearing high-heeled black shoes, one of which now dangled seductively from her toes. Grant tried desperately not to stare.

'So, as I said, you and I, we know where we stand, as did my father. But my mum? Well, how much of her past do you know, Grant?'

'Not much, the father of one of my DC's worked the East End, knew a bit about her, said she came from a decent background.'

'Yeah, that's right. When you were at the house my mum seemed to remember him. Well, he was pretty much correct. Her mum and dad, my maternal grandparents, were ordinary working-class Glasgow people, not wealthy, but decent, law-abiding, God-fearing folk.'

She paused and he raised an eyebrow at her questioningly. She continued, 'Sorry, I was waiting for you to say "not like you".'

He just shrugged but remained silent.

'Well, I appreciate your reticence, Grant. Anyway, for whatever reason, my mum fell hook, line and sinker for my dad. Mind you, he was a good looking boy, well-made, flash with the money and I dare say his status gave him a certain "edge". But, as I said, she lost her heart to him; and, to be fair, he lost his too. As far as I know, he has always been faithful to his dear "Ellie" and now, well...'

Grant wasn't sure where this was leading.

'Aye, he's not the man he was, I know that.'

'No. Ricky's death was the end of him, although he's got Alzheimer's now too. My mum is effectively his carer, won't hear of him going into a home. That's just the way their generation were brought up, I suppose.'

Grant was struggling to come to terms with this polarised, humane side of one of the city's most notorious criminal bosses. Her hard exterior seemed to have softened and it was extremely disconcerting.

'I'm sorry, Ronnie. About the Alzheimer's, I mean, it's an awful thing.'

She gave him a brief smile.

'Thanks. Yes, it is, same person, just without their soul. Horrible! Anyway, back to my mum.'

'Mm?'

'Well, I believe that you're now looking for someone else in connection with these murders?'

'Huh, news travels fast but, yes, we are.'

'Which, presumably, lets Molloy and Dougall off the hook?'

He didn't like where this was heading.

'Not necessarily. One of the victims choked to death on his own blood before he was dumped in the loch; they're still guilty of abduction and assault at the very least. I shouldn't be discussing this with you anyway.'

'As I said, Grant, this is all off the record. Right, let's say Molloy and Dougall *are* guilty of abduction and assault, manslaughter, even. I think we both know their reasons and I think we both know that they didn't actually set out to murder anyone.'

'Where's this leading, Ronnie? What are you after?'

She sighed.

'Look, I imagine that you must have enough evidence to convict them. Okay, my mum did have... well, you know...but other than that, she's completely innocent. She had nothing whatsoever to do with what happened to those two guys.'

'So who did, Ronnie?'

She paused and stared at him as if unsure whether to continue. Finally, she did, lowering her voice as she spoke.

'Okay, I can understand that my mum is a woman who still has physical needs but I wasn't at all happy about what was happening with those two...well, male whores, I suppose, and it would have finished my dad if he'd ever found out. I'd tried to warn them off, I waited outside the flat one day and caught them coming out. But no, they wouldn't listen, they were on to a good thing and they thought they were big hard men. I was just a silly lassie trying to stop their source of income. So... well, it had to stop. Call me old fashioned...'

He shook his head.

'Ronnie, there's many things I could call you. Old fashioned isn't one...'

She snorted and gave an uncaring shrug.

'Whatever. Listen Grant, I don't want my mum to have to go in the witness box and be cross-examined, it'll destroy her; and my dad, because he'd be sure to find out. He's always managed to keep most of his business matters from her, as have I and this would... well...'

Grant gave her a cynical look and she gave him a wry smile in return.

'Och, of course, she's not naïve, she knows a bit about our business, how could she not? But she's never had any direct involvement in any of it, she's just been a wife and a mother and, to be honest, she's had a pretty difficult life.'

Grant snorted.

'Huh, difficult? Life of leisure, living off the proceeds of organised crime. Oh aye, must have been a terrible hardship!'

She glared over at him, her grey eyes cold once again.

'Aye, looking over your shoulder all the time, wondering who's next after what happened to Ricky? If you ever had a son, ask yourself how you'd feel, watching him die, with all his joints shattered and a bullet fired up his arse. Think of my mother, an innocent girl married to a gangster, watching her only son's life slip away in agony and humiliation. She never did a thing wrong in her whole life except marry the man she loved, who just happened to be Michael Pettigrew. You don't begin to understand hardship and loss, my friend...'

She stopped suddenly and, again, her expression softened slightly. He looked across at her and she held his gaze.

'...actually, I suppose you do, Grant, at least a little bit. I forgot, and I'm sorry about what happened to your friend. Brian, wasn't it?'

He stared at her in surprise and she smiled back.

'Em, aye, it was, thanks.' he mumbled.

'Despite what you think, Grant, I'm not *all* bad...'

They looked at each other in a strange, silent empathy for a few moments, broken by the sudden appearance of a stray sparrow which landed on the table and pecked at a few crumbs before flying off, trying to find its way out. Grant's eyes followed it as Ronnie continued.

'So you see, my mum is fragile and, believe it or not, I love her dearly. She's been a good mother, she's always done the best she could for me and I don't want to see her suffer any more than she has already.'

'Fair enough, Ronnie, I can understand that. But you need to understand that we need her to testify, there's nothing I can do about that. I'm sorry.'

She bent down and picked up her exquisite Gucci handbag. Grant didn't doubt for one moment that it was genuine. She opened it, taking out a small plastic box and placing it on the table in front of her. He stared at it, his eyes widening as he realised what it was. He reached out to lift it but she pulled it back, her hand resting on top of it.

'You know what it is, Grant? She purred.

He looked at her, his dark brows furrowing as he mouthed 'You bitch.'

'Not a bitch, Grant, just prudent. A wee bit of history, let's just say. So, if you can see your way to keeping poor Helena out of the witness box, I'll see my way to giving you this tape.'

He shook his head.

'No.'

'No? You'd rather allow this to enter the public domain?'

'Do what the hell you want, Ronnie, I don't care. Like you

say, this is ancient history. And blackmail, of course, as well as perverting the course of justice.'

She laughed.

'Hah, you'd have to prove it first, Grant. Your word against mine.'

He smiled.

'And hers.'

Ronnie Pettigrew looked at him, her eyes widening as the penny dropped.

'Hers?' she hissed.

Ronnie Pettigrew's head turned as Grant pointed at the pretty, scruffily-dressed blonde-haired girl sitting a few tables away from them. She appeared to be looking intently at her phone, which was pointed in their direction. Sam Tannahill looked up, smiled across and gave Grant the thumbs-up; Ronnie Pettigrew jumped to her feet, knocking her chair noisily onto the floor. Shoving the tape back in her handbag, she turned, spitting out "you fucking prick, McVicar" as her parting shot. Grant watched her leave, her heels clicking on the floor and her shiny pleated skirt swinging angrily as she strode towards the exit. He rather liked pleated skirts...

Chapter 21

Pam Lawson woke from an uneasy sleep; stretched to ease her tired and aching body then rolled over. She felt old. The clock said ten-thirty but, somehow, it felt much later. She rolled on to her back. Last night had actually been quite pleasant; despite poor Delia's recent traumas, they had both enjoyed the take-away and the wine, although she realised that she had done most of the drinking. Still, no harm in that, once in a while...

She lay for another few minutes, then climbed out of bed; she would take breakfast in to Delia about eleven then they would have a wee chat. There was a great deal to discuss...

At eleven o'clock precisely Pam stood outside Delia's bedroom door, carrying a tray laden with two steaming china mugs of coffee, a jug of cream and two Belgian buns, her friend's favourite morning treat. She tapped the door gently with her foot.

'Delia! Delia, I've brought you breakfast.'

There was no reply.

Poor thing, she must be in a really deep sleep.

Pam balanced the tray on her knee and pushed down the handle, pushing the door open as she did so. The room was in darkness as she entered.

'Delia! Delia, my dear, break...'

The bed was empty. Pam stood for a few seconds, her mind racing. Where the hell *was* the girl? In the toilet, maybe?

'Delia' she called loudly; there was no reply. She put the tray down on the dresser and crossed to the en-suite, It, too, was empty and in darkness.

She took the tray back to the kitchen, clattering it down on the marble worktop; she ran through to the lounge and pulled back the still-closed curtains.

Fuck...

Delia's BMW wasn't in the drive.

Pam wasn't sure whether she should be worried or angry. She went back to her bedroom and took her mobile from her bag, scrolling to Delia's number. It rang three times.

'Hello Pam.'

'Delia! Where the hell are you? I was so worried!'

'Oh Pam, I'm so sorry. I didn't mean to worry you, but I...'

Pam decided that she should be angry and she raised her voice in reply.

'You didn't mean to worry me? I go in to your room and you've disappeared? How, exactly, do you think that wouldn't worry me, Delia?'

There was silence.

'Delia?'

'What, Pam?'

'Delia, I'm sorry, but you can't just hop off like that; how dare you, after all I've done for you?'

Again, Delia didn't respond and Pam was now struggling to keep her temper. She snapped at her friend.

'Delia? Are you still there?'

'Yes, Pam, I'm here.'

'Well, why aren't you answering me?'

'Because you're giving me a row, Pam and you sound just like my mother; which you're not, I may add.'

This time it was Pam who didn't respond. She felt as if she had been slapped in the face. Delia continued.

'Pam, I'm sorry, but I just needed some space. I came into the office during the night, mainly because I'd left my phone...'

'Oh, for fuck sake Delia, you didn't call that arrogant bastard Simon Hope, did you...'

'Yes, Pam, as a matter of fact I *did* phone Simon, because I needed to talk to him...'

'But I told you, you can talk to me...'

'Yes, I know that Pam, but you were sleeping and...'

'And wasn't he sleeping? According to you it was the middle of the bloody night. You're quite happy to waken Simon bloody Hope but you won't waken me when I'm right there, on hand...'

'He wasn't sleeping.'

'What? What do you mean? Why wasn't he sleeping? What the hell was he doing...'

Delia's voice was suddenly firm, interrupting Pam's near-hysterical rant.

'Pam, stop, please. I just needed to talk to Simon, that was all; and now I've decided to stay and clear up the office. I'm going to call all my clients, all my boys, it's over. I'm handing the keys back to Duncan tonight...'

Her voice tailed off and Pam decided to change her tack.

'Listen Delia, I'm sorry, okay. Let's not have a silly fall-out about all this. Look, I'll come over...'

'No Pam, please, just let me have one last day in what was once my own wee world. Please! I'll be home for dinner.'

Pam sighed heavily. 'Oh, well, I suppose. Okay then, I'll make your favourite, a wee rib roast, all the trimmings; then chocolate fudge cake. Let's indulge ourselves. How does that sound?'

Delia sighed.

'That sounds just fine, Pam, thanks. And I'm really sorry I worried you, I wasn't thinking straight. You've been so good to me, I don't deserve...'

'Oh, shoosh, lassie, as long as you're safe. Right, is six okay? Does that give you enough time to sort everything out?'

'Six is great, Pam, I'll see you then.'

'Promise?'

'Promise.'

Grant drove back to Paisley in a daze. Seeing Ronnie like that, so obviously dressed for effect, had seriously unsettled him; and all to try and keep her mother out of the witness box...

It seemed so long ago now, but the meeting with Ronnie Pettigrew had left the memories fresh and raw in his mind...

*

He had been a young beat policeman working in the same Paisley "K" Division, thoughts of becoming a detective only beginning to form in his fresh and enquiring mind. He had been called to an incident in the Albion Vaults, a disreputable and long-disappeared east-end drinking den located half way down Well Street but, when Grant and his partner, Jimmy Nelson, arrived they discovered that the incident had escalated into a full-blown fight involving rival football supporters. Celtic and the home team of St. Mirren. The two cops were hopelessly outnumbered but they did their best to contain the "rammy" until reinforcements arrived. Grant had noticed an attractive young barmaid cowering behind the bar, obviously too scared to attempt an escape. He struggled through the swearing, violent melee and vaulted over the beer-soaked counter top.

'You all right, Miss?'

She shook her head. He could see the terror in her eyes.

'No, not really.'

'Right, come with me, I'll get you out.'

He had helped her over the bar, her jeans and t-shirt soaking up much of the spilled beer in the process. He put his arm round her shoulder and was nearly out of the door when a burly, red-faced man, wearing a green-and-white striped Celtic top, smashed a bottle and tried to grab her round the throat, threatening Grant with the jagged glass.

'Ah'm havin' this wee tart fur ma'sel', pig.'

The man lunged with the bottle but Grant swerved, catching his attacker on the back of the neck with his standard-issue truncheon. The man went down like a pack of cards as Grant grabbed the girl and ran; once they were outside, she smiled up at him.

'Nice move, officer! So that's what they teach you at Tulliallan!'

He grinned back.

'Aye, among other things... are you okay, Miss...?'

'Em, Peters. Vera Peters. Yes, I'm okay now, thanks to you; listen, my car's parked up in Walker Street, could you maybe come with me, just in case?'

By this time about a dozen uniformed police had poured out of two police vans and were starting to drag the warring and the wounded out of the remains of the Albion Vaults. Grant hoped they were well insured! He reckoned he had done his bit and started to walk along the road with Vera. She gave him a coy look and hooked her arm through his; he didn't resist.

'And what's your name, officer?'

'It's Grant. Grant McVicar.'

'Grant the Vicar? Nice to meet you, your holiness.'

'No, McVica...'

She was grinning up at him again and he grinned back. She was very pretty, with smoky grey eyes and thick dark hair tied in a ponytail that hung down her back. She had lovely full lips, very kissable, he thought; that was when he felt the first stirrings...

*

He was brought sharply back to his senses when a van cut in front of him as he drove on to the M8 slip road at Dalintober Street. He blasted his horn as he stood on the brakes, narrowly avoiding rear-ending the offending vehicle. To make matters worse, the van proceeded to jump the traffic lights just as they turned to red, leaving Grant angry, frustrated and wondering just how the hell he had reached the M8 without noticing. He decided to concentrate on his driving. That lasted about thirty seconds...

*

Grant had plucked up the courage to ask Vera Peters out a couple of weeks after he had rescued her from the fight in the Albion Vaults; retrospect being its usual exact science, it now seemed to have been a very strange relationship. But at the time...

It was after only their second date that Vera had invited Grant into her surprisingly comfortable third-floor flat in Paisley Road West for a coffee, although they both knew that coffee was most definitely not on the menu; the alternative had been completely mind-blowing! Vera had actively and enthusiastically taken the lead and Grant had finally descended the stairs sometime after four in the morning, exhausted, exhilarated and hardly able to comprehend that he had found a girl who had fulfilled just about every one of his adolescent sexual fantasies in one evening.

The situation had continued for a couple of months, with both Grant and Vera managing to arrange several meetings each week between his shifts, Vera's part time bar job (the Albion having quickly recovered from its trauma) and her attendance at Strathclyde University, where she was studying English and Spanish.

Looking back, he now realised that they had actually spent very little time socialising. She had never introduced him to any of her friends and she had never asked about any of his. They had only occasionally eaten out, Vera usually suggesting more distant locations such as Dumbarton or Greenock. Mostly they dined in on Chinese or Indian takeaway food, subsequently worked off by their intense love-making. The reason was soon to become apparent.

Grant had arrived at Paisley's Mill Street headquarters one morning and, on entering the canteen (then still operational) he saw his boss sitting at a table and chatting with a tough-looking man with receding fair hair that he had attempted to disguise with a Brylcreem'd comb-over. He was dressed in the obligatory Ralph Slater suit, signifying that he was en route to a hearing or trial at Paisley's Sheriff Court. Grant's boss, Inspector Dennis Bogle, summoned him over.

'McVicar, this is the man you should talk to if you're interested in becoming a detective. Have a seat.'

Grant sat down and the stranger gave him a smile.

'So you want tae join the big boys, eh son? How d'you do, I'm Detective Inspector Jacky Winters.'

He held out his hand and Grant took it, returning the man's firm grip but aware of a peculiar movement as it was released.

'Pleased to meet you sir, PC Grant McVicar; and, yes, I'm keen to transfer.'

'Good stuff, son, good stuff. Aye, everyone thinks it's the glamorous side o' law enforcement but there's a lot o' bloody hard work involved, just sloggin' away tryin' tae uncover layer after layer o' dirt. Still, if you're interested...'

Dennis Bogle stood up.

'Right Jacky, I've a meeting with Superintendent King so I'd best be off. Good to see you, hope the trial goes well.'

Jacky Winters stood up and the two men shook hands; again Grant noticed the sight movement of the fingers that he realised identified both men as being members of the Masonic Order. The inspector sat back down, leaned across the table and, in a low, gruff voice started to speak.

'Right Son, a couple o' things.'

'Yes sir?'

'First, if you do become a detective then you'll be rubbin' shoulders wi' a lot o' very unpleasant characters, although I'm sure you're well aware o' that.'

Grant smiled.

'Of course, sir, but I suppose it's all part of the job.'

'Indeed it is, son, indeed it is. So, what I'm sayin' to you is this; *never* be tempted, d'you hear? Never take a single bribe, never turn a blind eye tae anythin' as a favour. Never let anyone threaten you. At the end o' the day, no matter what they think, our gang's bigger than their gang and we must never let the bastards forget it. Never allow yourself to be put in a compromisin' situation, ever. D'you understand me, son?'

DI Jacky Winters looked intently at Grant and it felt as if the man was trying to read his mind. He nodded.

'Yes Sir, I understand, absolutely.'

'Good. Because if you do, then you're buggered. You'll never be able to do your job properly again because, once you've crossed that line, there's no goin' back. They'll own you, heart, soul and bollocks.'

Grant didn't quite know how to respond; he just nodded.

'Right. Second thing.'

Again Winters stared intently at Grant; it was extremely discomfiting.

'Yes sir?'

'Ditch the girl.'

Grant wondered if he had mis-heard.

'I beg your pardon, sir?'

'I said ditch the girl. Now. Don't ever see her again.'

Grant just stared at the man.

'Em, but... why not, sir? I mean, surely we're all...'

'Yes, we are and God knows where I'd be without my dear wife, Mary. But no' this lassie, son. What's her name?'

'Her name? Em, it's Vera...Vera Peters.'

Jacky Winters sat back in his chair and folded his arms.

'Peters, eh? Close, I suppose. And Vera too...aye, clever.'

Grant could feel his hackles rise; surely he was allowed to have a relationship? And how the hell did Winters know...?

'What exactly do you mean, sir?

'Well, Vera is short for Veronica, although she normally goes by Ronnie; an' Peters? Well, actually it's Pettigrew; as in father Michael and brother Richard, better known as Ricky, of course.'

Grant stared at the man. Even in far-flung Paisley the name of Pettigrew was notorious as being one of Glasgow's most powerful criminal dynasties. Surely the Inspector must be wrong.

'But, sir, that can't be right. Vera's at University, she's doing languages. She's a really nice girl...'

'She may very well be a nice lassie, son. But that doesn'ae alter the fact that she's the daughter o' the bastard who goes by the name o' Michael Pettigrew and the wee sister o' the equally obnoxious Ricky. Trust me, McVicar, you do not want to become involved wi' them under any circumstances.'

He gave Grant a cynical smile.

'I take it that she hasn't introduced you to her parents?'

'No, but we've only...'

'Or any o' her friends?'

'No sir, but...'

'Have you been up the town wi' her? Been to a club, a Glasgow restaurant?'

'Well, no, but...'

'So where exactly have you been, son?'

'Well, we usually just stay in, have a carry out meal, you know, then...'

'Then you'd shag each other silly. Aye, I know the routine. Never strike you as odd, though, that she didn't introduce you to anyone, she never wanted to be seen wi' you in public, or go to a club? Helluva funny relationship for a young couple.'

Grant stared at the table. Winters was correct. Now that he mentioned it, it did seem odd. But surely...

'So, if you want to get anywhere in this game, son, whether as a detective or in uniform, you need to ditch her, no matter how pretty she is, no matter how good she is in bed, and you need to do it now. Do I make myself clear?'

'Yes sir.'

'Good lad.'

*

It had been a few weeks before the fateful conversation with DI Winters. Grant and Vera were recovering from a particularly adventurous encounter, which had involved his standard-issue handcuffs, his recently issued baton and a selection of esoteric bondage items whose existence he hadn't even been aware of, far less where to purchase them! They were lying naked, sweating and satiated, their limbs entwined, when Grant noticed the small silver object sitting on Vera's dressing table. A tiny red light was flashing on its corner.

'What's that wee thing, love?'

She sat up slightly, her skin sticking to his as she did so.

'What? Oh that? That's my new toy, Grant McVicar.'

'Toy? Wait, is that a video camera?'

'Yes, the latest Sony digital model, in fact. Particularly good in low light, the salesman told me.'

He stared up at the ceiling, wondering if he should be worried.

Och, no, Vera's a nice girl...

'Wait...were you taping us?'

She giggled.

'Yes! Dead sexy, isn't it? Better still, on the nights you can't come...'she gave his testicles a playful squeeze '...then I can watch it over... and over... and over.. and over....'

She punctuated these with further, increasingly hard, squeezes, which soon had the desired effect...

*

What a bloody fool he had been, trusting her, his ego flattered that she found their love-making...

No, it wasn't love-making, it was just sex. Great sex, but just bloody sex...

Anyway, a few days after the conversation with Jacky Winters, he had met her for the final time. She was looking lovely as usual, her red pumps, the pair of tight-fitting black ski-pants and the pale blue polo-necked sweater giving her the look of an American college girl. Vera knew exactly what Grant liked!

'Hi babe. How's you?' she had said, with a smile.

'Not so good, actually, Miss Pettigrew.'

The smile vanished instantly.

'Oh. You found out. I'm sorry, Grant, but...'

'Aye, you bloody should be, Vera— or is it Ronnie?'

'Listen Grant, I can explain...'

'No, you listen, Vera. We're done, got it? And I want that bloody tape. Understand?'

She smiled again. This time it was a different smile, one he hadn't seen before; a sneer, almost.

'You do, do you? And if I don't give it to you, what then? Will you handcuff me again? Naked. Well, except for the leather restraints, the nipple-clamps...'

He raised his voice.

'Shut up, Vera and just give it to me. Please.'

'Please? Oh yes "please"...as in "please, Vera, don't stop now, make me co...'

'For Christ sake will you bloody stop it!'

'Stop it? Ha! That wasn't what you were saying last week. Well, it's stopped now, officer, that's for sure. But you ain't getting that tape. I'll hang on to it as a wee reminder of all the good times; and they were good, weren't they, Grant McVicar, porn star? As in "Oh Grant McVicar, that's sooo good" or "please Grant McVicar, shove your baton...'

He had screamed at her then, before turning and storming away, his heart broken, his pride shattered and seriously worried about his future career. It seemed he had broken Jacky Winter's cardinal rule even before he had started...

Chapter 22

'Well?'

Sam Tannahill had just arrived back at Osprey House; she sat down, pulled out her phone and shrugged her shoulders in response to DS Briony Quinn's enquiry.

'Not really sure, Sarge. I got there first, before she arrived, sat myself at a table with a cup of tea and a scone and waited. She wasn't hard to spot, well-dressed, confident, but she sat a bit away; I couldn't very well get up and sit beside her, could I? When the boss arrived I turned on the video, that was pretty much it. To be honest I couldn't make out anything they were saying.'

'Bit of a waste o' time, eh?'

'Well, mostly. The only thing was that, towards the end, she took out what looked like a digital video tape —you know, in the wee plastic box— and put it on the table.'

Briony raised an eyebrow in surprise. This was interesting.

Or worrying...?

'So what happened then, Sam?'

'Well, the boss tried to take it but Pettigrew grabbed it back then he said something to her and pointed over to where I was sitting. She stood up, swore at him and stormed out.'

'Hm. Wonder what was on the tape...okay, that was well done Sam, you did the best you could under the circumstances. Listen, did the the boss say he was going anywhere else afterwards?'

'No Sarge, he just told me to head back and said he'd be behind me. He didn't seem in a particularly good mood, though.'

Briony gave Sam a questioning look.

'Och no, Sarge, he's been much better since you spoke to him. No, he was just a bit...well, distracted. I'd say...'

She paused, thinking.

'Listen, Sarge, maybe I shouldn't really ask but...well, did something happen between the two of them? It was an odd conversation, I kind of got the feeling that it wasn't all antagonistic, if you know what I mean. Maybe I'm just putting two and two...'

'No, Sam you're not, but let's just leave it at that. It was long ago and, at the time, he hadn't a clue who she was. He's well over it now, don't worry.'

But is he...?

*

It was another half an hour before Grant arrived, the slamming of his office door announcing his arrival. Briony gave him five minutes then walked along and knocked; there was no reply. She knocked again and received a surly, muffled response.

'Aye, what is it?

'It's me, Boss. Can I have a word please, eh?'

There was a pause.

'Aye, I suppose.'

She opened the door; Grant was sitting at his desk, his head cradled in his hands. He gave her a baleful stare as, uninvited, she sat down. He remained silent.

'D'you want to talk about it, Boss?'

'Not particularly, no.'

'Might do you good...'

'Aye, and just as likely it won't.'

'Sam said Ronnie Pettigrew had a tape o' some sort...'

He slammed his hands down on the desk, causing Briony to jump in alarm.

'Oh yes, the bitch has a tape all right, a tape she made one night, a tape that I've always suspected she still had. Eell, now I know.'

Briony looked at her boss in astonishment.

'Wait... you and Ronnie Pettgrew...'

He glared up at her.

'Aye, me and Ronnie fucking Pettigrew. Only she said her name was Vera Peters. It was Jackie Winters who told me the truth, told me to get rid of her before I became a detective.'

He dropped his head onto his hands.

'Is it bad, eh?'

He sat back, rubbing his face.

'Bad enough. Triple-x rated, I'd say.'

She decided not to ask for any further details. Not yet...

'But it was ages ago, Boss. What— twenty-odd years, eh? How much harm could it do you now anyway?'

He shook his head.

'Oh, God knows, Bri. What if she gave it to one of the tabloids. You know what they'd make of it "Senior cop in steamy sex-tape rumpus". Then there'd be the insinuations, did it affect my integrity, have I turned a blind eye, all that crap. You know, Jacky Winters told me never to put myself in that very situation and I fucking well did, before I even became a detective.'

She could see him starting to descend into the usual morass of self-pity.

'So what was she wantin' from you, Boss?'

He sighed.

'She wanted me to keep Helena Pettigrew out of the witness box at Dougall and Molloy's trial.'

'Really! That was it?'

'Aye, really. Told her she wasn't on, though, she can do what she bloody well likes with the tape. To be honest, I've been thinking about packing it all in anyway...'

Briony looked at her boss in astonishment. This was worse than she had thought.

'What? You're bloody jokin', Boss. Why?'

'Why do you think? I can't do my job right, can't think straight, my intergity's potentially compromised. Can't sleep...the list goes on.'

Briony shook her head. She hoped he was just sounding off and she tried to get the conversation back on track.

'Is this the first time she's ever tried to use it?'

'Aye. I was actually beginning to wonder if she still had it, although I suppose I knew she'd never get rid of it.'

'Strange, though when you think about it.'

He frowned at her.

'Strange how, Bri?'

'Well, if she thought it had any potential leverage, you'd think she'd have used it by now, unless she was savin' it for somethin' really serious. But no, she uses it to try and keep her mother out o' the witness box. Doesn't that strike you as a bit odd, eh?'

'What, are you suggesting that she actually has a heart, Bri? Because she fucking doesn't – she pretty much admitted that she was behind the assaults of Andy and Chris; "dishonouring her father" was how she tried to justify it, said she tried to warn them off first. Nothing I can use, of course, she's too bloody smart for that. But she claims that Molloy and Dougall weren't responsible for their deaths. Lying bitch...'

Before he could continue his rant, his phone rang. He checked the screen and put it on speaker.

'DCI McVicar'

'Hello, Sir, it's Sergeant Craig Morton here.'

'Hello, Sergeant. Anything?'

'Nope. Place remains deserted. Listen, sir, are you absolutely sure Danny Donald still lives there...?'

*

Delia felt numb; she had phoned everyone, all her clients, all her boys. It had been harrowing, heart-breaking and horrible, although deep down she had always known that her business was, technically, illegal. As she finished the last call, she felt as if part of her soul had been taken from her. She sighed and placed her phone on the desk. The only slightly brighter spot of the day had been a call from DCI Grant McVicar, although it had been on a purely "business" matter.

Is that how you refer to a call from the police...?

After a somewhat terse enquiry about her well-being, he had asked if she was aware if Danny Donald possessed any firearms. She was able to tell him that he had a couple of shotguns that he sometimes used to shoot rabbits (she omitted the occasional unfortunate off-season pheasant) and he had almost seemed anxious to end the call, leaving her feeling ever so slightly disappointed. He had gone on to ask about Donald's vehicle, which she had advised him was a silver pick-up, not unlike Grant's but with a rear cab fitted. Their conversation had ended rather awkwardly and now there was just one final call left to make.

She had packed up her few portable belongings in a couple of bags and a cheap holdall that she had bought at lunchtime. She also had a brown paper bag filled with goodies from Matonti's Deli, containing a few wee treats for Pam; a nice bottle of Barolo, some fancy Italian cheeses and some Tuscan sausages. Despite the vacuum wrapping she could smell the strong garlic aroma emanating from them and it was making her mouth water! Having eaten virtually nothing all day, she was now thoroughly looking forward to Pam's beautifully cooked rib roast, accompanied by yorkies, roast potatoes, mashed turnip...she smiled, realising that she really did now feel as if she was going home.

The smile faded as she glanced at her watch. It was past five; she stood up and had a final look around, casting a wistful glance over at her beloved chair. What use would it be to her now? She sighed and stepped out of the small office that, for so long, had been her sanctuary, then closed the door for the very last time. As it slammed shut, it felt like a door had closed in her heart.

She walked slowly down the stairs and stopped outside Duncan's door. She put her bags down and was about to knock when, suddenly, it opened and there was Duncan, reasonably smartly dressed and beaming at her; he reeked of an odd combination of after-shave and whisky.

Has he been drinking? It's a bit early...

'Hello Duncan. How are you?'

'Hello, Delia, my dear. All the better for sheeing you, of course. Come in, come in...'

'No, I won't, thanks, Duncan. I need to get on...'

He looked somewhat crestfallen and her heart went out to the poor, lonely old man who had been such a comfort to her over the years; well, for her financial dealings, at least!

'Actually, I came to hand in the keys; and to say goodbye.'

His crestfallen look turned to one of absolute despair.

'Oh no, Delia, shurely not? Bu... but... why?'

'Och, there's been a lot going on in my life, Duncan, and it's time to move on. You've been such a sweetheart over the years and I wanted to thank you. Here...'

She delved into one of the bags and brought out a boxed bottle of Bowmore malt whisky, handing it to him. As he took it she could see that his hands were shaking slightly. She had never noticed it before.

'... I hope you like it.'

He looked up at her, tears welling up in his rheumy eyes.

'Oh yesh, yesh, one of my favourites.'

He paused as if struggling for something to say.

'I... well... I'm really shorry to see you go, my dear. You've been an explem... exem, exemplary tenant, alwaysh on time with your rent...'

'It's been a pleasure Duncan, you've always been such a help with all my financial stuff. I'm hopeless, really... listen I've left the fancy chair, I won't be needing it so you can have it. It's very comfortable...'

They looked at one another in a slightly awkward silence.

'Well, goodbye then Duncan.'

Reluctantly he held out his hand but, on an impulse, she reached out and drew him into her arms. The aftershave was overpowering but she held her breath, squeezing his slightly podgy frame tightly. Then as she let go, she gave him a peck on his rough, badly-shaven cheek. She smiled, afraid that he was going to break down completely.

'Thanks for everything, Duncan. Take care of yourself. 'Bye.'

She turned and, lifting her bags, started off down the stairs, determinedly not looking back. Had she done so, she would have seen tears running down his stubbled cheeks as he carefully removed the Bowmore from its box.

*

Grant was seated opposite Superintendent Patricia Minto, having brought her up-to-date with the situation regarding Danny Donald. She steepled her fingers and pursed her thin lips; finally she spoke.

'Do you really think that you need firearms officers, Grant? I mean, just how much of a threat do you consider this man to be?'

'I'm not sure, ma'am. We know he has a firearms licence and his estranged wife says he has a couple of shotguns. Other than that I couldn't say. It was just a thought, in case he decides to start anything. Given the situation, with Delia leaving him plus the loss of her income, he may be mentally unstable. But we just don't know.'

'Hm. Pity this Delia character didn't report him for the violence though...'

To his surprise, Grant felt an irrational twinge of anger at this slightly disparaging reference to Delia but his boss continued, unaware of his thoughts.

'...then his licence would have been revoked, not to mention saving her from considerable grief. Still it's often the way...listen, I'll have a word with Jim Barcroft, the Tactical Firearms Advisor – see what he thinks. I have to say that on the strength of possession of a shotgun alone, it's unlikely that we would get approval but I'll let you know.'

'Okay, thanks ma'am.'

'So now you're just waiting until Donald makes an appearance then you'll proceed?'

'Yes, ma'am. The local boys are keeping us informed.'

'Good; and you're quite certain that he's your man?'

Grant paused— was he?

'Em, well, he certainly ticks all the boxes, ma'am. We know he's violent and he has a temper; we know he used his wife to obtain large sums of money, although just what these sums were used for remains to be seen. Apart from Delia herself, he seems to be the only one who had access to her database. I'm working on the basis that he knew who all her "boys" were and where they stayed. There's both motive and opportunity, as well as fitting with his character. He seems to have been pretty brutal, according to both Delia and Pam.'

'Hm. Bear in mind that Pam Lawson's input will be anecdotal, of course. Okay, let's see where it leads. Hopefully this'll be an end to the case. It's not been a pleasant one and I'll be glad to see the back of it. Right, I'll let you get on, good luck, Grant.'

He stood up. There was a vague, niggling doubt at the back of his mind but he certainly wasn't going to let Superintendent Patricia Minto know about it.

'Thanks ma'am.'

*

Pam Lawson placed the foil-wrapped slab of prime beef into the oven and closed the door. Despite everything, she was looking forward to tonight; with the Agency consigned to the past, she could spend more time with Delia. Maybe they could go away for a holiday, away from everything...

She was a funny wee thing, Delia; Just like Grant, Pam had had preconceived ideas about her; after all, the Domestic Services agency was, first and foremost, an escort agency, even if the more physical arrangements were made directly between the client and Delia's "boys". Over the past few months Pam had often wondered how someone so apparently innocent and naïve had managed to operate what was quite clearly an up-market sexual service for "discerning" ladies. But, despite herself, she had come to realise that it was that very naivety, as well as her gentle, caring nature that had been the keys to her success. The girl truly believed that she was helping her clients. No, if anyone was to blame it was that bastard Simon Hope...

She raised the sharp kitchen knife and brought it down with a heavy "thunk", neatly slicing off the head of a turnip.

*

Grant was pacing impatiently back and forth across the meeting room, watched by his team. He looked at his watch, pulled out his phone, dialled a number, then spoke.

'Sergeant Morton? DCI McVicar. Any sign yet?'

The response was clearly negative.

'Okay, he must be due back anytime. Can you arrange for a

couple of a cars to stay in the vicinity, check the traffic? ...yes, I understand, Sergeant, but I can get my SIO to authorise it if necessary... Okay, that's great, thanks, I appreciate your help.'

He ended the call and glowered at his assembled team.

'Still no bloody sign. That's after seven, where the hell is the man?'

'Delia said he's often back late on a Tuesday, Boss' said Briony. 'Suppose it all depends where he's been, eh.'

'Hm, I suppose. Listen, I think we should head over and be ready, rather than wait until the uniforms let us know. Right, let's be careful; once more, remember, we don't know much about his present state of mind, he may be violent although I think it's pretty unlikely that he'll attempt to use his shotgun. Faz, you and Kiera can take charge of searching the outbuilding. If he keeps it locked then it would indicate that there's something of importance inside. We should have four uniforms for backup and to keep the locus secure in case he decides to do a runner. Cliff, you and Sam go round the back of the farmhouse. Bri, you and I'll take the front door. Right, let's go...'

His phone rang and they all stared at him in anticipation, expecting it to be the uniforms advising of Danny Donald's arrival. He pulled it out and stared at the screen as "Message in a Bottle" blared out. He looked back up at them, obviously irritated.

'It's Pam Lawson.'

He answered it and put it on speaker.

'Pam. Not a good time, I'm afraid, we're about to head over to...'

'Grant, Delia's missing.'

The silence in the room was profound.

'What? What exactly do you mean by "missing" Pam?'

'Missing, Grant, as in I don't know where she is. She promised me she would be home by six and she hasn't arrived. I can't get hold of her on her phone, I'm so worried, it's not like her.'

Grant could hear a tone of alarm starting to rise in her voice. The woman was obviously genuinely worried.

'Calm down, Pam, please. Right, tell me, where had she been?'

Pam managed to compose herself.

'Oh, its a bit of a story, I'm afraid. I went in to her room this morning and she was gone, turned out she'd left in the middle of the night. She was in her office, closing it up. She was handing the keys back in today. I said I'd make her favourite dinner and she promised she'd be home for six.'

Grant looked at his watch again.

'Pam, it's only seven twenty-five, she's probably just been held up, or chatting to someone. What about that guy downstairs, the accountant. Duncan, wasn't it? Maybe she was saying cheerio to him.'

'What, Duncan McGrory? Huh, I'm pretty certain he's an alcoholic; Delia was quite fond of him but it's unlikely that she'd choose to spend any more time with him than necessary. No, the thing is...'

Her voice tailed off.

'What's the thing, Pam?'

'Oh, I'm probably being stupid. But...well, I'm worried that her husband may have taken her.'

'What? What on earth makes you think that? *We* can't even get hold of him. Delia said that he was away every Monday and didn't usually come home until late on the Tuesday. Does he even know where you live or where Delia's office was, for that matter?'

There was another pause.

'Grant, I probably should have told you but there's been a couple of times recently that I've seen a... well, a van, or a pickup, something like that... anyway, it's driven past the end of the drive a few times. I didn't think anything of it. We often get people turning at the bottom of the drive if they've missed a house or a farm road. But it was only after Delia gave you the description of... of Danny's vehicle that I started to wonder.'

'And have you seen it today, Pam?'

'Em, yes, a couple of times. Well, I think it was the same one, it didn't stop, it just slowed down a bit, as if the driver was looking for something...'

'Something? What – like Delia's car, maybe?'

'Yes, and now I can't get hold of her. Grant, I'm really worried. I mean, if this man is unhinged then... then...'

'Pam, please, try to stay calm. We'll send someone over to Partick and have a look at the office – we can also check if her car's about. It's a white BMW, isn't it? What's the registration again?'

He wrote it down then, with further assurances to Pam, he ended the call.

'Right, I take it you all got that. It may be nothing but we'd better check. Cliff, can you and Sam go over to Partick, check if there's any sign of Delia or her car. She could be parked anywhere in the vicinity so it might be worth seeing if there's a couple of uniforms available to help. And see if that accountant is in, Duncan McGrory. Delia said she thought he didn't always go home, he may still be around.'

He looked over at Faz and raised an eyebrow.

'Faz, I believe you've got a contact in Partick?'

The DC looked very slightly embarrassed but nodded in assent.

'Aye, Constable Lappin, Boss.'

'Right, give her a call and let's hope she's on duty; find out who's in charge over there and we'll see if we can get a bit of help. Tell PC Lappin to get her superior to phone me if they need authorisation but remind her that it is a murder enquiry.' He paused and shook his head. 'Christ, we could do without this. Hopefully she's just had a puncture or some...'

Faz was already calling Grace Lappin when Grant's mobile, still clutched in his hand, rang again; he answered immediately, raising his eyebrows and gritting his teeth. He really needed to change that bloody ring-tone. He swiped the screen and barked.

'McVicar.'

He listened.

'Great, thanks Sergeant, just keep an eye on him and make sure he doesn't slip back out, we'll be over right away. Cheers.'

He looked at his team's expectant faces. It was time.

'That's Donald finally arrived back home. The locals are going to stay at the end of the farm road until we get there. Okay, come in, let's get this over with. Cliff, keep me posted.'

Chapter 23

As DC Cliff Ford and DC Sam Tannahill drove out of the Clyde Tunnel and on to the Clydeside Expressway, the heavens opened.

'Good old Scotland' said Sam. 'I hope we can get parked near her office.'

He turned and winked at her.

'It's a murder enquiry. We can park where the hell we like!'

They did. Cliff pulled his Ford on to the pavement in front of Delia's office building, leaving the hazards flashing.

'Right, let's go an' brave these bloody elements.'

They jumped out into the downpour and ran over to the door. Cliff scanned the names and found the one for the Agency. He pressed the buzzer and waited. There was no reply and he tried again.

'Christ, ah'm gettin' bloody soaked here.'

'Looks like she's not there. For goodness sake, try another one, Cliff.' replied Sam, pulling the hood of her jacket over her face.

'Aye, okay, this one might be hopeful. Think it's her wee accountant pal.'

He pressed the button marked DM Accounting and waited; he was about to press it again when a tinny voice responded.

'Who'sh tha'?'

'Mister McGrory?'

'Yesh. who'sh tha'?'

'Police, Mr McGrory. I'm DC Ford. Can we come in please?'

The buzz of the lock sounded and they entered the shelter of the concrete lobby. It smelled faintly of disinfectant. One of the doors was already ajar, a dishevelled and rather pathetic-looking figure leaning on the jamb and staring balefully at them over an ancient pair of spectacles.

'Mr McGrory?' Sam asked gentl. She instantly felt sorry for the man.

'Yesh, my dea.'

'Hello, I'm DC Tannahill, this is.DC..'

'Yesh, Ford. He menshioned...'

Cliff and Sam gave each other a knowing look . The man was clearly very drunk.

'Mr McGrory, can we...'

'Oh, Duncan, pleash, Duncan...is thish about my little Delia.'

The constables exchanged another glance.

'Em, yes, actually' replied Sam. 'Listen Duncan, could we come in please. We just need to ask a few...'

But Duncan McGrory had already turned away and was walking unsteadily back through the door, leaving them to follow; he staggered into the wall and Sam prepared to catch him in case he fell. The place reeked of whisky as well as a few other underlying aromas, one of which was a slightly rancid-smelling after-shave. They entered what appeared to be his office and he turned back to face them.

'Have a sheat, have a…can I get you wee drinkie? I'm having one…' He lifted a half-empty bottle of Bowmore and splashed a hefty measure into a dirty crystal tumbler.

'No, Duncan, we're fine, thanks. We won't keep you long' replied Sam. She doubted they'd get much useful information out of the man. 'Duncan, we need to ask you if you've seen Delia today?'

He stared at Sam as if she wasn't there or as if he was looking at someone else.

'She'sh gone.'

He started to cry; Sam crossed over to him and squeezed his arm.

'Duncan, it's all right. Where has she gone, do you know?'

Duncan moved away and almost collapsed into the fancy office chair that, with a considerable struggle, he had brought down not long after Delia had left. He dropped his head and stared down at his whisky glass, then lifted it to his lips and drained it.

'Jusht gone, my dea'. She closhed up shop and…and left.'

He shook his head sadly as he continued to sob.

'Oh, if only I'd been twenty yearsh younger…'

Cliff interrupted. They didn't have time for this.

'Mr McGrory, please, can you try and concentrate? When did you last see Delia? Do you know where she was going? It's very important, we believe that something may have happened to her.'

Duncan stopped crying and looked up, his face twisted in anguish.

'Oh dear! Oh dear! What do you mean…'

Cliff was rapidly losing patience and hardened his tone.

'Mr McGrory, when did Delia leave?'

Duncan seemed to pull himself together and frowned, appearing to concentrate. He dropped his head down again as if in despair and looked at his watch.

'Em, oh, I think it was about a quarter pasht five. Yesh, yesh, I rem— memember thinking that was when my world had come to an end…'

Sam interrupted, speaking more gently.

'Duncan, I understand. Are you sure, though, it's very important.'

He nodded sadly, still staring at the empty glass.

'Yes, I'm sure, my dear. I remember checking my watch...oh, if only I had been twenty yea...'

'And do you know where was she going?'

Duncan looked up at her, his eyes red and puffy, his cheeks tear-stained. The idea of anything having happened to Delia appeared to have sobered him up considerably..

'Home. Home to that awful woman.'

They were driving through Bearsden. The roads were awash and Grant was peering intently ahead as the wipers were struggling to clear the windscreen. Briony was beside him, with Faz and Kiera in the back. Suddenly, his phone rang.

'Can you get it, Bri?'

She lifted the phone and looked at the screen.

'It's Cliff.'

'Okay, put it on speaker.'

She swiped the screen.

'Cliff, it's Briony, you're on speaker.'

'Aye, okay. Em, hello. All right, there's no sign o' Delia Donald but we spoke to Duncan, the old guy down the stairs, he says she left about quarter past five, right after she handed in the keys. Says she told him she was headin' to Pam Lawson's. The old boy's completely out his face an' greetin' on about bein' twenty years younger...anyway, we're now drivin' about an' havin' a look for her car. Bloody awful night though, can hardly see a thing.'

Grant felt a vague niggle of worry. Where the hell was the girl? Suddenly, a thought came to him.

'Cliff, the Agency van's still missing. Have you checked the car park at the back of the office? Maybe she parked there.'

There was an ominous pause before Cliff replied.

'Oh... no, we didn't. We'll go back now...'

'You do that, and keep me posted.'

Briony ended the call and looked at Grant.

'Don't be too hard on him, Boss.'

'He needs to use his head a bit more sometimes, though...'

A few minutes later his phone rang again and Briony answered.

'Hi Cliff, what have you got?' she said, leaving Grant to concentrate on driving.

'Em, it was out the back right enough. Sorry.'

'Aye, well at least you've found it.' said Grant. 'Anything...?'

'Well, it's definitely her car an' the strange thing is, it wis unlocked. Ah checked in the boot an' there was a couple o' bags o' stuff from her office, her laptop, some papers, kettle, just bits an' pieces, really. Oh, an' there was a brown paper deli bag on the driver's seat, looked as if it had split open; there was a pack o' those funny Italian sausages beside it, as if it had fallen out. Thing is, they were wet and a bit mucky, as if they'd fallen on the ground an' then been lifted up. But apart from that, nothin'. No phone, no keys, no handbag.'

'Okay Cliff, can you and Sam organise some uniforms and do a bit of door-to-door just around the immediate vicinity, see if anyone saw anything. I've got a bad feeling about this. Keep me posted, cheers.'

Again there was silence, then Briony turned to Grant; she had a worried frown on her face.

'What d'you think, Boss?'

He didn't reply immediately. He didn't know what to think. She continued to look at him, waiting for a response.

'Don't know, Bri but I don't like it. She's not at her office but her car's still there, to be honest I'm starting to get worried... listen, call Osprey House and get a scene of crime team over to Partick. He need to see if there's any prints other than Delia's or Pam's on that car. Just in case...'

Briony didn't say anything and took out her own phone – she didn't need to ask in case of what.

*

The flashing blue lights of two police patrol vehicles marked the entrance to Mid Blane farm. The rain had abated, turning to a thick, damp mist that reduced visibility to a matter of yards – it was as if they were enveloped in the clouds. Grant put on his hazard lights and pulled in behind the first car. Sergeant Craig Morton and Constable Pete Fleming walked towards his pick-up and he wound down the window.

'How long has he been here, sergeant?' asked Grant.

'Em, I'm not exactly sure, sir...'

'What? I thought you were patrolling regularly?'

'Well, we had an incident... look, I'm sorry, sir, but you know what it's like, we're stretched to the bloody limit...'

Grant shook his head. He knew.

'Aye, whatever, sergeant. I don't suppose you got a look at his vehicle when he went up, by any chance?'

'No, we just drove up far enough to check if anyone was there. When we saw his vehicle we reversed down again and phoned you. Any particular reason, sir?'

'His estranged wife has gone missing and the signs are that she may have been taken against her will. We think Donald is likely to be harbouring considerable grievance against the girl, which might well put him in the frame.'

The sergeant's face took on a serious expression.

'So is this a potential hostage situation we're dealing with, sir?'

'Well, he may be holding her against her will, if that's what you mean, so we'd better tread carefully. Right, we'll go first, you come along behind. Can you turn off the lights, don't want to give him too much warning in case he does anything stupid. My sergeant here and I will try the house, if you and your lads go round the back and watch the conservatory on the right-hand side. Faz, you and Kiera concentrate on that outbuilding. We'll see if there's keys inside the house, if not, just get in however you can. Have we all got gloves, just in case?'

Everyone nodded their assent.

'Good, right... oh bollocks, what now?'

His phone was vibrating in his pocket; he took it out, glared at the screen then shook his head in annoyance.

'Christ, bloody Pam Lawson, again.'

He was about to reject the call when Briony said.

'Best answer it, Boss, in case Delia's been in contact.'

He sighed.

'Aye, I suppose...hello Pam.'

They could all hear the woman's raised tones.

'No, we haven't...Pam, we're about to enter the farm...no, I don't know if she's here...Pam, listen...'

Pam's remote voice continued, sounding increasingly agitated. Briony could see Grant's self-control evaporating until, finally, he interjected, speaking in an authoritative and somewhat angry tone.

'Now listen to me, Pam, I am conducting an important and potentially dangerous investigation here and I cannot allow you to interrupt any further. I'm terminating this call and must insist that you do not call again. As soon as I have any news I will inform you. Is that clear?'

There was silence, then an indistinct response. Grant spoke more gently.

'Thank you, Pam. Now I know you're worried about Delia, as are we all. Rest assured that we are looking for her and I'll keep you advised, I promise....yes...goodbye.'

He terminated the call and scowled at Briony.

'Bloody woman. Right, let's go.'

*

The convoy made its way slowly up the uneven, rutted surface of the track; after a few minutes they arrived at the dilapidated farmyard and the three vehicles fanned out and stopped. Two automated security lights came on, flooding the area with a harsh white light, glaring in the mist. A silver pick-up with a rear cab sat to one side of the yard and, as Grant opened his door, he commented.

'Looks like he's home right enough, thank God.'

As soon as everyone had exited, Grant barked his commands.

'Right, Sergeant, you and your boys cover all the exits; two round each side. Bri, front door. Faz, Kiera, over to the outhouse, in case he's there. Okay, go.'

The uniformed officers disappeared round the sides of the house as Grant and Briony charged up the steps. He banged heavily on the door.

'Police. Open up.'

The banging echoed round the empty yard but there was no reply. He heard Faz doing the same on the outhouse door, with similar results. He banged again.

'Police, Mr Donald. We have a warrant to search these premises. If you don't answer the door we may have to...'

Briony had turned the handle and, as she pushed, the door swung open. He gave her a grim smile and put his head into the opening.

'Police, Mr Donald. We are entering your house.'

They walked through the door and into the gloomy hallway, illuminated by a bare fluorescent bulb hanging from the ceiling. The place smelt damp and dirty and there was a quantity of unopened mail lying in an untidy heap on a small table. They opened the door ahead of them and entered the kitchen.

'Jesus' muttered Briony 'what a bloody mess, eh?'

Every surface of the room was littered with an assortment of discarded take-away cartons, empty beer and whisky bottles and dirty clothes. The sink was full of filthy dishes and, as they entered, two mice scuttled along the worktop and into a crack in the wall. The floor crunched under their feet as they walked across it.

'Fuck sake!' exclaimed Grant. 'How can anyone live like this? Right, let's check the rooms, Bri, but I've a feeling that he's not here.'

Ten minutes later, everyone had re-assembled in the cold, misty farmyard.

'Any joy with the outhouse, Faz?'

'No, Boss, it's all locked up.'

'Okay, have a rummage inside the house and see if you can find the keys. Might take a bit of work to get access otherwise. Any ideas, anyone?'

Grant looked over at Constable Fleming, who was talking on his mobile. He glared at the young man who, sensing the DCI's gaze, finished the call.

'Was talkin' to my uncle Alec, sir. He says there's a track that leads off from the back of the farmyard, over at the left there. There's an old forestry cottage about a mile along it, been empty for years but he says it might be worth checking.'

Grant relaxed his glare and nodded.

Jumping to conclusions again...

'Good work, Constable. Right, let's go and have a look. Sergeant, might be best if you leave a couple of men here, just in case. Don't want him turning up then disappearing again when he sees he's got visitors. Kiera, you and Faz stay put and try to get into that outhouse. Have another look about the house too, see if there's anything of interest.'

The sergeant turned and spoke to the other two constables, who returned to their vehicle then turned it to face down the drive in case they needed to make a quick exit. PC Fleming spoke again.

'Uncle Alec says the road's in a hell of a state, sir, so just watch.'

'Okay, will do. Should be okay in the pick-up and your Shogun'll handle pretty much anything. Right, again we'll go first; Sergeant, you and PC Fleming follow; and keep the lights off.'

They got back in to their vehicles and set off; the track obviously hadn't been used for years and was uneven, rutted and littered with potholes full of water, making the journey slow and uncomfortable. It was five minutes or so before the outline of a low, squat house came into view in their headlights and to their surprise, there was a vehicle parked outside. Grant stopped the pick-up and they stared at it.

'Christ, who the hell's that? Bri, can you make out the number?' She peered through the gloom.'

'No, Boss. Listen, give me a minute...'

Before he could stop her, she had jumped out and sprinted up the track. She stopped for a moment then turned and ran back.

'Got it. Looks like one of those vans that's been converted to transport folk in wheelchairs.'

'Strange. Right, run a check. Might be another vehicle of Donald's, might not; I'll have a word with the troops.'

He climbed out and went back to the Mitsubishi. Sergeant Morton wound down the window.

'Okay lads, we don't know the lie of the land here so I suggest we do the same as before. On my word, you two cover the back, we'll check inside. Leave the cars here.'

They all got out and crept through the thickening mist towards the bleak cottage. As they approached, they could see that there was one central door, with two boarded-up windows on either side. Two cottage-style windows jutted out of the slate roof. These, too, were boarded-up. The place had a dismal, abandoned air, apart from the grey vehicle, which looked almost new. As they approached, Grant whispered.

'Right, lads, round the back, in case there's another door. Don't think we need worry too much about the windows.'

The two uniformed officers split up and went round the sides of the building. Grant and Briony approached the front door; he gave it a push and, as it swung open, he shouted.

'Police. Mr Donald, we're entering your house.'

Again the statement was greeted by silence. They stepped through the doorway and found themselves in a cold, damp room, with a rickety staircase directly across from them and running up the back wall. Grant reckoned the room had served as the kitchen; there was a cracked Belfast sink under the boarded-up window and a decrepit wooden table in the centre of the room. As they moved, they could hear the faint scuffling of unidentified vermin as they slunk for cover. Sitting on the table was an ancient storm lantern, it's flickering light casting eerie shadows around the dirty walls; beside it was a plastic container filled with what looked like paraffin. The floor was strewn with an assortment of rubbish —old newspapers, bedding—. It looked as if it had been used as a dump for unwanted household items. He wrinkled his nose in disgust.

'Hm, certainly looks like someone's here, Bri. We'll need to watch that lamp, though. Right, I'll have a look upstairs, you see if there's anything down here. Watch yourself, shout if you need me. And what the hell's that smell?'

'I think it's paraffin, Boss, probably off the lamp.'

He crossed the room to the bottom of the stairs and looked up. It was pitch black and he took out his phone, switching on the torch and pointing it upwards.

'Mr Donald, are you there? police, I'm coming up.'

He started up the stairs, aware of the dried-out wood creaking alarmingly as he did so. He reached a small landing that had three doors leading off it and he shone the torch around him. One was wide open and seemed to be a bathroom. The second was shut tight but the third door that faced the stairs was very slightly ajar. He decided to try it first. He stepped forward and opened it.

'Mr Donald, are you there?'

There was no reply and, gently pushing open the decrepit door, he entered the room.

In that one brief moment of time, his brain registered several things; the room was similarly illuminated by a flickering storm lantern, resting on a rickety dressing table; in the middle, their back towards him, a slight figure was sitting in a chair, hands and feet tied and with some sort of bag over their head. They also appeared to be naked; and there was a dark-clad figure standing to his right, almost behind the door. As he entered, the latter picked something up from the dressing table and pointed it at him. Instinctively, Grant turned away.

The flash and the bang were simultaneous, as was the sudden, sharp burning sensation in his left hip. He spun round, dropped to the floor and curled in a ball, aware of someone running towards him, jumping over his body and clattering down the stairs. He screamed.

'Fuck. Fucking bastard! Briony, watch out, he's armed...'

He struggled to his feet and put his hand on his side. It was damp and he could feel blood trickling down his leg. In the dim glow of the lantern, he could see a shotgun lying on the floor. He breathed a sigh of relief. He reckoned that he had only sustained a flesh wound and he realised that it could have been much worse; at least he was alive. He shouted out.

'Bri! Briony, the gun's still here...'

There was a shout downstairs, followed by a loud crash and the sound of breaking glass.

'Bri! Briony, are you...?'

His shout was cut short by the sudden "whoomp" of an explosion and he could immediately hear a crackling sound.

'Fuck!'

He took two painful strides towards the figure in the chair and pulled the sacking hood off their head. As he had expected, it was Delia but her eyes were unfocussed and he realised that she was either semi-conscious or in a state of severe shock. The hair at the back of her head seemed to be matted with blood.

Shit...

He grabbed her naked shoulders and shook her. Her pale skin felt cold but clammy.

'Delia. Delia, can you hear me?'

There was no response; the sound of the flames was getting louder and he could smell the sharp, acrid tang of smoke and burning kerosene. He looked about for something to cut the rope that was securing her hands and feet to the chair but there was nothing. Above the roaring of the fire that was now rapidly gaining hold of the dried-out building, he could hear a voice yelling his name.

'Grant! Grant, are you all right?'

He screamed.

'Aye, I'm okay, Bri.'

But am I...?

He could feel the panic rise in his chest as he realised he was now facing his worst nightmare. He looked at Delia, her dark curls falling down her naked back. He couldn't take her out like this, he couldn't let the flames sear that hair, that soft skin...

Jesus...

He looked around and saw what looked like a filthy sheet lying in the corner. He grabbed it, wrapped it round the inert figure and, mustering all his strength, he lifted Delia, still firmly tied to the chair, and kicked the door open with his foot, ignoring the sharp pain in his hip. As he moved, the chair seemed to catch on something and, looking down, he could see another piece of rope, tied to the chair-legs, that seemed to disappear through a hole in the rotten floorboards.

Fuck...

He put his burden down and managed to untie the knot, then lifted the chair and its occupant once again. The stairway was now starting to catch and the room below was a mass of flame, the thick, cloying smoke burning his eyes and making him choke. He realised it had to be now, Gritting his teeth and letting out a roar, he charged down the stairs and through the rising inferno. He felt the heat; he heard the hungry crackle of the flames as they greedily licked at his hands and his head; he was sure he heard screaming but the door ahead of him was open...and then he was out, gulping in the cold, fresh air. Briony grabbed him as he dropped Delia and stumbled into the welcoming damp of the long grass. Then he passed out.

*

'Boss? Boss? Fuck, are you okay? Grant?'

He opened his eyes; he had no idea how long he'd been out.

'Bri?'

'Oh, thank fuck. Jesus, are you okay?'

Is she crying...?

He managed to sit up and started to cough violently; however, he gave her a slightly manic smile as he rasped

'What, apart from being shot and nearly burned alive?'

She just gaped at him as another coughing fit took hold. He took a deep breath.

'Aye, I'll live, Briony. What about Delia?'

Briony looked over at the still-inert form, now released from the chair and covered with a survival blanket.

'Honestly? I don't know, Boss. Physically she seems okay but...'

He felt as if his lungs were on fire now but he managed to keep talking. He needed to know.

'And Donald?'

'The bugger came chargin' down the stairs and I tried to grab him. He jumped over the table and knocked it over, lamp and all. I came after him but he ran straight into the sergeant's lovin' arms, fortunately. That's him over there.'

Grant looked across. In the light of the burning building he could just make out a figure lying face down in the grass, with Constable Fleming now kneeling over him, radio in hand; he could hear a distant siren and knew that the place would soon be swarming with police, not to mention the other emergency services. The roar of the fire behind him was almost deafening but, over it, he heard Sergeant Morton's voice calling, his tone urgent.

'Sergeant Quinn! Quickly! Over here.'

Briony glanced at Grant then jumped up and sprinted off. She returned a couple of minutes later and knelt beside him, a strange look on her face.

'What, Bri' he croaked. His throat was parched and he was desperate for a drink of something.

'Craig managed to get the boards off one of the windows at the back of the property, in case there was anyone else inside.'

He looked at her.

'Turns out there was. But they were already dead.'

'What? Christ, not another...'

She shook her head.

'Nope. This one was hangin' from the rafters wi' the same nylon rope that wee Delia was tied up wi'. We managed to get him down and through the window just before...'

There was an almighty crash and a huge shower of sparks, then the flames dramatically shot skywards as the roof of the building finally collapsed. Grant looked at her, waiting for her to continue.

'...aye, well, let's just say we got him out.'

He was almost afraid to ask. He nodded in the direction of the inert shape of Delia Donald.

'D'you think it's another one of her boys?'

Briony stared at him with an odd expression and shook her head.

'No...'

He frowned as she continued

'...from the description we have I don't think there's any doubt as to who it is; Danny Donald.'

They stared at each other as the fire continued to roar and the sirens got closer. They both turned and looked over to where Constable Fleming was continuing to secure the man lying on the ground. Grant could now feel a strange, cold feeling creeping up his legs and it seemed that his world had started to spin. He looked back at Briony and, just before he lapsed back into unconsciousness, he mumbled

'Then just who the fuck is that...?'

Chapter 24

'Good morning, Grant, nice to have you back with us. How are you feeling?'

He had half-opened his eyes and now he made the effort to open them fully, although the brightness made him wince. He struggled to focus. A woman wearing a white coat and with a stethoscope draped around her neck was smiling down at him; he tried to respond, but all that came out was a hoarse croak. The woman put her hand behind his head, lifting him up slightly, then brought a plastic cup of water to his mouth.

'Have a drink. Your throat will be a bit raw after your ordeal...'
My ordeal? Oh shit...

She must have seen his change of expression as the memory returned.

'Now, it's all right, Grant, don't panic, everyone's safe and it seems that you're the hero of the hour. It's nice to know that we're being looked after by officers like you. Now, I suggest you lie back down and let us take care of you. We gave you a sedative last night so you'll still feel a little groggy...

He closed his eyes and drifted back into oblivion; well, apart from the dreams...

*

Grant was sitting up now, sipping another cup of water. It had never tasted so good. Briony had just sat down beside the bed, having eventually managed to persuade the charge nurse that her business was urgent.

'Christ, you gave us a right scare, eh, Grant McVicar!' she said with a relieved smile.

He put the plastic cup down on the bedside cabinet and sighed. Even that hurt his throat.

'Aye, gave myself one too, Bri.' he replied with a croak. 'Fortunately it was what's called "bird-shot" and it wasn't a direct hit, they ricocheted off the wall an' into me. A proper hit from larger lead pellets could have blown a hole in my thigh, apparently... listen, how's Delia?'

'They won't let me near her. Probably quite right too. Physically it seems she's much the same as you, a bit of smoke inhalation, nothin' too serious. Her mental state...well, that's anyone's guess, eh.'

They sat in silence for a moment, listening to the sounds of Glasgow's QEU Hospital. The evidence against Danny Donald was certainly mounting up, except for one minor issue.

'So, the big question, Bri, who the hell is the guy that shot me?' She sat back.

'You ever heard of Simon Hope, Boss?'

'Simon Hope... nope, doesn't ring a bell. Should I know him?'

'Well, there's this programme on Netflix called "Saint Mungo – Sinner." It's about a kinda shady Glasgow character, Mungo Harris. You know, tough guy with a heart of gold, ex-special forces, helps people out when the odds are stacked against them. Personally I think it's a bit o' a rip-off o' Jack Reacher, but who am I—'

Grant hadn't heard of either Mungo Harris or Jack Reacher; in fact, he seldom watched the TV. Briony shook her head in apparent dismay.

'Anyway, Simon Hope wrote it. He's had a load of paperbacks out too, worth a fair bit by all accounts.'

'So I'm presuming it's this Simon Hope that we have in custody?'

'Yup!'

'And what does he have to say for himself?'

She made a face.

'Sweet eff all, Boss...'

'Waiting for his solicitor, I'd imagine?'

'Aye, got it in one, eh. Tight as a bloody drum. An' I have to say I don't particularly warm to the man.'

Briony continued.

'Mind you, it doesn't seem likely that he intended to kill you, does it? If he *had* been shootin' to kill, you'd be a lot worse off!'

'Aye, thanks for reminding me, Bri. Well, we need to get a full statement from him and take it from there. And, by the way, that was a piece of luck getting Donald's body out. You and Craig Morton did well but you put yourselves at considerable risk, Bri. Christ, I don't want to lose another...'

Before he could continue, she squeezed his hand and smiled.

'You don't get rid of me that easily Grant McVicar, don't you worry.'

*

Grant finally managed to get himself discharged that afternoon. The "birdshot" hadn't done too much damage; they'd patched up his hip, given him a course of antibiotics plus a bottle of pain-killers and issued a warning to "take things easy!" Before he left he had tried to look in on Delia but, as expected, the nurse in charge had strict instructions that no-one was allowed in; well, except Pam Lawson, who had identified herself as next-of-kin, much to Grant's annoyance.

He had then phoned Briony, who duly arrived driving his pick-up, then they immediately set off for Osprey House, where the team was busy collating the fresh evidence and uploading it to HOLMES. When he entered the room there was a slight cheer from his team. It brought a brief smile to his brooding countenance.

'Thanks all and good job everyone. Right, Bri has brought me up to speed regarding this guy we have in custody, one Simon Hope. Anything else to report?'

Faz spoke first.

'Yup, we found the keys to the outhouse.'

'And?'

'Well, a dusty cross-trainer and a set of weights, both looking as if they hadn't seen any action for ages. A load of assorted power tools and other bits and pieces, including a roll of duct tape – although you could find that anywhere, I suppose. Oh, and his lap-top.'

'Excellent - did you manage to get into it, Faz?'

The Detective Constable grinned.

'Of course, Boss! Brought it back here and I've been working on it since; don't think there's any doubt where the money was going.'

'Oh? Where?'

'Gambling, Boss. On-line and in a high-stakes poker school.

Those Mondays that his wife thought he was having an affair? Seems he was down in Manchester.'

'Manchester? What, playing poker?'

'Aye, and he kept a diary with dates and amounts; and, let me tell you, by all accounts he was pretty crap at it. For a start, the buy-in was five grand, then on one particular occasion he lost over sixteen thousand in one night! No wonder he needed the cash.'

'Christ, no wonder right enough! Did he keep it up after Delia left?'

'Seems so. There were a couple of large cash injections earlier this year, that would tie in with the loans and the re-mortgaging of the farm, but given his losses, his account must be down a fair bit by now. No wonder he was pissed off at Delia.'

Grant considered this fresh information. It certainly provided a powerful motive for revenge and he wondered if Donald had maybe insured Delia's life. They would have to check.

'Did you find any weapons?'

'Yes, Boss,' said Kiera 'we found a shotgun as well as a couple of seriously nasty-looking hunting knives. They're with forensics as we speak.'

'Good. Did it look as if there was space for another gun?'

Faz and Kiera looked at each other, then Faz replied.

'Em, there was the usual gun cabinet bolted to the wall but there was space for four guns in it. Hard to say how many he kept, really. Sorry, I know that's not much help, Boss.'

'Never mind. Anything of interest in the house?'

Kiera shrugged and shook her head.

'No, nothing much' she replied. 'A lot of unpaid bills, I reckon he was just a few steps away from foreclosure. Place was an absolute midden, mice everywhere, I don't know how he could live like that. SOCOs are there now, seeing what they can find.'

'Hm. What about Donald's PM? Who's doing that?'

'Think the uniforms have organised it, Boss' replied Cliff. 'Ah phoned Doctor Napier but she said it was out-with her area an' gave me a bit o' an earful for disturbing her!'

Grant chuckled then winced. His throat was still raw.

'Aye, I bet she did! All bark and no bite, though; listen, I'll give her a call and see if she can at least liaise. Right...'

His phone buzzed, the ringer still being switched to silent. He looked at the screen. It was Superintendent Minto. He also noted that the charge was down to five percent.

Shit...

He swiped the screen, listened, said 'yes, ma'am' then ended the call and handed his phone to Briony.

'Three things, Bri. Can you charge it for me and can you get me a coffee? I've been called upstairs.'

She took his phone, raising an eyebrow.

'You said three things, Boss?'

'Oh aye. Wish me luck...'

*

Grant was staring at Superintendent Minto's desk, biting his cheeks and trying to control his temper. Her raised voice was shrill and angry.

'... an unmitigated disaster, Grant. I've got the Divisional Commander ranting at me, strongly suggesting that I relieve you of duty. For God's sake, first you arrest the wrong men, then your prime suspect hangs himself and now we have this bloody author, Simon Hope in custody, having shot a police officer! What the hell is going on?'

'I'm sorry ma'am, I know it doesn't look good but...'

'And why the hell did you leave the search of Donald's property until he came home? You should have carried it out whether he was there or not! He might very well still be alive if you had.'

'ma'am, with all respect, I decided to postpone it as I believed that, if he arrived and found us there, he may have made off again. I had the locals keeping an eye on the place...'

'Yes, once every...what, two hours...'

'Em, no, they were a bit stretched...'

'Exactly! And, as I mentioned, you go and get yourself bloody shot!'

'Again, with all respect, I did ask for firearms...'

She raised her voice a notch.

'You didn't need bloody firearms support, Grant. All you needed to do was be more bloody careful. Anyway, the whole thing's a complete fiasco. This is your last chance, DCI McVicar. If anything else goes awry, I'll be taking you off the case and suspending you until we've reviewed whether you're fit to continue in your present role. Right, away and sort this out. If you can...'

He stood up and nodded, aware of the colour rising in his cheeks. As he walked to the door, Superintendent Patricia Minto called after him in a more gentle tone.

'Grant!'

He turned, unsuccessfully trying to hide the scowl on his face. 'ma'am?'

'Believe it or not, I've had your back up 'til now. You're a bloody good cop but I think you still have some serious issues that you, or we, need to address. However, there's not much more I can do. Clear up this mess, please. Don't let me down.'

'No ma'am.'

Fuck...

*

Briony knew by the expression on Grant's face that the meeting hadn't gone well; she decided not to ask.

'Phone's chargin', Boss, and your coffee's probably cold.'

'Cheers.'

He slumped in a chair then looked up at her. When he spoke, his voice was flat.

'Right, I'm going to head up to Helen Street to have a word with this Mr Hope; Sam, you come with me. The experience will do you good. Bri, can you take Kiera and see if you can have a word with Delia? I doubt that you'll have much luck but it's worth a try. If not, see if you can speak to Pam Lawson. Delia may have said something to her. Cliff, Faz, chase up the SOCOs and see if there's anything further, either from Mid Blane or what's left of that cottage. They might have salvaged something. Oh, and Delia's BMW too. Speaking of cars, what about that other vehicle?'

'Registered to this Simon Hope, Boss.' replied Cliff. 'One o' those van conversions that'll take a wheelchair an' there was a chair in it. The vehicle had a bit o' damage wi' bein' close to the fire but it was intact so the SOCOs are goin' over it wi' the proverbial fine tooth comb.'

'Hm. What the hell would he want with a wheelchair? And it's an odd vehicle for a successful author to be driving too. I'll be interested to see what he has to say. Anyway, keep me posted, Cliff.'

He stood up.

'We need to get this wrapped up soon before the Mint gives yours-truly a free transfer – don't want to be issuing parking tickets for the remainder of my career. Right, chop-chop, busy-busy, work-work...'

Briony gave him an odd look.

'It was an advert on the telly...och, never mind.'

'Thought you never watched the telly, eh, Boss?'

'Used to. Where do you think I got all my detective skills?'

She raised a questioning eyebrow.

'Taggart. *Come on, there's been a murder...*'

*

Grant had to admit that Simon Hope had a certain charm; dark, slightly-greying curly hair, dark eyes and full, sensuous lips that were currently set in a slightly ironic smile, as if he was amused to find himself being held in custody. But there was an underlying supercilious, almost cruel aura about the man and Grant was in no doubt that he was up against a powerful personality, capable of both deception and manipulation. Maybe that was what made him a successful author. He and Sam sat down and started the interview.

'Mr Hope...'

'Oh, Simon, please.'

'Very well, Simon, I'm DCI Grant McVicar and this is DC Sam Tannahill.'

'Hello. I should say "pleased to meet you" I suppose, but, with all respect, I'm not really. But wait... DCI McVicar?'

Grant stared at Hope.

'That's me.'

'Oh my God, I am so, so sorry about what happened. I honestly didn't mean...'

He stopped suddenly and smiled.

'...actually, that's it, I'm afraid.'

'Em, what do you mean by that, Simon?' asked Sam.

'I mean that I'm not going to say anything further, other than to repeat how sorry I am to your superior, Sam.'

He switched on the same smile that had charmed Delia all those years ago; Sam just gave him a disparaging look. She had already decided that she didn't like the man.

'So that's it, Mr Hope? ' Said Grant. 'You're not prepared to discuss anything further?'

'No. I'm really very sorry to inconvenience you, officers but, as

I'm sure you'll understand, my solicitor really needs to be here and, unfortunately, she's in court in Edinburgh today. That's where her offices are, by the way. So it'll be tomorrow before she can attend and I should be able to give you a full statement then.'

'That's very kind of you, Mr Hope...'

'Really, there's no need for sarcasm, Mr McVicar. I've already made your colleagues aware that I wouldn't speak to you without her being present.'

'Aye, maybe, but I wasn't aware that she was unavailable until tomorrow. Given that you shot a police officer, you'll be held in custody at least until then. Interview terminated...'

*

Grant was sitting in his office, his mind reeling with the events of the last few days. How could things have gone so wrong? His left side was aching and he was only too well aware that the gunshot could have had much more serious consequences. Maybe the Mint was right, maybe he wasn't fit for front-line policing any more. But what else could he have done? Should he have searched Donald's house before the man came back? He still didn't think so but it seemed that everything he did at the moment was wrong, at least in the eyes of Superintendent Minto. As for that smarmy bastard Simon Hope, just where the hell did he fit into all this, and why was he present at a murder and kidnap scene?

He dropped his head onto his hands and groaned, then jumped as his phone gave an unfamiliar ring. He picked it up. It was Dr. Napier.

'Hello Doctor.'

'Hello Grant. I heard about your escapades. How are you?'

'Well, I'm still in one piece, thanks. Just a flesh wound, should be fine in a week or two.'

'I see. It must have been difficult, though. I heard what you did, Grant. That was very heroic.'

'Em... thanks, Doctor, but, you know, all in the line of duty and all...'

'... that crap? Yes, I know, but you should still be proud, considering... anyway, on to this hanging.'

'Yes, the unfortunate Mr Donald?'

'Tell me, Grant, do you believe that he was the murderer?'

'Well, that's the theory at the moment, Doctor, and the evidence certainly seems to point that way. Of course, we'll never get the opportunity...'

'...to ask. No, unfortunately not. Or to punish him for his sins either.'

She paused for a moment.

'So, as far as the PM goes, it's a Dr Patel who'll be carrying it out. He's a young chap, full of modern ideas, and he's extended the courtesy of inviting me to attend and to have an input, which I'm very much looking forward to.'

'That's good news, Doctor... well, of course, not that I don't think he'll...Well, you know...'

'Yes, Grant, I understand, you know me and my methods but Dr Patel is every bit as qualified a pathologist as I am so you needn't worry on that score. He's just a bit more "CSI" rather than my "old school tie". We'll be carrying it out first thing so I'll call you as soon as I have any relevant information, although from what I can gather it should be a pretty straightforward case of suicide.'

'Yes, it looks that way. Okay, Doctor, thanks for calling, I'll hear from you tomorrow.'

'You will, Grant, 'Bye.'

*

Grant decided to call it a day. Briony and Kiera's visit to the QEU Hospital had, as expected, been fruitless. They weren't permitted to speak to the heavily-sedated Delia and Pam Lawson had already gone home. The ferocity of the blaze at the derelict cottage had destroyed virtually everything and the SOCOs had found no further evidence amongst the smouldering ruins. There was little left of the shotgun and only a few fragments of the lanterns, making fingerprinting impossible; SOCOs had found no further relevant evidence at the farmhouse. Faz was still working on Donald's computer but, other than links to the high-stakes gambling and a few, public-access pornographic sites, there was nothing sinister lurking on the hard-drive. As expected, Delia's BMW had yielded fingerprints belonging to Delia and to Pam, but no-one else. Forensics were now working on the bag of food, which they had traced to Matonti's delicatessen in Partick. Cliff had spoken to the proprietors, who seemed genuinely shocked at what had happened and had happily given their fingerprints in order to eliminate them from police enquiries. All they needed to do now was to speak to Delia and to Simon Hope. Grant said a brief goodbye to his team and left Osprey House. At this stage in the case he should have felt a sense of satisfaction and of closure. However, with three murders, a victim hospitalised and the prime suspect having committed suicide, not to mention his own trauma, he felt nothing but frustration and unease.

Chapter 25

Grant knew it was early. He also knew he hadn't the slightest chance of getting back to sleep. He had wakened in a blind panic, sweating, writhing and mumbling incoherently, his left side aching where the shotgun pellets had been removed. He had lain on top of the bed, waiting for his heart-rate to drop and, as he did so, his mind filled with unbidden thoughts of the last few weeks' events. They were neither positive not productive and, after what he reckoned to be nearly an hour he got up, pulled on a t-shirt, limped through to the kitchen and switched on the kettle. After he had brewed a mug of coffee and swallowed some more painkillers, he sat down at the counter, gazing out of the window; the sky was already light, which meant he must have had a reasonable amount of sleep. So why did he feel like shit...?

He took a slug of the coffee and opened the lid of his laptop, gazing at the screen as it came to life; his own, uploaded photo of a snow-capped Ben Lomond appeared, bright, fresh and inviting...

If only life was that bloody simple...

He started...paused...deleted...started again...

Half an hour later, it was done.

"Dear Superintendent Minto,

Following very careful consideration and a great deal of soul-searching, it is with the deepest regret that I am writing to tender my resignation from my position as Detective Chief Inspector, K Division, Police Scotland..."

The pointer of the mouse hovered over the print icon for a few seconds, then he moved it away; he would put the matter on hold meantime and make a final decision later. As he stood up, a thought occurred to him; he gave a wry smile as, with great clarity, he realised that what he needed to do more than anything else was to talk to Briony Quinn.

Grant and Briony had just pulled out of the Osprey House car park en-route to Helen Street police station and their forthcoming interview with Simon Hope. The other members of the team had remained at the office, waiting for any results from the SOCOs and their subsequent forensic investigations. They would also be starting work on the final report, which would conclude that Danny Donald was presumed to have been the killer of the three young men and that, after abducting his estranged wife, he had committed suicide. His motivation for the brutal murders would go to the grave with him, although revenge against Delia seemed the likeliest explanation. Given the circumstantial evidence and his record of domestic violence, the conclusion was almost inevitable. As they pulled on to the M8, Grant turned to his sergeant.

'Bri?'

'Aye, Boss?'

'Em, can I run something past you?'

'Aye, of course you can. Fire away.'

'I've been thinking...'

She looked at him and raised an eyebrow, but remained silent. He continued

'...well, actually, the thing is...I wrote a letter to The Mint this morning, tendering my resignation.'

She gaped at him, opening and closing her mouth. Finally, with a stern look, she responded, in a broad, stacatto Fife accent.

'Ur ye bluidy stupit ur whit, eh?'

He turned and stared at her, his brows furrowed.

'Pardon?'

She shook her head and sighed.

'Basically, it's Glenrothes for "are you off your head?" So I'll ask again, are you bloody stupid... sir?'

He managed a grim smile as he shook his head.

'Christ, I don't know, Bri. Thing is, I'm really starting to wonder if I'm still up to the job. I mean, this case, it's been a complete disaster...' Bri interrupted,

She'd had enough of her boss wallowing in self-doubt.

'No it bloody hasn't, Boss. You need to stop this... this, Christ,

I don't know what it is! Okay, maybe we *were* a bit hasty in the murder...'

Grant interrupted with a shout, banging on the steering wheel.

'No! There was no "we" Bri. It was me, my responsibility, and I was so bloody desperate to nail Ronnie Pettigrew that I let it get in the way of common sense. That's what I mean. Am I able to move on from my fixation with the Pettigrews; am I able to move on from... well...'

She put her hand lightly on his arm.

'Of course you are, Grant. Look at what happened at the farm...'

'I'd rather not, actually.'

'Aye, I know that, but when the chips were down you faced the danger and you saved Delia – and yourself. If you weren't up to it would you be here just now, eh?'

He thought about it for a moment.

'No, I suppose not. So you don't think I should hand in my resignation then?'

She frowned at him.

'I thought you said you had?'

'Well, I wrote the letter but I didn't actually print it, thought I'd run it past you first.'

She rolled her eyes.

'Aye, well, you know my answer, Boss.'

'What?'

'Dinn'a be bluidy stupit, eh!'

*

When Grant and Briony arrived at the Helen Street office, they were told that Simon Hope's solicitor had been delayed and it would probably be eleven-thirty before she arrived from her office in Edinburgh. They had managed to procure a coffee and were sitting chatting about the case; eventually a civilian employee sought them out.

'That's Mr Hope's solicitor here, officers. She's asked for half an hour with her client, then you can proceed.'

'Aye, thanks' said Grant with a sigh, as the young woman disappeared with a click of heels.

'Bloody cheek. Thinks we've nothing better to do than hang about waiting for her. Probably charging him a fortune too; still, serves him right for shooting me... oh bugger...'

Grant's phone was ringing and he struggled to remove it from his left-hand trouser pocket, grimacing with pain as he did so.

'That looks a bit sore, Boss. Are you sure it's okay?'

'Aye, just a bit tender . Christ, it's Pam Lawson. What the hell does she want now?'

He swiped the screen and answered in a decidedly official tone.

'Good morning Pam. Listen, it's not a great time... what?... oh, right, I see. Listen, I'm about to conduct an interview, I'll call you back as soon as I know when I'll be free... yes, thanks very much, I appreciate it...bye.'

He ended the call. Briony was looking at him with an odd half-smile.

'Well?'

'Well what, Bri?'

She raised a questioning eyebrow.

'Och, she was just calling to say that Delia's feeling a lot better today.'

'And?'

Grant sighed again and shook his head; Briony Quinn was getting to know him very well indeed.

'And that she'd like to see me.'

'Who, Pam?'

'No, not bloody Pam! Del...'

Briony was grinning at him now.

'You...'

But he couldn't help himself . He smiled too.

*

Grant was in a slightly more buoyant mood when they finally entered the bleak, window-less interview room. There was no point in denying it, the thought of seeing Delia later in the day had improved his mood considerably. However, as soon as he set eyes on Simon Hope's solicitor, his heart sank to his boots. The attractive, blue-eyed blonde looked up at him and gave him a business-like smile.

'Good morning Grant. You're well, I hope?'

Briony's gaze shifted from the blonde to her Boss as Simon Hope smiled and spoke.

'Oh, you two are already acquainted. That should make thing's a lot easier.'

Jackie Valentine turned to her client and spoke in a rather condescending tone, tinged with an acquired Morningside accent.

'I wouldn't count on it, Simon. Actually, the Chief Inspector and I were married for a short while but I'm not quite sure that he's ever got over it...'

It was Briony who interrupted. Grant had never seen such an expression of anger on her face as she leaned forward and hissed at the woman sitting across the desk.

'How dare you? Might I remind you that this is a police interview, your client having shot my superior officer, I expect a considerably higher level of professionalism. To bring a previous personal relationship into this conversation is extremely disrespectful and, to be quite frank, brings both you and your profession into disrepute. I want your comments noted...'

Grant put his hand on her arm.

'Thanks Sergeant, I think the point's been made...' he glared at his ex-wife 'but I have to say that I totally agree with DS Quinn. Jackie, your comment is beneath you and I refuse to rise to the bait and respond.'

He sat down, the still furious Briony taking her place beside him. Jackie Valentine had the good grace to look very slightly embarrassed and Grant waited a few moments before starting the recording and proceeding with the interview.

'Right, Mr Hope...'

'Simon, please...'

Grant ignored him. He was starting to seriously dislike the man.

'... Mr Hope, we are at Helen Street police office, I am DCI Grant McVicar, this is DS Quinn and you are accompanied by your solicitor, Jacqueline Valentine. Do you understand?'

'Yes' replied Simon, with a slight smile.

'Good. Right, Mr Hope, we need to...'

To Grant's annoyance Jackie Valentine now interrupted.

'Actually, my client has prepared a full statement, if I could pass this to you and let you read it.'

She slid over two sheets of paper, a flamboyant signature at the bottom of the second; Grant took them, glaring over at Jackie as he did so, and held them so that Briony could also read Hope's statement; he had the feeling that it would read like one of the man's literary works and the heading confirmed his suspicions.

Statement
by
Simon Mackie Hope.

After years of writing about the incarceration of a variety of fictional characters, it is strange indeed to find myself in that very situation. Strange, yet in a peculiar way, somehow thrilling, although I must confess that, when the door slams and the lock turns, the thrill quickly gives way to a feeling of deep dread. Despite being an author of fiction, I am fully aware that it is in my best interest (as the old cliché goes) to tell you the truth, the whole truth and nothing but the truth...so here it is.

Already Grant could feel his hackles rise. It was supposed to be an official statement, not another chapter of one of Simon Hope's books...still, he read on.

Delia Donald and I go back a very long way. You may or may not know this but, some time ago, she and I had an intense relationship (both physically and emotionally) that lasted for a good few years.

It was as if an icy hand had suddenly reached inside Grant and was squeezing his innards – he felt vaguely nauseous.

Alas, it came to an end and we went our separate ways, but we have kept in touch over the years. Now, I feel that I have to make this absolutely clear. The whole concept of the Domestic Services Agency was mine! Although it was devised in the spirit of "hauf-jokin', hale-earnest", like many such crazy ideas it decided to take wings and fly. To be honest, I think that, for Delia, the Agency was born out of sheer desperation and, for many years, it provided respite from what had become an extremely difficult, unpleasant and, as far as I can gather, abusive marriage. Danny Donald was an absolute bastard (I make no apology for saying that) and Delia was well rid of him, although I do wonder if her new-found friend Pam Lawson isn't equally emotionally controlling. Still, I digress...

Grant took a deep breath. The man wasn't bloody joking...

Despite running what was, in effect, an Escort Agency, Delia is a gentle, caring and rather vulnerable woman. There is no doubt (and it is not in the least surprising) that the death of the first two young men upset her very deeply. She phoned me just after she found out and, at that point, I wanted to come down and comfort her. However, she asked me not to and I respected her wish. The next death served to compound the poor girl's misery and, again, I wanted to come and see her; again, she refused, in the mistaken belief that I wanted to re-kindle our relationship. Now, make no mistake, I still find Delia very attractive but, at that point, nothing could have been further from my mind. My only concern was for her mental well-being which I believed had been badly compromised by the brutal deaths of three of her young men, men that she knew well and was extremely fond of.

Grant could now sense Briony bristling beside him. He glanced across at Simon Hope, who was staring impassively at a space above Grant's head, whilst Jackie Valentine was studiously perusing something on her phone. He looked back down and continued to read.

Delia phoned me very early on Tuesday morning —sometime after about three, I think— and I knew that she was close to the edge. She was in her office, having sneaked out of her friend's house, and she had decided to close up the Agency once and for all. I knew how much the business meant to her and I understood the emotional cost of walking away from it. However, there was another concern. She told me that Pam had seen a vehicle passing her house on several occasions and she was worried that it was her estranged husband. Delia had also told me about the vile man's fraudulent use of her name to take out a variety of loans and it was obvious that, having lost his main source of income, the man would probably be out of funds, frustrated and angry, not a good cocktail of circumstance and emotions, one would imagine.

After speaking to her I came to the conclusion that it was time to take matters into my own hands and I seriously considered travelling down to see her. I had some arrangements made for later that day (my mother is in a nursing home in Aberdeen and I had arranged to visit her) and I had decided to drive straight down to Glasgow afterwards. However, the visit to my mother took longer than I anticipated and, in the end, I decided that it might be for the best to abandon my plans. That was until the text...

I was returning my mother to the nursing home when Delia texted me. Of course, I had her number stored and I knew it was her. It was a brief message – she was still at her office but she was concerned that her ex-husband was stalking her and she was afraid that he was intending to harm her. She asked me to come down immediately. It was the sign that I had both hoped and waited for.

Having deposited my mother at the home, I immediately drove down and went straight to her office. Alas, I had missed her and I was unable to get a response from her phone. I was worried. I knew she was in a fragile state of mind and I was concerned that Danny Donald was now actively searching for her. The only other location that I knew of was the farm where she had lived with Donald and I drove straight there.

When I arrived, Donald's vehicle was parked in the farmyard but there was no sign of him. I went up to the house, finding the door open, but it was empty (apart from the vermin that roamed freely...)

By now I was in a panic. I was certain that Donald had taken her, but where? Then I remembered; Delia had once spoken about an old property along a farm track; she had wondered if it could be renovated as a holiday-let but, to be honest, Danny Donald wasn't the least bit interested in anything that involved either hard work or financial investment. It was the only place I could think of and, seeing a track disappearing up behind the farmhouse, I decided to investigate, I found what I presumed to be one of Delia's trainers lying a few feet along the track. Sure now of my reasoning, I continued onwards.

I crept in to the semi-ruinous building (you saw it, of course), keeping as quiet as I could. There was a container of some sort on a table and a small paraffin lamp burning beside it. Donald's intentions now seemed only too clear. Then I heard what I thought was a whimper, coming from upstairs. With scant regard for my own safety, I ran up the rickety steps and into the only illuminated room to find poor Delia just as you found her shortly thereafter – naked, tied in a chair and with a sack over her head. I was also horrified to see that there was a shotgun lying on the floor. Was that how he had managed to abduct her, perhaps? I was looking for some way to free her when I heard footsteps, the door opened and, assuming it was Donald returning to finish the job, I lifted the gun and... Well, as you are only too painfully aware, it went off.

I can assure you that I was every bit as shocked as you undoubtedly were and, dropping the gun, I ran. I was now in a blind panic. So much for my great heroic action in saving the girl! As I entered the downstairs room, another figure appeared and, in my haste to escape from what I believed to be an accomplice, I barged into the table, knocking it over, spilling the contents of the container and smashing the paraffin lamp.

You know what happened next, of course; and, thank God, you saved poor Delia. The thought that, on account of my careless and cowardly actions, she might have perished in the ensuing fire will haunt me for years to come. But at least she is safe; that was my only concern. As to Danny Donald, I had no idea that he had hanged himself, although I'm not really surprised. He was an abusive bully and, most likely, a worse coward than I, underneath his rough, brutish exterior. When it came down to it, presumably he lacked the courage (or the insensitivity) to carry out his final act of violence and, instead, he decided to take the coward's way out; and good riddance (again I make no apology.)

So, my confession. Yes, I shot a police officer, for which I am truly sorry. I believed that it was Danny Donald returning either to murder or to torture (probably both) his estranged wife. In my defence, I had no idea the gun was loaded and, having little experience of firearms, I should never have lifted it up in the first place. But I was afraid, I panicked and, whilst I am ready to accept the consequences of my foolish actions, I will plead the mitigating circumstances that I have stated and hope for leniency.

Simon M Hope.

Grant placed the letter down on the table and glanced at Briony. Her expression gave nothing away. He looked across at Simon Hope, sitting with a very slightly smug smile on his face; Jackie Valentine appeared to have finished the business on her phone and her attention returned to the matter in hand. Grant took a deep breath and exhaled slowly.

'Well, Mr Hope, that's quite a statement. When is it due to be published?'

Simon Hope glared at him but said nothing. Jackie gave him a dark look.

'There's no need to take that attitude, Grant. Sarcasm doesn't become you...'

'No, it's fine, Jackie' interrupted Hope, flashing his smile once again. 'I can understand that the Inspector isn't used to such...well, such eloquent statements, I suppose.'

Although Grant could see that the man was a natural charmer (he was beginning to understand how Delia had fallen for him) he was also developing a strong dislike for Simon Hope. The feeling of nausea also made a brief re-appearance before Briony spoke, her tone harsh.

'Can I ask, Mr Hope, as a successful author...'

Grant could see Hope's ego preen itself as he turned to face Briony, the smile widening. He had clearly missed the sarcasm in the sergeant's tone.

'...why are you driving a van converted for wheelchair use?'

Simon Hope chuckled.

'Yes, I suppose you may think it's a funny vehicle of choice for someone in my position, I agree. But, as I said in my statement, my elderly mother is in a nursing home in Aberdeen; she can't walk far so I bought a vehicle that could accommodate a wheelchair.As you will have discovered, it's kept in the back. As I also said in my statement, I had been up in Aberdeen that day visiting her and, following the phone call, I decided to come straight down to see Delia rather than detour to my house and pick up my...well, my Porsche, if you must know.'

Briony didn't respond; Jackie Valentine shuffled some papers impatiently.

'Well, as you can see, Simon's statement pretty much covers everything. Now, if...'

Grant had been aware of Briony's phone buzzing and she was now looking down at the message on the screen. He was annoyed. He didn't like being disturbed during an important interview and he had switched his own phone to flight mode. She held hers in front of him so that he could read the message. It was from Cliff.

"Sarge plz get Boss 2 phn me ASAP. V V urgent. C"

He disliked text speak; he made a face, sighed, then stated 'I need to make a call. Interview suspended...'

Once outside, he switched his phone back on and dialled Cliff's number. The DC answered on the second ring.

'Cliff? This had better be bloody good...'

*

He finished the call, put the phone back in his pocket and stood for a moment, his mind racing; he took a deep breath and went back into the interview room, aware that all eyes were watching him. As Briony looked at her Boss's face, she saw an expression that she couldn't quite fathom. He sat down, looked at the desk, then across at Simon Hope.

'Mr Hope.'

'Yes, Chief Inspector?'

'When you took your mother out the other day, where, exactly, did you go?'

Simon Hope smiled.

'I took her down to the beach at Aberdeen. We used to go there when I was a boy, I'd play on the shingle while my mum and dad sat on the grass bank. She still loves it there. I walked her up and down for a bit then we sat and ate chips. The simple pleasures, you see.'

'Indeed. Yes, I know the beach at Aberdeen, nice place. Fresh, though.'

'Yes. Actually, it was extremely fresh the other day and we didn't stay out for too long.'

'So after you left, where did you take your mother?'

Jackie Valentine interrupted.

'Can I ask the relevance of this, Grant? What has my client's mother got to do with anything?'

'Please, Jackie, I'm just...'

Simon Hope interrupted.

'Really, it's fine, Jackie. After all, there's nothing to hide and the Chief Inspector could easily confirm the details with my mother; although I'd rather you didn't, as it would only get her agitated. After we ate our chips, I wheeled her back to the car then we went back to the nursing home...'

'Which is?'

'What, the home? Oh, it's called Hawkswood Hall, in Milltimber. Lovely place, she's very happy...'

'I'm pleased to hear it, Mr Hope. Can I ask, did you use the wheelchair when you returned your mother to the home?'

'No, she's able to walk the short distance from the car.'

'So the only recent use has been to walk your mum along the promenade at Aberdeen Beach?'

'Yes, just that.'

'Can you think when you would have last used the wheelchair before Tuesday?'

'Let me see...'

Jackie's face was now turning scarlet with suppressed anger.

'Really, Grant, I can't see what this has to do with anything. Mrs

Hope is an elderly...'

Simon turned and bestowed the full radiance of his smile on his agitated solicitor.

'Honestly Jackie, I'm more than happy to answer the Chief's questions if it helps him in any way.' He turned back to Grant, a slightly pained expression on his face.

'Well, it's usually my wife who visits my mother but she's... em, overseas at the moment, although her schedule is pretty much the same as mine was. The previous week I picked mum up, went to the beach, had a walk —or a wheel, in her case— we got chips, I took her back to Hawkhill. Exactly the same routine, but it makes her happy and that is my only concern.'

'And do you ever use the wheelchair for any other purposes?'

Briony was watching the exchange intently and wondered if there was a fractional hesitation before Simon Hope replied.

'No, never. Why would I? It stays in the back of the van, which I, or my wife, only ever use when we take my mum out. Well, of course, I used the van when I came down on Tuesday, but those were exceptional circumstances.'

'I see.'

Grant sat back in the chair, clasped his hands and, looking down, started to slowly twiddle his thumbs; Briony was fascinated at the change in her Boss's demeanour and she was desperate to know the cause. He placed his thumbs together and looked back across at Simon Hope.

'Mr Hope, are there geese on the Aberdeen seafront at this time of year?'

Simon Hope looked surprised, then he chuckled.

'Geese? Honestly, in all the years I've been going, I've never set eyes on a goose! Seagulls aplenty. One tried to steal my mum's chips last week. But never geese. They're not sea birds as far as I'm aware. Why on earth do you ask?'

'Oh, just curiosity. But, yes, they're not seabirds, they prefer inland water, as far as I know. Right, that's all for now, Mr Hope. We may have more questions later. Interview terminated.'

He stood up but Jackie was on her feet before him.

'Grant, we haven't discussed bail...'

He turned and put on his more official tone.

'And we won't be either, Jackie. For a start, and by his own admission, your client shot a police officer. Anyway, this is an ongoing murder investigation and I'm going to ask for an extension to your client's custody.'

'On what grounds?'

'As I said, it's part of a larger ongoing enquiry...'

'I strongly object...'

'Aye, I'm sure you do. Right, Bri, let's go, work to be done...

Chapter 26

'Geese?'

'Aye, geese, Bri.'

She waited for an explanation; when none was forthcoming, she asked.

'So what exactly did Cliff have to say, Boss. I'm presumin' it had somethin' to do with said geese.'

He smiled; they were making the short journey from the Helen Street offices to the QEU hospital.

'Aye, it did. Well, not geese, exactly, more their, em, shit!'

Briony's eyebrows shot up in surprise as Grant continued.

'So, among other things, the SOCOs have had a good look at the wheelchair in the back of Simon Hope's vehicle. They reckon it's been pretty thoroughly cleaned. Recently too, by the looks of it. Nice and shiny, they said.'

'Okay, so maybe he just likes it kept clean for his mum, and for the back of his car too, I suppose,'

'Maybe, but the thing is, the tyres on it are quite chunky, with quite a heavy tread on them; when they examined the treads, they found residue lodged in few of them. Some of it was heavy clay, hard to trace but less common up in Aberdeenshire, where the soil is fairly light. Anyway, once they'd removed that, underneath they found...'

'Goose shit?

'Aye.'

'Okay, but what's the significance of goose shit, Boss? Well, other than you've established with him that there are no geese on the Aberdeen seafront.'

'Well, think back to Castle Semple loch, Bri; the first two murders. Actually, to give him his due, it was Cliff who made the connection; remember the pontoons, where the boats set off from. They were covered with little piles of excrement; I stood in it myself. It's the only place I've been aware of it. Well, it's not something I keep a look-out for, to be fair – but Simon Hope has said that the seafront at Aberdeen is the only place that he uses the wheelchair. And now we find goose shit in the treads of said wheelchair. Co-incidence?'

She looked at him, realising the implication of what he had just said.

'Wait, so you're saying you think that Simon Hope might be involved in the loch murders in some way?'

'Let's just say I'm hedging my bets for the time being; the SOCOs are investigating if it's the same type, apparently they can check the excrement for what the geese have been eating and determine if the two samples are from the same area. Right, here we are. Listen, Bri, can you do me a big favour?'

She had a feeling she knew what it was going to be.

'Aye, go on then.'

'Could you try and keep Pam Lawson busy while I have a chat with Delia? You know what the bloody woman's like, she'll answer every question for the girl and she'll object if she thinks I'm upsetting her. I need to talk to Delia on her own. Please?'

Briony sighed.

'Okay, I'll do my best...look, there's a parking space, someone's just pullin' out...'

*

Briony had been true to her word and had managed to keep Pam Lawson engaged in conversation on the pretext of taking an informal statement whilst Grant entered the bright little hospital room. Delia was propped up on pristine white pillows, her dark curly hair spilling out against them. She was wearing a set of expensive-looking soft-pink lacy pyjamas, presumably brought in by Pam. She looked pale and slightly gaunt but nonetheless she smiled at him as he entered, causing the familiar fluttering of his stomach. He smiled back, desperately trying not to imagine Simon Hope...

No...don't...

'Hi Grant, thanks for coming. How are you?'

She had managed to ask after his well-being even before he had spoken. He felt slightly guilty and he wished he'd remembered to bring her something. But what did you bring nowadays? Were flowers still acceptable? Chocolate?

Shit...

'Em, well, not too bad thanks. And it's good to see you looking...'

And just what does she look, Grant...?

'...anyway, how are you, Delia?'

She sighed.

'I've been better, I suppose. But I'm alive, and it seems that I have you to thank for that.'

He sat down on a chair beside the bed and immediately she reached out to take his hand, squeezing it tightly and gazing intently at him. He didn't know what to say. Somehow he felt like a clumsy teenager, but he didn't resist...

'Em, well...you know, I was just doing my job...'

'Crap! You got shot and you nearly got burned alive rescuing me. The doctor told me what happened...'

'But how the hell did he know. I mean, it's not really public knowledge?'

'Oh, there's a healthy grapevine, it seems. The local cops, the paramedics, they all appear to know what you did, they know that you covered me up with an old sheet and carried me through the flames, still tied in the chair...'

Despite her brave act, he saw the tears welling up in her eyes as she relived the terror. He squeezed her small hand firmly.

'Don't Delia, please. Of course I saved you. How could I not? Do you think I would have left you?'

She sniffed, managing to stem the flow.

'No, no, of course not; but look...'

She leaned forward and brushed his short beard.

'... you've still got singed bits...'

As she rubbed away the burnt hairs, he felt a shiver run down his spine. Her smile returned as she looked into his eyes, her soft hand still resting on the side of his face.

'You're a good man, Grant McVicar. You know that? Good, solid, kind, dependable. God knows how you're still footloose and fancy free!'

He could feel the colour rising in his cheeks.

'Aye, well, long story... anyway, speaking of stories...'

She lay back on her pillows, knowing he was changing the subject to hide his embarrassment.

'Yes?'

'Well, I'm really sorry to have to go over all this, Delia. I know it won't be easy but...'

'It's okay, really. I'm still struggling to come to terms with the fact that Danny was responsible for those...well, I mean, I know he was a brute, but murder? God, when I think back, if Pam hadn't taken me in I might not...'

The tears welled up once more but, again, she managed to fight them.

'It's over now, Delia, you don't have to worry anymore.'

'No, I suppose not. Anyway, ask what you want, Grant, I'll be okay.'

Somehow, he believed that she would.

'Well, really I just need to know what you remember. First of all, I take it you know that he's...well, your husband's dead?'

She closed her eyes.

'Yes. They told me.'

'Okay. Listen, I'm sorry...but before...well, did you see Danny. I mean, did he ask you to go with him...?'

She interrupted him.

'No, that's the thing. I was back at the car, just about to head home to Pam's; I'd parked round the back of the office and it was pouring by this time. I'd bought her a few things from the Deli, just as a wee thank-you... actually, it was more of an apology Did she tell you?'

'What— that you left in the middle of the night?'

'Yes. You see, I'd had a really bad dream and, when I woke up, I was all confused. Somehow I felt that I needed to talk to Simon but I realised I'd left my phone on the desk at work. I don't know what made me do it but I just sneaked out and drove over to Partick.'

'And did you speak to...him?

Grant was reluctant to mention the man's name but Delia didn't seem to notice.

'To Simon? Well, he seems to keep odd hours. He's an author, after all, I suppose he doesn't have to get up at the same time as us mere mortals. But, yes, I spoke to him.'

'Did he say that he was coming down to see you?'

'He wanted to come but I told him not to. Whenever I phone he wants to come down but I always ask him not to. He's been very good, he's always respected my wishes. He's married, you see...'

'Yes, I know...'

Grant paused. Somehow this didn't seem to fit with Hope's story. He continued.

'But you texted him later. You thought your husband was stalking you and you asked him to come down?'

She gave him an uncomprehending look.

'Sorry... I what?'

'Didn't you message Simon Hope and ask him to come down?'

She shook her head.

'No, I didn't, Grant. At least, I don't remember... oh, I don't know, I don't remember much, to be honest...'

She was struggling again and he squeezed her hand. He realised that she didn't know about Simon Hope's involvement. He supposed he would have to tell her.

'Delia, it was Simon Hope who shot me.'

She stared at him, her brows furrowing and her dark eyes widening in surprise.

'But... but... I don't understand. I mean, I thought it was Danny! I though he shot you then he... he...'

This time the tears started to roll down her cheeks and her head slumped forwards.

'Delia, when I came into that room, it was Simon Hope who grabbed the shotgun and fired it at me. I hadn't a clue who he was. The only light was from a little storm lantern, it was pretty dark and I hadn't even heard of Simon Hope until recently! Anyway, he's given us a full statement; he said that you'd texted him, he said that you'd been worried that Danny was intending to harm you so he drove down and, when he couldn't find you, apparently he went to the farmhouse looking for you. When neither of you were there he remembered that you'd mentioned the old cottage and eventually he made his way up to it. He said he'd just discovered you tied in the chair and was looking for something to cut the ropes with but, when I walked in, he thought it was Danny coming back for you. As I said, he picked up the gun, fired it at me then he ran down the stairs. When Briony appeared, he panicked, jumped over the table and knocked over the lamp and the container of fuel that, presumably, Danny was going to use to torch the building once he'd...'

His voice tailed off; Delia was staring at him, a horrified expression on her face.

'... once he'd killed me?'

Grant shook his head.

'I don't know what he intended, Delia, but it didn't look good. Anyway, Danny had already killed himself by the time Simon arrived. He says he was about to save you and just panicked when I showed up.'

'Danny's dead... he was a brute, but he was also my husband. I must have cared for him once.... How did we end up like this?'

She shook her head sadly.

' Oh Grant, I'm so, so sorry. I never meant for any of this to happen, what with you getting shot...'

She started to sob loudly. Grant was worried that it would bring Pam Lawson scurrying in.

'Shh, Delia, it's okay, really. It appears that what happened with Simon was just an unfortunate accident, he says he didn't mean for the gun to go off. Anyway, it was only a few pellets in my side – could have been much worse.'

He smiled what he hoped was a re-assuring smile; at least the tears stopped.

'Simon was really upset about all of this too, of course.'

Grant raised his eyebrows in surprise.

'Oh! Why, Delia?'

'Well, he knew all my boys, you see.'

'Knew them? How did he know them?'

Delia looked at him as if he were missing something.

'Didn't I mention it before? Oh, I'm sorry, I thought I had, it's just there's been so much...well, you see, all my boys were introduced to me by Simon. That's why I always felt safe with them. They were all friends of his. Well, maybe not friends, exactly, but certainly acquaintances, and I knew that he wouldn't send anyone... dodgy, I suppose. He was really protective of me, you see, and I'm sure he's as upset as I am about what's happened.'

Grant didn't reply. This fresh piece of information had taken him by surprise. She looked at him plaintively.

'So what now?' she asked in a small voice.

'What? Oh, sorry... well, can we go back to what happened, if you're up to it?'

'Yes, yes, I'm okay now. It was just a shock, hearing that it was Simon... well, anyway, I had arrived at the car, I was upset, flustered, sad... It's pretty dark round behind the offices, the rain was lashing down and I was rushing to get in when the stupid Deli bag burst . You know, it was one of those flimsy brown paper things and it was soaked. A pack of sausages dropped out and went underneath the car so I put the bag on the seat then bent down to pick them up when... well, I don't know. I seemed to black out, somehow.'

Grant gave her hand what he hoped was a re-assuring squeeze. Somehow it seemed the natural thing to do.

'We think you were hit on the back of the head, Delia. You were knocked out.'

She thought about this for a moment.

'Yes, yes maybe I was. It seemed to be so sudden; anyway, the next thing I knew I was being driven somewhere, I had something over my face, a splitting headache and my hands and feet were tied.'

Grant could see the pain on her face. He knew it must have been terrifying and he hated having to make her re-live her ordeal.

'I'm sorry, Delia. What happened next, do you remember?'

'Well, the pick-up —at least, I'm assuming it was Danny's pick-up— stopped and I was carried out. To be honest, I think I was in shock. I felt like I had lost all the power in my body. Then he stripped me. I think he cut my clothes off, actually, because I don't think he untied me. He sort of half-dragged, half-walked me up a flight of stairs then tied me to the chair, still with the bag over my head. I was sure I was going to die— or worse.'

Her voice tailed off and he squeezed her hand again.

'It's okay, Delia. You didn't die and you're safe now. We're nearly done.Can you remember anything else?'

She shook her head.

'No, not really. I think I heard the gunshot but after that... nothing, until I woke up in hospital.'

'So Danny didn't speak, he didn't say anything to you throughout the whole ordeal?'

'No, nothing.'

She paused and frowned.

'Actually, now that I think of it, that's really strange, because he always used to tell me exactly what he was going to do to me when...'

Her pupils started to dilate.

Shit...

Grant jumped up, ran over to the door and wrenched it open.

'Briony— quick, she's having one of those attacks...'

*

Once again, Briony's ministrations had managed to bring Delia back to the reality of the hospital ward. Pam Lawson was standing beside the bed, a dark look on her face as she glared at Grant, clearly assuming that he was responsible for her friend's breakdown. Finally, Delia recovered sufficiently to speak.

'I'm so sorry. Thanks, Briony you're such a star.'

As Delia grasped the sergeant's hand, Pam spoke in an authoritative tone

'Right, I think the poor girl has had quite enough for one day. Come on, it's time to...'

Grant's phone was ringing and he glanced at the caller display. It was Dr Napier.

'I'm sorry, I really need to take this...'

Pam bestowed an even darker look upon him but he ignored it as he swiped the screen.

'Doctor Napier. Can you give me one minute, I'm just concluding an interview...'

The response was terse but, to his relief, she didn't hang up.

'Right. I'm sorry, Delia, but I really need to go. You take care of yourself...'

There was so much more that he wanted to say but the circumstances made it impossible. Delia just smiled at him.

'It's fine, Grant, off you go. Listen, come and visit me again...'

'I will, right, I'll see you...'

Fuck...

He was just leaving, with Briony at his heels, when Delia called out.

'Grant!'

He turned, conscious of the pathologist holding impatiently on the other end of the phone.

'Aye?'

She smiled across at him.

'You're a hero. You know that?'

He simply stared at her. He had no words...

*

'I'm so sorry Doctor, I was speaking to a witness. I'm all yours now.'

'Yes, well, you're bloody lucky I didn't just hang up, Grant. I haven't got all day. Anyway, we've finished our examination of Mr Donald and I thought you might be interested in our results. If you're not too busy, that is...'

He gritted his teeth, ignoring the sarcasm.

'No. Doctor, I'm really sorry. Of course I'm not too busy.'

There was a slight pause, then the Doctor continued.

'Well, as I think was patently obvious, Danny Donald died from strangulation as a result of hanging.'

This was what Grant had expected.

'I see. So it was suicide, then?'

Another pause.

'Well, not unless Mr Donald achieved a remarkable act of resurrection and untied his wrists and his ankles...'

Grant froze, staring blankly at the door of Delia's room. Briony stared at her boss until, finally, he responded.

'I'm sorry— what?'

'Yes, I thought that might get your attention. Our examination has shown that Danny Donald's wrists and ankles were bound until after his death. By the looks of it, by a thin nylon rope of a similar type to that used on the previous murder victims. It's quite obvious from the indentations that the restraints were removed after death. You see, these indentations would...'

Grant opened and closed his mouth a few times before he managed to think of anything to say. He interrupted the pathologist's technical explanations.

'Em...sorry, Doctor... so you're saying that it wasn't suicide?'

Nippy Napier sighed impatiently.

'Exactly that, Grant. Mr Donald was most certainly hanged but, in our opinion, it was definitely not suicide. His hands and feet were bound, these bonds being removed after he was hanged, as the indentations are clearly post-mortem. Of course, had you not retrieved the victim's body, this evidence would have been destroyed by the fire. However, as you did manage to retrieve the unfortunate Mr Donald, the evidence is clear. Mr Donald was securely tied until after his death, which certainly doesn't indicate suicide.'

Grant was assimilating this new evidence when Dr Napier spoke again.

'Oh, and another thing, Grant...'

Here we go...

'Yes, Doctor?'

'He had a blunt trauma injury to the back of the head. I would say that he was struck with something and knocked unconscious.'

Grant looked at Briony, who seemed as astonished as he was.

'Right... thanks, Doctor, I appreciate it. I take it there's no doubt...'

The silence was profound.

'I hope you're not questioning my...'

'Absolutely not, Doctor Napier, no, I just need to be completely certain...'

'Then you can be certain, Grant. Mr Donald was rendered unconscious by a blow to the back of the head then tied until after he was hanged, which suggests only one thing.'

'Yes, it does. Listen, thanks again, and thank Doctor...em...'

'Patel? Yes, I will, Grant. Right, I must dash. 'Bye.'

She was gone, leaving Grant staring at Briony. She broke the silence.

'Well, that kinda' casts a different light on things, eh, Boss?'

He didn't reply. Yet again, he seemed to have arrived at the wrong conclusion, believing Danny Donald to be the murderer. But now...?

*

They were sitting in a desultory silence outside the QEU Hospital, sipping take-away coffees. Finally Briony broke the slightly awkward silence.

'So what now, Boss?'

He looked at her with an expression close to despair and shook his head.

'Fuck knows, Briony. Yet again, it looks like I've cocked it up, doesn't it?'

Briony barked back at him.

'No, you haven't bloody cocked it up, Boss. The case wasn't closed and Danny Donald hadn't been finally named as the murder suspect. It's a complicated ongoing enquiry. I told you, stop being so bloody hard on yourself!'

He sighed and finished his coffee.

'Aye, well, maybe I deserve it. I was all set to put Donald in the frame and, if it hadn't been for a bit of luck...'

'And how often does luck play a part in an enquiry, Boss? You know that as well as I do. The lucky break that "breaks" the case? Come on, lighten up and let's consider this. Right, what've we got?'

He sighed heavily. Briony Quinn seemed to be an eternal optimist

Thank God one of us is...

'Okay, so it seems that, despite his treatment of Delia, Donald is now actually a victim, knocked unconscious, tied up then hanged. Delia was abducted by person or persons unknown. There were traces of goose crap on the tyres of Hope's wheelchair– said crap not being present at Aberdeen, the only location he told us that it had been used. However, it *was* found at Castle Semple...'

Briony interrupted him.

'...an' a wheelchair would have been an extremely useful way of gettin' the bodies of two fit, healthy young men down the pontoon and into the water...'

He paused. He hadn't thought of that.

'Of course it would! We'd assumed that it took two people to move the victims but it would have been relatively easy for one person with a wheelchair...'

'Exactly! And Euan Johnstone, for that matter. Did you not say there were traces of mud found in the wheelchair tyres? Might be worth checkin' against the second locus, eh? Then there were all the co-incidences about Simon Hope comin' down to see Delia, who claims she doesn't remember phonin' him. Of course, her phone was conveniently destroyed in the fire, wasn't it? Then Hope being at the farm when it all happened, "accidentally" shootin' you and "accidentally" knockin' over the container of paraffin. Then Delia told you today that Hope knew all of her boys, three of whom were murdered. An' that statement of his, a work o' bloody fiction if you ask me.'

Grant nodded. Simon Hope's statement *had* seemed far too good to be true. He gave Briony a grim smile.

'Right, Bri, we need a search warrant for Hope's house. It's time to nail this bastard, once and for all.'

Chapter 27

An hour later and Grant was no longer smiling; on their return to Osprey House he had been summoned to his superior's office and the interview with Superintendent Minto wasn't going well. She was standing up behind her desk, her voice loud and harsh with suppressed anger

'Christ, just what the hell is going on, Chief Inspector? First you charge those two thugs, Molloy and Dougall. And whilst I have no doubt that they're a couple of rotten apples, it appears that they most certainly weren't the murderers. Next you have this woman Donald's ex-husband as the guilty party, who then conveniently manages to hang himself; now you're telling me that it's this author fellow, Simon Hope, whom you believe to be responsible and that Donald was, in fact, murdered? Who's next, may I ask?'

Grant bit his tongue and tried his best to look apologetic.

'No-one, ma'am. I'm in no doubt that he's the guilty party. That's why I've asked for a warrant to search his property. I'm certain that he intended us to presume Donald was the murderer and, by all accounts, his plan nearly succeeded. Had we not recovered Donald's body, then the forensic evidence would have been destroyed in the fire and Hope would have been the hero of the hour.'

She glared at him.

'Yes, as opposed to your good self. At least that's one positive outcome, saving that girl, and it was fairly heroic, I have to say.'

She paused to draw breath.

'But if this man Hope *is* responsible, what in God's name is his motive for all these murders?'

'Well, according to his statement...'

'Statement! Huh, pure fiction, if you ask me...'

'Yes, ma'am, but it does seem that he and Delia go back a long way. My feeling is that he was trying to drive her back to him.'

Patricia Minto gave him a sceptical look.

'What, by killing her... employees?'

'Yes, I think he hoped that it would upset her so much that he could win back her affections. He'd been pursuing her without success for years, according to the statement. I think he wanted to make her vulnerable; the kidnap and the staged "rescue" were simply the final parts of the plan. As I said, he'd then be the great hero and she'd presumably fall back into his arms...'

The superintendent considered this for a moment.

'Well, maybe you have a point. But, of course, I've now got your bloody ex-wife ranting about holding her client. I've spoken to Sheena and, at this point, she doesn't think we've got enough evidence to charge him with anything other than an accidental firearms discharge, apparently in presumed self-defence, according to his statement. Although your evidence may be fairly compelling, it's still entirely circumstantial and, with a good QC, Sheena thinks he's got a reasonable chance of slipping off the hook. No, if you don't come up with something more concrete by tomorrow, I think we'll have to let Hope out on bail.'

Grant was furious.

'But surely not. I mean, he shot a police officer: me, in case you hadn't noticed... ma'am...'

She glared at him.

'Don't be stupid. Of course I know who he shot, but as his statement has clearly stated, it was a complete accident and, if his story is true...'

'"If" being the operative word...'mumbled Grant.

'Point taken, but he has clearly admitted he fired the shot under some very challenging circumstances. No, if you don't come up with more compelling evidence then I'm afraid he'll be out. I'll sort out the warrant for the search of his house but, believe me, you'd better come up with something concrete...'

She stopped speaking and, shaking her head, sat down with a weary sigh. Grant remained standing, towering sullenly above her desk like a recalcitrant schoolboy summoned to the headmaster's office.

'Grant, Grant, what are we going to do with you? This wouldn't have happened with Brian, would it?'

He bristled.

'What do you mean, ma'am?'

'Well, let's face it, the two of you *were* a great team. You thought things through, reasoned, discussed your cases; and, of course, you were good friends. You trusted each other implicitly. There was never a false move or a cock-up like this, was there?'

She hesitated before continuing.

'But you and Sergeant Quinn...' she shook her head. 'Well, you haven't really seen eye-to-eye, have you? I blame myself. Although she requested the position as your sergeant, I sanctioned it, but I should have known better. You're a law unto yourself sometimes, Grant, and it's quite obvious that this pairing isn't working. Once all this is over...'

'NO!' snapped Grant.

Patricia Minto looked up at him in surprise.

'I beg your pardon?'

'I said no, ma'am. I don't want another sergeant, thank you very much. Briony and I have sorted our differences and we're working really well together...'

She was shaking her head again as he spoke.

'No, I don't believe that's the case, Grant, you see...'

Suddenly he leaned forward to face his superior officer, staring down at her as he spoke in a low, angry voice.

'With all respect, ma'am, it *is* the bloody case. To be quite honest, I don't know what the hell I'd do without her. She's been a bloody Godsend! We're a great team. Break us up now and I'm gone... with all respect, ma'am.'

She narrowed her eyes and gave him a shrewd look as she sat back in her chair, steepling her fingers.

'Well, if you're *quite* sure, Grant...'

He stared back at her with the sneaking suspicion he'd just been hoodwinked.

*

Grant had been sitting in his office for about forty minutes. He needed some peace and quiet and he had a feeling it was going to be a long night. He jumped when his phone rang but, once he had ended the call from the Mint, there was a smile of satisfaction playing on his face, Grabbing his jacket, he stormed out of the door and into the team's office. They all stopped their activities and looked at him.

'Right, we've got the warrant for Hope's place. Who fancies a trip up to deepest Perthshire?'

There was a resounding chorus of "me" and he smiled.

'Bugger it, we'll all go. Many hands make light work, as they say. I'll phone Helen Street and ask Hope to hand over his keys. Otherwise we'll threaten to force an entry, which I'm sure he won't want. Cliff, are you okay to take your car and collect the keys en-route?'

'Aye, no problem, Boss, filled it up earlier.'

As he answered, the DC looked surreptitiously at his watch. Grant noticed and addressed them again.

'Aye, my stomach's rumbling too, Cliff. Listen, there's a service station with a good restaurant on the way, we'll meet up there,. My treat. Right, chop-chop, sooner we're there, sooner we're fed...'

As they walked along the corridor, Cliff caught up with Grant.

'Boss, Hope's place is near Huntingtower, on the road to Crieff. I've Googled it, it's a tidy wee estate, about fifty acres. It's off the A9, after the Broxden Roundabout. We should be there in just over an hour. I've requested local SOCOs but we're happy to do whatever is needed.' They exited the building, climbed into their cars and set off on what Grant hoped would be the last lap. He was sick to his back teeth of this case and would be glad to see the end of it.

*

It was getting dark when, suitably fed and watered; they had finally arrived at Lower Almondglen House. The entrance was guarded by two uniformed officers who waved them through after careful scrutiny of their credentials. Grant was no longer on home territory, after all. The two vehicles drove slowly up the winding gravelled driveway and stopped outside the front entrance.

'Nice place' commented Grant, as they stood outside staring at the beautiful, creeper-clad sandstone mansion house.

'Aye, he's no' short of a bob or two, eh. Think I'll take up writin' when I retire.' replied Briony.

'As long as I'm the main character... right, let's go. Gloves and shoe-covers on, folks. I don't want anything going wrong...'

The team walked up the half-dozen worn sandstone steps and entered the house. It was beautiful. The furniture was understated and expensive, topped with a variety of antique clocks, vases and

other ornaments. Numerous pieces of original artwork adorned
the dark-painted walls, each piece exquisite, tastefully-framed
and well-lit. There were a few silver-framed photographs of Hope
and a woman, presumably his wife. She looked vaguely familiar.
Grant wondered if, perhaps, she was an actress; after all, Hope was,
apparently, moving in esteemed theatrical circles these days! Good
taste abounded and Grant had a brief flash-back to the Pettigrew
residence. The level of investment was probably similar but as far as
taste went, it was at the opposite end of the scale.

They split up, searching for something... anything...

*

Grant heard the sonorous chime of a distant clock striking nine.
Somehow he felt it was later and looked at his watch, nine forty
five; the clock was slow. He gave a long yawn; he was painfully
aware that they needed to find something or he would be faced
with having to release Hope the next day, charged only with a
minor firearms offence. He was getting desperate; he could see the
weariness amongst the team and was about to call it a day when
Sam Tannahill shouted from the hallway.

'Boss, Sarge, can you come through here for a minute?'

They padded wearily back through to the main entrance, a
large, wood-panelled hall complete with antique furniture and a
magnificent set of stag antlers. It had a runner of beautiful, soft,
Turkey-red carpet, around which, in true country house style, was
a border, about a foot wide, of dark, polished floorboards. Sam
was staring at a wonderful old grandfather clock that was ticking
comfortingly, its pendulum swinging mesmerizingly to and fro,
it's hands registering nine oh-five. Grant felt that if he stared at
it for too long he would keel over and he did his best to sound
enthusiastic.

'Aye, Sam, what is it?'

'Look at the clock, Boss.'

He gave her a small smile.

'Actually, I'm trying not to. It's putting me to sleep. Okay, go on,
I'm looking. It's running slow.'

'I know, but that's the thing, Boss. Everything else in the house is
perfect, neat, tidy, all the other clocks are running to perfect time.
So why is this one running slow. After all, it's a beautiful piece of
furniture, a feature, one of the first things you see when you come

in. You'd think that he'd make sure it was accurate, wouldn't you?'

He cocked his head to the side and stared at the handsome, decorated clock-face.

'Hm, so what's your point, Sam?'

'Well, I wondered if, maybe, it had been moved. Or if someone had been inside and stopped the mechanism...och, it's probably a silly notion...'

He lowered his gaze to the long, polished and glass-panelled door, the pendulum within continuing its gentle swing.

'Have you checked inside the case, Sam?'

'Not yet, Boss.'

'Right, let's have a look. Hopefully it's not locked...'

It wasn't; Grant knelt down and gently eased the door open, then paused; he stood up again.

'Your call, Sam. It was you who noticed it. '

Sam knelt down and reached inside the clock; her hand hit the chimes, causing them to jangle noisily.

'Sorry... it's a bit dusty, hope there's no spiders... or mice... hang on, there's something loose...'

She grappled with the unseen object then, as if performing an amateur magic trick, she pulled out a tan-coloured cigar box, the words "Cohiba Esplendidos" emblazoned across its top. She held it up and smiled.

'Voila!'

*

The six officers were seated round the large, polished-oak dining room table, each one still wearing a pair of thin latex gloves. In front of them, still unopened, sat the cigar box. As Grant stared at it, a memory sprang into his mind. Were these not the cigars smoked by Fidel Castro himself? As with everything else in the house, it seemed that Simon Hope had impeccable taste. Almost reverently, he reached forward and prised up the little brass clasp.

'Right, let's see if it's really cigars that Mr Hope's been hiding.'

As soon as the lid was opened, they could spell the sharp, aromatic tang of the contents that it had once contained. Although Grant had never been a smoker, it was a smell that he rather liked; however, not on this particular occasion... the box contained only three items, a smart-phone, a plastic folder containing some folded A4 sheets and a shiny red Nikon digital camera (Grant had a similar one somewhere at home). The batteries in both the phone and the camera were out of charge but, after rummaging in the kitchen drawers, Faz had managed to locate the charger for the Nikon and Cliff had brought in a spare phone charger from his car. As expected, once the phone was fired up it asked for the six-digit pass-code. There was nothing that they could glean from it's hidden contents. Faz stood up and fetched the battery for the camera, now partly charged, inserting it before handing it solemnly to Grant. They all had an inkling of what the contents might show.

Grant switched on the little camera and started scrolling through the picture library. There were a number of grainy shots of a building at night. It looked like Danny Donald's farm. These were followed by images of Pam Lawson's house and it appeared that Hope had been stalking Delia for some time.

The next images were inside an unidentified but dilapidated industrial unit and showed the first two victims. Initially they were tied and fully clothed but the next set of images showed them naked, still with their hands and feet tied and duct tape over their mouths. He scrolled on. Euan Johnstone, similarly naked, bound and gagged. The location appeared to be inside a very confined area.

'Could be the inside of a van' mumbled Grant, scrolling to the next image. He stared at it with a feeling of revulsion. This was what he had hoped for... dreaded... the team watched him as he quickly scanned through the remaining photos, then he switched the camera off and carefully placed it back on the table. He spoke softly.

'Enough. We've got all we need now.'

They knew by his expression what he had seen.

'I don't think that there's any doubt that we're dealing with a true psychopath here. It seems that Hope hadn't the slightest compunction when it came to Delia's boys. No remorse, no guilt...'

Briony turned and looked at him.

'But why, Boss? What in God's name was his motive?'

Grant repeated the conversation he had had with Superintendent Minto.

'Well, to be honest, I think he did it to try and win Delia back. She said that he'd been chasing her for years but she had always refused him. What better way than to create some sort of trauma that would make her more vulnerable to his approaches?'

'Seriously?' interjected Sam. 'But how is killing her boys... hang on though, he wanted it to look like Danny was the murderer, didn't he? Then he'd be the hero who saved her... oh my God...'

'Aye, that's my guess, Sam. Each time there was a murder she phoned him. She told me that, And each time he said he was coming to see her. She resisted, so he decided to stage her kidnap, pretending it was Danny Donald. Then he'd come along, like the proverbial knight in shining armour, and rescue her. How could she resist him after that? He *was* a writer of fiction, after all! It wouldn't be hard for him to think up a story like that.'

Briony had unfolded the sheets of paper and was reading the neat, typewritten text.

'It's pretty much all in here, Boss. Clandestine night-time trips to spy on Delia —hence the photos I'd imagine— dates that she phoned, plus a few thoughts of his own and... oh Christ...'

'What?' asked Grant.

'It's here too, what he planned for the boys. As well as all their details: names, addresses, phone numbers...oh my God...'

She handed it to Grant and he started to read.

'Faz, how likely are we to crack open his phone?

Faz shook his head.

'Unless he gives us the pass-code, not very. There's not a hope that Apple will help. That's their policy. Complete and utter privacy.'

'Bugger, it might have been useful to see if he'd phoned any of the victims before he...well, it's pretty unlikely that he'll give us access.'

He folded the sheets of paper and placed them carefully back inside their folder.

'You know, it doesn't actually matter that much. The evidence on the camera will be more than enough to put this bastard away for a long time.'

He slid his seat back and stood up.

'Right, pack the stuff back in that box and let's head down the road. I'm bloody knackered but I'm looking forward to tomorrow and wiping the smug smile of Simon Hope's face. Listen, great job, everyone...'

He looked over at Sam and winked.

'And especially you, DC Tannahill. That was a great wee bit of observation with that clock. Wish I'd bought you a dessert now.'

Her smile told its own story.

*

Despite the lateness of the hour, Grant had phoned Superintendent Minto to relate their findings. Although she wasn't delighted about being roused from her sleep, the news obviously pleased her and she had arranged to meet Grant the following morning, along with Sheena McPartland, the Fiscal. On the journey down they had just passing Stirling when Faz had leaned his turbaned head over between the two front seats.

'Boss, can I ask you something?'

'Aye, sure, Faz, go ahead.'

'Well, remember you said you were looking for another member of the team?'

'Did I?'

Briony smiled and glanced at him in the darkness.

'Aye, you did. Said we were a bit stretched at times, eh.'

'Och well, if you say so. Got someone in mind, have you?'

Faz sounded slightly embarrassed.

'Em, well, do you remember that constable over in Partick? Grace Lappin.'

Grant and Briony exchanged a look. She turned in her seat and raised an eyebrow at the DC

'The one you were takin' for a "proper" curry?'

'Aye, em, well, the thing is, she's really keen to become a detective. Honestly, Boss, I think she'd be really good. She's dead enthusiastic, smart, she's got a good degree...'

'Have you got a vested interest here, young man?' Grant asked, in a stern tone.

Faz shook his head and, in the mirror, Grant could see his expression turning more serious.

'No, no, of course not, Boss. Although, em, well...what do you think?'

Grant gazed at the dark ribbon of road ahead and smiled. He *was* needing another DC and he trusted Fazil Bajwa's judgement; it was also fortunate that the young DC had caught him in such a benevolent mood.

'Aye, well, tell her to give me a call next week, Faz, and I'll see what we can do. Maybe get her over for an interview. How's that sound?'

Faz beamed.

'Brilliant, Boss, cheers, really appreciate it, I'm sure you won't regret it...'

Briony interrupted.

'When're you takin' her for the curry, eh?'

Without thinking, Faz replied.

'Wednes... shit... oh, sorry...'

Grant chuckled.

'Ach, get back in your seat, sunshine, and think of something more useful to take your mind off it!'

Aye, as if I can talk...

The young DC grinned and sat back in the darkness of the pick-up; Grant looked in the mirror and could see Kiera stifling her laughter, her hand across her mouth. He smiled at Briony and half-whispered.

'Christ, love's young dream, that's all we bloody need. Still, I trust him. He's shit-hot with all the IT stuff, let's see how he is with recruitment...'

Briony, too, was grinning, caught in the buoyant atmosphere of a job well done, a case almost closed and a team now bonded by their first major operational success.

'Indeed; an' it's been a while since I was at a weddin'...'

*

Grant pulled the pick-up in to the near-deserted Osprey House car park and stopped.

'Right, let's make it nine-thirty tomorrow, we've pretty much cracked it now and you all deserve a bit of a lie-in. Bri, can you text Cliff and Sam to tell them? We should be in a position to charge that smarmy so-and-so tomorrow morning. Pity you can't all come, mind you. You'd enjoy it!'

They said their good-nights and Grant headed for home. Despite his exhaustion, he was now feeling a morsel of the elation that usually came when a case was finally cracked. It was a good feeling...

Chapter 28

Grant entered Osprey House at nine-fifteen to find the whole team assembled; they looked tired but there was a palpable sense of excitement in the room. He grinned.

'Right, troops, I know we're on the home straight but there's still work to be done. We need to try and find that bloody van, although it could be almost anywhere, I suppose. Cliff, is the stuff from Hope's house off to forensics?'

'Aye, Boss, first thing. I was in at eight.'

'Good lad. That should give us the final proof. Any word on Delia's car?

Kiera answered.

'Plenty of prints inside and out, Pam Lawson's and Delia's, just as you'd expect, They're double checking the doors, just in case we can find any of Hope's.'

'Good. Right, I've been thinking about the location where the first two victims were stripped and I seem to remember that there are a few old, empty industrial units down near the Renfrew Ferry. Sam, you and Cliff head along there and see if there's anything. Dougall and Molloy might just have been headed in that direction, it would be one less lie for them to tell, after all. Hope was probably following them, must've thought it was his lucky night when the job was half-done for him.'

The two officers stood up.

'On it, Boss' said Sam, a look of enthusiasm on her face.

'Right, Bri, we'll head up to Helen Street and speak to the delightful Mr Hope. I phoned on the way, so my equally delightful ex-wife should be attending...'

The two remaining DCs gave him a questioning look.

'Long story. I'll tell you later. Faz, Kiera, you start compiling the report, don't miss anything and let me know as soon as you hear from forensics. We want this case watertight, otherwise you might be getting a new boss...'

Half an hour later, Grant and Briony arrived at the Helen Street police offices for what he hoped would be the final interview in this case. Having passed through the various security protocols that guarded the formidable brick edifice, he pulled the pick-up into a vacant space.

'Right, here we are, Bri. Last lap.'

She let out a long sigh.

'Aye, an' it's been a right bloody marathon, Boss.'

'Indeed...'

Finally they entered drab, depressing and window-less interview room number two, where Simon Hope and Jackie Valentine were, once again, sitting beside each other. Grant briefly wondered if there was more to their relationship than that of solicitor and client. He wouldn't have been in the least bit surprised. He and Briony sat down and his ex-wife nodded across to him.

'Grant.'

'Jackie.'

He had a folder containing the charge sheet, which he placed on the table beside the laminated sheet of standard legal wordings. He looked up at Simon Hope, whose full lips were set in the same faint, cynical smile, his dark curly hair ever so slightly dishevelled; but was there slightly less of a twinkle in those dark eyes? Did he suspect...? Grant spoke in a monotone that belied his inner feelings of excitement. This was what it was all about, after all. The recording started.

'I am Detective Chief Inspector Grant McVicar, I am accompanied by Detective Sergeant Briony Quinn. We are interviewing Mr Simon Hope, also present is Mr Hope's solicitor, Jacqueline Valentine. We are within interview room two at Helen Street police station...'

The formalities complete, he sat back in his chair, trying his best to adopt a friendly, conversational air.

'Mr Hope, as you are aware, we obtained a search warrant for your property, Lower Almondglen house. Last night we discovered fresh evidence, hidden in the base of a grandfather clock, in the hallway of said property.'

He paused for effect.

Now for it, Grant...

'This evidence clearly implicates you in the murders of Andrew Watt, Chris Findlay and Euan Johnstone. It also implicates you in the later murder, by hanging, of Mr Danny Donald.'

A puzzled look appeared on Simon Hope's face, a look that, somehow, Grant hadn't anticipated.

God, he's good...

'*What*, Inspector? Just what the hell are you talking about. I had absolutely nothing to do with...'

'What evidence is that?' interrupted Jackie, a look of extreme alarm on her face.

Doesn't she trust him...?

Grant swivelled his gaze towards her.

'The evidence, secreted in a cigar box, consists of a number of typewritten pages containing personal details of the victims, as well as numerous references relating to Mrs Delia Donald, the Domestic Services Agency and its entire staff. It also contains detailed plans for the capture and murder of said victims, including the emasculation of Euan Johnstone, the subsequent abduction of Mrs Donald and the murder of her husband. These acts were presumably carried out with the intention of re-establishing relations with Mrs Delia Donald, who...'

'Rubbish!' shouted Simon Hope.

Grant leaned forward.

'No, Mr Hope, it is not rubbish. The evidence is there and the items recovered are being checked for your fingerprints as we speak.'

Simon Hope opened and shut his mouth as if unable to think of anything to say. Grant sat back again.

'Mr Hope, can you account for your movements last Saturday and Sunday?'

'What? No, of course I bloody can't. My wife's buggered off to Africa for a month and I was at home writing... listen, I don't need to account for anything...'

Jackie Valentine put her hand on his arm and he stopped speaking. She glared at Grant.

'Chief Inspector, can I ask again, other than these circumstantial items, which could have been produced by anyone, what tangible evidence do you have to back up your allegations?'

He sat back again and folded his arms across his stomach.

'What— apart from these rather incriminating lists of personal details and plans? Well, among other things, we have a Nikon camera containing full, graphic images of the acts you carried out...'

As he spoke, he was aware that Briony was reading a text message on her phone and he could feel his anger rising at the distraction; this was his moment, the climax of the case. She turned to him, a concerned expression on her face.

'Sorry Boss, we need to talk...'

Fuck... not again...!

'Sergeant...'

'*Now*, Boss.'

*

'Briony, what the fuck's going on' he hissed. 'Christ, we're about to nail this bastard...'

They were standing in the corridor outside the interview room, where two uniformed officers were staring at the opposite wall, pretending to ignore the altercation that was taking place. Grant's voice was a barely controlled hiss, but Briony's phone rang before he could continue.

'It's Faz, Boss. You *really* need to talk to him.'

She put the phone on speaker.

'Go ahead, Faz, we're on speaker.'

'Boss, Sarge, listen, I'm really sorry to interrupt...'

'Aye, you bloody should be, Faz. What the hell is it now...'

Briony put her finger to her lips; he glared at her but paused. Faz continued.

'We've just had the forensic reports on the stuff from Hope's house. Covered in his prints...'

'Well?'

'So, they took the zoom lens off the Nikon camera and checked inside. There was another thumb print on the inside element of the lens...'

Grant stared at his phone.

'...but it wasn't Simon Hope's...'

Grant's eyes met Briony's as Faz continued to speak.

'Fuck...!'

*

The interview had been terminated abruptly without explanation, much to the anger of Jackie Valentine; Grant couldn't have cared less. A phone call to The Mint had, after much cajoling, elicited the necessary search warrant which Kiera and Faz were now bringing. After a strained forty-minute journey, they pulled in at the side of the road a few hundred yards from their destination; ten minutes later, Kiera and Faz came up behind them and flashed their lights. Grant indicated, pulled out, then, moments later, the small convoy turned into a gravel drive. Grant took the three steps in one stride and knocked loudly on the door. Pam Lawson opened it and stared at him.

'Grant. This is a surprise. I was just about to head over to the hospital. Delia should be well enough to get out today...'

'Mrs Lawson, we have a warrant to search these premises...'

'What? What the hell are you talking about? You can't just waltz in here and...'

Briony interrupted. Grant could see the expression of satisfaction on her face.

'Actually, we can, Mrs Lawson...'

She held up the warrant.

'...now, if you'll excuse us, eh.'

Briony and Grant pushed past her and entered the house, leaving Pam Lawson staring at them in silent astonishment before she turned and followed them, Kiera and Faz bringing up the rear. Pam's voice finally returned, angry and shrill.

'This is a piece of bloody nonsense, Chief Inspector. Delia had nothing to do with these... these... crimes, she's completely innocent. I don't know what you expect to find...'

Briony, who had gone ahead, came back out of the kitchen.

'Is this your handbag, Mrs Lawson?'

Pam glared at her,

'Just you put that bag down, my girl, that's a Birkin...'

She made to grab the bag but Kiera put a firm hand on her shoulder and pulled her back.

'I think it best if we go into the lounge and have a seat, Mrs Lawson.'

*

They were seated in the comfortable lounge. Pam's expression was murderous and Kiera was standing behind her, with a hand on her shoulder, ready to restrain her again if necessary. Carefully, Briony opened the exquisite Birkin bag and took out a purse.

'Right... is this your purse, Mrs Lawson?'

'Of course it's my bloody purse, you stupid little...'

'Mrs Lawson, I must warn you...' interjected Grant.

'Don't you dare presume to warn me, Grant McVicar' she screamed, spittle flying from her lips.'You're all the same, all so bloody high-and-mighty... but I've seen the way you look at Delia. I know what's going through your dirty little mind...'

Briony had checked the contents of the purse. All was in order; receipts, some cash and a number of debit and credit cards. She rummaged at the bottom of the bag and took out a neat leather case with a small brass lock securing it.

'Do you have the key for this, Mrs Lawson?'

'No I don't . It's in my house in Peterhead. Don't you dare damage that...'

She made to stand up but Kiera's grip prevented it. Faz went through to the kitchen and returned with a pair of scissors, which he handed to Briony; she looked across at Pam Lawson.

'I'm very sorry, Mrs Lawson, but I'm goin' to have to cut this open, unless you can provide me with the key?'

Pam was now scarlet with fury but she remained silent, Kiera's hand still resting firmly on her shoulder. With a bit of difficulty Briony managed to cut through the leather strap that was keeping the note-case secured; finally it opened. She looked through the contents, removing an item and handing it to Grant; he took the familiar red-bound United Kingdom passport and opened it.

Like most passport photographs, the face that stared back up at him didn't bear a particularly close resemblance to the woman sitting across from him, although he felt he had seen the likeness somewhere before. He looked up at Pam Lawson, whose expression was impossible to read, then back down at the image. It was definitely her.

He read the name on the passport.

Francesca Mary Hope...

*

The same drab, dreary interview room, the same metal table. This time, however, it was Pam Lawson who sat opposite Grant and Briony, accompanied by an anonymous and somewhat disinterested female duty solicitor, her own lawyer being based in Aberdeen and unable to attend until the next day; the interview commenced. Grant looked at Pam Lawson. Her eyes were distant, her expression veiled and he felt it didn't bode well...the formalities having been observed, the interview commenced.

'Mrs Lawson...?'

She looked at him but didn't respond.

'...or should I say Mrs Hope?'

Again, silence, although her eyes narrowed slightly.

'You are, in fact, Mrs Francesca Mary Hope, wife of Simon Hope, currently being held...'

Suddenly the woman's eyes blazed into life.

'Don't you dare mention that bastard's name. Don't... I hate him, I hate him...'

The young lawyer turned to her client in alarm.

'Em, Mrs...

She looked helplessly at Grant.

'Hope. She's Mrs Francesca Hope.'

'Mrs Hope, are you sure you're up to this? You don't need to answer anything if you don't want to...'

But, in the end, she did...

It only took Grant a few minutes to realise that the confession he and Briony were hearing was more of a religious nature than a criminal one, the main difference being that he would be unable to offer absolution. He also realised that any attempt at interruption would be pointless. Pam Lawson, or Francesca Hope, as he now knew the woman to be, talked without pause, in a voice devoid of emotion, telling her tragic, warped story.

It took him only slightly longer to realise that the woman was, quite probably, insane.

She had suffered years of psychological abuse at the hands of Simon Hope. Her husband was a serial philanderer, he knew that her strict religious upbringing would never permit divorce and he relied on her strong moral fibre to take care of the inconvenience that was his aged mother. Of course, her job as a pharmacist had provided for them during the lean years of his writing career, long before "Saint Mungo – Sinner" became the enormous success that it now was.

In the end, the catalyst that triggered the series of catastrophic events had been Delia Donald. Francesca knew about the affair, and she knew that Simon had consistently pursued Delia after the affair ended. She was an intelligent woman, well-versed in computers and IT and it hadn't taken her long to access Simon's laptop and clone his phone; she monitored every conversation, she knew all about the Domestic Services Agency; and, as most of Delia's "boys" had been referred by Simon, she knew all their personal details. When Simon started pressurising Delia to see him again, obviously hoping to re-kindle their relationship, she knew that action needed to be taken; otherwise she might lose him—forever.

Grant and Briony sat in a slightly stunned silence, listening to the outpouring of the distressed and remote-looking woman sitting across from them. The duty solicitor's indifference had vanished and she was now staring wide-eyed at her client as if watching the latest episode of a soap-opera; Grant briefly wondered just how much criminal defence experience the girl actually had.

As was often the way, there was a strong element of truth in her story. Her aunt had, indeed, died and left her the bungalow outside Milton of Campsie, along with the car and a considerable amount of money. Her aunt's name was Pam Lawson...the plan was hatched...

Adopting her aunt's identity, she had made contact with Delia's agency; she had booked some strictly "non-sexual" services, usually with Andy and Chris; she had engineered the "chance" meeting with Delia in Matonti's delicatessen; she had, in effect, become Delia's stalker. What she hadn't bargained for was discovering that Delia was, in fact, more of a victim than Francesca and, as such, actually needed protection rather than punishment. That was when things became complicated; and, during the interview, that was when Francesca Hope suddenly took on the persona of Pam Lawson...

Chapter 29

Francesca Mary Hope, aka Pam Lawson, was duly charged with numerous offences including murder, assault, abduction and fraud, not to mention perverting the course of justice. Whether she would actually be tried, still remained a matter of debate, she might be judged mentally unfit; only time would tell...

After some rather lengthy and serious discussions with Superintendent Patricia Minto, Grant remained employed as a front-line Detective Chief Inspector, albeit with the warning that he had to "pull his socks up", an instruction with which he fully intended to comply. Better still, Briony Quinn remained as his detective sergeant; the outcome could have been much worse...

Grant had thought long and hard about it but finally decided that it was time to re-join his friends, the Holy Trinity. With one proviso – he had asked Briony.

'Seriously? I'm not sure, Boss, might be best if you go by yourself.' He shook his head.

'No, Briony, I'd like you to come. It's been a while... I've spoken to them on the phone a few times but, well...'

She waited for an explanation but, as always, none was forthcoming.

'So what do you say, Bri? They're great company, exactly what we need right now.'

'Aye, okay then. By the way, where did the name "Trinity" come from?'

'Did I not tell you...'

*

Not long after Grant had moved to the dilapidated Bluebell Cottage, he had decided to pay a visit to Howwood's Railway Inn, a relic from the days of the long-abandoned station. He had opened the door and stepped into the small, comfortable public bar; although a hush didn't quite descend, a few looks were certainly cast in his direction. Sometimes it was hard to disguise his profession. He ordered a pint and turned round; the room had a homely feel, with assorted railway artefacts displayed on the walls. Two men, both about his own age, were seated at a table nearby and the nearest smiled at him. There was the faintest trace of an Irish accent in his voice as he spoke.

'Join us if you like, mate.'

He walked across and sat down.

'Cheers. Always a bit awkward, first time in a strange pub.'

He took his first, welcome drink of beer; the other man did the same, then placed his glass on the table.

'You're new to the village then?'

'Aye, just moved a few weeks ago. Up in Newton of Belltrees, actually.'

'Here, it wasn't you that bought the old gamie's cottage, was it?'

'Aye, it was.' He smiled. 'Bluebell Cottage. Starting to regret it very slightly already!'

He drank again, placed his glass on the table and extended his hand to the man who had first invited him over.

'It's Grant, by the way. Grant McVicar.'

The other two men looked at each other and burst out laughing. Grant stared at them. His name wasn't that unusual, surely?

'Seriously? McVicar?'

Grant was now becoming annoyed; he glared at the man.

'Aye. Is there a problem with "McVicar"?'

The man laughed again and finally took Grant's hand.

'No, not at all... how do you do. I'm Father Eddie McKee, occasionally known as Father Ted, but not if you value your health...and this is my friend and, of course, great Christian rival, the Reverend Fraser Ballingall. Between us we provide the necessary spiritual sustenance for the good residents of Howwood.'

Grant shook Eddie's hand, the smile already forming on his lips. He then shook Fraser's hand and laughed.

'Right, I've got you now...'

And, from that point on, they became great friends – and the Holy Trinity...

Saturday night; Grant, Fraser, Eddie and Briony were ensconced at a cosy corner table in the Railway Inn, each with a pint of frothing liquid before them. The Reverend Fraser Ballingall lifted his glass and proposed a toast.

'Well, first of all, welcome back, Grant. We've really missed you...'

Father Eddie McKee nodded his assent.

'...and, next, to Briony. We've heard all about you, of course...'

He gave a mischievous grin as Briony turned towards Grant, arching her eyebrows.

'All good, Bri, all good...'

'Aye, it bloody better be, eh!'

They each took a long, welcome draught of beer (none more so than Grant) then Eddie raised his glass once more.

'And here's to Scotland's finest, the men and women who keep our streets safe.

*

Grant's two friends had made small talk initially, mainly asking Briony about her background.

'I'm detecting a bit of an East Coast accent there,' remarked Fraser. 'My son, Ian, is studying medicine at St. Andrews so I'm reasonably familiar with the lilt.'

'Actually', Bri grinned,' I'm from Dunoon originally, believe it or not. My dad was US navy and, when the USS Simon Lake went home, so did my dad, leaving me behind with my mum. She took up with one Mr Quinn and we moved to Glenrothes. He worked in the whisky industry.'

'Oh, good man' said Fraser.

She pulled a face.

'Turns out he wasn't, Fraser. Long story...'

'Speaking of which' interjected Grant. 'The Mint said something to the effect that you'd requested to work with me. What's the story there, Bri?'

Eddie McKee stood up.

'Sorry, but before you start, I'd say it was time for something nice. I see they've got a new bottle of Springbank eighteen-year-old that requires opening. Briony, do you...?'

Grant looked up at his friend with a grin.

'She's a bloody detective, Eddie, of course she does!'

*

'Slainte'

Grant took a sip of the golden, viscous liquid, his first since...
Since Brian died...

He swirled it around his mouth. A second on the tongue for every year in cask... he placed his glass back down on the table.

'So, Briony, you were saying?'

She smiled and sipped her whisky.

'Aaah, that's good. Well, my mum eventually took up with another gentleman. Still with him, I'm glad to say, although he retired last year.'

'And?'

'He was a cop too. Actually, a Divisional Commander latterly.

'Aw, come on, Bri, the suspense is bloody killing me!'

She smiled over the rim of her glass.

'Alastair Young?'

'What? You're joking! Big Al? He was Chief Super when I worked under Jacky Winters. He was great with me after... well, I was considering leaving the Force and Al talked me out of it. Haven't seen him for years though. So he's your mum's partner!'

'Aye, one and the same. Still doesn't miss a trick either. Followed your career from a distance, always spoke really highly of you I'd already decided I wanted to become a detective, he said you were the best, and so, here I am, eh.'

Grant looked at her in astonishment.

'So you really *did* ask to be assigned to me?'

'Aye. Alastair pulled a few strings but it was at my request.'

Grant shook his head in surprise. Fraser grinned wickedly and looked at Briony.

'Regrets?'

She winked at him.

'I've had a few, but then again, too few to mention...'

Grant threw his head back and laughed. Briony smiled. It was a good sound.

They sat in a companionable silence for a few moments, then Eddie put down his glass.

'So, I gather this has been a particularly trying case, Grant?'

'Aye, you could say that...'

His companions just looked at him.

'Sorry, guys... well, where do I start? Pam Lawson, aka Francesca Hope...'

'Is she insane, do you think?' asked Fraser.

Briony nodded..

'I reckon so, Fraser. But the sad thing is, she's as much o' a victim as Delia. She's a deeply religious woman who's suffered years o' psychological abuse at the hands o' her husband, the delightful Simon Hope. In the interview, she seemed to be able to switch between the two characters, dependin' on which part o' the story she was tellin.'

'But murder?' asked Eddie. 'I mean, she's killed four people! And, yes, I know all about Christian forgiveness but...'

'Technically, it was only three' interjected Grant. 'One of the boys was already dead when she placed him in the loch. I think that was the turning point. Francesca had effectively been stalking the boys and assumed that Dougall and Molloy had killed them before dumping them in that old industrial unit and it might have been weeks, months even, before they were found. She saw it as the perfect opportunity to bring the dealings of the Agency to light.'

'But why Castle Semple?' asked Fraser. 'Why didn't she just dump them in the Clyde?'

'Because she needed them to be discovered, she needed questions to be asked that would implicate the Agency; that was why she stripped them. Remember, at this point she only wanted to discredit Delia and, if they'd gone in the Clyde, well, they might never have been found. No, she'd been down to the loch before, helping with underprivileged kids, she knew that numerous water-sports took place there, she knew that they'd soon be discovered. But the shock came when she found out that she'd actually become a killer herself and that was just too much for her conscience. I suspect she suffered a serious breakdown at that point and retreated into the persona of Pam Lawson from then on.'

'But how on earth did she move the bodies? 'asked Eddie.

'The wheelchair. She'd taken Hope's van conversion that was used to transport his mother.'

'But didn't he notice it was gone?'

Grant gave a wry smile.

'It stayed at the nursing home. Neither he nor Francesca wanted to be seen in such a...well, humble, vehicle so they left it parked at Hawkswood Hall. As Hope himself seldom visited his mother, he wouldn't know that his wife had used it.'

He took another sip of whisky.

'Anyway, Hope believed his wife to be in Africa on her humanitarian duties. We checked, she *had* been numerous times, and he decided that he'd better visit his poor old mum, taking her out in the van. Francesca had managed to put one of these location apps on his phone. She knew exactly where he was at any point in time...'

Fraser's eyes widened in surprise.

'That's clever. Maybe I should get one for our Ian so I know what he's up to at Uni...'

Grant grinned.

'Anyway, she texted him using Delia's phone, saying that she thought her husband was trying to kidnap her. Of course, he came straight down without going home for his Porsche, which shows how keen he was.'

He took another sip of the whisky. It was starting to loosen his tongue.

'So, at the end of the day, she *has* admitted to the three murders. The first, Andrew Watt, she claims was unintentional which, to be honest, it probably was; and, of course, the fact that Chris Findlay died prior to being put in the loch puts Molloy and Dougall back in the frame for his death. However, the third one— well, Francesca... or Pam, as I think she was now, was out to destroy Delia and she had been certain that the discovery of the first two victims would do just that by bringing the dealings of the Agency to our attention; which it did. But when we inconveniently overlooked what the Agency was actually doing. We had two murders to investigate, after all. She was stunned. Her initial plan had failed so she decided that she needed something a bit more brutal. Something that would *really* get our attention.'

'So this other poor bugger... Euan, wasn't it, was just unlucky?' asked Fraser.

'Well, she claims that she contacted him, but when he arrived, he made a pass at her and then tried to rape her. But given how screwed up she is about sex, I think it's more likely that he was just playing the part he thought she expected.'

Briony picked up the story 'we did track down the Agency van; her prints were all over it and there was no doubt about what she'd done inside the back... That was his punishment for the attempted rape, the... well, you know...'

They knew.

'And Delia's husband? Was that just more revenge?' asked Eddie.

'In a way.' Grant replied. 'By this time Pam knew all about the vile Mr Donald and how he had treated "her Delia", as she had come to think of her. She had completely fallen under Delia's spell...'

'That's no' entirely fair' interjected Briony' I don't think Delia actually tried to influence Pam, do you?'

Grant swallowed another sip of whisky.

'Hm, maybe not, but Pam certainly seemed to consider herself to be Delia's "protector" by this time. After all, the girl does have a certain, well...'

Three pairs of eyes turned and looked at him. He held up a hand in protest.

'What? Come on! You know what I mean, Bri?'

She smiled.

'But I don't think Delia does. And that's what makes her all the more attractive. But, by the end, she pretty much had Pam eating out the palm of her hand...excuse the pun!'

'Anyway' Grant continued 'Danny Donald was obviously rotten to the core. He beat Delia, he raped her, he used her name to raise funds for his gambling habit. By this time, I think that Pam saw herself as some sort of avenger on the male species and Danny Donald most certainly deserved to be punished! She believed that, at the same time, she could implicate Simon Hope; the perfect solution! It's ironic that she would rather suffer the ignominy of having her husband jailed for murder rather than the humiliation of being divorced.'

'But how on earth could she have known that this Donald character would be at home?' asked Eddie. 'Surely that was leaving a lot to chance?'

'No' replied Briony. 'she was pretty clever about it; she'd cloned Delia's mobile by that time. She sent him a convincing sob story about how she'd made a mistake, how she wanted to come back. She asked him to message her when he was nearly home and it worked; once he arrived, Pam was waiting for him inside the farmhouse. A quick blow to the head, tied up, then into the back of the van. She's a pretty strong, capable woman, after all.'

'But how did she get into the farmhouse, you said it was locked ?'

'She'd copied Delia's keys when she helped her move out.'

'What about the fire, though? 'asked Fraser.' Did she really mean to kill Delia?'

'I don't think she cared anymore.' Briony replied. 'By this time, I don't think that she even knew who she was herself! Danny Donald had been suitably punished; if Delia died, then she was out of the way forever. If Simon died, then so was he – and if Simon arrived too late, then he'd see the love of his life go up in flames and, in all likelihood, be charged with murdering Delia's boys. What better punishment?'

'But how could she be so sure that it would all go according to plan, I mean, with the fire and everything?' asked Fraser.

Grant put down his empty glass.

'Remember, this woman had worked in some of the worst places in Africa. It seems she'd learned a thing or two. We found the remains of a car battery in the ruins of the cottage. She's admitted it was attached to a rudimentary timer and a broken light bulb. Oh, and the chair that Delia was tied in. There was a cord leading through a hole in the floor that was attached to the paraffin lamp. Anyone moving the chair would upset the lamp and, if that didn't start the fire, the timer would have eventually set it all off . She'd doused all the old rubbish with paraffin. Remember the smell, Bri? One way or another it was going to go up although, in the end, it was actually Simon Hope trying to escape that caused the blaze.'

'Weren't you watching Donald's place, though?' asked Eddie.

Grant gave a sigh.

'Aye, we were watching the front entrance, what we didn't know was that the old forestry road turns back on itself and comes out nearer Blanefield. We found mud from the track inside the wheel arches of the van and on Pam's Range Rover. Unbeknownst to us she was going in and out, setting the whole thing up. All she needed was to phone Hope, she knew he'd come running.'

Briony gave a grim smile.

'Aye, the bastard just couldn't resist the bait...'

The two clergymen looked at her in mild surprise.

'Oh... sorry guys... but he came, straight into Pam, or Francesca's trap. And we nearly fell for it too.'

'Aye, we did, Bri' said Grant. 'We had Hope in custody for shooting me, Pam —or Francesca — knew we'd have found Danny Donald and hopefully assume that Hope had murdered him too. She knew that we'd look at the van, that we'd search Hope's house and she'd set the whole thing up beautifully; the clock, the cigar box, the notes, the camera, knowing we'd be likely to check it all for forensic evidence. She deliberately set the clock slow to attract our attention but, even if we hadn't noticed, the SOCOs would certainly have checked inside, so it would have been found sooner or later. But she was just a wee bit careless. She left that stray print on the inside of the camera lens.'

'So, in the end, it all came down to one fingerprint?' asked Fraser, with a slightly puzzled look. 'But how did you have Pam...or Francesca's prints in the first place?'

'We didn't' Grant replied. 'But the print matched those found inside Delia's BMW. More importantly, we'd also found a match on the handle of the wheelchair; we'd assumed —wrongly—that it belonged to one of the staff at the nursing home. Then we found the print again, on, of all things, a pack of sausages that had fallen out when Delia was getting into her car . That must have been where Pam attacked her; it was pretty secluded round the back of the offices, after all. But Pam was the common denominator, the only person who could have left the prints at all four locations. The sausages had fallen on the ground and she must have lifted them and put them in the car, which placed her at the locus of the assault. It left a fair bit to chance but she wasn't thinking rationally by this point. Actually, she hadn't been for some time...'

There was another pause as they finished their whiskies. Finally Eddie asked.

'And has she shown any remorse?'

Briony shook her head.

'That's the strange thing, Eddie. As Pam, she feels it was all completely justified, a means to an end in bringin' those "evil and depraved bastards to justice" as she put it herself...sorry again... but as Francesca, she seems to be genuinely horrified and refuses to accept any guilt. She only ever wanted to get Delia safely out o' Simon's clutches. She's such a complex, troubled character. I wish I could spend more time with her, find out what makes her tick. After all, as I said, she's as much o' a victim as Delia but, from here on, she'll be treated as a criminal, if not criminally insane. It's tragic, really...'

'What do you think'll happen to her?'

Grant considered Fraser's question.

'Honestly? I suppose it depends whether she's deemed fit to stand trial; but, one way or another, I don't think there's much doubt that she'll be put away for a long time...'

He shrugged and shook his head sorrowfully; there was another lull as they sipped their drinks.

'And what about Delia? I mean, what on earth will she do now?'

Briony sighed.

'Well, Fraser, she's absolutely devastated, of course. She'd trusted Pam; the woman had given her sanctuary and now it turns out it was all a pack o' lies. She's lost her home, her car, even the bank account was in Pam's name so, technically, it all belongs to Simon. She's bankrupt too and, of course, the Agency's gone. It was a huge part of her life for ages, she knew and liked her "boys". But I phoned her mum down in Dumfries an' she's goin' to take Delia back in until everythin's settled. Presumably Danny Donald had a will, although there's probably bugger all left, given his gamblin' habit. Still, at least the poor woman's got somewhere to go, eh? She's a survivor, mind, she's tougher than you'd think, but it'll take her a while to get back on her feet. She *is* an English graduate, though, she'll find somethin'...'

She looked across at Grant.

'...by the way, she said to tell you...'

He looked up and raised a dark eyebrow; Briony grinned.

'Em, what was it? Oh yes, that you were her hero...'

'Do you think she might get back together with this Hope character?' asked Eddie, failing to notice Grant's expression.

Briony shook her head.

'Not a chance, Eddie. No, she's had her fill o' him, she recognises him for the lyin' bastard...sorry...'

'Briony, please stop apologising' said Eddie with a smile. 'Your profanity is rather refreshing, in fact...!'

She grinned at him.

'Okay then; but, as I said, there's no way Delia's goin' within a hundred miles o' Mr Simon Hope, thank Christ...aw shit, sorry...'

They laughed again. Grant stared down at his empty glass, his thoughts straying to the pretty, dark-haired woman whose world now lay in ruins.

'It'll be tough, though' he mumbled. 'Poor girl, she's not had much luck...'

His three friends nodded as they sipped the last of their whisky. Only Briony noticed the strange, unfathomable expression on her Boss's face. She stood up.

'Same again, lads, eh? Or somethin' different?'

Eddie smiled.

'Here, I'll help you, Briony. There's a lot to choose from on the gantry...'

*

Grant and Fraser had gone to relieve themselves, leaving Eddie and Briony alone at the table. She took a deep breath; it was time...

'Eddie, can I ask you something?'

He smiled.

'Sure, Briony. Fire away.'

'What's the story with Grant and Brian? I keep trying to get him to open up but he point-blank refuses. I know Brian died in an accident but that's about it and Grant just doesn't seem to be able to move on.'

Eddie swallowed the remainder of his whisky and shook his head.

'I don't know, Bri. Grant *did* tell me but I think it was in confidence. I don't even think Fraser knows, to be honest.'

'Please, Eddie. I was in victim support before. If I knew just what the hell's was goin' on, then maybe I could help him. Please...?'

Eddie looked about surreptitiously then lowered his voice.

'Well, I suppose... but it's not a happy tale, I'm afraid. You see, Grant blames himself for Brian's death.'

'But why, Eddie. Surely he had nothing to do with it?'

'No, he didn't, really. Brian seemed to be, well, "going off the rails" was how Grant put it. He'd started drinking heavily, staying out late. They'd had a couple of really difficult cases. All the classic signs of a stressed-out cop, it seems. Louise had phoned Grant a few times, she was pretty upset...'

'Well, that's understandable, I suppose...'

'... yes, but the thing is, Brian suspected that Louise was having an affair. He'd caught her on the phone to Grant, she'd hung up quickly and she wouldn't tell him who she was talking to. The situation started to get out of control...'

Eddie cast a furtive look in the direction of the gents' toilet.

'Anyway, things came to a head; Brian stormed off one Sunday, said he was leaving her, drove to a pub in Paisley and started drinking. After an hour or so, he messaged Grant, saying he needed to speak to him; but the problem was, by this time Louise had phoned Grant, begging him to come over. She was distraught, needless to say. The poor man faced a terrible dilemma. Brian or Louise? Well, he reckoned Brian was safe enough in the pub, drowning his imagined sorrows, so Grant decided that Louise needed him more and went round to their house.'

He looked down forlornly at his empty glass.

'What then, Eddie?'

'By this time, Grant was trying to reassure Louise, he promised that he'd find Brian and sort things out between them

'Fifteen minutes later, Brian rammed his car into a tree. He was trapped, the car went on fire and exploded. Grant was called but, by the time he got there, they were pulling out what was left of his best friend...turns out it's one of Grant's greatest fears. He's got a real phobia about fire, it seems. Anyway, he reckons if he'd gone to Brian instead of Louise, his friend would still be alive..

'But surely Grant can see that it wasn't his fault, Eddie, I mean...'

'Well, you try telling him that...watch, here they come...'

*

Closing time; a great deal of fine whisky had been consumed and Briony staggered slightly as she stood up and pulled her mobile phone out of her jeans pocket.

'Right, best call a taxi, eh... bugger, no signal in here..'

Eddie stood up and took her arm.

'You need to go outside to get one. Come on, I'll escort you...'

Grant and Fraser finished their drinks in a companionable silence; finally, Fraser drained the dregs of his whisky, placed the glass on the table and leaned over towards Grant.

'That was a memorable night, my friend. It's great to have you back.'

'Aye, it was indeed' replied Grant. Fraser leaned closer and grasped his friend's hand in a firm handshake.

'Briony's a great lass Grant, and she's a bloody Godsend for you, you know that?'

Grant gave a rather lop-sided smile.

'Aye, I know, Fraser. To be honest, I don't know just what the fuck I'd do without her...'

Briony smiled. She was standing right behind him.

*

There had been the usual nightmare; flames, screaming...Grant

awoke suddenly, in a panic and sweating profusely. He pulled
down the covers, waiting for his heart to stop racing. As always,
in the dead of night, the outlook seemed considerably bleaker.
He sat up and reached down to the drawer in his bedside cabinet,
taking out the little, Chinese-silk-bound notebook and the pen that
was attached with a rubber band. He thought for a moment, then
started to write.

*If we were absolutely certain of what lay ahead of us, what would
we do? Would we stay at home, barricade the door and hide under
the covers? But then, if we really did know, how could we possibly
change it? Can we hope to change or to conquer fate? Anyway, as far
as I'm concerned, there are only two certainties in life. Yes, I know,
most people say there's only one – death! True, but there's another
certainty – the moment! That single instant in which you exist is
absolute, irrevocable, unchangeable. What comes after – who knows?
And what went before? Yes, that's absolute, irrevocable, unchangeable
too, surely?*

*Take dementia... Michael Pettigrew, gangster, villain, crook...now
just another lost soul, not knowing what day it is. Does he remember
what he was, what he did? What a bastard he was? Unlikely.*

Irrevocable? Not for him...

*So here we are; continuing recovery, if that's possible.
Rehabilitation, maybe. Must try harder. But maintaining the
constant brave face is difficult, sometimes I just want to give up...*

*Speaking of which, it is time to give something up; time to stop the
midnight sorties, in the hope of...what, exactly?*

What do I expect from my visits to Louise Thackray's house?

*At first I was just making sure Brian's widow was okay; I was
concerned, I was responsible, I was guilty... but, in the end, did it
become stalking? God only knows, but I do know that it has to stop.
Right now! And it will.*

*Then, of course, to add to my woes, there's a new...well, what,
exactly? I find it hard to get her out of my mind. She's kind,
affectionate, gentle, caring...vulnerable?*

And she says I'm her hero, ffs...

*Then there's Ronnie Pettigrew; she was something to me once too.
Now... oh, God knows...*

Face it, Grant McVicar, you should be out of the Force! You're a disgrace... etc... etc...

Bollocks! What else is there for me to do? Anyway, I can't change the past and I can't foresee the future, there's just "the moment" and "death". And, to be honest, if you were to ask me at this particular point in time, I'd be very hard pushed to make a choice between them.

"Oh sleep, why dost thou leave me, Why thy visionary Joys remove..."

Acknowledgments

My publisher told me that the final version of "Sins" would be a team effort – how right she was! There are many people to thank and mention and I am eternally grateful to you all.

First of all, a huge thanks to Lesley Affrossman, my wonderful publisher at Sparsile Books, and to Jim Campbell, my patient and helpful editor (or "gnarly old coach" as Lesley so succinctly described him...) You believed in me and I hope that I have come up to the mark!

Thanks to all the people who have given me great advice when asked, especially my good friend Davy (you know who you are) for superb information on police procedure, protocol and politics. Michael Connolly, the cigar man, Kirsty Mac for handbag advice, the staff and customers at the Railway Inn, Howwood (even though you did all turn and stare at me when I entered...), Castle Semple Rowing Club (well, they taught me to row, after all...), Claudia, my friendly pharmacist (minor ailments – "where would I get hold of…?")

Finally, to my dear friend, Jill Bryceland, for invaluable help with "English as she is Spoke" and for her unending encouragement and support.

Thanks and apologies to my staff at Look, who have had to listen to my endless "self-publicity" on a daily basis (well, you`ve got to try...)

Thanks and much love to my long-suffering but supportive and wonderful family, Joanie, Kirsty and Lindsay. I`m sorry I took up the kitchen table for so long...!

And, of course, to you, the reader. Thank you for taking a chance on a new author and buying "Sins". I hope you enjoy reading it as much as I have enjoyed writing it – hopefully this will just be the first of many DCI McVicar mysteries!

Further reading

The Promise
When promises can cost lives

Simon's Wife
Time is running out, and history is being rewritten
by a traitor's hand.

The Unforgiven King
A forgotten woman and the most vilified king in history

L. M. Affrossman

Comics and Columbine
An outcast look at comics, bigotry
and school shootings

Tom Campbell

Science for Heretics
Why so much of science is wrong

Barrie Condon

www.sparsilebooks.com

Lightning Source UK Ltd.
Milton Keynes UK
UKHW041820261019
352365UK00001B/6/P